SNAPSHOT

ABOUT THE AUTHOR

During his 20-year career in Glasgow with a Scottish Sunday newspaper, Craig Robertson interviewed three recent Prime Ministers, attended major stories including 9/11, Dunblane, the Omagh bombing and the disappearance of Madeleine McCann, was pilloried on breakfast television, beat Oprah Winfrey to a major scoop, was among the first to interview Susan Boyle, spent time on Death Row in the USA and dispensed polio drops in the backstreets of India. His debut novel, *Random*, was shortlisted for the CWA New Blood Dagger.

Also by Craig Robertson

Random

SNAPSHOT

CRAIG
ROBERTSON

London · New York · Sydney · Toronto

A CBS COMPANY

First published in Great Britain by Simon & Schuster UK Ltd, 2011
A CBS COMPANY

1 3 5 7 9 10 8 6 4 2

Simon & Schuster UK Ltd
1st Floor
222 Gray's Inn Road
London WC1X 8HB

www.simonandschuster.co.uk

Simon & Schuster Australia
Sydney

A CIP catalogue record for this book
is available from the British Library

ISBN 978-1-84737-728-9

Typeset by M Rules
Printed in the UK by CPI Mackays, Chatham ME5 8TD

To Alan and Aileen Robertson, my mum and dad,
with love and thanks for everything.

CHAPTER 1

Sunday 11 September

It was raining. Of course it was raining, it was Glasgow. It didn't get to be the dear, green place without more than its fair share of rain.

The hundreds of hunched, angry shapes who were lined up in a disorderly queue outside Blochairn Market were getting pissed on and pissed off.

Pitches were allocated on a first-come, first-served basis and so people made sure they got there early. Some of them had been queuing since four in the morning. It was now just after seven – although to Tony Winter it still felt like the middle of the night – and these people had probably been crabbit even before they were told they had to leave their stall and get back outside the gates because some inconsiderate fucker had got himself stabbed.

Winter lifted his camera and took a quick shot of the entrance to the market. Scene setting. Not strictly procedure but it was always his way. It was the way Metinides did it and if it was good enough for the man then it worked for him.

They were all facing the entrance, some back in their cars and others pacing about on foot like mental bears in a zoo. It meant he was able to take a shot of them from behind without risking getting his head kicked in. Rows of cars and vans that had been stacked full to the gunwales with everything under the sun. Views out of rear windows still blocked with boxes and piles of clothes, impatient people crammed between paste tables and plastic sheeting. Bottled-up humanity, simmering in the rain and not giving a damn for the poor bastard that was dead, just desperate to get back inside and flog second-hand shoes and remnants of make-up.

The Sunday car boot at Blochairn, minutes north of the city centre, is the biggest in Scotland and one of the biggest in Europe. You can buy everything from nearly complete jigsaws to designer coats, second-hand books to antique jewellery and everything in between. You wouldn't believe what people will buy.

He'd been before and saw two women fighting over threadbare dishtowels selling for ten pence each. There was probably a decade of grease and dirt on them but it was that or nothing. This was real poverty. Okay, maybe it could be eased by buying a few less packets of fags or less booze but that was the way it was and who was he to judge?

Cars would roll up to the market entrance from the early hours and they'd sit in the dark and wait for opening time, steaming up windscreens with half-hearted expectancy. They'd be there no time at all before torches would be shone at them and there would be a knock at the window. Sharp faces and searching eyes would reach in from the dark. What you selling? You shifting mobile phones? You selling gold? How much you looking for it?

The idea is to sell everything they bring as fast as they can and get out again. Not this day though. This day, one of those miserable September mornings doing a passable impression of a nasty December afternoon, was different. Two cops stood in front of the newly relocked gates at Blochairn, others were at work inside and Winter was about to join them.

He nodded at Sandy Murray and Jim Boyle, the two PCs on the gate, as he passed them and headed into the market.

'Awrite, Winter? Another day, another dead body.' Boyle made the same crack every time he saw him.

'Word of warning, Tony. That cunt Addison is in a bad mood. As usual.' Murray and Addison had never seen eye to eye and the DI had booted the constable's arse on a couple of occasions. Chances were Addison wasn't as grumpy as they were making out. It was just the same old, same old.

The body was waiting for Winter at the back. The early morning wake-up call had already told him much of what he needed to know. A lifeless heap in a dark puddle of blood, a knife wound to the heart. Found by a woman who had gone in search of carrier bags to keep the rain off teapots. The dead man was a number, a statistic. He might as well have had 'cliché' scrawled in blood on his forehead. Getting yourself stabbed to death in Glasgow showed a spectacular lack of originality.

They already knew his name. As the chip wrappers would put it, he was known to the police.

Sammy Ross, two-bit drug dealer, professional low-life. Now a no-life.

It was only September but this was already fatal stabbing number forty-six in Glasgow. There had been too many non-fatal ones to count.

Winter had personally photographed fourteen of the previous forty-five and it was becoming very dull. Number fifteen was likely to be no more interesting than the rest.

It wasn't his job to do so but off the top of his head he could think of a dozen reasons why someone might have killed Sammy Ross. You didn't work with cops all day without learning something.

Someone might have wanted to pay less. Someone might have wanted to pay nothing. Maybe Sammy was cutting his heroin with too much sugar or powdered milk. Maybe Sammy had been selling worming pills as ecstasy tabs again. Maybe he had made promises he couldn't keep. He could have been shagging someone he shouldn't have. He might not have been shagging someone he should. He could have owed money, he might have been defending a pal, he could have been done for the cash in his pocket. Maybe he just looked at someone the wrong way. Maybe he supported the wrong football team. In Glasgow there was no end of ways to get yourself stabbed.

It didn't matter. Sammy Ross was Winter's mess to photograph that morning. Happy days. There he was, lying empty, having leaked his life at the foot of Derek Addison. The DI had his hands thrust into the pockets of his raincoat, studying Ross with all the interest of someone finding shit under his shoe. Only September but it had already been a long year. Winter focused the camera on the two men, one live, one dead, and fired off a couple of shots. Scene two. The rapid clack-clack-clack of the motor made Addison whirl round angrily.

'Where the fuck have you been, Tony? Some of us have been here for almost an hour. And stop taking my fucking picture.'

Winter knew he didn't really mean it. Addison was just as pissed off at being there in the rain as he was.

'Ah piss off, Addy,' he fired back. 'Some of us don't have a flashing light and a car that goes nee-naw. Sammy Ross, I presume?'

'You been watching *CSI* again? Aye, Sherlock. One dead drug dealer with regulation stab wounds. Hurry up and take his photo. I'm starving.'

'You're always starving.'

Police photographers didn't always talk to cops this way, especially not detective inspectors, but Winter had earned the right over countless pints and drunken nights. He knew where Addison's bodies were buried.

The thought of food was doing nothing for Winter. His head

throbbed from the effects of the night before and his body was rebelling at being hauled out of a warm bed to come to this shit-hole. He couldn't help thinking that she was still in there, curled up soft, smooth and cosy where he'd left her. Every splash of teardrops from the Glasgow heavens was taunting him, reminding him how much he'd rather be tucked in behind her.

Instead he was in the rain with a dead man. And the worst of it? Nobody would give a toss. Short of maybe Sammy's mammy – and even that was doubtful – no one would care that he was lying in a pool of his own blood.

No one had time to be bothered. Not about Sammy at any rate. The next body would be along any minute. There would only be time to roll Ross out of the gutter to make way for the next scumbag who had drawn a target on his own chest and had to be immortalized on digital.

Pick up a Sunday paper any week and you'll likely find a couple of paragraphs on someone stabbed to death. Two paragraphs. That's all it was worth. Somebody's wean knifed into oblivion and all they could be arsed giving it was half a dozen lines. Said it all.

Winter could see on their faces that everyone else on site was as scunnered with stabbing forty-six as he was. Scumbag stabbed by scumbag. City is one scumbag less. Only another few thousand to go. Case closed.

Uniforms, fed up with it. The DI, fed up with it. Campbell 'Two Soups' Baxter, the crime scene manager, clearly fed up with it.

It didn't mean that any of them wouldn't do their job. Sammy Ross would get the same duty of care and attention as the rest. He would be measured up, dusted down, forensically examined and given a good wash before going to a hole in the ground or the burny fire.

In the unlikely event that there would be witnesses then they would be questioned; doors would be knocked on; known associates would be talked to. Maybe, just maybe, the cops would find out who shanked the dealer. Maybe, just maybe, the great Glasgow public would give a monkey's if they did.

There were probably worse places to be early on a wet, miserable Sunday than a damp corner of Blochairn, but right at that moment Winter was buggered if he could think of any. The natives at the gate were getting restless and Winter imagined he could hear the sound of pitchforks being sharpened. Little splashes of rain were falling into the burgundy pool that Sammy had drowned in, making waves that screwed up any blood splatter calculations that Two Soups and his forensics would try to make. Not that it mattered much.

Winter had just seen it too many times.

You were more likely to be murdered in Glasgow than any other city in Western Europe. And when it came to stabbings, the 'no mean city' was a match for anywhere in the world. It kept you in work if your job was to photograph the leftovers.

He'd been doing just that for six years and this moment, the point where he was about to look at the body for the first time, was always the same. From day one to this, it hadn't changed. Excited and scared, fifty-fifty. What he was scared of was also exactly what he wanted to see. And part of the reason he was scared was because he knew just how much he wanted to see it.

Tony could kid himself all he wanted about how dull another stabbing was but he was still interested in the business end. It was what got him out of bed whether he liked it or not.

Being there, in the moment before the flowers and the football tops mourn another victim, when blood still runs hot in a body that has given up its ghost, is a strange privilege. You can see much of what the person had been and some of what they might have been if the city hadn't cut them down. It was a moment that messed with his head every time.

You saw them caught in the very moment that they were claimed. He was already feeling the ache to see and to photograph the expression on Sammy Ross's face as much as the wound in his belly. He knew that made him a sick fucker but it was his itch.

There's a Gaelic word that he loved. Winter only knew a handful of words and phrases, the obvious ones like *uisge beatha* and *sláinte*: whisky and cheers.

In fact when he thought about it, the words that he knew in Gaelic either said a lot about his drinking or about Scotland. Apart from words about boozing, he could count to five – *aon, dà, trì, ceithir, còig* – and trot out *ceud mìle fàilte*, a hundred thousand welcomes.

His favourite, though, was *sgriob*. An old boy from Skye named Lachie, who used to drink in the Lismore, taught him it. It means the itchiness, the tingle of anticipation that comes upon the upper lip just before taking a sip of whisky. Brilliant. The Eskimos may have a hundred different words for snow but trust the Gaels to have a word for that.

Another old teuchter later told him that you had to say *sgriob drama* or *sgriob dibhe* for it to refer specifically to whisky or else it just meant a scratch or scrape. He preferred Lachie's version, though.

Everyone had an itch and this was Tony's. *Sgriob* death. The hot, smooth, soft woman that was lying curled up in his warm bed once called it necrophotographilia. It wasn't sexual though. Not that. Every bit as much as he was tired of death, sick of it, he couldn't help looking. He knew he was making himself wait. Prolonging the *sgriob*. Savouring the final seconds before he looked, wondering if Sammy boy would be scared or shocked, outraged or questioning. Would that stab wound be angry or clinical, lunatic or clean? How much blood and where?

The first dead body he ever saw was the first one he photographed. Day one on photo cop duty and called out to a car smash on the M80 just north of Muirhead. A woman no more than twenty-five had gone head first through the windscreen. No seat belt, no chance.

He'd been told what had happened on his way to the crash and his stomach was already doing somersaults. He nearly threw up when he saw her lying in a shroud of broken glass in front of her Renault Clio. A smart silver car with a pair of pink hanging dice that she had vaulted past on her hurry through the glass.

The cop on the scene said she must have managed to duck her head forward because there was barely a scratch on her face. The top of her skull was smashed and the steering wheel had wrecked her chest but her face was all but unmarked. She had this clear look of determination, had been doing all she could to stay alive and protect herself. Everything that is apart from putting her seat belt on in the first place.

Tony took one photo. He had knelt a few feet away from her, snapped one then was backing away towards the barrier when the uniform came over and hissed in his ear. Asked him what the fuck he thought he was doing. Told him he had to photograph the woman from every possible angle, make sure there was no doubt whatsoever as to position, trauma, depth, scale, everything, and then when he had done that he had to photograph tyre depths, skid distances, glass shatter and all approaching junctions. Winter had known all that of course but every bit of his training disappeared from his head when he saw the woman lying on the road.

Finally, he did what he was supposed to but he didn't stop there. Beyond the caved skull and the battered torso, the glass pattern and the skid signature, he photographed the look of business on the face of the uniformed polis that covered her up and the frightened stare of the witness who couldn't tear his eyes away from her.

Looking back, he wondered at the nerve of tucking his own Canon SLR away in his bag beside the digital Nikon that the department provided but was glad that he did. Something about the grain of the black and white film gave it a feel that he liked. More importantly, the shots weren't on the official memory card.

Avril Duncanson, exhibit one. He didn't suppose he would ever forget her name if he did a million jobs. Anyway, her photographs were in his collection so there was always something there to remind him. As if it was needed. Some things you never forget. Close your eyes and they are hiding there behind your lids.

Winter snapped backed to the dreich reality of Blochairn and realized that Two Soups was huffing about him getting on with it, pushing for him to get his photographs done so that the examiners could get in about the body. He was a miserable old sod, easily Winter's least favourite of those that could have been on scene. If the lovely Cat Fitzpatrick was at one end of the scale then Two Soups was definitely at the other. He was a pain in the arse. An old-school type who had a hatred of amateur forensics, particularly cops, who had learned all they knew from the rush of telly programmes on the subject.

But sadly for Baxter, photography always comes first at a crime scene, recording everything as is before the SOCOs get in to touch anything. It meant his time was dictated to and that wasn't the way he thought it should be. Monkeys with cameras ought not to take precedence over highly trained scientists. This morning he was clearly pissed off that Winter hadn't been on site earlier as well as being annoyed that he was on site at all. He didn't say anything, just glowered. Well, he could get to fuck. Winter only had one chance to record this scene and he wasn't going to rush it even if it was just yet another stabbing.

He lined up a full-length shot of the body and focused. Two Soups was shut out and so was the rest of the world. It was just him and Sammy Ross.

He took in the look on the face below him for the first time. Resignation. Total defeat. Not shock though. Sammy Ross had seen this coming. Now he had this thousand-yard stare and it didn't look as if he liked what he saw.

Winter did, though. For all its ugliness, it was a thing of beauty.

Rigor mortis had begun to kick in so he must have been dead for a few hours. The knees that had given way as he buckled and fell were already locked. One arm bent under him, clutching at the hole in his chest, the other twisted at his side where he had tried to break his fall. No chance of breaking a fall like that though – it descended straight into hell.

The burgundy bloodspill soaked his jeans and drenched his light-blue T-shirt but was already drying on both. His skin was alabaster pale, his lips kissed with blue.

It was a deep incision. Through the torn, bloodied scraps of cotton, Winter could see the ripped skin where the knife had been stuck. An initial entry wound then it rose sharply up the chest tearing skin as it went. The killer had stuck it in then twisted the knife before pushing it up deeper and deadlier, seeking out vital organs to destroy. Whoever did it had used a knife before. In Glasgow, that narrowed it down to maybe a quarter of the male population between twelve and twenty-five.

Winter focused on the wound. It was almost big enough to reach inside and grab those punctured organs, enough room to get in and search for the spirit that was no longer there. The skin was split and smiling up at him, the treasures behind already starting to fester without the beat of life to sustain them.

Focus. Shoot. Every detail, from every angle. So tempting to lift the T-shirt and see the full extent of the damage but that was strictly forbidden. Look but don't touch. Record but don't interfere. Observe but don't violate. Chronicle but don't contaminate.

Designer trainers, at least £120 the pair. Hideous, flash shoes in black and gold. The Burberry cap that had tumbled off his lank, unkempt hair and lay by the side of his sleeping head. The navy-blue Ben Sherman jacket sprayed with his own blood and the Tag Heuer that was smashed on his wrist but still ticked even though his heart had stopped. It all said money. It all said bad taste. It all said trash with cash.

His blue-purple lips said no. His eyes said please. A rabbit caught in the headlights of his own destiny. Bastard child of greed and poverty.

All that was laid out in the broken body before him, writ large in the wound in his middle and on his freeze-frame face. Sammy was a picture all right.

This was why Winter took photographs. To show it how it was, every wart, every insult, every injury, because every city is defined just as much by its ugly wounds as its architecture. He'd always imagined that if you cut Glasgow's gutterbelly, you'd see it run blue and green with bitterness but with as much hope as there was bile. It was a great city where terrible things happened, things that should never be ignored but should be captured for ever.

His job had taken him to dark places that most civilians never go, seeing bloody puddles where life used to be, recording the moment before the mourners descended. All life was there, sitting cosy right next to death.

That was the bit that always got to him, just how close they sit next to each other. A split second, a nanosecond, an angstrom from one to the next. And he was there to ensure that that precise moment, where life turns to death and hope turns to shit, is always recorded right there on their face. Recorded for ever by a Nikon FM2 and a Canon EOS-1D.

A thing of beauty really.

CHAPTER 2

'If I remember right then Sammy boy is from Royston, east end somewhere for sure.' The voice came from behind Winter and dragged him out of his dwam. It was Addison. 'He's thirty-two, thirty-three. Old to be still knocking it out on the street. Sure-fire sign he was going nowhere fast. Kind of bam that pushes out coke, heroin, jellies, ecstasy, dope, uppers, downers, steroids; whatever the junkies want, this cunt would stuff it down their throat, in their arm or up their nose. '

Addison was angry and it was obvious in his voice. He'd seen way too much of this shit.

'Just a foot soldier in Malky Quinn's army,' he went on. 'Funny how Malky and his like never end up lying stabbed in the rain. It's always the Sammy Ross's that get it. One of Malky's boys ... brilliant. Means trouble for someone. Probably means trouble for everyone. Fuck's sake, it's not even eight o'clock and the day's already turned to shit. I want a bacon roll.'

Winter had finished his photographs but hadn't stopped looking. He was irritated at Addison for shaking him out of it but when he caught the look on Two Soups's face he thought maybe it was just as well. The old sod looked fit to burst. Winter ignored his glare.

'You ever stop thinking about your stomach, Addy,' he said as he stood up. 'No wonder you are such a fat bastard.'

The DI was six foot four and skinny as a rake, his height just making him look even thinner. He was just about to come back with a smart-arse remark of his own when his DS, a haunted-looking guy with dirty fair hair, name of Colin Monteith, wandered up towing a human skelf wearing trackies, a heavy white jacket and the obligatory baseball cap. Junkie ned. Monteith must have had the uniformed boys talking to the walking dead that were anywhere near the market at that time of the morning. Though if any of them had ever known anything, chances were they had already forgotten. Addison rolled his eyes as if to say, jeez, this better be good.

Monteith told the skelf to stay put and came up to where the pair were standing.

'Might have a live one, Addy. This guy was dossing in the market but he actually knows what day it is, so I'd say he's worth a wee word. Says he heard noises that sounded like it was our man meeting his maker.'

'Knows what day it is?' Winter butted in. 'Does that qualify him for some award scheme? Junkie of the Month maybe.'

Monteith fired him a dark look.

'I'll have a word,' said Addison with a sigh. 'He might be as near to compos mentis as we are going to get from the zoomers round here. Bring him over.'

The inspector's lanky frame towered over the undernourished user, leaving him in no doubt who was in charge. The skelf looked up at Addison uncomfortably, shifting from foot to foot.

'So, you heard noises?' It was as much a statement as a question. 'Tell me about them.'

'It's like ah telt the other polis. Ah'd been sleeping. It was still dark o'clock. Know what I mean, man?'

Addison looked like he was resisting the temptation to tell him to get on with it but settled for a nod instead.

'Aye well, it wis still pure dark an ah heard voices. Arguing, man.

But no that loud. It went on for a bit then there wis this bit eh a mad scream that stopped quick an ah heard the guy hit the deck.'

'What did you hear after that?'

'Nothing, man.'

'Nothing? Anyone walking away, anyone running? Anyone crying for help? A car starting, maybe a motorbike? Something hitting the ground after being thrown away?'

'No. Well, aye. Someone walking away. I'd say he wisnae running, kinda slow like he was maybe dragging something. Naebody crying for help though. Would say he was well deid.'

'And what did you do? Call the police like a good citizen?'

'No way, man. Sorry but no way. I was jist laying low in case the guy came back. Nae point in me getting offed as well. I might have fell asleep again. No sure. Next thing I know the place is full of polis.'

'Did you see the person that did it? Height, hair colour, anything?'

'It wis dark, man, telt ye. Anyways, didnae lift ma heid tae look. Just listened.'

'What did you mean when you said he was dragging something? Carrying something with him?'

'Mibbes. Ah've nae idea. Carrying, dragging. Mibbes.'

Addison shook his head despairingly then nodded Monteith back in to take the junkie away and finish taking notes.

'Tell him anything and everything you remember and don't go booking any foreign holidays any time soon.'

'Aye, very funny. Any chance of a few quid for coming forward?'

'Sure. See the officer at the cash desk on your way back out the market. Mind and duck in case there are any pigs flying past.'

The skelf's comeback about pigs died on his lips and he slunk off with Monteith's meaty paw on his arm.

'Sunday, bloody Sunday,' moaned Addison. 'Hurry up and finish photographing that muppet and bring your camera with you,' he told Winter. 'There's a van down the street that does good grub even though most of the folk who go to it are too shit-faced to know the difference. You can photograph me eating two bacon rolls. Brown sauce on it and a cup of coffee. You're paying.'

Winter didn't bother asking why. Just as Addison didn't bother asking why he'd been photographing the dealer's body with his Canon EOS-1D as well as the standard issue Nikon FM2. The same reason Addison didn't ask why Winter had sneaked a shot of the haunted look on the skelf's face as he stared down at Sammy's corpse. Addison was one of only two people who knew about Winter's collection. He'd even said Winter should stage an exhibition but that was usually when he was pished.

Suddenly, Two Soups barged in between them, asking if they were quite finished. Big mistake. He could pull that shit with Winter but not with Addison.

'Mr Baxter,' he glared down at the forensic and growled. 'I was interviewing possibly the only witness to whoever killed this guy. Tony Winter was photographing the body. Both of these tasks are vital to this investigation and it was imperative that they be done without delay. The body, on the other hand, isn't going anywhere. I take it you have no fucking problem with that?'

Two Soups blinked in disbelief at being spoken to that way and struggled for a reply. 'Well I was just ...'

'Fine. I'm glad you agree. We are both finished so now you and the lab monkeys can begin your equally invaluable work. Winter has footprints to photograph and I've got stallholders to interview. We won't keep you.'

With that Addison took Winter by the arm and led him away from Baxter and the body, leaving Two Soups spluttering with discontent behind them before calling his forensic soldiers to the battlefield.

'That man is an arsehole,' said Addison with a grin on his face.

'Where are these footprints?' Winter asked him.

'Two pairs of them together on soft ground near a wall on the north side. Suggestion is that it could be our man Sammy and whoever came in with him because they were heading in the direction of where Ross was found before they were lost on tarmac.'

'So if they are on the north side, why are we heading this way?' asked Winter with a quiet laugh.

'Because I want bacon rolls. Jesus Christ, do you never listen to anything I say? Two uniforms have got the area secure and covered over, the footprints can wait but my stomach won't.'

Addison drove his hands deep into his pockets as he led Winter towards the van.

'How many times are we expected to do this?' he moaned. 'If I'd wanted to sweep the rubbish off the street I'd have joined the council bin squad. At least I'd have been back in my fucking bed by now.'

Bed. She'd still be lying there, thought Winter, probably sprawled over onto his side by now. Addison was still whinging but all he could think of was her. A dead dealer and a bacon roll didn't really cut it in comparison.

It was less than a five-minute walk. A dark-haired fat guy who was far cheerier than anyone had a right to be at that time in the morning was serving two teenagers as they arrived. The pair immediately spotted Addison for police and couldn't wait to get their grub and leave. Their hurried departure didn't bother either Addison or Winter. If there was a soul in Glasgow whose conscience wasn't bothered by the sight of a cop then chances were it was another cop. 'Four bacon rolls, Charlie,' Addison said to the fat man.

'Three,' Winter corrected him.

'Four,' he repeated. 'I'll have your other one if you don't want it.'

'Brown sauce, Mr Addison?' asked Charlie.

'Does the Pope shit in the woods? Of course, brown sauce.'

Addison turned his collar against the morning chill and took in the smell of pork and fat coming from the van's grill.

'This place should have a Michelin star,' he said to Winter. Then, 'What time did you start this morning, Charlie?'

'Half six. Think your boys and girls were already at the market by the time I turned up if that's what you were thinking.'

'Who was on before you?'

'Jimmy Frize. He'd been on since eleven last night. Never mentioned anything out of the ordinary. Usual shit.'

'Drunks and druggies?'

'Does a bear wear a big hat?'

'Aye, aye. Where can I get hold of Jimmy?'

Charlie wrote Frize's number on a piece of paper and handed it over to Addison who had already scoffed his two rolls even though Winter had only managed half of one.

'Another roll, Mr Addison? On the van.'

'You trying to bribe a police officer, Charlie? Aye, go on then.'

'No as if you are going to put on any weight, is it? Put a slice of black pudding in there too, Mr A. Ah know how you're partial.'

'Plenty of brown sauce, Charlie.'

Addison started on his third roll as they turned their backs on the van and ambled back towards Blochairn, the debris of a good night out still kicking at their feet. Like its people, Glasgow looked at its gallus best on a Saturday night and at its worst on a Sunday morning. Empty Buckie bottles, vomit and broken windows. This was the Glasgow they didn't put in the glossy ads. It was a ten-minute drive from Princes Square and the designer shops on Buchanan Street but it was a world away.

Two seagulls fought over the cold remains of a fish supper dropped by a drunk. The wind and rain made an empty can of Irn Bru scoot along the gutter.

'Fuck this,' complained Addison. 'There are times I hate Scotland and it's usually when it's raining. Which is most of the time. Having to scrape a dealer off the floor of the market sure isn't doing much for my mood either.'

'Ah, cheer up, big man,' Winter laughed. 'Maybe by the time we get back that twat Monteith will have solved the case and we'll know the secret of the mysterious death of Sammy Ross.'

Addison snarled.

'Sammy Ross? Waste of fucking space, waste of fucking time. He's just more paperwork.' The DI's phone rang and he swore as he transferred the remains of his roll from one hand to the other, digging his mobile out of his jacket pocket. Swallowing food down, he held it to his ear and grunted a hello.

'Yes? Yes, sir . . . You're fucking joking me . . . No sir, I don't suppose you are. Sorry . . . Shit. Okay, I'll be there in half an hour.'

Winter was stuck between trying not to smirk and worried about what he'd been told.

'What's up?'

Addison shook his head wearily.

'This town will be the death of me. They've found the body of a hooker in Wellington Lane. Some bastard's strangled the poor cow.'

Winter tried to conceal the look that wanted to flitter over his face, a look that would register somewhere between disgust and excitement.

'We finishing up here before we go?'

'*We're* not going,' replied Addison. 'Just me. Monteith can run the show here but forensics are already photographing the prossie so you're not needed. And don't even bother arguing, it's out of my hands.'

'Fucksake,' blurted out Winter. 'They pull you off one fucking murder for another. Why? Because it's more important. Yet they don't want to photograph it properly!'

Addison smiled gleefully at his friend's irritation.

'You know how it is, wee man. Everything's got its place in the scheme of things. Some scumbag getting stabbed on a Saturday night is worth about the same as an A in Scrabble but a murdered prossie is a J. And photographs of deid bodies are the same whether they are taken by you or a trained monkey.'

Winter knew that he was winding him up but, despite himself, he bit.

'Fuck you. Fuck right off and stick your letter J up your A for arse.'

Addison laughed loudly.

'Nice comeback, wee man. And so eloquently put. And now if you'll excuse me, I've got to go. I've got a date with a young lady.'

CHAPTER 3

It was raining harder by the time Addison got to Wellington Lane, one of the handful of narrow alleyways that cut their way across the lower city centre. With just enough room to drive a car or van through, the lanes acted as a service for the rear entrances of upmarket shops, offices and hotels. At night, dark and out of sight, they serviced a different type of business altogether.

The DI parked on West Campbell Street, cursing at the downpour that forced him to turn his collar up and hustle past the rain-soaked constable who guarded the entrance to the lane. Up ahead, spotlights and a tent had already been set up where a knot of uniforms, CID and forensics gathered in the gloom. Addison, head down, marched by a procession of large red, industrial wheelie bins and found his DS, Rachel Narey, waiting impatiently by the last of them – the one that was covered by the white crime scene tent.

Addison walked straight past her, only a raising of his eyebrows letting her know that he was duly pissed off, stopping inside to pull on coveralls and a pair of disposable gloves. She shook her head and followed him inside the tent where examiners were huddled over the woman's body.

'Okay,' barked Addison. 'Let the dog see the rabbit.'

The white protective suit immediately in front of him turned and looked up.

'The epitome of decorum as ever, Detective Inspector.'

Addison saw the green eyes of Cat Fitzpatrick looking up at him disapprovingly but he wasn't in the mood to be lectured to.

'Aye, aye, whatever. I know it's not even opening time yet but it's already been a very long day. So if you don't mind, doll, I've got a job to do.'

'That's fine, don't mind me. I'm just waiting for my nail varnish to dry,' she replied sarcastically.

'That's nice,' replied Addison, not remotely listening but taking Fitzpatrick's place as she moved out of the way.

The girl lying tangled on the pavement was in her early twenties, her eyes and mouth wide open in shock, her short skirt rucked up above her waist and her underwear round one ankle. Her pale neck bore violent compression marks where her young life had been strangled out of her.

The girl's platinum-blonde hair was darker at the roots and her make-up was as thick as her lipstick was red. Her arms were skinny and her face gaunt behind the war paint. Addison noted the discolouration of her fingers, her decaying teeth and the raw red marks at her nostrils. They were as sure signs of her habit as the black platform boots, the micro skirt and the halterneck top were of her employment.

The DI moved slightly to the side and saw a dark patch of dried blood on the back of the girl's head that made a good match with her lipstick.

'So which killed her?' he asked the scene examiner. 'The strangulation or the blow to the head?'

'Either could have done it,' Fitzpatrick replied. 'But I'd suggest the injury to the skull was secondary, or at least incidental to the primary attack. As he compressed her neck, he forced her back and in doing so banged her head off whatever was behind her. Which wasn't here, by the way.'

'So where?'

'Twenty metres further up the lane. There are flecks of blue paint in her skull which matches an opening there. If it took place here then she'd have traces of this brickwork but she hasn't.'

'We got a name for her yet?' Addison asked.

'No,' replied Narey from behind him. 'There was nothing on her, no bag, no ID. She'd either stashed it somewhere before she began working or someone stole it from her.'

'Robbery?' asked Addison doubtfully.

'Doesn't seem likely, I agree. It looks as if he killed her during or immediately after sex and that suggests a whole different kind of motive.'

'Fucking great,' muttered Addison.

He gently lifted up one of the girl's hands, noting the dirty fingers and cracked nails and, more importantly, no obvious signs of skin beneath the nails where she might have clawed at her attacker.

'It looks like she didn't fight back.'

'Stoned out of her head, most likely,' offered Narey. 'She didn't know if it was Friday or Falkirk and by the time she did, he'd strangled her.'

'Looks that way,' agreed Fitzpatrick. 'I'll need to wait on the toxicology tests and have a more thorough look beneath her nails but I think DS Narey is right.'

Addison nodded soberly, their opinions confirmation of what he thought.

'Okay, Rachel, seeing as you are on form, what do you make of this?' he asked, pointing his finger at a patch on one side of the girl's face where her make-up had been partially scrubbed away from her cheek.

'It's strange,' admitted Narey. 'Might just be part of the struggle or it could be some weird attempt by the killer to leave his mark on her.'

'Could be,' murmured Addison. 'See the sweep of it? Looks like it was done with fingers then gone over again with something like the sleeve of a shirt to wipe away any fingerprints. Who have you got here with you?'

'DC Corrieri,' Narey replied. 'She's outside.'

'When you get back to the station get her onto the Police National Computer and see if this marries up with any known sex offender, marking his territory kind of thing. It's probably a long shot but if this fucker has done this before then we need to know about it. And I need you to find out who she is. You got people you know down here?'

'I've got a contact over at the drop-in centre,' Narey nodded. 'But there's not going to be anyone around at this time of day.'

'Same goes for the other girls who would have been working down here last night. Okay, I'll organize a sweep of the place for tonight and see if anyone will talk to us. In the meantime I'll get someone to go through the CCTV. You find me a name for her.'

'Will do.'

'Ms Fitzpatrick, do you have an approximate time of death for me?' Addison asked.

'For you, Detective Inspector? Any time soon, one would hope.'

'Funny. I did mention that it had been a long day, didn't I? When do you think she was killed?'

'Best guess right now is around midnight. I'll be able to give you a slightly better idea later.'

'Okay, I guess that will have to do for now. Rachel, talk me through how and where she was found. I take it the cops who were first called are still here?'

'Yes, PCs Dwyer and Watt. They're outside with Corrieri.'

'Okay, let's go talk to them. Cat, do what else you need to then cover her up and get her out of here for fuck's sake. The poor cow has suffered enough for one day.'

Constables Stevie Dwyer and Kenny Watt had been called to

the scene just before eight that morning after a man taking a shortcut along the lane had spotted the heel of a black platform boot sticking out from behind the big red bin. Something had made him take a closer look and he discovered the owner's body still attached to the boot. After nearly crapping himself on the spot, he called the cops.

Dwyer and Watt were there in minutes from the cop shop at Anderston and had the full forensic cavalry join them not long after. Neither of the cops recognized the girl and witnesses were thin on the ground. The man who'd found her had a solid alibi for the night before. The girl had been photographed in situ behind the bin before it was eased away so that she could be examined. When Fitzpatrick noticed the residue of blue paint in the girl's hair, she'd looked up and down the lane, seeing likely locations nearby. The first was a window frame and doorway just a few feet away which were in the same shade of dark blue as the paint but neither area contained the blood spatter she would have expected from the blow to the girl's head. Further down the lane, however, was a garage entrance, set in a few feet from the road and decked out in dark blue. It had taken Fitzpatrick just a few seconds to look around head height on the metal shuttered entrance to find skin tissue and blonde hair strands matted in blood where the girl's skull had been cracked against it.

'Looks a likely place for a girl to take a punter,' Addison was saying to Narey. 'Dark, set in off the lane, no street lighting, no cameras.'

'A good place to kill someone for the same reasons,' she replied.

'Hm. So, premeditated or impulse? Stand up against the wall here. Next to where she would have been.'

'You wish.'

'Fucksake, just do it. Assume the position.'

With a shake of her head, Narey placed her back to the wall and looked defiantly at the DI.

'Okay.'

He stood in front of her, far too close for her liking, and positioned himself with his hips close to hers. He raised both hands to her neck and mimed strangulation.

'Sir?'

'Yes?'

'Fuck off, will you?'

'Not just yet.'

Addison parodied the motion of knocking Narey's head against the wall, then moved down in the direction she would have fallen, noticing further tiny traces of blood on the ground.

'Now he wants to hide her,' he continued. 'He carries her, drags her maybe, towards the bins.'

The DI moved slowly along back towards the tented crime scene, careful to avoid stamping all over the actual route, finally standing by it.

'Okay,' he said eventually. 'Thoughts?'

Narey could have done without the theatrics but could see some value in the process.

'Okay,' she began. 'So he's big enough to have hauled her along there, twenty metres or so, without getting seen.'

'But –'

'But perhaps not big enough or brave enough to put her *in* the bin where the body would have stayed longer without being found.'

'Yeah,' he agreed. 'I reckon if he could carry her that far fairly quickly - and he wouldn't have wanted to hang about - then he could have got her in the bin. But he wanted away from there as quickly as possible. So, not premeditated. I'd say, rushed.'

'An impulse sex killer,' she concluded.

'Rachel, do you ever get days when you wish you'd just never got out of bed?'

'Boss, whenever you use sentences with the word "bed" in them I get nervous,' she replied.

'Because I certainly do and this is one of them,' he said, ignoring her. 'There's something about the mess on that girl's face where the bastard tried to remove her make-up that really bothers me. You know what I mean?'

'Your second body this morning,' she sympathized. 'Hardly surprising if you are a bit spooked.'

Addison threw her an indignant look.

'Spooked? Get to fuck. I'm hungry, that's what I am. Starving. But the scrubbing of that make-up? The bastard that did that is making a point. You mark my words.'

CHAPTER 4

Afternoon, Sunday 11 September

Winter had been stuck in his office in the bowels of Strathclyde Police HQ in Pitt Street since returning from Blochairn. The room was empty but for him and his photographs of Sammy Ross's plundered chest. If the pics had been more interesting, like Addison's murdered hooker, then it might well have been enough for him. But Sammy just wasn't cutting it.

Winter hated paperwork every bit as much as Addison did. The mindless purgatory involved in filing and barcoding his crime scene photographs was bad enough but even worse was when he was forced to do the same thing for other people. Being his own secretary was dull as either dishwater or ditchwater, whichever it was. Being someone else's made him want to puke.

He wanted to be out there, at the scene of car crashes, shootings and suicides as soon as they happened, hitting the shutter minutes after the body hit the ground. Not stuck under diffused lighting, filling boxes and killing time.

Winter hadn't given up what passed for a career in IT and retrained at college just to be a frigging data processor. Or maybe he had. It had taken him six years to get to the stage where he was doing something that was this dull. When it was like this, suddenly running network applications didn't seem quite so bad. In fact, worse than that, it didn't seem so different.

Of course the irony was that the cops were where he'd wanted to be in the first place. Uncle Danny Neilson had been in the force all his days and when he was young there wasn't much that Winter wanted more than to do what Danny did. So he'd applied and strolled through the Standard Entrance Tests and the fitness tests at Jackton but managed to stuff up the formal interview by telling the truth. Maybe if he had kept that fascination with death to himself then he wouldn't have had to fall into computer programming instead. Still, he always wondered how he'd been considered too much of a risk to be allowed to walk around the city centre all day but it was perfectly okay for him to be in charge of millions of pounds of software or to photograph dead people. Winter settled for believing it said more about the police and psychometric testing than it did about him.

People told him he was crazy when he gave up his job as an IT hunchback to become a police photographer. Everyone said he was nuts throwing away his degree but what they didn't understand was that he hadn't wanted to spend any more time at a keyboard. He'd had the itch from the moment he first saw Metinides's photographs in London. It wasn't exactly following in Danny's size elevens but maybe it was better. Winter had got such a buzz looking at the Mexican's work and he'd known that was going to be multiplied by ten when he took his own. The photos he was filing for one of the scene examiners, Caroline Sanchez, had been taken on the corner of Dullsville. A Mazda MX-5 had gone through a red light and had been smacked by a bus going smartly through green coming the other way. The driver of the car had escaped with a fractured arm but there was a lot of broken glass to be photographed and filed. Give him strength. Sanchez was back out there working the skid marks from an assault and robbery in Summerston and he was stuck deep in the Pitt, doing her electronic paperwork.

It was all part of what Winter thought of as his bargain with the devil, the strange set-up that allowed him to be one of only two proper photographers to be still working for Strathclyde cops. The rest of the work was now done by the monkeys in bunny suits, button-pushers who didn't know their aperture from their exposure. Oh, they knew everything there was to know about grave wax, petechial marks and ridge characteristics, but they knew bugger all about taking photographs. Point, fiddle with the focus and fire off as many shots as they could in the hope that one of them would be on the money. And, of course, money was what it was all about. Getting the scene examiners to double on the camera was all to do with saving cash at the expense of expertise. There were so many times that not only was a proper photographer needed but that it cried out for film rather than digital. Something like bite marks could never be done well enough on digital, you needed film to get the depth of detail you needed when you went into court. Winter had learned his trade on an old Hasselblad H4D that gave you just twelve shots and you had to make damn sure that every one of them counted. As far as he was concerned, the forensics wielded their cameras like scatterguns.

Winter knew he didn't have too much room to complain on that front though because at least the previous Chief Constable had sense enough to value what he did, and didn't kick him into touch with the rest of the snappers. Of course it hadn't hurt that Sir Ed Walker was a camera buff and appreciated the finer points of agitation and hyperfocal distance. Nor did it do any harm when Winter made a first-class job of the Chief's official photo for the Pitt Street reception wall and did a freebie family portrait of him with the wife and kids. Even when natural wastage and the ravages of Inhuman Resources took their toll on the force's photographers, Walker ruled that someone should be kept on for specialist purposes. Winter was the cockroach that survived the nuclear holocaust.

Being the exception didn't endear Winter to everyone but that was hardly his problem. Two Soups could moan all he liked about wanting to standardize the department but Winter's work spoke for itself and there was nothing he could do about it. The new chief, Grant Gordon, was happy enough with the arrangement.

The only other proper snapper left in the west was an old-timer named Barrie Marshall who worked out of Argyll, Bute and West Dunbartonshire, covering everything from the edge of civilization to the islands and southern teuchterland. He'd been in with the bricks so long that HR seemed to have forgotten he was there so he'd also managed to escape the cull and spent his days happily photographing ransacked birds' nests and break-ins at distilleries. Not that that would have worked for Winter; he needed more.

He needed more than Sammy Ross too. It had been dull fare spending forty-five minutes filing every available bit of information they had on him. Twenty-two photographs from twenty-two angles and distances, every curl of skin, every tear of tissue, every bruise, entry point, exit wound and expression. It was all pretty mundane stuff.

Only the disappointed look on Sammy's face was of real interest on the basis that a glimpse into eternity is always worthwhile. Back in the day they believed you could see the reflection of the killer in the eyes of a murder victim. Of course it sounded bollocks but maybe no more ridiculous than Winter thinking he could see death through a lens. Look into the eyes of any of Glasgow's victims and you'll be staring into the same deep pool of murky darkness that Winter saw in the drug dealer's pupils. All the very same shade of black.

The phone mercifully rang and he found himself wishing for a bit of murder, mayhem or carnage. Maybe a nice shooting. Whatever it was, he wasn't for sharing it.

Two minutes later the phone was back on the hook and he was shutting down his PC. It wasn't great but at least it was getting him out of there. A seventeen-year-old kid had been beaten up and one knee trashed with a baseball bat. The teenager was now holed up in the Royal where the cops were about to interview him.

The Infirmary was a mile away across the city centre so he had the choice of taking twenty minutes to walk there from Pitt Street or nineteen minutes to drive. He'd drive.

Glasgow Royal is like so many of the city's hospitals. A two-hundred-year old maze that costs a fortune to heat and to repair. Next to no parking, under-staffed and under-funded, over-used and always in the crosshairs of the bean-counters' sniper. It sits on the north-eastern edge of the city and has been on the same spot near Glasgow Cathedral and the Necropolis since George III was barking mad on the throne of the Empire and Glasgow was its second city. Which was about the last time the Royal had a lick of fresh paint.

Millions of Glaswegians had been born there, died there, broken and mended there. It had seen more blood and guts than World War One and bits of it looked like they had been patched up with a bicycle repair kit. Over the years they'd torn down blocks, tagged on new buildings and added to it when they could and where they had to. New building here, maternity division there and plastic surgery unit somewhere else. It was an amazing building, architecturally stunning in parts and ugly blocks in others, so much more than the sum of its parts.

It was the nature of the job and the city that Winter found himself in there much more than he'd like. Saturday night, Sunday morning in a city like Glasgow was odds on that someone got an injury that was going to end up in court and needed photographing. It wasn't the same thing as getting them at the scene, nothing like it, but it paid the bills.

It meant Winter knew his way round the labyrinth well enough, particularly around A&E, and there were a few doctors and nurses that he was on nodding terms with. Truth be told, there were a couple of nurses that he'd done more than nod to in the past but that was another story.

He'd just turned into the corridor leading to A&E when he saw two cops coming the other way. Detective Sergeant Rachel Narey and a young uniformed constable. Well, well.

Narey was looking good. Her dark hair was tied back and shining, her trim figure filling the dark suit and white blouse rather nicely indeed. No matter how businesslike she aimed for, this girl couldn't help but look sexy. Winter didn't know the constable but he looked like he was straight out of the cop college at Tulliallan. He also looked like he might have a sex wee just looking at Narey.

'You here for Rory McCabe?' Narey asked by way of a hello.

'Sure am,' Winter replied with a smile. 'What's the script? I just got a few details on the phone and headed over.'

'Seventeen-year-old from Dennistoun. Found by two of his mates, screaming his lungs out in the middle of Craigpark Drive with a busted knee. They couldn't get a car to stop so they picked him up and carried him here. McCabe's saying nothing other than he's no idea who did it or why. Lying little shite. He's scared out of his mind and he knows a lot more about who did it than he's letting on.'

'Didn't think they would send a DS for this,' he teased her.

She scowled at him but her brown eyes flashed.

'Yeah, it's not like I don't have enough on my plate today but this falls under the Chief Constable's pet project. Gordon wants us to come down heavy on gang stuff at the moment so here I am.'

'That what it is, gang stuff?'

'Looks that way but it's usually knives with that lot. Baseball bats are more a big boy's way of doing things. But like I said, the wee bastard isn't saying. We've spoken to his parents and they swear blind he isn't involved with any gangs. Was at college and had been looking to go on to uni. He'll be hobbling there now.'

'What's the damage?'

'Left knee smashed to bits. Taken a whack to the face as well and his arm's nearly been twisted out the socket. They've got him on morphine for the pain.'

'Nice.'

'We're going to let him stew and maybe talk to him tomorrow. Maybe. I've got some proper work to be getting on with. Your pal Addison has got me trying to put a name to a girl who doesn't seem to have one, so that is going to take priority. Happy days.'

'The girl that was found in Wellington Lane?'

Narey narrowed her eyes at him curiously but didn't bite.

'Happy photographing, Mr Winter.'

With that the DS and the young PC, who hadn't said a word the whole time but just made puppy eyes at Narey, headed towards the exit and Winter headed into A&E. In the family waiting area outside, he locked eyes with a young muscular guy with close-cropped hair and got an angry glare for his trouble. He had no idea what the guy's problem was but given that he was about six foot two and built like a brick shithouse, Winter wasn't about to start arguing with him.

Inside, a nurse directed him to a curtained-off bed and he pulled back the screens to get a reproachful look from a bald surgeon in green scrubs who, along with a plump blonde nurse, was standing over the teenager in the bed. Winter just gave him a shrug in return and the surgeon shook his head before slipping through the curtain and letting him get on with it. The nurse, Karen according to her name tag, stayed.

Rory McCabe was a big lad for his age but soft with it. A tousled mop of reddish hair fringed his eyes and he'd barely begun shaving. Most local kids his age were seventeen going on thirty-seven but this one didn't have the hard-edged look that they wore.

He looked a stranger to Buckfast and baseball bats. Well, except the one that had wrecked his knee.

Narey said his mum and dad had sworn blind that Rory had never been in any bother but then lots of parents don't have the first clue what their kids get up to. Winter was inclined to think the McCabes might be right though. No scars, no tattoos, no ned hair cut, no missing teeth, no needle marks. Just a busted knee, a big purple bruise on his jaw and a rash of skin torn off his face, presumably where he fell.

It seemed standard practice. Teenager gets the shit kicked out of him and he remembers nothing. No names, no pack drill. Cops take notes then close the book and the case. Next.

Rory was wearing a gown open to the waist and pulled off one shoulder, which was already bandaged and strapped to his side, his left leg hoisted up in a pulley. He looked at Winter but seemed far more interested in the pain that was coming from his knee. Aye, that knee, it was quite a sight. His amateur physiology said displaced patella and a severe haematoma. In new money, that's a broken kneecap and badly swollen knee. Winter knew there were three bones that made up the knee joint – the patella and two others that he couldn't remember. The odd, awkward angles pushing angrily at the skin around the knee suggested that all three of them were fucked. Someone had made a very good job of this.

There was already violent bruising colouring the sides of the knee; it was now blood-red and would turn purple then black before long. It had ballooned up to nearly the size of a football and looked ready to pop. The docs would be draining that soon to ease the pain but he had to do his stuff first. It was the same old routine. On the outside chance that anyone was nicked for it then the extent of the boy's injuries would need to be shown in court so that the sheriff could decide between a smack on the wrist or a really stern telling-off.

Winter snapped off a photo without asking, catching the boy

off guard. McCabe turned and just looked at him. Sullen. Glowering. Dour. Unsure. Resentful. Lost.

'Awrite, Rory? My name's Tony. I've got to take your photie.'

'So I see,' he muttered.

'What happened to you anyway?' he chanced. No harm in keeping in Narey's good books if he did let something slip.

McCabe spat out the words. 'Don't know. No idea. Leave me alone.'

His mouth said no but his eyes said no way. The boy was scared shitless.

'Fair enough,' Winter said. 'I'll just do my job and leave you in peace. Couple of those nurses look pretty hot, eh?'

That gained him a sheepish smile from Nurse Karen but no reaction from the boy beyond a grimace. He guessed that was down to the pain in his patella rather than a lack of interest in the nursing staff. No problem, wee man. I'll stick to the photographs and you stick to your story, he thought. See where that gets either of us.

This wouldn't be a pic for Winter's collection, too run of the mill. Something didn't quite fit either because the scared rabbit look on McCabe's face wasn't right either. He'd seen more than enough of these kids and he would have expected angry and vengeful. The full-on, rebel-without-a-cause, going-to-get-my-mates-to-break-some-legs kind of angry. Not this; it was all a bit pitiful.

Winter shot the knee from every angle, seeing the bones that threatened to poke through the skin, closing in on the bruises and the distortions of the joint.

Next he pulled the Fuji IS Pro from the bag, a dedicated ultraviolet infrared camera that can pick up bruising that's invisible to the eye. It wasn't needed to see the mess round his knee but you never knew what else was hidden away. Winter took a shot of Rory's face and chest too and sure enough there was a contusion on the right-hand side of the teenager's chest that couldn't have been seen without the filters.

Enough was enough. He was in no hurry to get back to the lab but what more could he do?

'You take it easy, Rory,' he told him. 'Don't go running after those nurses mind, let them chase you.'

The boy glared at him.

'Fuck off.'

Winter got the feeling it was maybe the first time Rory had ever told anyone that. The blonde nurse scowled at him as well; it looked like he'd overstayed his welcome. As Tony pushed his way through the door out of the ward, he saw the close-cropped brick shithouse guy get to his feet and make for a water dispenser on the other side of the room. It took him within a couple of feet of Winter and the photographer had no doubt that it was deliberate. The guy was aged about twenty and looked like he could handle himself – and wanted Winter to know it.

'You alright?' Winter asked him when the man was almost in his face.

'What's it got to do with you?' he growled back. 'What's your problem?'

'No problem, none at all,' Winter replied, without breaking his stride.

'Keep it that way,' said the voice at his back.

Fucking Glasgow, Winter thought. Every conversation is a confrontation. He sighed, realizing that he was on his way back to Pitt Street with as much admin to do as he had started the day with; a fresh bunch of photographs to file and precisely none that were worthy of a place in his collection. A pint of Guinness was sounding like a better idea with every passing step.

He didn't know if it was intuition or some sense of being watched but Winter turned at the end of the corridor and looked back towards the door to the ward to see the tall, muscle-bound guy glaring at him from the other side of the glass.

CHAPTER 5

Monday 12 September

A day after being in the red-light district, Rachel was back there again. She had ditched the rookie constable and instead had DC Julia Corrieri in tow again, heading for the Wish drop-in centre in York Street. Narey had explained that that was where her contact worked and was currently their best chance of finding out the name of the murdered prostitute.

Corrieri was a tall, angular woman in her early twenties with a mop of dark hair and an uncoordinated air about her. Narey knew that she was smart enough but wasn't convinced that she always knew what day it was. The DS had been allocated the job of big sister and it was already proving a tiresome task.

Corrieri had spent the previous day going through the PNC as Addison had directed in the hope of finding a record of something similar to the killer's act of trying to wipe away the hooker's make-up but had come up empty-handed. Actually, that wasn't entirely true. In her determination to be thorough and her fear of missing something, she had produced a long list of weird offender fetishes including ear biting, house cleaning and tampon theft. All of which she handed over with an endearing solemnity that made Narey want to both hug her and slap her.

York Street was in the south-west area of the city centre, connecting Argyle Street to the Broomielaw, and only a few hundred yards from where the hooker was killed in Wellington Lane. Wish occupied the street level of a formerly imposing row of Georgian buildings but now the upper floors were largely deserted and the drop-in centre was squeezed between a Cantonese restaurant and a boarded-up shop. The place provided support and health care to the sex workers and had done for nearly twenty years. Cops weren't exactly welcomed in with open arms but the people that ran Wish knew that they were basically on their side.

A few yards away from it, Narey stopped and explained a few dos and donts to Corrieri before they went in.

'Let me do the talking, particularly at first, but feel free to chip in later. If any of the working girls are in then don't stare at them, for God's sake. They are bound to have heard about the girl on Wellington Lane and will probably be shaken up as it is without us blundering in. We don't talk to them without the centre's say-so. Just treat them with a bit of respect. They are all on the game but they are still women, remember that.'

Corrieri nodded earnestly and followed the DS inside.

A couple of young women who were drinking steaming cups of tea immediately turned their backs when the officers came through the door. Their movement caused a weary laugh from a middle-aged woman sitting behind a desk facing the door.

'Jeezus, we aren't getting many clients as it is without Cagney and Lacey coming in to scare them away. How are you, Rachel?'

Joanne Samuels was originally from Newcastle and had worked at Wish since it opened in 1992, working her way up from shoulder to cry on and chief tea maker to running the place. The centre itself had moved a good few times as leases ran out and rents rose when the red-light district became the international financial district. Samuels was a plump, pleasant woman in her mid-fifties who always had a kindly smile and a waspish sense of humour no matter what tales of horror were heard behind the door.

'I'm doing okay, Joanne, how are you? Cagney and Lacey? Christ, you are showing your age.'

'Hard to hide it, pet,' the woman laughed, pulling a hand across the greying locks that were pulled back into a fat bun behind her head.

'Away with you,' Narey said. 'Joanne, this is Julia Corrieri.'

Narey had instinctively not used Corrieri's rank but there was no way that anyone would have taken them for anything other than police.

'Nice to meet you, Julia. I take it you're here about Melanie.'

Narey's heart skipped a beat at the fact that Joanne knew the girl's name.

'You knew her then?'

Joanne shook her head sadly, a stray strand of hair flicking across her face.

'No, I didn't. But she is obviously the talk of the steamie around here. She didn't come into Wish but a couple of the girls that do have put a name to her. It'll be her working name, mind, I don't have a real one for you.'

Narey's heart sank again, even though she knew she ought to have expected it.

'I was hoping you'd have something,' she admitted.

'Very little,' the woman conceded. 'She was a local girl but she didn't appear to want any help from us. She seemed to think she was getting all the help she needed from somewhere else, if you get my drift.'

Narey thought that she did.

'Okay, so have you heard the women talking about anyone particularly violent recently? Someone that might be capable of this?'

'No, just the usual collection of bastards that want to use them as punch-bags and the ones who don't think twice about giving them a kicking to get a refund. Not that they're all like that. Some of them treat it the same way as going into a shop and buying a new pair of shoes. The thing is, Rachel, we don't have the same handle on it as we used to simply because there are less of them working down here now. Between mobile phones and websites, sex isn't bought the way it was before. More and more of it is taking place indoors after a quick finger shuffle through the internet.'

'That's a good thing though, surely?' Narey asked. 'If the girls aren't on the streets.'

Joanne's mouth became very small as she lowered her head and shook it.

'Nope. I can see why you'd think so but no. When they all worked the old red-light district down here then we knew where they were and they knew where we were. Now they are all over the shop and we might only see a handful of girls in a night. These women are vulnerable. We want them out of sex work altogether, not just off the street.

'The ones who are still working round here are usually the ones who don't have whatever it takes to organize themselves with a phone or a bloody website. The addicts. Their lives are in complete disarray and arming themselves with a sim card or hitching up their skirts to Google is beyond them.'

'That what Melanie was then? An addict?' Narey asked the question, already sure of the answer.

Joanne gave a brisk nod.

'From what I'm told, yes. Big time. I'd have been sure of it anyway but the few girls that knew her said she had a very heavy crack habit. It's par for the course, whatever any woman's reason for getting into prostitution – whether it's to feed a habit or feed their child – drug use spirals once they are involved. That's simply a fact.'

Narey looked towards Corrieri, encouraging her to get involved in the conversation. Willing as ever, Corrieri nervously took up the invitation.

'Yes,' she butted in. 'I read a survey saying that there were a thousand women on the game in Glasgow and that 950 of them were drug users.'

Corrieri immediately saw Joanne's eyebrows shoot up and a look of disapproval cross her face.

'But,' Corrieri continued hastily, 'even if they are on the game, they are still women. We must remember that.'

'Jeezus Christ, where do you get them, Rachel? Listen, young lady,' she shouted at Corrieri. 'That is a phrase that's always got on my tits. The Game. It's not a fucking game. Tiddlywinks is a game, croquet is a game, hide-and-seek is a game. These women face violent attacks, rapes and robberies at the hands of punters every day of their working lives. That's why our efforts are all put into getting them the fuck out of this "game".'

Julia turned a despairing glance towards Narey who gave her a supportive look to suggest that it was okay and that she would sort it.

'We know that they face these dangers, Joanne. That's why we're here. The women that knew Melanie, can you give me their names?' she asked.

'What? Sorry, no. You know how it is, Rachel. They talk to me in confidence and they're not going to keep doing that if I run off to the cops with whatever they tell me.'

The anger was clear in Samuels's voice, years of hard work taking their toll on her good humour.

'All I know is that the women who knew her were in here in tears,' she continued testily. 'From what I could make out they weren't particularly friendly with Melanie but when there's an attack then it scares the shit out of the lot of them. All I can tell you is that they say she was a proper looker before the crack got to her and that she had a room in a flat in Maryhill, although my guess is she is the kind who would be moving around on a regular basis. Oh, and there was talk of a heavy-handed boyfriend. That's it.'

'Joanne, I'm not trying to lay a guilt trip on you here but one girl has already been murdered and this guy could strike again. Surely that makes a difference. Let me talk to them?'

The woman massaged her temples in an attempt to keep her temper under control and emerged with a forced smile.

'No guilt trip, really? My responsibility is to all the women working out there and I can't put my relationship with them at risk over one incident. Their safety is everything to everyone that works in here so don't lay emotional blackmail on me. They are in danger every bloody minute they spend on the street. I will speak to them and *if* they want to talk then I will get back to you. Best I can do.'

Narey nodded thoughtfully.

'Okay, fair enough. I appreciate it, Joanne. It's in all our interests that the bastard that did this is caught as soon as possible.'

Samuels smiled again, her natural demeanour returning.

'I know. They are all dirty jobs and we all have to do them. As soon as I hear anything, I'll call you.'

Moments later, Narey and Corrieri were back on the streets, shivering as the cold hit them after the warmth of the drop-in centre. The DC looked apologetically at the senior officer.

'Sergeant, I'm sorry for messing up in there. Getting her back up like that.'

'Don't worry about it,' Narey reassured her. 'Joanne likes to let off a bit of steam sometimes. It's good for her.'

Corrieri smiled but still seemed doubtful.

'But if she wasn't annoyed then she might have given you the name of the girls that knew Melanie.'

'No,' replied Narey. 'She was never going to do that. But I

thought if she was pissed off enough then she might not notice that her talking to the girls for me was the best that I was hoping for in the first place.'

Corrieri looked thoughtful.

'So it wasn't entirely a bad thing that I blundered in by mentioning "the game" the way that you mentioned it to me earlier.'

Narey smiled quietly.

'Not entirely, Julia, no. Let's go get some lunch.'

CHAPTER 6

Tuesday 13 September

Winter parked his car in the Cambridge Street car park and made his way along Renfrew Street past the back of the Savoy Centre, dodging rain showers and dangerous lunchtime umbrellas. The earlier throb from the beers that he'd shared with Addison the night before had gone and he still had a few hours before his shift started and he'd have the pleasure of finishing off filing Rory McCabe. He was heading for the shops on Buchanan Street, intending to get a birthday present for his young cousin Chloe.

He'd just crossed West Nile and was a hundred yards from the Royal Concert Hall steps at the end of Sauchiehall Street when he was assaulted by a long-haired smiley face doing a half-arsed tap-dance routine.

'Hi there. How are you today? Got a minute, just a minute? I don't want any money.' No, of course you don't, you lying git, thought Winter. Walking down Buchanan Street was a lot harder than it used to be. Apart from a couple of streets cutting across it, it was pedestrianized all the way from the Donald Dewar statue at the top of the hill down to St Enochs, which should make it a dawdle of a stroll but instead you have to fight every inch of the way past crowds, kids, chuggers and street entertainers.

The chuggers hunted in packs under Dewar's short-sighted gaze and also down on the flat where the top-end designer shops were. If you could dodge past one then sure enough there would be more of them asking for a minute of your time and your bank account details.

The eejit in front of Winter was still smiling away, moving his weight relentlessly from foot to foot.

'Sorry, I don't have time,' Winter said as patiently as he could muster.

'Ah go on, it will only take a minute. You know you want to.'

'I said I didn't have time.'

'Ah but you didn't really mean it,'grinned the chugger.

'Look, just fuck off.'

'Hey, no need for that. It's for charity!'

Suddenly Mr Charity began muttering swear words under his breath. Winter allowed himself a grimace of satisfaction, his work was done and another prat had been converted to his miserable version of Glagow.

He kicked on down Buchanan Street, the smirry rain slowly eating into his clothes. Winter was annoyed at letting the chugger get to him but he had been a persistent sod. Worse than that it had got him irritated enough that he knew the crowd he could see gathered down the street would mean his anger level going up another notch. It meant a street entertainer.

He hated them. The escape artists, fire-eaters and magicians were bad enough but even worse were the living statues. He'd always wondered what kind of way that was for a grown man or woman to make a living. Getting yourself tarted up with paint and standing still for a while was not a talent. He walked on, past Diesel, Tiso's and the White Company, past a statue decked out in black and with make-up, perched on a bicycle with a basket in front of him. Winter had the sudden but not unfamiliar urge to kick him off to see if he managed to stay still when he hit the ground. However he guessed the rest of the people in the street, some of whom actually seemed to be impressed by this crap, might not have understood so he let it go. Another barely living statue had got off his perch and was having a fag while making a call on his mobile. That was more like it.

Winter knew he could be bad-tempered and intolerant but he spent most of his time on the dark edges of the city where most of these people never ventured and it meant he could get annoyed at them simply for living normal lives. His temperament wasn't quite up to photographing a suicide or a fatal pile-up or the victim of a drug overdose then watching halfwits gawping in wonder at a man who could stand still for five minutes. He'd stare through a lens at a fifteen-year-old kid stabbed through the heart then see people staring in shop windows at shoes costing three hundred quid and dresses going for a grand a time. So far he'd always resisted the urge to smack their heads against the window.

He'd passed the huge Vodafone store, with Princes Square, Hugo Boss and Frasers up ahead. He managed a laugh at a Hare Krishna with a crazy smile and a ponytail, asking some bewildered granny if she was a rocker. He guessed the answer was no. He had to be more tolerant of these muppets, it really wasn't doing him any good to . . .

The noise hit him as he came to the corner of Gordon Street. He realized that until then it must have been drowned out by the towering high walls of shops and flats but it smacked him as soon as he reached the gap. Sirens. Both cops and ambulances. Shouting. Something big was going down. Winter bolted in the direction of the noise, driven by the itch to see what was happening. Judging by the number of 999s on scene it was major and he didn't want to miss it. Fuck! He didn't have his gear with him. He had a decent camera on his mobile but that was it. Everything else was in the boot of his car in Cambridge Street.

There was nothing he could do about that though, nothing

else but run. The corner of Buchanan stayed pedestrianized till it reached the point where the road hit West Nile Street and Winter charged along it, dodging between two cars and onto Gordon Street. Ahead was Central Station and he knew that was where the clamour and the blaring were coming from.

The crowds grew thicker as he got nearer and he had to barge his way through, hearing swearing at his back and taking a couple of swipes for his trouble. The throng was even thicker at the sand-blasted corner of the Central where Gordon Street ran out and Union Street started. Winter could see that four cop cars had cut off access points and were only allowing emergency vehicles through. What the hell had happened? There was already police tape up creating a cordon but he got the impression no one had been there too long.

Winter shouted 'Police' as he shoved his way through the undergrowth of the human jungle, cutting a swathe through the swearing till he was just a couple of ranks back from a front-row seat. There were uniforms forcing the crowd back as best they could and beyond them a no-man's-land before there was another ring of cops shielding detectives and white-togged forensics. Two of them, Paul Burke and Caro Sanchez were his best guess under the bunny suits, were firing off cameras. There were anxious faces everywhere. Winter was pushing his way past two guys in leather jackets and getting a hard kick on his ankle when the high-vis screen suddenly parted and he saw a body lying in a pool of crimson blood, the head angled violently to one side. Just as suddenly the view disappeared again and his frustration began to boil over.

'Gaz!' he roared at a cop he recognized and was rewarded with a glance. 'What the fuck's happened?' Winter asked him.

Gaz McKean looked round to make sure none of his bosses were watching and stepped a few feet away from his position just long enough to talk to Winter without the entire crowd hearing.

'It's Cairns Caldwell. Shot through the head. Looks like it was a sniper. No one saw a thing. Could have come from anywhere. The impact turned him round so they're struggling to work out an angle. Look, I've got to get back.'

'Christ's sake. Can you have a word with your sergeant and get me past the line?'

'Are you serious? We're a wee bit busy, Tony, in case you hadn't noticed.'

Cairns Caldwell. Major gangster. Responsible for bringing in most of the heroin that came into Glasgow. Ex-public schoolboy now worth multi-millions. Well he was until some fucker put a bullet through his napper. The shit had officially hit the fan.

Winter had to get in and photograph this. Damn, why was his gear back in the boot of his car?

Then suddenly he saw Two Soups. Baxter had stood up, shaking his head and firing off an order. Winter managed to catch his eye and gestured that he wanted to get across the cordon. Baxter laughed, swiftly followed by a curt shake of the head. Damn him, thought Winter, he's loving this. He tried to shout but his voice was taken away by the noise of the sirens and the crowd. There was no way that Two Soups was for listening anyway.

Winter pushed his way along the crowd till he was between two cops he knew, Rob Harkins and Sandy Murray. He put on his most confident face and strode between them.

'Cheers, guys. Fucking crowds are mental. You'd think they'd never seen anyone shot in the head before.'

Murray didn't even blink while Harkins only counted to five before he nodded Winter past him. Winter knew he was never getting past the inner ring, it was protecting the good stuff not just holding back the natives, but this was a start. He found the best gap he could in the cordon and slid onto his arse, then pulled his mobile out of his pocket to see what six megapixels could do from ten yards away.

Winter was aware that some of the cops were looking down at him in bemusement but was hopeful that enough of them would know him by sight that they wouldn't ask why he was armed with a mobile phone rather than couple of grand's worth of kit. He didn't care anyway. He only had eyes for Caldwell.

The gangster's eyes were wide open, forever shocked and horrified, his flop of fair hair soaking in an ocean of pillar-box red, his arms spread wide in an unheard plea for mercy. You'd think that someone who does what Cairns Caldwell did for a living might think there was a bullet out there with his name on it. Comes with the territory. The look on his face, though, gave the lie to that. Sheer surprise. Caldwell was so far up the ladder that he thought he was untouchable. But he'd been touched big time.

Winter bumped the focus on his iPhone up to the max and saw right away that he'd get nothing, scaling it back down a bit and hoping that technology in the lab or his own PC would sharpen it up. He saw a nice suit, easily £800 a throw, blood spray over a crisp blue open-necked shirt, a mouth wide open in a silent scream. Other legs and feet were walking by, alternatively blocking his view and framing Caldwell in a uniformed letterbox.

A big space opened up and he zeroed in as best he could on the hole in the drug lord's head. A beautiful round hole, oozing dark life. Fuck, this was just what he wanted. Not even a single regret at thinking that. Not for a second. He knew what Caldwell was and he certainly wasn't going to apologize for feeling like that. Bingo. House. Result. A quote from an interview that Metinides did suddenly fired into his mind. *'I got to witness the hate and evil in men.'*

Winter fired off the iPhone as best he could, cursing the slow shutter and the age before it was fit to go again. Eyes, mouth, scream, blood, hands. Cops, forensics, scene setting. Eyes, eyes, eyes. Nothing existed except the inch by two-inch world that he could see through the phone. He caught cops and forensics, a patchwork of expressions set grim on their faces. Anger, fear, worry, intent, humour, maybe even satisfaction.

Instinctively, he swivelled on his bum and turned away from the cordon. Few of the rubberneckers were interested in him. They were all staring over his head, desperate to get another glimpse of the man with a bullet in his head.

Some were stunned, a few were laughing. Most were desperate to have something to tell when they got home or to the pub. They craned their necks and pointed, they gawked and drank in every drop of bloodlust that dripped from their lips.

He snapped a red-faced man, his eyes bulging at what was being played out before him, jostling shoulders with his neighbour in an effort to get that inch or two closer to the action. He caught him open-mouthed and impatient, desperate to see and to know. Agog, that was the word.

A couple of feet from him was a woman in tears, crying for a man she almost certainly didn't know, maybe hadn't even heard of. Her sensible jacket and cardigan said she lived in a different world from the man with the hole in his head. Would she have wept for Caldwell if she knew what he did for a living, knew how many lives he had ruined with the shit that he peddled? All Winter knew was that the tears that streamed down her face causing strands of fair hair to stick to her cheek were wasted on Caldwell. But for him they made a picture.

The woman must have become aware of Winter on the edge of her vision because her eyes fell onto him, causing him to turn uncomfortably back to the scene. All he could now see was the bulky, shaking body of Two Soups gesturing angrily towards him. The man was purple with rage and looked like he was about to have a fit. He was roaring at Winter but the photographer realized he could hear nothing. Not Baxter, not the sirens or the crowds, just the rush of blood that filled his ears and the pounding of his own heart. It was photographic gold. Dark gold that Metinides would have approved of.

Winter's self-imposed deafness was the reason that he didn't hear the scuff of oversized copper's boots on the road or them asking him to get the fuck out of there. He knew nothing till his collar was grabbed and he was hauled off his feet.

Harkins and Murray were looking down at him, at once angrily and apologetically. He'd probably dropped them in it but they still didn't feel comfortable throwing him about. Over their shoulders he saw Rachel Narey standing open-mouthed, looking at him in nothing short of disbelief. It broke a spell and the sound of the crime scene suddenly burst in on him, all discordant, angry and chaotic. He was breathing hard, elated yet embarrassed, like a teenager caught having a wank. This was not going to be good.

CHAPTER 7

Evening, Tuesday 13 September

'As far as I can see the only thing they can say you're guilty of is over-enthusiasm. Two Soups is just getting his oversized knickers into a twist as usual. It'll blow over in a couple of days. Although every cop on the shift will take the piss out of you for weeks. Sitting on your arse taking pictures of the crowd? I've never seen anything like it.'

'Is that your considered professional opinion, Detective Sergeant Narey?'

'I am never anything other than professional, Mr Winter.'

'So how come you're naked then?'

'Are you complaining?'

'I've never complained before, Sarge. Not going to start now.'

Rachel pushed Winter onto his back, leaning over him and grinning wickedly.

'Good.'

He grabbed at her and rolled so that he was on top, pinning her arms. Just because she was a sergeant didn't mean she was always in charge and he had to remind her of that. It was a mistake though. In her defensive position she lashed out.

'You should have heard Baxter's rant. He wanted us to do you for anything from breach of the peace to public indecency. The old bugger was virtually foaming at the mouth.'

She laughed.

'He's never liked you. Too pally with Addison for one thing and just too cocky for another.'

'Thanks.'

She sniggered again.

'Hey, I like you being cocky. It just doesn't go down so well with everyone else. But Two Soups is an arse. He doesn't like anybody. I'm not even sure he's that good at his job. The man's a dinosaur. You sometimes think he wished Watson and Crick hadn't bothered discovering DNA.'

'He's a dick. Mind you, I can sort of see why he might not have been too pleased at me taking pics on my phone.'

'Hm, just a bit. Everyone was stressed out of their boxes though. Cairns Caldwell. Jesus, it's going to kick off big time. The papers and the telly are already going mental. That won't be the end of it though. No chance.'

Cairns Caldwell ran most of the cocaine that came through Glasgow and had his fingers all over every gram that was sold south of the river. A former pupil of Kelvinside Academy and Glasgow Uni, he was born west-end middle class and worked his way up to south-side scumbag. His parents died in a car crash when Caldwell was seventeen, left him a bundle and a townhouse on Clarence Drive, and six years later he was shipping enough coke into Glasgow to turn the dear green place white. He worked his way up by the standard route – although he short-circuited it big time by having a lot of dosh to kick off with – undercutting the competition, freebies to draw in the mugs, arming himself with the best muscle that money could buy and stamping over all opposition. They also said he smoothed his path the middle-class way, greasing palms and making promises, shaking hands and giving nods in the right direction. The Kelvinside accent opened doors; his bully boys kicked them in. Either way, Caldwell was where he wanted to be.

Apart from coke, he ran hookers and security firms, private taxi hires and nightclubs. It was grey money – the dirty dosh funded the clean cash and it funded more dirty stuff. The snow laundered money till it was as clean as the driven slush fund.

Caldwell was untouchable of course; hard cash made sure of that. He supposedly earned deference from the lowlifes that worked for him by putting an axe through the head of a hard nut named Barney Reid who at one time fancied his chances of muscling him out of the way. That kind of thing tends to buy you respect.

It was reckoned he cleared four million a year. Spent his life putting two fingers up to the cops and coke up the noses of everyone he could.

Untouchable until someone put a bullet through his head. Twenty-nine years old and the brains educated at Glasgow's finest were spilled over a pavement. Not so clever now.

'What do you reckon is going to happen?' Winter asked her.

'Shit, I don't know. You know the old Sean Connery film line about "they put one of yours in the hospital so you put one of theirs in the morgue"? Well, they've started off with the morgue so I hate to think where this is going to end up. One thing's for sure, there's no way his people are going to sit back and take it. Unless they did it but that seems unlikely.'

'Why not? A man like that has as many dodgy friends as enemies, surely?'

'For a start they never want to bite the hand that feeds them. And if they did then they would have a million opportunities to knife him, strangle him, push him off a high building. Shooting him from a mile away seems to be going to a lot of unnecessary trouble. Couldn't rule it out but I'd say it wasn't one of his.'

'So who?'

'Who knows? Could be anybody.'

'And who cares?'

'Never said that. I don't care that he's dead apart from the fact that all hell is going to break loose and we are going to have to deal with the shit. I *do* care about who killed him. So don't start.'

Her eyes flared at him and Winter liked it.

'Oh, calm down. You know I'm winding you up. You shouldn't be so easy.'

'Oh, easy is it? I won't be so easy then, see how you like that.'

She ducked away from him with a giggle but he wrestled with her, pulling her back towards him. She fought for a bit and just as he was thinking how perfect her breasts were, her mouth fell onto his and her body disappeared from his view. All talk of murdered gangsters went out of sight. For half an hour at least. It was hard to worry about things like that when her dark hair tumbled over his face and her smooth curves locked onto his body. When her hands teased and taunted and worked their magic. When he rose to meet her and she smiled with satisfaction.

It was only when she fell off him again, laughing and panting, her hair sticking to the side of her glistening face in a way that reminded him of the woman who stared at Caldwell's dead body, that it started again. He knew it would because she couldn't leave it at that. She could never leave it.

'So just what were you doing at Central Station?'

'Christ, Rachel. You know what I was doing.'

'Okay. I know what you were doing. Let me rephrase. Why the fuck were you doing it?'

'Is this where you get the rubber hoses out?'

'Only if it turns you on. Come on, why?'

'Again, you know why. We've been through it before.'

'Fucksake, Tony. What the hell are you worried about? It's me. I know most of it. Spill the rest.'

He sighed. He really didn't want to get into this. He didn't want to get into it because he didn't really understand it himself, so how could he expect her to.

'It's my thing. I like photographing accidents and the people. You know that.'

'Yes, but I didn't know you had it as bad as that.'

The bitch was as persistent as she was sexy, he thought.

'How did you get into this anyway?'

Rachel had an annoying habit of asking questions she already knew the answer to. It was the price he paid for sleeping with a detective, even if one look at her was enough to know it was a price worth paying.

She knew all about Enrique Metinides and the exhibition that Tony had attended in London back in 2003 at the Photographers' Gallery, just two minutes from Oxford Circus. He'd gone with a blonde named Jodi, a London girl. He didn't really have much interest in going to a gallery or an exhibition but she was keen and he was keen on her. As soon as he was in the gallery, though, Metinides's photographs blew him away. They were like nothing he'd seen before and tapped right into something deep inside him.

The images messed with his head, being truly brutal and yet truly beautiful at the same time. Car crashes. Floods. Suicides. Train crashes. Plane crashes. Fires. Murders. Accidents. Anything bad that resulted in death or destruction in Mexico City for over fifty years, Metinides was there and had photographed it for their red-top tabloids. Metinides started out taking photographs when he was just eleven. Chasing ambulances, running to fires and hanging out in front of the local cop shop waiting for criminals to be dragged in or out. The reporters and the other photographers called him *El Niño*, the kid, and the nickname stuck.

His photographs were intimate and unsettling, poetic and haunting. The critics said that he found humanity in catastrophe.

It was the faces that got to Winter, not the flames or the tangled wreckage. Nor was it just the faces of the dead but also those that had turned up to gawp at them. Metinides was the rubberneckers' rubbernecker.

It was Mexico City and much of it was decades ago but to Winter it could have as easily been Maryhill or Mount Vernon right here, right now. The photographs reached the dark places inside him and Narey knew that too, although neither of them had ever said it. She knew how Metinides had inspired him, she just didn't quite know why. That was why she teased and tormented him to try and get to the bottom of it.

'Don't be shy about it,' she mocked now. 'It's cool that you are so into something. The passion is a turn-on. Tell me more.'

Part of him wanted to tell her to fuck off. Not in a bad way, just in a leave-it-alone kind of way. He reached an arm around, pulling her close and feeling her body yield to his touch.

'A turn-on, is it? Come here then.'

'I want to hear more first,' she continued. 'You've never really told me why you are so into it.'

Yeah well, there's a reason for that, he thought. Guilty secrets. They'd played this game too often though, and he wasn't ready to offer up any more of himself just yet.

'There's something you haven't told me about either,' he tried, to change the subject.

'Oh yes?' She looked doubtful. 'What's that then?'

'The hooker that was found murdered in Wellington Lane. What's happening with her?'

Rachel's eyes narrowed and it was obvious she didn't want to go there, which suited him just fine.

'You're right,' she conceded. 'I didn't tell you about it.'

'Well?'

'There's not a lot happening,' she admitted. 'Our enquiries are continuing, as they say.'

Her tone was changing, warning him off, but it wouldn't have been the first time he'd taken a kicking to veer her away from places he didn't want her to go.

'What is this? The ten o'clock news? That's all I get?'

'We're getting nowhere with it, okay? The poor girl was left dead with her knickers round her ankles. It's been the shittiest part of an already shitty week and I don't want to go over it all again.'

She paused and Winter sensed a counter-punch coming.

'I bet your creepy Mexican guy would have loved to have photographed her though ...'

'He wasn't cree–'

Damn her. She was grinning at him and he was annoyed at himself for falling for it.

'Come on,' she continued. 'Photographing dead bodies? What else would you call it?'

'Ha bloody ha. Fuck off.'

She giggled.

'Come on, tell me about him, then. What was his thing? And why is his thing your thing?'

No, he thought, enough was enough.

'Forget it. Talking time is over. Playtime again.'

He made a grab at her but she easily ducked away from him, twisting her body out of reach and asking again. 'And why have you got it so bad?'

He grabbed her, placing a hand over her mouth but she playfully bit it. He pulled her on top of him, happy to wrestle rather than talk any more. Just as he was thinking that they were heading for round two, her mobile rang and she rolled off him to answer it, laughing as she picked up the receiver.

'Hello? Oh, hi. What's ...'

The smile froze on her face.

'Shit ... No way ... Fuck. What happened? Uh huh ... Right, okay. Soon as I can.'

The look on her face as she hung up left Winter in no doubt that there wouldn't be a second round. She sat looking vaguely at the wardrobe but he knew she was looking much farther away.

'Well?'

'That was Addison. Malky Quinn has been shot. Through the head. By a sniper.'

CHAPTER 8

'Shit.'

'That's pretty much what I said,' Narey intoned, her eyes briefly closed. 'Right, I've got to go in. Happened half an hour ago. Quinn stepped out of his car to go into his converted ranch thing in Kinnear Road and bang. Place is going fucking mental.'

'Retaliation for Caldwell?'

'Maybe. Seems the obvious thing. Need to go see what they are saying. Love you and leave you.'

The L word hung awkwardly between them for a second until she pulled her top over her head and poked her tongue out at him.

'Figure of speech. You be here when I get back?'

'I was thinking I could come with you.'

'Aye right. How are we going to explain that one, Einstein? You show up without Addy giving you a call. What you been doing, listening in to police scanners? That's an offence, you know.'

'Well . . .' The thought that she could actually tell people that they had a relationship clearly wasn't obvious to her at that moment. And maybe it wasn't the time to discuss it.

'Well, let me know what's going on. Maybe see you when you get back, depends how long you will be.'

Rachel planted a quick kiss on his lips, at the same time grabbing at his cock under the covers. With a fleeting grin she stood up and left, closing the door behind her.

Cairns Caldwell. Malky Quinn. Either somebody had it in for the bad boys or they had it in for each other.

The man they called the Mighty Quinn was an old school thug. Not renowned for his brains but well known for his ruthlessness, he and his family ruled the east end the hard way, breaking heads and legs as he saw fit. They had the bulk of the city's heroin trade locked up through links to Turkish gangs, a dirty business that didn't bother them for a second. What did it matter to them if anyone was stupid enough to inject that shit into their veins?

Now Malky was lying somewhere in Kinnear Road in the east end, a hole in his head and blood on the pavement. Some lucky bastard would be photographing it, Winter thought. Probably some scene examiner who wouldn't value it, wouldn't see it for what it was. Would just be thinking evidence and court, dispassion and objectivity.

He wanted to follow Rachel. Sneak out of the window like a teenager and head for Kinnear Road. No point though. He knew he'd already shat on his copybook enough for one day and, anyway, it was pitch black outside. The only way he'd get any worthwhile picture was to be standing right over the body. And Two Soups or whoever was on duty was never going to allow that.

Pitch black. If a sniper took out Quinn in the dark then it was one serious motherfucker. If he took him out from the same kind of distance as they reckoned the shooter took Caldwell from then it was a professional motherfucker.

Winter turned on both the television and the radio in search of news. Nothing.

Cairns Caldwell and Malky Quinn. Even if this stopped right now it was enough to have the gutterbelly shitting golf balls for months. So much about it said it wouldn't stop. Two of the biggest, hardest, most untouchable villains had been nailed in the most vengeful, macho-ridden city on the planet. It never stops there. There is always another one who wants his name above the door. An eye for an eye, a life for a life, somebody must die for the death of my strife. Someone else was going to be killed, he'd lay money on it.

Never mind golf balls, there would be people all over Glasgow who would be shitting bowling balls at the thought of what might happen next.

For an hour and a half he flipped between TV and radio, trying to find any mention of the shooting. It came in a trickle: police incident, reports of a shot being fired, man seriously injured. The media was way behind. His itch had subsided a bit, knowing that he'd missed the photograph and that there was nothing he could do about it, but he was still keen to know what had happened and why. Winter knew he'd get his balls in his hands if he phoned Rachel. Addison and the other cops whose names were in his phone were out too because he couldn't explain or justify calling them. There was someone else who might know and could certainly find out though. He reached for his mobile and waited till a gravelly voice growled hello.

'Hi, Uncle Danny? It's Tony.'

'Jeezus, is it Christmas already?'

'Aye, I know. Sorry it's been so long since I called.'

'Aye, that's what you always say. Don't worry about it, son. How you doing anyway? Still photographing the ones that can't run away?'

'It's the only way I can get them to sit still, Dan.'

'Very good. Okay, enough of the small talk. What do you want?'

Winter laughed quietly.

'That obvious, huh?'

'Christ, son. It's after two in the morning, you haven't called for weeks and you sound like you've seen the ghost of Jinky Johnstone wearing a Rangers top. Aye, it's that obvious.'

Danny Neilson was ex-police. He was in the job for thirty years, man and boy, and could never quite stop being a cop. He never rose higher than a detective sergeant even though he had twice the brains of most of the men above him. Most of his career he was happy just catching crooks even though Auntie Janette was always on at him to go for a promotion. By the time she had finally convinced him of the idea, he was too old. Suited him fine though, he always said he was born a sergeant and would die one.

These days he worked even though he didn't have to. His police pension was better than a decent wage and Danny was kicking on to sixty-five but he couldn't or wouldn't sit on his arse and collect the money. He worked as a superintendent on the taxi rank at Central Station, keeping drunken wasters from jumping queues and battering lumps out of each other. Winter had given up asking Danny why he wanted to stand outside in the rain dealing with the arseholes of the morning hours. Too young to watch *Coronation Street* and drink milk was the only answer Uncle Danny ever gave him but they both knew it wasn't the truth.

'You're right, Dan. There is something. I wanted to know if you'd heard about the shooting in the east end. Malky Quinn.'

There was a slight pause and then a deadpan answer.

'I heard.'

'It's not on the news. Not his name, anyway, so how did you . . .'

'Fucksake, Tony. If you wanted to know what was on the news then you'd have put the fucking telly on rather than phoned me.'

'Aye. True.'

'So ask me what you want to ask for and stop dancing with me. I'm tired and you know I've no time for that shite.'

Big Danny Neilson wasn't much for small talk or ceremony and always made a point of calling a spade a shovel.

'What have you heard, Dan? Has one of Caldwell's boys shot Malky Quinn in retaliation for shooting their gaffer?'

There was a long sigh on the other end of the phone before Neilson's gruff tones responded.

'Not from what I'm hearing, no. It could be. You couldn't rule anything out with these cunts but it's not looking that way right now.'

'How come? It's surely the most obvious thing?'

'That's right, Anthony. And how many times have I told you not to jump to the obvious conclusion?'

'More than once. What are they saying, then?'

'Mate of mine says that they are spooked by how similar it is to the Caldwell shooting. If Caldwell's guys wanted to take out Quinn then there's a hundred, a thousand ways they could have done it but this was near as dammit the same.'

'Same guy, same gun?'

'Fucksake, Tony. Did we not just have the jumping to conclusions conversation?'

Winter ignored him and ploughed on regardless.

'So what have we got then, Uncle Danny? Claim jumpers? Someone wanting to huckle these guys and move in on their operations?'

'Christ. Do you know how long I was out in the pishing rain tonight, son? Do you know how tired my bones are? I finally get in and think I can get on the outside of a glass of Jura and listen to a bit of Dean Martin but instead I get one half of the Hardy Boys on the phone asking me all kinds of shite. How the fuck do I know, Tony? Eh? How the fuck do I know?'

Because you always know more than you are letting on, Uncle Danny, Winter thought but didn't say. Instead he pushed his luck a bit further.

'Alex Kirkwood? Think he might be behind it? I know he's banged up but these guys can pull any strings they want from the nick. Maybe he just wants a bigger cake to cut from when he gets out.'

Danny growled again.

'Jeezus, son. Phone me at Christmas like you usually do. It's past your bedtime. Night.'

The phone went silent in Winter's hand and he couldn't help looking at it and laughing, thinking that they broke the mould when they made Danny. He threw the mobile onto the bed and crawled after it, getting beneath the covers and lying back to seek answers on the ceiling. Caldwell and Quinn. Quinn and Caldwell. Bullets and blood. They swirled around in his head and he saw them behind his eyes as they closed over just for a second. Quinwell and Cald. Caldquinn and Well. Blood and more blood. He fell into one of those strangely drowsy, part-dreaming, thinking-too-much states that go on for ever and you're never sure what is awake and what is dreamt. It ran for nearly two hours till it was shattered by cold flesh slapping him immediately awake.

Rachel had crawled back into bed, freezing cold and wide-awake tired, wrapping herself round him despite his half-hearted protests. How could a woman so hot be so cold? The shock of her chill had him fully conscious in a split second.

'Thanks,' she mumbled into his shoulder.

'For what?'

'Being here and being warm.'

'You're welcome. Freezing but welcome. Want to talk about it?'

'In a minute. Let me heat up first.'

She hugged herself in tighter, the frost of a Glasgow night sneaking into his skin as she stole his warmth. Her long brown hair tickling his face, smelling of the chill that she had brought home with her. Winter knew she was thinking before she spoke to him, debating with herself just how much she was going to divulge. He was hoping it would be everything. He wanted to know every detail of Quinn's killing. The who, what, where, when and why. The facts and the speculation. Danny had given him some but he wanted more. She wanted to tell him the lot, he was sure of that, but police protocol was always the problem. So what was she going to settle for?

'It was mental out there,' she said at last, burying her head even deeper into him before coming up for air. 'People running round like headless chickens. Some of them are shit-scared of what's coming next. Not a good night.'

He knew from experience that the best thing was just to shut up and let her talk. Asking questions would either annoy her or cause barriers to come down. Winter was on the payroll but he wasn't a cop. It wouldn't pay for him to remind her of that by saying something stupid.

'Shirley was already at the scene by the time I got there. You know it's serious when he's dragged out of his bed at that time of night.'

Alex Shirley was the chief superintendent. Variously known as 'Shirley Temple' or 'Don't Call Me Shirley' by the troops. The way Tony heard it from Rachel and Addison, he was liked and respected, which was no mean feat for a chief when the Indians were a bunch of cynical, moaning-faced Glaswegian smart arses.

'He looked spooked, to be honest. Never seen him that way before. Hardly surprising, I suppose. Just one day after Cairns Caldwell gets shot and one of the city's other main dealers goes down the same way. Enough to shake anyone, never mind if you are the one who has to clean the fucking mess up.

'Not that he wasn't in control of the situation. He was. Just that he looked rattled. He gave a uniform a hell of a bollocking for not keeping the locals back when they fell out of their pits to see what was going on. Poor guy looked like he was going to shit himself when the Temple gave him what for. Not like Shirley to do that.'

She fell silent for a moment, her head falling back toward his shoulder, thinking again. He silently pleaded for her not to stop.

'No sign of who had done it,' she eventually continued. 'No real idea of where the shot came from except that it was a mile away. Maybe literally. That was what was bugging the Super as much as what might happen next. I'm sure of it. It was the same scenario as Caldwell. Exactly the fucking same.'

Trust Danny, Winter thought, bang on the money as per usual. Then, even though he knew he shouldn't have, he asked the question.

'So you're thinking it wasn't a revenge hit for Caldwell?'

She rolled away from him, falling face down onto the bed.

'I'm tired. Long, long night.'

'Okay, come here and I'll warm you up,' he tried.

After a bit she pulled herself back into him, legs round and over him. She lay with her head on his chest, her eyes fixed on some spot on the far wall, her head rising and falling with his breathing. Winter ran his hand through her hair and her eyes closed but he knew her mind was still racing.

'He'd been coming home from some night out,' she said at last. 'A meeting was all his crew would say. He had walked halfway from the car to his front door when the bullet caught him bang in the middle of the back of his head. He was on his way down before anyone heard a sound. The guys with him threw themselves to the pavement but that was all there was. A single bullet. The Mighty Quinn died immediately. Dead before he hit the path.

'Some woman across the street saw it and began screaming her lungs out. After that the hired help had no option but to call the cops whether they liked it or not. Weren't exactly forthcoming at helping the polis with their inquiries, funnily enough. Some of them were shaken big time. If some bastard could take out Malky then they were all at risk, that's what they were thinking.'

Winter couldn't help himself again.

'If they could hit big Malky then all the wee Malkies were in deep shit?' he suggested.

Thankfully she laughed a bit.

'Ha ha, very good. Big Malky was the hand that fed them, like I said. The one that was supposed to keep them all safe and put bread on the table and drug money in their pockets. If he's fucked then they're all fucked. Unless one of them steps up to the mark and takes over. And whoever has the balls for that better do it soon before some other fucker decides to help himself to Quinn's business.'

'That what's happening? Someone after Quinn and Caldwell's operations?'

'Don't know.'

Her reply was curt.

'Far too early to know. But someone will be after the business whether he was the one who pulled that trigger or not. It's the way of the jungle and there's far too much money not to have someone do it. Fun times ahead, that's for sure.

'The Temple took Bobby McGurk into London Road for questioning. Malky's second-in-command. Not that he particularly thinks Bobby had anything to with killing Malky but maybe he fancies him for having done Caldwell. Maybe. Maybe he was just fishing. Hard fucker, McGurk, but he was knocked off his feet by Quinn getting shot. Not exactly shitting himself but his jaw dropped all the same. Couldn't take his eyes off Malky's head. He watched that blood spreading over the path like he was hypnotized.'

Winter let her linger for a bit. Not pushing, waiting.

'Press will have a field day too,' she said eventually. 'Newspapers and TV were there within half an hour of us getting there, crawling over the place like locusts. Shouting out pish like "turf wars" as if they were going to get an answer. I hate those turds.'

Rachel had got a raw time from the media when she led the investigation into the Cutter murders and she still held it against them. Not that she'd ever been their biggest fan but since she was publicly slated when a serial killer randomly murdered six people in the city, she hated them with a passion. They hounded her from the minute she took over, questioning why a mere detective sergeant was in charge, why she couldn't catch the guy, until they finally got her turfed off the case. She wouldn't talk about it but Winter knew it still grated.

'If those morons think I am spending my day fielding their idiot questions then they've got another think coming. They can talk to media services all day long if they like but they can get tae as far as I'm concerned. This shit is bad enough without them making it worse. Know that Lindsey Richardson from the *Express*? Addison told her to fuck off. No messing. She asked him about vendettas and who's next. Got to admire your pal's attitude sometimes. He wasn't a happy bunny out there tonight.'

'How come?'

'How many reasons do you want? Got my own theory but you better ask him yourself.' Winter raised his eyebrows by way of a question but she blanked him and he knew he was getting nothing. Their relationship had always been based on the concrete fact that she was police and he wasn't. There was blue and white police tape between them and she'd have arrested him if he tried to cross it.

'Anyway,' she went on. 'Dead gangsters, who needs it? At least I'm back in bed. Forensics will be picking pieces of skull and tissue off Kinnear Road for the rest of the night.'

'Who was on camera duty?'

She shook her head wearily.

'Mulgrew and Burke.'

'Fucking forensics,' he spat out, more angrily than he knew he should have.

'Fucksake, Tony. Leave it. They were doing their job and they do it well. It was a murder scene, not an art exhibition. A dead man. Bullet hole. Blood and brains on the path. That's it. No one's going to put it in a fucking frame and hang it on a wall.'

'Aye, okay.'

'Sorry, but it just gets on my nerves sometimes.'

'Aye, I said okay. I get it.'

Her face softened.

'Sorry, long night. Very long night. And I'm back in at nine. I love that you can see all that stuff when I can only see scumbags but not tonight, okay?'

'No, I'm sorry,' he mumbled. 'You're right. It was out of order. Come here, you better get some sleep.'

She kissed him and snuggled in. Within two minutes she was dead to the world.

He knew that she was right about the photographs but she was so wrong about the rest.

The picture of Quinn spilling all over that pavement flooded his mind. He imagined the pool being dark, warm and lustrous. Streetlamps glistening on the claret sea and causing highlights that his Canon EOS-1D could pick out beautifully, the pavement washed in the price of the drug king's sin, painted from a palette of scarlet dues. Quinn laid out on a concrete canvas, glassy eyes not looking up to the glowering heavens but cast down to his maker.

He envisaged heavy-set, scarred men with mouths open wide in shock, seeing their protector thrown to the ground. Movie-still flash, capturing guilt and fear. Inch by inch, the creeping realization dawns that retribution has stepped out of the shadows. Deep down they'd always known there would be a price to pay.

Death's sheen shimmered bright in his camera's eye; Malky Quinn's tainted juices seeping through Glasgow's stone floor. A perfect picture of bloody comeuppance and inevitable consequence. A picture he didn't have the chance to take but one that he could still frame in his memory.

CHAPTER 9

Wednesday 14 September

Winter was due to be in Pitt Street till it was dark. Two Soups had moaned the previous day about his Central Station performance until Winter was effectively grounded like a teenager. Filing, answering phones and lobbing crumpled balls of paper into the bin was the order of the day.

He'd hauled his arse in two hours after Rachel had left for the crime scene or the operations rooms. She hadn't said which, just kissed him, saying she'd catch up later, and left him to the newspapers and the TV.

The *Record* had splashed it all over the front and four pages inside. They had gone absolutely tonto over it. Massive, lurid pictures of dire quality. Grainy, badly lit shots of vague shapes on an indistinct canvas. Crap photographs that Winter would have killed to have taken. One of those occasions for the papers when content is worth much more than quality. The same could be said for the writing, he thought. Vast slabs of speculation, innuendo, background and bollocks. Screaming headlines and scaremongering text. And their coverage was the best on offer.

At his desk in Pitt Street, Winter grabbed a copy of the *Sun* which had been left lying around and saw much the same in there.

Three pages this time but less didn't mean more. Where there was speculation they brought conjecture, where there was innuendo they brought insinuation, where there was bollocks they brought more bollocks. Killings of two underworld figures in as many days let the tabloids run wild, foaming at the mouth with alarmist indignation. It was a sensation, it was stunning, it was unprecedented. SLAIN, shrieked the *Record*. BLOODBATH, yelled the *Sun*.

The *Sun*'s pictures made the *Record*'s look like something Enrique Metinides would have told his grandchildren about. They'd been there later and were further away. Quinn's body might as well have been a sleeping dog for all you could tell. It didn't stop them using them the size of the page and leaving readers to use their imagination the best they could.

He stuck the radio on for a bit and Clyde offered a verbal version of much of what he'd read. Caldwell and Quinn were dead so contempt laws went out the window. They were called all the names that they couldn't while they were alive – gangster, drug runner, criminal, crime lord – the euphemism 'well-known businessman' wasn't heard once. At last the media could call them for what they were. Caldwell was said to be a prime suspect in the murder of Barney Reid while Quinn was said to be responsible for a 'string of unsolved killings'.

The reporter from the end of Kinnear Road spoke in hushed, almost reverential tones as he told how the residents of the quiet east end street were stunned, shocked and altogether clichéd about the shooting in their midst. He had to up the tone quite considerably when a local ned started shouting, 'Hey wanker, ur you on the radio? Ur ye? Ur ye on the noo? Wanker, ah'm talking tae you!'

They had to cut to one he'd done earlier, an interview with an unnamed concerned citizen whose name Winter was betting was Sadie or Magrit. She'd lived in the street for seventeen years and had never seen anything like it (as if gangster executions were a common occurrence elsewhere). She hadn't exactly heard the shot and she didn't exactly know Mr Quinn but she knew who he was and it was absolutely terrible. Her weans were off the school because they were so traumatised, so they were. Fucking bollocks, the lot of it. Not least the fact that he was stuck there while all the fun was on the other side of the city. The way it was, he'd have been as well still being in IT, asking halfwits if they'd tried switching it off and on again. He wanted to be out there on the streets where the blood was, where the dirt lay thick and the dark shadows were long, where the people were. Real people, bad people, good people, scared people. He wanted to be where they lived and died, particularly where they died. Winter couldn't make out the hole in Quinn's head from the newspaper photos but nor could he get it out of his mind. Bone fragments, blood spatter, open mouth, open hole, a clean kill by an expert, dead centre, dead shot. The pavement damp eating into his jacket, nibbling at the fabric, the earth reclaiming its own a millimetre at a time. The dampness clambering up his shoulder as the blood ran down, passing each other like strangers never destined to meet. Life and death on parallel tracks.

Suddenly, his phone beeped with a text message, making him jump and slamming the shutter down on the photograph in his mind.

It was Addison, asking if he was being a good boy today. Just what he needed. Less than a minute later he texted again, moaning about how he was having to deal with the hooker killing as well as the fallout from the Caldwell and Quinn shootings.

The pecking order was clear to see. The going rate for a pound of drug baron flesh was a lot higher than for the living variety sold around Anderston. Just as the killing of the hooker was a step above the stabbed dealer Sammy Ross, so Malky Quinn was way above whatever had happened in Wellington Lane. Anything else had to take second place.

Winter's mobile rang and the display screen flashed up Addison's name.

'Alright, loser? How's life in the cupboard?'

'Fuck off. This is doing my head in as it is and I don't need your shit as well.'

'Ah, don't wet yourself, wee man. Has Two Soups stolen your sense of humour as well? This city's going crazy and I could do with a pint before the day's out. Up for it?'

'Aye, of course. So what's happening out in the real world?'

'Real world? If this is reality then they can keep it. I take it you heard about Malky Quinn? I've had calls from all over the city and it's kicking off big time. I've already heard of three cases of guys getting dragged off the street into cars and having the living shit kicked out of them, two separate drive-bys with clowns taking potshots at windows and umpteen stories about knuckle draggers holding meetings that nobody is supposed to know about. They're running around booting and shooting at anyone and anything that they think might be responsible. It's open season.'

'Any of them have any idea what they're doing?'

'Do they ever? Best guess from me is that they are lashing out, knocking heads and capping knees in a panic to get any information they can. They don't have the brains to work out what the fuck's going on so they are resorting to what they do best. They will beat the crap out of anyone they can get their hands on in an effort to force some line out of them.'

'Tell me to keep my nose out, Addy, but is it one guy that's done them both or was Quinn in retaliation for Caldwell?"

'Keep this to yourself but the early word from the lab is that it was the same gun that took out the pair of them. So it doesn't look like some tit for tat hit. More like one tit with big ideas.'

'Fuck. Oh well, I guess if he's killing gangsters then it can't be all bad.'

'Don't be fucking stupid,' Addison snapped. 'No matter how

many you kill, there's always an even uglier one waiting to take over.'

That wasn't like Addison. Time to change the subject, Winter thought.

'Awrite. Keep your hair on. So what's the deal with the killing in Wellington Lane?'

'Oh God knows. We're getting nowhere. The timing couldn't be worse either. I'm in danger of getting lumbered with this when I should be investigating Caldwell and Quinn. I've got to go. See you later.'

So much for Winter's change of subject. The line went dead and he was left wondering what nerve he'd touched. Addison had been treading in the brown stuff at the bottom of the sewer for a long time but hadn't made a habit of blowing his stack, not at him at any rate. Maybe this was just the shit that broke the camel's back. Something chimed in the back of his head that Rachel had said, about Addison not being a happy bunny at the scene of the Quinn killing and that she had a theory about why. He dismissed it. Addison had plenty on his plate and was five or six hours away from a pint, easily enough to make him grumpy. Winter expected normal service would be resumed soon enough.

The pair of them went way back, almost to Winter's first week on the force. It was just after he'd photographed Avril Duncanson after she'd gone through the windscreen of her Clio. The very tall, moaning DI with vicious one-liners that made other cops duck didn't seem like someone Winter was going to get on with, not till Addison heard him say he'd been at Parkhead the night before to see Celtic beat Kilmarnock. That was all it took, a simple bond between two guys that supported the same football team.

They were Tims and they had to stick together. Tims as in Celtic fans, not as in Catholics; they understood the difference. Winter hadn't been to Mass since he was fifteen, much to the disappointment of his family, while Addison was a Proddy who'd seen the light. Like Winter, he didn't give a damn for religion but was mad for Celtic.

Addison liked to tell people that he used to be a Protestant atheist but that he was now a Catholic atheist. He was thirty-six but if anyone asked, he'd tell them that he was twenty-seven. It wasn't that he was vain about his age, it was just that he didn't count the years when Rangers won nine league titles in a row. As far as he was concerned, those years didn't happen.

They had Celtic in common and then there was beer. They both liked that quite a bit and demonstrated it whenever they got the chance. Winter knew it helped that he wasn't another cop – Addison didn't want to talk shop when there was drink to be drunk but equally the nature of the photographer's job meant he knew enough about what was going on if the DI did want to bitch about it. They also both liked women, just as much as they liked Guinness or Caledonian 80. Winter liked to think he was more discerning but Addison would have shagged the hole in a dolphin's head. If he was in the mood, which was most days that ended in a Y, his motto was 'go ugly, early'. He was a terrible man.

He knew something had been different with Winter the last year or so but had never come out and said it. There was no way he could have known about him and Narey, she'd made sure of that, but Addison had seen his mate was much less likely to disappear into the night with some piece of skirt. He'd done so a couple of times but it was never more than a diversion, dropping whoever it was off at theirs and continuing home in the taxi on his own. Addison knew he was no longer in the game but didn't say anything. Winter was the wingman that no longer flew.

Winter knew that Addison got flak from the plain-clothes boys for being so pally with a photographer but he got that info from Rachel rather than Addison. She also told him that anyone who tried to slag off Winter got a verbal pasting from the DI. He was a good man to have your back. As far as Addison was concerned, if anyone was going to be giving Winter pelters then it was him. His current favourite was Winter's insistence that Didier Agathe had been Celtic's best right-back since Danny McGrain. Addison reckoned he should be shot for even mentioning Agathe and McGrain in the same sentence and that Didier was a diddy, a speed merchant who couldn't cross the road. Winter would usually just tell him to shut the fuck up and that someone who'd written Henrik Larsson off after one game had no right to an opinion. That was the way it was between them.

Sometimes they talked, sometimes they didn't. Winter remembered the time they'd met in Jinty McGinty's the night after Addison had to attend to a seventeen-year-old girl who'd died of an overdose. When Winter arrived in Jinty's there were already two pints of Guinness poured and Tony had said, 'Cheers'.

'For fuck's sake,' Addison complained. 'Are we here to talk or to drink?'

Winter's phone rang, waking him again from his memories. Talk of the devil. An hour after he first phoned, Addison was back on the line, sounding more like himself, the snap gone from his voice.

'If you've been stuck in your broom cupboard then you won't have seen the early edition of the *Evening Times*,' he chirped. 'Don't know if they were guessing or some dick has tipped them off but they are running with the one-killer angle. It wasn't you, was it?'

'That killed them?' Winter joked.

'That phoned the *Times*.'

The photographer took the bait.

'Fuck off, ya prick. I'd be less insulted if you *had* asked if I'd bumped them off. You know full well I would never go to the press with anything you tell me.'

'Course I do. Calm down, wee man. Jeezus, you are too easy to wind up. Takes all the fun out of it. Anyway, the *Times* is going with one killer. They're calling him an executioner. Bunch of dicks.'

'They are that right enough. You'd fit in just fine.'

'Ha. Cool your jets, wee fella. Still up for that pint? I should be finished here by six and I'll get you at Pitt Street.'

Winter was just over six foot tall and Addison was one of the few people that had the opportunity to call him 'wee man' and the only one that had the cheek to do it. Hang on, he thought, why would Addison want to meet at Pitt Street if they were going drinking?

'Why meet back here? Why not in the pub?' he asked.

'I'm going to have to sit through some CCTV before I can hit the boozer. It's already been watched once and there was nothing but I'd like a look for myself. I thought you could keep me company.'

'Oh, wait a minute . . .'

'Look, just sit on your arse for half an hour then we can hit the pub. My shout. Deal?'

'You want me to sweep the fucking floor while I'm waiting?'

'I'm sure the cleaners would appreciate that. Thanks.'

'Fuck off. Okay, I'll wait. But we go to the Griffin, okay?'

'You know I hate the Griffin.'

'Exactly. Deal or no deal?'

'See you at six.'

CHAPTER 10

Winter was sitting with his feet up on the desk in front of the bank of CCTV screens, knowing full well it would irritate Addison. Small pleasures, he thought. It also earned him a disapproving glance from the CCTV operator, a WPC named Rebecca Maxwell.

Addison nodded at her and she began running the tapes from cameras around the red-light area in the time before and after the prostitute – who, thanks to Rachel, they now knew was called Melanie – was murdered. It didn't make for pretty viewing. Men skulking round West Campbell Street and Waterloo Street and points in between, collars up and heads down. Hookers standing under streetlights, taking their chances with passing trade. All just two minutes' walk from where they sat in Pitt Street.

It was a long, slow trawl. Sulphur-lit shadows loitering with intent didn't make for riveting viewing. Maybe it was a voyeur's paradise but it did nothing for Winter. Addison had Rebecca stop every now and again, freezing images of likely lads but more in hope than expectation. It was a needle in a haystack job. The girls might have a quiet word with the passing customers and direct them somewhere for business to take place. When the punters disappeared into the darkness of the lanes and the doorways there was no way of knowing who did what to who. Including strangle them.

'Even if we could identify every punter in those frames, even if we pulled every one of them in, then we have to know which of them went with Melanie,' said Addison. 'And we have to know which of them killed her. If it even was one of them.'

For half an hour there was a succession of stops and starts and swearing while all the time the taste of the Guinness with Winter's name on it was tickling his mind.

'So who do you fancy to take over Quinn's operation?' he eventually asked Addison. 'McGurk? Brother Lenny?'

Addison didn't take his eyes off the tapes but shook his head.

'McGurk lost his balls the second he saw Malky's head blown open by that sniper's bullet. I saw the look on his face and I'd say there's no way he fancies some of the same. People I talk to say he was always a natural number two. Same with wee brother Lenny. He just didn't have the *cojones* for the big job in the first place and certainly doesn't now. The gunman might as well have shot them with the bullet that took out his brother.'

'So who?'

'Ten-million dollar question, mate. A name that's kept coming up since yesterday is Ally Riddle. You know him?'

Winter shrugged.

'Young guy, maybe only twenty-five but a smart cookie. Been with the Quinns since he was in his early teens and fast-tracked through the organization. He's been running a scrap yard of Malky's off London Road for a few years now and there's a helluva lot of money goes through there. Shows Quinn rated him highly. He never put McGurk or Lenny's nose out of joint by bigging it up but word is it was well known Riddle was the coming man.'

'He in the frame for killing him?'

'Doubt it. He was much better off with Malky alive than the mess there is now. Might be too soon for him, too. And it's stretching it a bit to think he did Caldwell as well. We're keeping our eye on him though. Well, I say "we" but if I'm stuck with this one,' he nodded towards the screen, 'then it might be someone else's job. Fuck that for a game of soldiers.'

Winter drank in Addison's words and a game plan began to form in his head.

'Biggest case round here in a long time . . .' he began.

'Like I haven't noticed,' Addison replied. 'What's your point?'

'And it could get bigger yet. They really should have the top men on the job. Is that you?'

'Damn right it's me. There's no way they should be running something on this scale without me being involved.'

'So what you going to do about it, Addy?'

'What do you suggest?'

'Go see Alex Shirley. Tell him straight out that you want it. Direct approach never fails.'

Addison looked at him thoughtfully, chewing it over in his mind. Just as he was about to answer, there was a knock at the door and Cat Fitzpatrick strolled through, all flame-red hair and sparkling green eyes. The DI's attention to the tapes was instantly forgotten and Rebecca Maxwell switched it off when she realized he was no longer watching.

'I was told you boys were hiding in here. Got a minute?'

'For you, Ms Fitzpatrick, I've got all the time in the world,' Addison grinned.

Cat rolled her eyes and shared a mutual look of despair with the WPC.

'Given how discerning you are, DI Addison, that's very flattering to know,' she replied with as much sarcasm as she could muster.

Addison took no offence whatsoever and misguidedly thought of it as flirtation.

'You wanted to see my report as soon as I was done with it so here you go,' Cat continued, handing him a folder. 'Do you want details or highlights?'

'Highlights.'

'*Quelle surprise*. My best estimate of time of death is half an hour either side of midnight. Cause of death was asphyxiation and the bruising to the neck indicates manual strangulation. There was also some internal haemorrhaging caused by the blow to the skull but that was not, in itself, fatal. The angle of the fingermarks suggests someone approximately six inches taller than the victim, so just under six foot. The body was, as you know, moved after death and that has been confirmed by lividity.'

'That it?'

Cat smiled sweetly and shook her head, determined not to rise to Addison's bait.

'That's it for now. You did ask for a rush job.'

'Ah, don't take offence, Cat,' he soothed. 'We're going for a drink once we're done here. Why don't you join us?'

'No offence, boys, but I'd rather not. Today has been rough enough without ruining it completely by drinking with you pair.'

'She loves us really,' Addison mouthed to Winter in a stage whisper.

Winter said nothing. Cat was about to answer instead when Addison broke in again.

'You do love us, right?'

He was nothing if not persistent.

'Boys, I love chocolate. I love Petit Chablis. I love Matt Damon. I love shoes. You two? I love cellulite more than I love you two. I'm dropping this back at the lab then I'm going home. You boys have fun though.'

'Methinks she doth protest too much,' said Addison as Cat left, the door closing behind her.

'Sexy bitch and what an arse. Oh well, back to reality. Rebecca, you can start the tapes again.' Maxwell rolled her eyes at Addison.

'Addy, I've been thinking. If I'm going to sit through the rest of these tapes for you, there's something I'd want in return.'

'Guinness?'

'No. Well, yes, but something else.'

'Oh aye?'

'You're convinced there will be more killings by whoever topped Caldwell and Quinn, right?'

'I'd bet on it.'

'Well, if you speak to Alex Shirley about getting on the sniper case, then I want you to ask him if I can be designated to photograph anyone else that gets hit.'

'Fuck's sake, you don't want much, do you?'

'No, I just want to photograph anyone else that gets hit.'

'Yeah, I heard you. Okay, I'll ask.'

'Thanks, Addy.'

'Don't thank me yet. I'll try. Best I can do.'

'Good enough.'

They both turned their attention back to the turgid task of viewing the tapes from the red-light district even though they both knew it was hopeless. If their man was in there then he was hidden from plain view. The area's natural camouflage of shadows and alleyways came with the territory and meant it suited the hunter and the hunted a lot more than it did those viewing it through a lens. After another half-hour of fruitless observation, Addison called an end to it.

'Enough's enough,' he muttered. 'We're out of here.'

'Right, the Griffin it is then and not before time,' said Winter enthusiastically.

'Not quite yet, wee fella. I'm fed up with this game already and I'm going to do what you suggested. I'm going to see if Shirley is still in the building. You go ahead, I'll see you in there.'

'Good move,' Winter replied, with more than half a mind on his own vested interest in the outcome. 'And if he says yes . . .'

'Christ, enough already. Will see what I can do. No promises, mind.'

'None expected. Thanks, Addy.'

It was only a few hundred yards to the Griffin but the walk was far enough for Winter to get a proper thirst on. He wanted his favour from Addison but he also wanted a few pints of the black stuff. His tongue was aching for it. The old *sgriob* was working overtime. But his other *sgriob*, his real itch, was tingling more.

The thought of Shirley giving him the go-ahead to join the case, the only real case in town, was overpowering. Two pints of Guinness and he'd be dreaming about a hole in the middle of a drug lord's head. And he'd like it.

CHAPTER 11

The Griffin was always more Winter's kind of pub than it was Addison's. For him it was a local in the city centre, the kind of everyman bar that Glasgow did best. Old man's pub, student hangout and theatre crowd all thrown in together. For Addison there were never enough women in it to keep him happy but then again there was never a pub with enough women in it for him.

It had stood on the corner of Bath Street and Elmbank Street for over a hundred years, curving round the corner in splendid wood and leaded glass. Between the Griffin and the lounge bar, the Griffinette, the exterior looked massive with more than enough entrances to make it confusing but inside it was split into three rooms making it much more intimate than it appeared from the street. The leather speakeasy seats facing each other across wooden tables meant the place filled up without a lot of people actually being in it.

That night there were maybe twenty people in the main bar and it gave it the busy, cosy feel that Winter liked. He and Addison were propped up on stools at the bar and the DI was refusing to say how his meeting with Shirley had gone, simply saying that he was waiting for a phone call and didn't want to jinx it. Instead he was moaning about the lack of talent and suggesting they move on elsewhere. Winter dragged the conversation back to the gangster killings every chance he got.

'Tell me more about this Ally Riddle,' he began. 'Is he going to be able to run Quinn's business? Surely the hyenas will be moving in to pick over the bones.'

'Course they will,' nodded Addison. 'Jo-Jo Johnstone, Bumpy Scott, Tookie Cochrane or the Gilmartins, you can bet they're interested. Their kind always have an eye on someone else's territory if they sense it's ripe for taking over. But Ally Riddle is still the bookies' favourite. The word is that he'll be able to hold Quinn's mob together.'

'What about Caldwell's operation?'

'Same thing. A couple of his lieutenants, Fraser Gray or Tommy Wright maybe, will have first crack at it but if they don't show enough balls then Johnstone, Terry and Davie Gilmartin et cetera will be chapping at their door. Whoever killed these two bams has created a vacuum that needs filling. And it *will* be filled.'

There were some questions he knew were better not to ask but Winter never could help himself.

'Addy, if you guys know so much about what these cunts are up to and who is running what for who, then why aren't more of them in the nick?'

Addison's eyes narrowed.

'Oh right, why didn't we think of that? Tony, if it was that simple . . .'

A tune suddenly burst from Addison's jacket, saving Winter from whatever was coming next. It was the theme tune to *Top Cat*, the indisputable leader of the gang, and by the time Addison had wrestled the phone from his pocket Winter had worked out that meant it was Alex Shirley. His guess was on the money.

'Yes, boss,' answered Addison as he got off his bar stool, taking the call outside and away from interested ears, including Winter, who was left admiring a full pint of Guinness, thinking not for the first time that it was a thing of beauty. Deeper than the darkest night and topped by a perfect full moon. If it was a sunset they would paint it.

The door swung open again and Addison burst through with a look of triumph on his face.

'Put your money away, wee man. Drinks are on me.'

Winter could have told him that they already had full pints and that he'd paid for them but there was little point. He knew Addison in full flow and there would be no stopping him.

'Whisky,' he shouted to the barman who was in the middle of serving someone else. 'Two large Highland Parks and one for yourself.' The last comment removed some of the scowl from the barman's features and completely washed over Winter's protests that he didn't want whisky.

'Okay, wee man, do you want the good news or the bad news?'

Winter just shook his head wearily and took a gulp of his Guinness. The only thing worse than Addison in a bad mood was him in a good one.

'What's that you say? The bad news?' chirruped Addison, regardless of his silence. 'There is no bad news just some really fucking good news.'

'Just tell me.'

'Okay, that was Superintendent Shirley. I'm on the team for the Quinn and Caldwell shootings! The Temple had already said he'd wanted me on it but the hooker killing threatened to screw that up.'

'Very inconsiderate of her,' Winter interrupted.

'Ach, you know what I mean. Anyway the point is that I was able to convince Shirley that such a sensitive case would benefit from the female touch and that anyway, DS Narey was overdue the opportunity to run an investigation on her own. So he's agreed to let Rachel take it on from here.'

Winter winced at how well Rachel would take that.

'Oh, she'll love you for that,' he managed sarcastically.

'Ah, it's all thanks to you,' Addison responded with a wicked grin. 'It was your idea that I ask to get a run on the sniper killings. Great idea, and I'll make sure Rachel knows it.'

Great, thought Winter miserably. That was all he needed.

Addison was his best mate but he couldn't help feel a kick of jealousy. He was in where Winter wanted to be. A slideshow played behind his eyes, his mental photographic album of Quinn and Caldwell with single bullet entries through their skulls, in crimson pools that ran city-wide and city-deep. He wanted it more than he could tell anyone, probably more than he could even admit to himself. Now Addison was on the inside and he was still on the outside, his chances of getting anywhere near it relying on Addison putting in a good word.

'Brilliant,' he told him. 'Happy for you. Now remember that—'

'It's huge,' Addison cut across him excitedly. 'This is potentially the biggest case to hit Glasgow since the Cutter murders. Okay, there's only two dead but fuck knows where it's going to end. No way we've seen the last of it. Everything I'm hearing tells me it's going to get a whole lot worse before it gets better. My money's on another body before morning.'

Winter realized that Addison was beginning to get on his nerves.

'So if you are at the heart of the biggest story in town since Jesus went to Dumbarton,' he asked him, 'should you not be out there knocking on doors rather than in here knocking back halves?'

'Not at all, wee man. It's been a long enough day and they will still be dead when the sun comes up. Tonight I deserve a drink and so do you.'

With that Addison pulled back his arm in an exaggerated gesture to pat Winter on the back but only succeeded in banging his elbow into the guy standing behind him. He was young and looking the worse for wear and Addison's elbow caused him to spill a few drops of his pint.

'For fucksake,' he shouted. 'Watch it, eh?'

Addison turned slowly and apologetically.

'Sorry, mate. My fault. I'll get you another one.'

'Too fucking right you will. Get me another pint then you can get tae fuck.'

The guy was about twenty, just five foot four with a close cut of red hair and looking decidedly rat-arsed. He was bridling with some kind of indignant rage, the kind that is fuelled by drink, being ginger and from Glasgow.

Addison just looked at the kid, obviously biting his tongue.

'Like I said, I'll get you another one.'

'Aye, and like I said, you can then get tae fuck, ya cunt.'

'Hm,' was all Addison said, nodding to the barman who was anxiously hovering nearby that he should get the guy another pint of lager. The drink was poured and sat in front of the still-seething twenty-year-old.

'I should fucking think so an' all,' he snarled. 'Fucking eejit.'

Addison shook his head, his patience wearing thin and the good mood he was in from the Temple's phone call gone out the window.

'I've bought you a pint even though you just spilled a mouthful,' he told the boy. 'I've said sorry. Now behave yourself, drink it and shut your fucking mouth.'

Addison turned away from the drunk and took a mouthful of his own pint. As he raised the glass, the boy pushed out an elbow and deliberately bumped Addison's drinking arm causing the glass to chink into his teeth.

Enough was enough and Addison put his glass down slowly before stretching out an arm and shoving the drunken kid clean off his feet. He fell stupidly, trying and failing to grab at the bar counter on the way down but only catching thin air on his way to a hard landing on the pub's tiled floor. All noise in the Griffin stopped like a needle being lifted off an old LP and there were sniggers and shouts from the speakeasy seats. Out the corner of his eye, Winter saw the barman reach under the bar and take hold of something that was undoubtedly as heavy as it was handy. Addison gave him a level stare to say he'd seen the movement as well and that to bring out whatever was under the bar would be as silly as it was unnecessary. The barman knew Addison was a cop and probably took Winter for one as well. He nodded but didn't look best pleased.

The boy was flat on his back, embarrassment raging in his eyes, so angry he was almost in tears. He lashed out with his feet, succeeding in kicking the foot of Addison's barstool.

'Away home,' sneered Addison. 'Your mammy will be wondering where you are.'

Somebody else sniggered and there was a fair chance this didn't do anything for the ginger guy's mood. He jumped to his feet, furiously wiping beer puddles from his jeans. In a flash he'd reached inside his coat and whipped out a knife, its blade twirling and glinting under the lights of the pub.

Instinctively Winter stepped off his stool but Addison had beaten him to it and had already pushed an arm across in front of him to hold him back.

'For fucksake,' he growled at the kid. 'More paperwork. I don't need any more fucking paperwork. I hate fucking paperwork. Do you have any idea how much I hate paperwork? Do you?'

The boy roared and lunged at Addison's face, slashing towards his cheek. Addison was more than ready for him though, stepping quickly to one side and catching the boy's wrist as it came through and twisting it till the knife tumbled onto the floor, turning the kid's arm tight behind his back, grabbing his head back by his hair with the other and making him squeal.

'I'll tell you how much,' Addison continued into his ear. 'I really, really hate paperwork. So much so that I'm prepared to kick your sorry little arse out into the street on the understanding that you get as far away from here as quickly as you can and that you never set foot in this place again. Everyone is entitled to a second chance and you've just had yours. There won't be another. Understand?'

The bampot muttered an 'Aye' and tried to pull away from Addison's grasp. The DI abruptly let him go and the boy staggered forward comically until he ran through the pub doors without a backward glance. Seeing him go, Addison sat himself back down, throwing the Highland Park down his throat and soundlessly signalling to the barman for a replacement in one seamless movement.

Winter had barely begun to complain that he didn't want one when Addison shrugged, picked up Winter's glass as it arrived on the counter and sent it chasing down after his own. 'Please yourself,' he muttered.

He was staring past the barman into the mirror behind the bar and he didn't look – how had Rachel put it? – like a happy bunny at all.

'What is it with these wee dicks?' Addison asked without looking at him. Maybe it wasn't even Winter he was asking.

He sat for minutes, breathing hard and staring alternatively from the glass behind the bar to the one in front of him that held his whisky, pensive and angry. He finally gave up his thoughts to his drink, low enough so that only Winter could hear.

'You ever watch wildlife documentaries?' he asked.

'What?'

'David Attenborough, *Life on Earth*, National Geographic Channel, that kind of stuff?'

'Well, sometimes. If there's nothing else on.'

'Should watch them. Might learn something. There's this animal, the honey badger. Just a wee thing, no more than a foot high, but it's scared of nothing. Get them in Africa and western bits of Asia – Iraq and Pakistan and the like. They take on anything and back down from nothing. Reckoned to be the most fearless animal on the planet. They tackle scorpion, porcupine, meerkat, mongoose, gazelle, python, you name it. They even take on small crocodiles and water buffalo.

'Hard wee bastards and dirty fighters. They say one of its favourite tactics when it's up against something much bigger than itself, like a buffalo, is to go right for the balls. Bites them clean off and waits for the fucker to bleed to death before ripping it to bits. But for me, the most amazing thing is that when something does get a hold of it, the honey badger still has a trick up its sleeve. It's got this ability to twist inside its own skin and bite whatever is holding it. Whatever you do, you don't fuck with a honey badger. Fucking brilliant, isn't it?'

'Aye, wonderful. Addy, what's your point?'

His face hardened.

'My point is that if a honey badger could speak then you could bet your last fucking dollar that it would have a Glaswegian accent. Too small to be continually picking battles with the big boys but programmed not to know any better. Just too brave or too stupid to know when to back away from a fight.'

Winter laughed. It was the wrong answer apparently.

'The thing is it's not funny, Tony, not funny at all. Every fucking day in Glasgow some stupid wee dick dies because he was born in the wrong place at the wrong time with the wrong attitude. And, just to be clear, every single one of them, every single one of *us,* is born with the wrong attitude. If you don't have it then you get the shit kicked out of you. Or get it kicked into you. Chicken or egg. Hit the fucker with the stick and if that doesn't work then hit him with the carrot. Or stab him with the stick. Either way, you stand on your own two feet or you die on your arse. It's the Glasgow way. Fuck them or they fuck you. Learn quick or be a victim.

'That's why this place is full of wee boys who are dying to be hard men. The cemeteries are full of them. Wee boys with what they think is courage instead of brains, all of them ignorant of the single piece of wisdom that might just keep them alive. The brave thing to do is run, the cowardly thing is to stand and fight just because you are scared of being labelled a coward. The ones that can find the guts to realize that it's all right to be afraid are the ones that just might live to see their next giro rather than become another statistic. The rest end up the same place that stupid wee fucker out there is going. I give him five years tops till he's pushing up daisies.'

Addison knocked back the last of his Highland Park, closing his eyes and savouring it as it slipped down. When he opened his eyes again, he turned to Winter with a grin replacing the grimace that had been stuck to his face.

'Okay, lecture over. I've drunk enough for one day. Home time.'

With that he lurched off the bar stool and headed for the door without looking back.

'Remember to talk to Alex Shirley for me?' Winter shouted after him. 'Get me doing photographs on the case?'

'Och, no chance. You've burnt your bridges on that one.'

Winter jumped off his stool and caught the door before it hit the latch.

'Come on, Addy, you said you'd speak to him. You know how important this is to me.'

The DI still didn't look back but shouted to him over his shoulder as he headed towards Sauchiehall Street.

'I've told you, wee man, you bite too easily. Takes all the fun out of it. Trust your Uncle Addy. Talk to you tomorrow.'

Winter could still hear him laughing as he disappeared down Elmbank Street in search of a taxi.

CHAPTER 12

Thursday 15 September

Alex Shirley's office in divisional HQ in Stewart Street was more functional than decorative, a bit like the man himself. The carpet was plain but sturdy, fit to take the boots of a thousand coppers marching to his solid oak desk. It was sparsely decorated, with just one framed award on the wall and a photograph of his wife and two teenaged children propped up on the desk next to his computer.

DI Addison was sitting in front of the desk, examining the family group shot and thinking, not for the first time, that Mrs Shirley was a bit of a looker and would have been pretty hot about a stone and a half ago. Alex Shirley himself was a dapper man, five foot ten with a close crop of steel-grey hair and a wide, muscular build making up for any lack of height.

The Temple's blonde daughter was in her late teens and Addison's opinion of her was mercifully cut short by the door opening behind him and Superintendent Shirley striding in with DCI Iain Williamson following behind. Addison wrenched his eyes from the photograph and made a half-hearted attempt to get to his feet until the Temple shooed him back into the upholstery.

'Thanks for coming in, Derek,' the superintendent began.

'We're all up to our eyes in it today so I'll keep this as quick as possible. The briefing is in half an hour and I've got other calls to make before then. The chief is going in front of the television cameras this afternoon and he's not looking forward to it one bit.'

'That makes a change, sir,' chipped in Addison brightly.

'Aye, very good, Inspector,' drawled Iain Williamson. 'Keep those thoughts to yourself. No point in making this week even worse than it's already lined up to be, is there?'

The DCI was a dour Dundonian who had been working in civilization for the past ten years or so. He was a good, solid cop but permanently wore the expression of a man who had found out his dog had died.

'No, sir,' Addison agreed.

'Correct answer,' interrupted Shirley, who was far less bothered about Addison's quip than his DCI was. 'Okay, tell me that you have brought DS Narey up to speed on the Wellington Lane girl so that we can get on with this other shit. It's to be Operation Nightjar, by the way.'

The codenames came from an approved list generated by a computer and one was picked at random from it. One month, all the names could be trees, the next it might be breeds of dog. It was meant to avoid using names that were connected to the case and might end up muddying the water.

'Catchy,' replied Addison. 'Nightjar? Makes me think of last orders. Or is that just me?'

Addison was looking at the superintendent but was aware of Williamson on his right, shaking his head disapprovingly.

'Just you, Derek,' replied Shirley. 'A nightjar is a medium-sized nocturnal bird. Or so Iain tells me. So, DS Narey?'

'I'll make sure she is fully briefed today and I'm going to assign DC Julia Corrieri to her so she won't be short of support. They've both been involved with the case to date so that will help.'

'Two female officers? Should work well with parents. How does Narey feel about taking over the case?'

'I haven't spoken to her yet but I'm sure she'll be delighted with it,' Addison lied. 'Narey's good, sir. Very good. Allowing her to run the Wellington Lane case means we can put every other resource towards the sniper killings.'

The Temple raised an eyebrow.

'Yes, you convinced me of that last night. And it also allows you to be free for the bigger case.'

'Well yes, sir. I can't deny that is something that appeals to me.' Addison quickly tried to shift the conversation away from his motives. 'But as I say, I feel these shootings are going to need every resource we can give. And on that front, I'd like to make a suggestion.'

'I'm listening.'

'I think it might be a big help, particularly further down the line, if we use Tony Winter on this.'

'The photographer?'

'Yes, sir. If it does pan out to be the Gilmartins or Riddle or whatever bampot out there is responsible for these shootings, then the last thing we want is for it to slip loose in court because of some evidential problem. I'd want to make sure that everything is nailed on.'

'You don't think the SOCOs are up to the job?'

'It's not that, sir. We all know how huge this is going to be when it gets to trial and that added expertise is certainly not going to go amiss. At the end of the day, he is a specialist and this is what we pay him for, sir.'

Addison gave himself a metaphorical pat on the back for that one. Alex Shirley was a big fan of specialists and had been around long enough to remember the benefits before half the force was turned into Jacks and Jills of all trades.

The Temple nodded slowly.

'Agreed. But this is assuming there is going to be something else to photograph. Which you think there will be?'

'Which I'm certain there will be,' Addison replied.

'Yes. Me too, unfortunately. Iain, what do you think?'

Williamson was equally aware of what the superintendent thought of specialists and could think of no good reason to argue against the principle.

'It can't do any harm,' he agreed. 'But hang on, is Winter not the same twat who turned up at the scene of the Caldwell shooting, taking pictures on his frigging mobile phone?'

'Er, yes, sir,' Addison admitted.

Shirley's head slid briefly into his hands.

'Great. Just great. Campbell Baxter is going to go mad at the very suggestion of this,' he muttered.

Addison allowed a sly smile to sneak across his lips.

'That's just an added bonus, sir.'

Shirley laughed despite himself and even Williamson seemed vaguely amused.

The superintendent sat in thought for a few seconds before swearing briefly under his breath, picking up his telephone and waiting for his secretary to pick up the other end.

'Phyllis, get me Campbell Baxter. Ask him to drop whatever he's doing and come over to see me as soon as possible. Like now.'

Shirley swore softly again.

'That awkward sod is going to bend my ear about this. I can't bear the pedantic prick at the best of times and he's going to be a right pain in the arse when I tell him what I want. This will be worthwhile, right?'

'I'm sure of it, sir.'

The phone rang and Shirley picked it up immediately.

'Yes? Thank you, Phyllis. Baxter will be here in twenty minutes. Okay, you two, what else is happening out there? I want to know every frigging incident that even sounds like it might be connected.'

Addison detailed the beatings and manoeuvrings that had erupted in the aftermath of the shootings. Those that had been officially reported and the far greater number that hadn't. The ears of Strathclyde cops were flapping overtime to get an idea of just how much of it was going on.

When the door to Shirley's office burst open after the most cursory of knocks, the three officers looked up to see the heavily bearded, heavy breathing presence of Two Soups looking down at them questioningly. Baxter was clearly eyeing Williamson and Addison with suspicion, as if he was being led into some kind of a trap.

'Campbell, sit down. Please.'

'I'll stand if you don't mind, Superintendent Shirley. We are extremely busy and I really ought to be back in the lab as soon as is practicable.'

All three cops sighed internally but let nothing show.

'Thanks for coming over at such short notice, Campbell. I do appreciate you are under pressure at the moment.'

'Yes, we are.'

The superintendent's voice hardened.

'We are *all* exceptionally busy. That is why I shall take as little of your time as is possible. I'd like to ask if you have any objections to Tony Winter being placed at the disposal of the team investigating the recent sniper shootings.'

Baxter bristled. An angry flush emerged on his cheeks and his words spluttered out in a barely concealed fury.

'What? Winter? Absolutely not. I would have to post the most strenuous objection to any individual, particularly *that* individual, being allocated to a specific investigation. It goes against the very grain of the established bi-partisan working arrangement and I would take it as a personal affront and an attack on the integrity of the Scottish Police Services Authority itself.'

Shirley tried to let the old goat blow himself out, seeing with some satisfaction the distress of Baxter's heaving paunch and the dismay of the sneering, pursed lips that peeked out from his salt and pepper beard.

'Well . . .' he began, only to be interrupted by Baxter's continued bluster.

'There is a matter of protocol here, Superintendent, and it strikes me that you intend to drive a coach and horses through that understanding. While I understand that Mr Winter is neither an officer of your constabulary nor a member of the SPSA, neither quite fish nor fowl as it were, I must make clear my objection. I would consider him to be something of a maverick, his behaviour being quite unsuitable to the task at hand and falling considerably below the standards I would seek in scenes of crime examiners. Furthermore . . .'

The Temple did not wish to hear furthermore.

'Campbell, I have had to consider the advantage, in such an inevitably high-profile case, of expert photography and the beneficial effects this will have with a jury.'

If human beings were actually capable of blowing a gasket, then Baxter's cylinder head was suddenly in severe danger of separating itself from his engine block.

'Am I to take it,' he raged, 'that you consider my department incapable of taking acceptable photographs? Because I can assure you that is far from being the case. The supposed *art* of photography is greatly exaggerated in terms of courtroom presentation but there is no crime scene examiner under my aegis who cannot produce perfectly satisfactory work in this regard.'

Addison wanted to get out of his chair and punch Baxter in the head to see if that would deflate some of his insufferable pomposity. But he didn't. Instead he smiled directly at him and nodded as sweetly and sarcastically as he could. He knew what Baxter couldn't – Alex Shirley had already made his mind up.

'*Mr* Baxter,' the superintendent emphasized his civilian title in order to stress his own superiority. 'When I asked if you had any objections to Winter being assigned to the sniper killings, what I actually meant was that I was telling you he was being assigned to the sniper killings. That was by way of courtesy. I had assumed, perhaps wrongly, that you would have had the sense to realize the difference.'

Baxter's mouth opened then closed again. He repeated the motion, succeeding only in looking like a rather stupid, bloated fish.

Addison was torn between laughing in Baxter's face or kissing his boss on the cheek but decided that neither was the correct course of action. At least not until Baxter had closed the door behind him.

Baxter pulled himself up into what he must have assumed was a position of moral indignation and said curt goodbyes before leaving with a scrap of his self-respect intact.

Shirley stared almost disbelievingly at the door as it closed behind Baxter, shaking his head.

'That man gets right on my tits. I hope that Winter is aware that Baxter is going to make his life a merry hell for as long as he is on this case and for a good while after that. He's never liked the idea of us having specialized photographers and this isn't exactly going to help. Just keep Winter in line will you, Derek, and keep that fat oaf Baxter out of what's left of my hair.'

'Not a problem, sir.'

'I don't give a frigging fuck if it's a problem or not. Just do it. Now move your arse, we're due at the briefing in two minutes. Phone Winter and get him down there, too. He may as well see what he's getting involved in.'

The squad room set aside for the operational briefing was in one of the bigger rooms in Stewart Street and out of the way of random cops walking the corridors, so it suited the purpose just fine. When Shirley, Williamson and Addison pushed their way through the double doors, they saw that most of the team that had been hurriedly put together to investigate the Caldwell and Quinn shootings had already assembled. Narey was among them, sitting expectantly in the second of three rows of eight chairs. The superintendent nodded in her direction and saw Addison groan at the prospect of explaining the change of plan to his feisty DS in front of a squad room of cops.

Addison eased his way past a couple of CID officers to get to a point where he could catch Narey's attention and signalled for her to step out of the row and speak to him. She quickly excused herself and went to the side where Addison leant in close and began explaining what was to happen.

'What? You are kidding me, right?'

Heads turned at Narey's angry outburst. Addison again spoke quietly but it didn't go down any better.

'And that means you can take your seat at the top table here, does it? While I have to bugger off and–'

Shirley's voice barked over them and brought the argument to a close.

'Ladies and gentlemen,' he began loudly. The greeting might have been aimed at the whole team but Narey and Addison knew it had been meant for them. They pulled back from each other and took their seats.

'Ladies and gentlemen,' he repeated, more calmly this time before turning somewhat theatrically to the large posters behind him.

'Cairns Caldwell.' He paused slightly for effect. 'Malky Quinn.'

Everyone in the room already knew the names tagged to the bloodied bodies on the posters but Shirley wanted to remind them just how huge the consequences of the killings might be. It had the desired effect and every pair of eyes in the room was fixed on the superintendent.

'I don't want anyone in this room thinking that their murders are in any way good news,' he continued evenly. 'It isn't. There's no good news in this for us. We get it nipped in the bud right away or all hell will break loose. I will not have this become a free-for-all for either the press or the dealers. We stop it here and now.'

No one said a word. Heads turned though as the Ops room doors swung open and Winter sidled silently, almost embarrassed, into the room.

'Welcome to Operation Nightjar,' Shirley continued to his audience. 'It starts in this room, it reaches out to everyone in Strathclyde Police, and it ends in this room. We find out who did this and we put them away. It needn't be any more complicated than that.'

Shirley again looked around the room, his authority unchallenged, as Winter slipped into a seat in the back row, which he felt suited his position in the scheme of things.

'Forget rotas, forget overtime,' Shirley was telling them. 'We are here till this is done and I want that to be sooner rather than later. If you need something you will get it. DCI Williamson is going to talk us through what we already know and what we need to know. Iain . . .'

DCI Williamson pushed back his chair and joined Shirley in front of the PowerPoint presentation, setting about monotonously recapping everything to do with the two shootings and might well have lost his audience but for Alex Shirley's stern gaze searching the room for anyone's eyes daring to wander. Williamson was a details man and was missing nothing out. He divided the room up into three teams of six and specified their different roles.

Winter did his best to listen but his gaze kept switching to the hypnotic sight of the two blown-up photographs of Caldwell and Quinn that grabbed the stage above Shirley and Williamson's presentation. He stared at them, drinking in every dot per inch, wishing it had been him that had taken them, seeing violated bone and singed flesh, guilt and penance, blood and more blood. It was all he could do to tear his eyes away from them.

Williamson was saying that shift patterns had been torn up and every bit of available manpower was to be directed at what had happened at Central Station and Kinnear Road and what may or may not happen from that point on. The baw was on the slates, he told them, and it was their job to get it down again.

As for Winter, he was to be where he was needed and at the beck and call of all and sundry. In other words, he thought, he'd be where the action was and that suited him just fine. More than fine. He stared hard at the photographs of Quinn and Caldwell again, wishing something that he could never have voiced in that room. He wanted more.

Williamson was still in full flow – explaining how the SPSA had verified that the bullets that killed Caldwell and Quinn were fired from the same gun, almost certainly a variant of the army's L115A3, a designated sniper rifle – when a telephone rang in front of Shirley. The superintendent glared at it for daring to interrupt before picking it up and barking into the receiver.

'What is it?'

Every pair of eyes in the room were locked on Alex Shirley. All of them, even Winter, knew that it would have to be something important to disturb the super in the middle of a briefing as huge as this one.

As Shirley listened intently, the granite look on his face began to slowly but visibly crumble. His eyes widened and his mouth dropped for just long enough to cause a shiver to pass through the entire squad room.

'Harthill Services,' he said quietly as he hung up. Then louder, 'Harthill Services. Now!'

CHAPTER 13

Half an hour earlier

The white transit van swung off the M8 at pace and headed deep into the first corner of the motorway services at Harthill, coming to an abrupt halt in an acre of space without another car within shouting distance. The driver, his head covered in a black balaclava, immediately opened the door and jumped out of his seat, making for the rear of the van.

He pulled the doors wide and bundled out the two men that were inside. They were both tied at the wrists and ankles and fell onto the ground at his feet. Without saying a word, the driver swung back a boot and crashed it into the midriff of the first man then the knee of the second.

Reaching down, he untied the ankle binds on one man, then the other, delivering a savage kick as he did so. As the two men writhed on the concrete, the masked figure pulled each towards him and undid the ties on their wrists. Standing behind them, he put a boot hard behind the back of each man and pushed them away from the van and in the direction of the services, a few hundred yards away, with only a few articulated lorries in between.

The men stumbled forward, the momentum bringing them unsteadily onto their feet. Both glanced behind them, blinking but uncomprehending. He was letting them go? Given what he had already done to them, the blood and the bruises evidence of it, they were wary of thinking that he would just let them run.

They looked at each other and back to him, then began moving forward, slowly then more quickly, a final glance back then into as much of a run as they could manage. Their injured legs took them as fast as they could allow, heading in the direction of the lorries further along the barren concourse and the petrol station beyond. Their hearts were pounding and they sweated heavily, joints aching and burning, but they didn't dare stop. They had to get away, to the safety of the lorries. Maybe if they got in among people then they could survive. It hurt, it hurt a lot but they had to run for their lives.

Behind them, they heard the engine of the van start up and knew immediately what it was. They had heard it loud and clear as they hurtled along the M8 and thought it might be the last sound they'd ever hear. The transit had turned over its engine like a pistol signalling the start of a race.

They ran harder, trying to shut out the pain and the fire and the sweat that was blinding them, bursting a gut to get towards the juggernaut lorries and then the petrol station that just might be their salvation. The driver must have stepped on the accelerator because they suddenly heard the engine leap and roar in the distance behind them, taunting them, chasing them.

Stevie looked across at Mark running almost level with him and instinctively knew that it would be better if he got away from him. Sure, they were together in this but the chances of them both getting out of it were slim. He veered off to the left, trying to put some distance between them. Mark saw his move and changed direction to go with him, his arms pumping at his side to keep up his momentum.

Stevie arrowed even further left and when he was followed again, he roared across at Mark.

'Fuck off!'

'What?'

'I said fuck off. Go right. Go the other way from me,' Stevie panted, blood dripping from his burst lip.

Confusion passed across Mark's face but he must have decided he didn't have time to work out why. He swerved right again, putting yards then more yards between them. The pair passed by the lorries, glad to have the sheer size of them temporarily between them and the van. Stevie clambered onto the plate of the first one, pulling himself up to the cab only to find the door locked and no one in. From his vantage point he could see that none of the lorries had drivers in them. He threw a glance back at the transit and jumped to the ground again, the pain shooting through his battered knees as he landed. He shook his head at Mark who was watching him hopefully and they both ran again.

Across either side of the patch of grass that separated the lorry park from the car parking area, onto the forecourt where there were a bunch of cars and drivers up ahead in front of the petrol pumps. It was really hurting now but another two hundred yards and they'd be safe.

They'd passed the first of the parked cars when Stevie heard the noise. He couldn't be sure if he heard the gunshot first or the sound of Mark hitting the ground or the scream; it all seemed to reach him at once. He knew one thing though, the screaming wasn't Mark's. The bullet that tore into his head had killed him before he could make a sound.

Stevie didn't stop. It had only meant that he'd been right to get away from him. He ran harder, his heart fit to bursting. There were people up ahead, standing with their mouths open, a woman screaming. He would go to them. They'd save him. They had to.

A car door suddenly opened to his left and a middle-aged man got out, obviously unaware of what had happened to Mark, just intent on walking to the services shop. This was his chance.

'Help me,' Stevie roared with what breath he had left. 'Please.'

The man stopped and turned, his eyes widening at the sight of the bruised and bloodied man, bathed in sweat, who was running at him and he took a step backwards.

'No, you've got to help me! Fucking help me!'

Stevie was on the man now and grabbed him, intent on twisting him so that he was between him and the transit van. But almost the second he had his hands on the driver, he felt his own body desert him. His legs couldn't support him and he was crashing to the concrete, darkness descending on him at a speed he'd never known before. His head hit the ground and he felt the cold rush through his skull like a too-cold ice lolly. There was a big hole somewhere and he was falling into it.

As he slipped away, he failed to hear the third shot, the one that took out the man who had done nothing more than to go for a newspaper or a packet of cigarettes. They'd been the death of him all right, them and the bullet that had exploded into his head. The poor man had already fallen into the same pit of death as Mark and Stevie.

As people gathered round the bodies, hardly any of them noticed a white transit van driving along the roadway that led to the slip-road onto the M8 towards Glasgow.

CHAPTER 14

As soon as Shirley had given the order, eight officers got to their feet, kicking back chairs and pulling on jackets in their haste to get out. Winter was aware of resentful looks from the cops, Rachel included, that were stuck there while he was on his way to the scene. She fired him a glare that didn't seem to be in jest and he returned it with a shrug that hopefully said that it wasn't his fault and she shouldn't hold it against him. She simply glared at him harder for interacting with her in public and he knew it would be a shag-free zone for him for a while. So be it, he thought, the truth was if it was a straight choice then he'd opt for the chance to photograph whatever it was lay at Harthill. Crazy maybe.

Instead he picked up his camera bag, comforted by the weight that told him everything he was going to need was in there. He hefted it onto one shoulder and his photo documentation kit – with its collection of photo markers; gray, white, black and transparent scales; photomacrographic scales; ruler tape and steel tape measure – onto the other and tagged on to the back of the small scrum that was filing through Stewart Street en route to the car park.

When they got there, the group split into two, Shirley leading one and Addison the other. Addison signalled for Winter to follow him to where his Audi A5 was parked and nodded towards the back. Winter had asked him in the past about why he needed such a flash motor but Addison would just look down at his expensive suit and give a self-satisfied wave of both hands as if to say, 'Hey, I'm worth it.'

Two other CID officers joined them in the car, Colin Monteith in the front and a sombre-looking blonde woman in the back. Winter had barely closed the door when Addison accelerated away, throwing him back in his seat and scrambling for the safety belt.

'Colin, you and Tony obviously know each other. DS Jan McConachie, this is Tony Winter. He photographs dead people.'

The blonde cop looked over disinterestedly for a moment before turning her gaze back to whatever she was finding so fascinating out of the window.

'Okay, here's what we know,' Addison said as he pulled out of the gates in second gear, hammering onto Glenmavis Street and towards the motorway. 'We have three dead at Harthill, two beaten up and shot in the back of the head from a distance, the other shot in the face. It doesn't take much of a stretch to link them to Quinn and Caldwell. Witnesses told uniform that they saw two of the men running, almost staggering, through the car park on their way to the area with the petrol pumps and the shop.'

'I take it we don't have any idea who they are?' asked McConachie.

'Nope. Uniform won't touch them till we get there and Tony photographs them. Once he's done that we can go through their pockets. They're looking through the CCTV now though and hopefully they'll have something to show us by the time we get there.'

'So what were they running from? Or to?' asked Monteith. 'Staggering means they could have been drunk or already hurt?'

'Hurt,' replied Addison. 'One witness reckoned they came from the far end of the services where you come in from the motorway and they had blood on them. Thought they might even have been hit by a car.'

No one had reported an accident. There was no sign of a vehicle abandoned anywhere nearby. The description of the victims rang no bells. If they were drug dealers on the scale of Quinn or Caldwell then they'd have been recognized right away. Forensics was going to examine the bullets for a match to the L115A3 but that would obviously take time. Not that anyone doubted it would prove to be from the same gun. This wasn't a time to start believing in coincidences.

The cops batted theories back and forth, Addison sure that the dead guys would also be dealers of some stature, Monteith saying he hoped that they were, McConachie saying little. Winter wasn't involved in any of it though, he was just the hired help along for the ride. It didn't bother him, he was there and that was all that mattered.

Addison belted along the M8 towards the Heart of Scotland services, his foot to the floor the whole way. He didn't have a siren on his Audi but didn't need one, simply overtaking everything in his path. The whole way, Winter's *sgriob* was itching like crazy at the thought of the men with the holes in the back of their heads. He closed his eyes and tuned out the chat in the car, seeing the blood, smelling it, almost tasting it. How much of the heads would be left, how much blood, how much of their brains would be spilled over the car park? Focus, check the ambient light, adjust aperture, assess the depth of field, focus, focus, focus . . .

He didn't open his eyes again till he felt Addison jump on the brakes and bring the car to a sudden halt. He saw the services were flooded with cops, Strathclyde blue everywhere, keeping back the open-mouthed masses. They'd parked up a fair bit away from the main event so as not to pollute the scene and walked to where a group of uniforms stood over what they had all come to see.

Shirley and three others were ahead of them obscuring the view but Winter could still make out a splayed body, blue jeans, a white shirt and a navy jacket, arms wide, cop tape and space marking out where he lay. About twenty yards further on a knot of blue was huddled round another two shapes on the ground. As they walked towards them, officers were being directed back across the car park to search every inch of the route the dead men had taken across the tarmac. Winter's nostrils twitched and his throat was dry. Game on, he thought.

Shirley beckoned him past, the hired help invited to the party and first to get fed. The sooner he did what was needed then they could get on with the real work, was what they were thinking, but Winter knew what was real and it was just a few feet away. He licked his lips and hoped no one noticed, covering it with a wipe of his hand. As he went to the body, he saw Campbell Baxter glare at him and knew that if looks could kill then he'd be lying on the concrete beside the three stiffs. Baxter was loathing him more with every step. Too bad, thought Winter.

First, he pulled the spherical camera out of the bag to take the 360-degree shots for the Return to Scene programme. They'd been using R2S for a few years now since it was created by the forensic investigation people in Aberdeen. When he got back to the office it would help him set up a virtual crime scene that the officers could add to with audio clips of witness statements, CCTV footage and whatever else might prove useful. Then, once he'd taken in the whole world view, he got out his own camera.

On the first victim he saw brushed navy boots with good, thick soles made for walking and dark denims with knees bent strangely where he'd hit the ground. A white cotton shirt was a good look if you were going to be shot in the head and then photographed.

Blood isn't red. At least, it isn't simply red. It is cornelian or vermilion, it's pillarbox or Venetian, Persian or scarlet. It can be anything from alizarin to carmine depending on the effects of oxygen or carbon dioxide. When you see fresh blood it will be crimson, signifying power and danger, glistening bright with vitality and pumped with oxygen. But let it simmer and watch it turn rosso corso, passing through lust by way of coquelicot.

Winter had never ceased to be amazed at the colour of blood because you never knew quite what you were going to get. See it vivid when the haemoglobin is oxygenated and you will be seeing amaranth, candy apple or American rose. See it dull, listless and dying and it will be sangria, rufous or burgundy. Smell hot firebrick or cool falu. Taste flame-grilled cardinal or coppery upsdell like the tang of two-pence pieces.

The flowing blood of a suicide where someone has cut their own wrists runs dark and gloomy because of the deoxygenated juice that runs through the veins whereas the blood of a victim of cyanide poisoning will be redder than red because the body cannot steal away its oxygen. When you know blood, when you love it, then you can tell lava from ruby, rose madder from coral. You can look at blood and know how long it has been exposed to the air where it cannot breathe, where it withers and dies like a fish out of water or a rose torn from the ground.

This guy was lying in a pool of sangria. Winter wasn't sure if that was appropriate or ironic given that the word comes from the Spanish for blood. His was full-bodied Rioja, all smoke and spice and everything that's nice.

He was in his early thirties with close-cropped hair intended to hide the fact that he was losing it. A scar maybe three inches in length and washed in muted, hour-old firebrick ran down the left-hand side of his face from ear to jawline. His mouth hung open like a rusty hinge, a flycatcher of a mouth, stuck before it could scream. You could almost make out the beginning of the final word that fell on his lips. This was Glasgow, whatever he was about to say it probably began with F.

Winter focused on his head and on the wound, the crater that had been driven through his skull by the sniper's bullet. Death through a lens. The murky light offered by the September sun lent his photographs a muted hue, casting them drab and downbeat. He fastened on a daylight fill-in flash and lit it in its full glory. Colours flooded the aperture, filling his viewfinder with everything he wanted. He shot, shot and shot.

He couldn't hear anyone talking. It was Central Station all over again, locked in his own little world of death. He heard blood, pounding in his ears and thumping at his heart. He saw blood, already drying on the man's face and drenching his long sleeved white. It swam round him like a velvet pillow, soaking up his soul.

His clothes were designer-expensive, the kind of bad taste cool pumped out by Italian designers and worn by overpaid footballers. Mr Hole in his Head flaunted his money, wore it as a badge.

The guy's face spoke to Winter of a life lived in the scumbag lane. The tanning studio glow and taut skin said nightclub poser. The scar shouted hard man in a hard town. Then there were the wide, cold fish eyes that had learned the light at the end of the tunnel was an oncoming truck and had screamed for help. His eyes roared fear.

His shirt was opened, ripped open maybe, almost to the waist. This guy had had the shit kicked out of him, with ugly red welts forming on his chest where he had been punched or kicked. He focused in on the marks one by one, all the time a bell going off in the back of his head. Something he'd seen before but couldn't think what. He also photographed his wrists which were telltale red and scored as if they had been bound tight.

A voice behind him burst his bubble.

'Done with this one?'

No, he thought. No, I'm fucking well not done. I want to stand here for ever, toe to toe with the eternity that this guy has slipped into, stand here and see if he blinks first. I want to see his soul slip away and his flesh peel.

'Winter, are you done?'

This time he recognized the voice as being Alex Shirley's. The detective superintendent sounded testy and impatient. He had to drag his eyes away from the entry wound and remove the scowl from his face before he turned to look at him.

'Two minutes, sir.'

'Make it one. I need to find out who these arseholes are.'

He stood back to take a final full-length shot in situ, framing the victim amidst stern-faced polis. He raised his lens slightly and pushed it left, catching a cop looking down at the body with a mixture of curiosity and disgust. Something about the whirr of the motor made the officer turn his head and look at Winter suspiciously but he'd already turned the camera away and blanked his stare. Job done.

Just a few feet away yet a world apart going by his clothes and the Ford Focus was the older man who was sleeping unhappily in a bath of burgundy. Winter guessed he might be in his mid-fifties even though the only clue apart from his clothing was that the man's hair was flecked in creeping grey. The area formerly occupied by his face was a gory hole of violent carmine, the soft flesh, bone and gristle having been blown away by the sniper's bullet.

Winter saw sensible, casual brown shoes with soles that would stand up to wet autumn leaves or a rain-soaked garden. He saw dark brown corduroy trousers and a dark-green jumper that emphasised a middle-aged paunch. He saw a father and a grandfather, a hard-working family man, an ordinary man.

That night, someone was going to have to sit down with a wee girl and boy and explain why they wouldn't see grandpa again. They'd have to try to make a seven-year-old understand how their papa could die when all he was doing was going for petrol.

Still, it was doubtful that they could be more shocked than the ordinary man was. Even without a face, there was no disguising his astonishment. He had fallen back flat with his arms wide, confused, questioning, pleading and utterly lost.

Winter got in close on the faceless face, picking out every detail where the bullet had done such horrendous damage. It was hard to see what had happened to this man as a thing of beauty, by all accounts the wrong man in the wrong place with the wrong people. And with no eyes to reflect his crossing, neither he nor Winter could see where he was going or where he'd been.

Winter stepped back and got both men in the one shot, something that even the sniper had failed to do. Two men whose paths should never have crossed and if there was such thing as a heaven or a hell then surely they'd be going in separate directions.

As he stepped away from the older man's stricken body and headed towards the third, a slim figure moved past him in the opposite direction. Even in a white scene suit, overshoes, a hood and a mask, Cat Fitzpatrick looked great. He couldn't see her hair but there was no disguising her green eyes or the curve of her rear. He briefly watched her begin to reach inside the victim's jacket as requested by Shirley but he had to stop staring, he had another body to look at.

The third victim was twenty paces away, face down in a rufous puddle and clinging onto the concrete for dear death. His white trainers were blood-sticky, as were his faded denims, brown leather jacket and reddish hair. The little brains he once had were sitting in an untidy pile next to him. The guy's face was squashed to the ground where he lay, making his nose snubbed like a boxer. His eyes were slumped and his jaw slack, giving in to the inevitable and paying no more than passing interest to the dirt beneath him. He wasn't much more than twenty years old and looked ready to cry for his mammy but for the fact that it was all too late.

He knew what was coming, he must have. He might have heard the shot that killed his mate, heard the scream or the cry and the body hitting the deck. He'd have run faster but there are some things you just can't outrun. Then bang, his lights would have gone out in an instant and he crossed the line into nothingness. Or somethingness, who knew.

Winter focused on his dull green eyes and tried to capture what he'd last seen. He had the look of someone who had decided none of it had been worth it. He'd made a bad decision the day he'd started getting into cars with the man in the white shirt with the scar on his cheek. His mammy had probably told him that and now he knew she was right. Mammies are always right. Too late to learn that lesson now.

Above him, three cops were chatting, paying little attention to the dead kid at their feet. Seen one body, seen them all. One of the three had obviously cracked a joke and they were barely suppressing grins and one was sniggering. Winter caught a beautiful wide shot with his Canon, the three of them looking one to the other, everywhere except at the body that threatened to dirty their boots. Above them, glowering Scottish clouds, fit to burst, were deciding just when to unleash their load and wash away the blood of the sinner. Drama above and below and couldn't-give-a-fuck in between. The picture was a winner.

'Hey. You miss your shot there?'

The accusing voice was from the tallest of the three cops, glaring at Winter, obviously realizing he was in the frame and not best pleased about it. You should show a bit more respect for the dead and you wouldn't be caught out, Winter thought.

'Just getting a scale,' he told him. 'Need to put everything into perspective.'

'Aye? Well, get your fucking scale somewhere else or I'll shove it up your arse. You're here to photograph the stiff, stick to that.'

'Don't wet yourself. I'm just doing my job and don't need you to tell me how to do it.'

'I know what you need, ya cunt, and if there weren't brass about then you'd be getting it.'

'Fuck you, Officer. If you . . .'

He wasn't sure what the rest of that sentence was going to be but he knew it was going to contain a threat he couldn't back up. So maybe it was just as well that it was cut short by a soft voice just to his right.

'Behave yourself, Tony. You can't win that one.'

It had been his turn not to notice what was at his feet. Cat Fitzpatrick had her hands in the pockets of the dead guy's leather jacket and had found a wallet from which she produced a driving licence. Those eyes, the colour of wet Irish grass, were laughing at him.

'I took it you were finished since you had the time to play wee boy's games with the nice constable,' she said. 'Okay, I've got names for all of them. Come on.'

She stood up and walked a few yards before holding out the licence for Shirley and Addison to see.

'The old man is called Alasdair Turnbull. And as for these two . . . the brown leather jacket is Mark Sturrock and the first guy, the white shirt, is Stephen Strathie.'

'Strathie?' said Addison. 'Name's familiar.'

'Strathie's a courier, I'm fairly sure of it,' piped up Jan McConachie. 'Stevie Strathie. If I'm thinking of the right guy then he runs drugs for Malky Quinn. Or did. Don't know the other one.'

'Fucking great,' replied Addison ironically. 'Phone it in and have the names run through the computer. Get me everything there is on both of them. Probably a waste of time but get me the licence of any car or van that's registered in either name too.'

McConachie nodded and pulled out her mobile to contact Divisional HQ.

'So, assuming this is the same guy . . .' Winter began.

'It is,' muttered Addsion.

'If it's him then why go to all the trouble and all the risk of shooting them so publicly?'

'So that we would know it was him.'

McConachie held up her hand to signal for attention and began nodding confirmation to Addison and the rest of the team. Strathie was a courier all right while Sturrock had previous for dealing and worked for the Mighty Quinn. Then her eyebrows furrowed and her jaw dropped. She looked up at Shirley, almost apologetically.

'Sir, a white van has been abandoned in the middle of George Square with two petrol containers sat away from it. They say there's what looks like twenty kilo bricks of cocaine sitting next to the petrol cans.'

'*What?*' Addison was stuck like Winter had never seen before. 'What the fuck is going on?'

'Who's at the scene?' demanded Shirley.

McConachie blinked. 'Three cars and two fire engines and more cars on the way. They've got the square cordoned off but they can't get near the van.'

'Why not?'

'One of them tried and a shot was fired at his feet. From a distance.'

'Jesus Christ,' recovered Addison. 'I don't suppose the van is registered to either of your men here by any chance?'

'Nope, but one of them might well have been driving it till an hour ago. DVLA say it's Malky Quinn's.'

CHAPTER 15

The call from Joanne Samuels had been left on Narey's answering machine and hadn't left much room for manoeuvre or much time to get there.

'Rachel, it's Joanne. I hope you get this soon. I've managed to talk to one of the women who knew Melanie quite well. Be at the Criterion Café at the beginning of the Gallowgate at two o'clock. She's very jumpy so if you're late then I don't know how long I'll be able to keep her there. Criterion Café. Two o'clock.'

It was nearly one-thirty when Narey, still fuming from the bombshell at the morning conference, picked up the message and she didn't have much time to get across the city centre to the east end. She jumped in her car and battled her way across Cowcaddens Road and George Street before crawling down High Street, cursing the traffic and the never-ending succession of red lights. As the digital clock on her dashboard shifted ever nearer to two, Narey became less convinced that she would make it on time. With just two minutes to the hour, she spotted a space near the Tolbooth Steeple and braked sharply, ignoring the horns that complained at her, and threw her car into the opening so she could run the rest of the way.

At last the powder-blue sign and low roof of the Criterion were in view. Surely the woman wouldn't have left yet, surely Joanne could keep her there that long. With thirty yards to go, she slowed to a walk in order to get her breath back, knowing she would now be able to see anyone leaving the café. As it happened, no one came through the door by the time she reached it and as she pushed her way inside she saw Joanne at a corner table, sitting with her back to her. Opposite her sat a young woman with short, spiky dark hair who was nervously fidgeting with a napkin and looking around anxiously.

Narey didn't take the chance of asking if she could join them, instead just pulling back the chair next to Joanne and sitting down. The girl continued to look round the room as if worried that someone would see Narey with her.

'Sorry I'm late, Joanne. Hi, I'm Rachel,' she said, holding her hand out to the girl opposite. No handshake came back though, the girl holding on to the napkin and twisting it below the table where a cup of coffee had been barely touched.

'This is Pamela,' Joanne explained. 'She was a friend of Melanie's.'

As Narey looked at Pamela she could see that her nervousness wasn't just down to meeting a cop. The girl was an addict. The paranoia went way beyond their meeting; Pamela jumped every time the door opened or someone at another table laughed. Her bloodshot eyes and dilated pupils might have been many things but Narey knew what they really were. With barely any make-up on, the dark circles under her eyes were as obvious as the sour smell from her breath. When she finally spoke, there was a noticeable tremor in her speech.

'I'm doing this for Melanie, right?' she slurred. 'It's the only reason I'm here.'

'Okay,' Narey nodded. 'I understand that. Did you know her long?'

'Long enough,' the skinny girl said quietly. 'A year maybe.'

'Did you meet her on the street?' Pamela's eyes briefly flickered with resentment.

'Yeah.'

'Okay, what can you tell me about Melanie, Pamela? Anything you know could help us find out who did this to her.'

The hooker looked at Joanne for reassurance and must have got it because after another fretful look round the café she leaned in towards Narey.

'She was awrite. Some people didn't like her 'cos she could get a bit full-on when she was high but she was awrite really, know what ah mean? Never did me any harm.'

'Where was she from?' Narey asked.

'Like where did she come from, you mean? Glasgow, south side somewhere, I think. She didn't talk 'bout it much. I think she fell out with her mum and dad.'

'Can you remember where on the south side?'

'No. Told you. She didn't like talking about it.'

'And she was living somewhere in Maryhill?'

'Aye. She had a room there in the high flats in the Valley.'

'You know the address, Pamela?'

'It was the big block in Collina Street but ah cannae remember the number. She hudnae been there that long.'

'That's okay. Did Melanie have any children?'

Pamela looked at the table then the door.

'Aye, she had wan. A wee girl. She's six.'

Narey and Joanne swapped a quick glance.

'Where is she now?' Joanne asked.

Pamela was twisting the napkin furiously now, her interest seemingly taken up by her shoes.

'Where is Melanie's wee girl?' Narey repeated anxiously.

'The wean's wi her dad,' Pamela answered quietly.

'And who's her dad?' Narey pushed.

Pamela just shook her head, still staring at the floor. Her anxiety levels had just rocketed.

'Please, Pamela,' Joanne Samuels broke in. 'It could be important, pet. I think if you know then you should tell her.'

The girl's hands went unconsciously to her face, wiping under her nose.

'He's trouble. A real bad bastard,' she hissed. 'He'd kill me if he knew.'

All Narey's senses were telling her that this was a name she had to know.

'He won't know, Pamela,' she assured the girl. 'No one will know except the three of us round this table. Melanie was your friend and I think she deserves for the person that killed her to be caught.'

Pamela was tilting her head to one side and repeating the gesture: anxious, thinking, afraid. 'Tommy Breslin,' she whispered.

'Okay. Tell me about Tommy,' Narey pursued.

The girl repeated her head-tilting routine and nibbled on the inside of her cheek.

'They call him T-Bone. Or he calls himself it, anyway. He was Melanie's boyfriend. Sort of. Thinks he's some kind of gangsta but all he is is an arsehole dealer.'

She looked up suddenly, remembering who she was talking to.

'It's okay, Pamela. He'll never know we've spoken to you. This is between us. How did this T-Bone treat Melanie?'

She shook her head bitterly.

'Like shit. Like a piece of shit. He was always laying into her for nothing. He broke her arm once and was always leaving marks on her. Kicks and punches. And he was the bastard that got her onto the shit in the first place.'

She looked up at them fearfully again but the thought of what Breslin had done to her friend gave her some steel.

'He was her dealer too. And mine.'

Narey nodded, grateful for the girl's information.

'Do you think he could have done this to Melanie?'

Pamela said nothing but looked Narey straight in the eyes and nodded.

Narey mentally crossed her fingers and asked the question she hoped for an answer to more than any other.

'Did Melanie ever tell you her real name?'

'Yeah. She told me once when she was out of it and after that it didn't matter. Her name was Una. Said she'd always hated it.'

'Did she tell you her surname?'

'No sure. She told people her name was Melanie McCulloch. Don't know if that was real or not. Look, I've had enough. I need to go. Told you enough.'

Narey still had a head full of questions but could see that Pamela was right on the edge and had made her mind up to go. Anyway, she thought, she had a hell of a lot more to work with than she had when she sat down.

Joanne said that she would take Pamela home, noticeably refusing to say where that was, and Narey left them after picking up the bill for the coffees. She saw Joanne's hand comfortingly placed over the girl's but by the agitated look on her face it was going to take more than that to put her mind at ease.

The door of the Criterion swung closed behind her and she was immediately hit by the cool afternoon breeze that had picked up. Her first thought was to telephone Addison with what she'd learned until she remembered that the bastard had dumped her with this and she was the one in charge. Well, sod him and whatever he was attending at Harthill, she was the one with the breakthrough.

When she got to the Tolbooth she found a parking ticket stuck to the windscreen and swore at the paperwork that was going to be involved getting it overturned. Fuck it, it had been worth it. She turned her car round and threw it headlong back into the traffic heading for George Square and from there would go on to Stewart Street. Christ, it seemed even busier than it had been earlier. The traffic was at a complete standstill and there was nothing at all coming the other way. What the hell was going on?

Up ahead, she could see flashing lights, blue as well as red. For the second time that afternoon, she abandoned her car in the nearest available space, this one with double yellow lines, and continued on foot. The closer she got to George Square, the more she realized some serious shit was going down.

She pulled out her phone and got onto Stewart Street, demanding to know what was happening. As the answer came through, so the old red square came into view. Narey couldn't believe her eyes.

CHAPTER 16

Narey arrived at George Square no more than fifteen minutes after the white van was parked up and about ten minutes before it began snowing. When the response came from the desk at Stewart Street, she raced the last couple of hundred yards until she reached the politburo splendour of the City Chambers itself.

A large crowd of shoppers and office workers had already gathered round the square and Narey pushed her way through them, alternately shoving, shouting and waving her ID card. She could see a ring of yellow-jacketed uniforms and two fire engines and headed for them as quickly as she could.

A uniformed inspector was standing at the nearest corner of the square, speaking into a walkie-talkie and looking like he was ready to punch someone or shit himself. Narey made a line straight towards him, trying to remember what his name was. Benson, Bett, something like that.

The guy saw her coming, looking her up and down in a way that made her want to puke. Prick, she thought. What the hell was the sleazeball's name?

'Inspector?' she started. 'I'm DS Narey, I–'

'Yes, I know who you are. I'm a bit busy, Sergeant. What is it?'

'We have reason to believe this is connected to an ongoing CID case and I need to ask you what you know about what's happened here.'

'Oh, do you now? What case is that then?'

'The shootings of Cairns Caldwell and Malcolm Quinn. I'm sure you are aware of them.'

To Narey's satisfaction, the inspector blanched, his eyes widening as he took in the consequences of what she said.

'From what we're told, the van came along the Queen Street side,' he began. 'It drove off the street and onto the square where it is now. No one's got a clue where the driver is but we're told he ran off as soon as he'd laid things out. You see the petrol canisters?'

Narey nodded.

The two green canisters sat close together about twenty feet away from where the van had been abandoned with its doors wide open. It sat on the red concrete, shunned by the statues that ringed the square, all with their backs turned to it.

Beside the canisters were a couple of dozen bricks, quite obviously kilos of cocaine, wrapped in white paper and stacked in four hurriedly constructed piles. She knew if it hadn't been for the presence of the cops, the bricks would have been nicked in two seconds flat.

'So did any one of your guys try to approach the van, sir?' she asked the inspector.

'Twice,' he answered with a curt nod. 'Both times they got shot at. Nothing too close the first time, maybe a few feet away but enough to scare them off. After the first try we got someone togged up and had another go but the second time the shot missed him by inches. We haven't tried again.'

'Okay. Where are the shots coming from?'

He shook his head.

'We think it might have been from the north of the square, the City Chambers end, but to be honest, the place is in such chaos that no one's sure. Everything was so quick that I don't think anyone could have told you where their arse was. The only way to find out would have been to send someone in a third time but I couldn't sanction that.'

'Fair enough,' she agreed, having to shout now above the growing clamour around them. 'But what's been done to find out where he might be? He's got to be somewhere high up, right?'

The inspector stared hard at her, nodding but looking up and around him to prove his point. The square was surrounded on all sides and beyond by towering buildings that could have hidden a hundred snipers.

'Which way did the driver run, sir? And do we have a description of him?'

The inspector – suddenly she remembered his name, Begley – began to answer but he was immediately interrupted by a huge roar behind him. He spun and they both saw a surge in the crowd near Queen Street station and the start of a punch-up as people barged into each other.

Narey looked around her and saw that a huge crowd had now gathered and the cops were struggling to hold them back. George Square was bang in the middle of the city centre and there were always hundreds of people walking along one of its sides or across it. Closing off the four streets that formed the square had immediately created a growing bottleneck and was continuing to draw a curious swarm. More people were joining the throng every minute and the human dam was threatening to burst at every access point.

The surge at the station seemed to be caused by another commotion a hundred yards down the same stretch of the street. A Sky news crew had somehow managed to talk and push their way through from North Frederick Street and had taken up a vantage point near the Millennium Hotel, not giving a toss for the people that had been standing there. Two officers had run over and were arguing with the reporter while the cameraman and sound guy were busy focusing on the white van.

Much later, it occurred to Narey that maybe it was all that the sniper was waiting for. Right then, though, when it happened, she had no time to think. Like everyone else round George Square, all she could do was duck.

The air exploded with a gunshot that had hit before anyone knew it had been fired. The first she was aware of was the result of the bullet thudding into and through the petrol cans. They burst into flames with a roar that immediately had police and public instinctively stepping back from the square. In seconds, the newly burning petrol had ensnared the cocaine bricks, setting them alight with a snarl.

Narey saw Begley's jaw drop. To be fair, she could hardly blame him. In seconds there was a Class A funeral pyre. At first it was just the petrol that leapt high and violently in dark, furious flames. But as they subsided it was clear to see the bricks breaking and burning and a wispy, creamy smoke snaking across the square and into the city beyond, seeking bloodstreams to invade.

The reaction among the crowd was a loud, excited chatter but that was silenced when another bullet suddenly rang out, the sound hitting them a split-second after it drove straight through the fuel tank of the white van, exploding it and wiping out the potential forensic evidence inside. The transit roared into an orange fireball and blazed away in support of the cocaine.

Begley seemed transfixed, staring at the flames with his mouth open. Narey wasn't though. She'd seen the impact on the canisters and how they'd moved towards them as they exploded.

'The north of the square,' she told him, part explanation, part order. 'The shots are coming from beyond the City Chambers. Get your men over there, sir.'

Begley looked at her as if he wanted to reprimand her but settled for spinning on his heels and barking orders at the nearest uniforms.

Narey's attention was caught by the blare of a car horn coming from North Frederick. She saw a car bulldozing its way through traffic and ploughing through the crowds. It was a wonder that they didn't run someone over because everyone that they were pushing past was gawping at the scene on the square. The car doors opened and as people emerged, Narey realized with a snort and a shake of her head that it was Tony, Addison, Colin Monteith and Iain Williamson. She took in the looks of disbelief on their faces and saw Tony pull a camera out of the bag over his shoulder. Christ, this will be right up his street, she thought. It was undeniably an amazing sight and she found herself wishing she had his gift of seeing the beauty in it.

George Square like you'd never seen it before, snowing as if it were Christmas and bonfires as if it were Guy Fawkes Night. The air was thick with smokes and smells: one the familiar pungent tang of petrol and the other a sweet, rubbery whiff that reminded her of caramel.

The cops could hold the crowd back as best they could but they could do nothing about the air. It and the burning coke went where it pleased, like rumours disappearing into the night. Luckily for those in the city centre, or maybe unluckily for some, the burning cocaine didn't give anywhere near the hit that it would have if it had been snorted or smoked. One of the forensics later told her that when you burn powdered cocaine you lose about half of the potency. It still burns and smokes, just very inefficiently. It was still enough to put a smile on a few faces for half an hour. Some of the locals were sniffing at the air like rabbits twitching for signs of a fox, taking as much of the free hit as possible.

She saw Tony walking between the crowds, photographing as many as he could. Inevitably some of the fuckwits thought he was getting evidence of them taking drugs and a few of them covered their faces while others looked like they were threatening to rearrange his. Any risk was worth it for Tony, though, she knew.

She saw him capture two teenagers grinning at each other like idiots while sticking their tongues out as if they were catching snowflakes. They'd probably never had any more than bottles of Buckfast or White Lightning, so graduating to cocaine was a big step for a Wednesday afternoon when they should have been in Double Maths.

A wee old wifie with blue-rinsed hair obviously thought it was the funniest thing she'd ever seen, giggling away to herself and pointing at the sideshow even though no one was paying her much attention. Maybe it was the nose candy in the wind, maybe it was the lunchtime sherry or maybe she was just a bit crazy to start with but the old girl was in fits. Tony captured her weather-beaten face as she screwed her eyes up and howled with laughter.

A pink-faced bank manager type in an overstuffed overcoat and a peppered beard looked horrified at the events around him and seemed desperate to avoid breathing in even a whiff of the coke. He had pulled out a white handkerchief and held it over his mouth as if he'd been bombarded with tear gas. He'd clearly never taken drugs in his life, as long as you didn't count nicotine or industrial quantities of whisky, and wasn't about to start now.

Other bampots were just welcoming the wind with open arms, quite literally, wafting it towards themselves with as much gusto as they could muster. Fuck the polis, fuck the CCTV cameras. Breathe it in, man, pure magic. They were even fighting for their share of the air, elbowing each other out of the way to snort a bigger nostril-full of next to nothing. These eejits didn't need much encouragement to be off their heads and their stake in twenty-odd kilos of cocaine floating over George Square would certainly do the job.

Addison and Monteith were by Narey's side now and for that moment there was little for them to do but watch and wonder what was going on, a state of affairs they were all well used to. None of them could take their eyes off the cocaine snowstorm; it was as if someone had turned the city upside down and shaken it hard.

'Burn,' Monteith was muttering angrily. 'Go on, burn, you fucker. Burn. Better off with that stuff up in flames than up someone's nose.'

Addison turned to look at the DS, seemingly amused at Monteith's rage.

'Moral righteousness, Colin? It's not Sunday, is it?'

Monteith's eyes darkened but never left the free show that was falling over the square. 'I just don't find it funny, sir,' he replied. 'I'm fed up having to clean up the mess this stuff makes.'

'Well you've got to laugh sometimes, Col. Otherwise it will eat you up.'

'Thanks for the advice.'

'No problem, sergeant. Oh aye, what have we got here then?'

A burly PC in high-vis yellow was leading a terrified-looking young guy towards them by his arm.

'DI Addison. This is Douglas Charlton. He says he drove the car onto the square.'

Dressed in faded denims and a blue waxed jacket, Charlton was in his mid-twenties and looked like he was near to shitting himself and was shaking like a leaf. Surely this guy didn't have the nerve to pull the trigger or hold it steady long enough to hit a barn door. He was attempting to blurt something out and Addison was trying to calm him down so he could get some sense out of him.

'I didn't have any choice,' he was stammering. 'No choice.'

His eyes were nervously darting left and right, he was moving from one foot to the other and it was a safe bet that his arse was going like a threepenny sponge.

'I didn't have a choice,' he said again.

'Aye, we get that,' said Addison with his usual diplomacy. 'What didn't you have any choice about?'

'He made me drive that van to George Square. Said he would shoot me. Made me drive it the wrong way down the one-way street. Said he would kill me if I didn't.'

'Okay, calm down and talk us through it from the top. Where was he? Tell us everything that happened.'

'I was in Livingstone Tower. You know, the Strathclyde Uni building?' The student pointed back up George Street where the corner of a high-rise structure could just be seen in the distance.

'Okay, hang on a second. Was that the last place you saw him?'

'Yes. He said he'd be watching me from there. Said he'd see.'

'Inspector Begley!' Addison roared above the chaos. 'Livingstone Tower. Get everyone you've got there now! Rachel, go with them and make sure they don't fuck things up.'

The remark got him a sharp look from both Narey – who doubly made up her mind not to tell him about her conversation in the Criterion – and Begley, but their reaction clearly didn't bother Addison in the slightest.

'Okay, Mr Charlton, as quickly as you like, tell me the rest of it,' he said hurriedly.

'He said he'd see all the way down the street and would know if I stopped,' the young man continued, almost babbling. 'Said he could hit anything between there and George Square. I'd been going up to the fifth floor and someone stepped out from the stairwell behind me. I didn't see him at all. First I knew, what felt awfy like a gun was pushed into my neck and he asked me if I could drive. I said yes and the barrel of this rifle slipped past my ear so I could see it. He dropped keys in front of me, told me there was a white transit parked out front and that I was to get in and drive it to George Square. The one thing I wasn't to do was look round.

'I didn't have any choice, man. He said if I tried to turn off the road or get out then he'd put a bullet through the fuel tank. He was making me go the wrong way on the one-way, said I was to go at full speed with my horn to clear cars out of the way. I was shitting myself. Had to do it.'

'Aye, okay. Whatever,' interrupted Addison, turning to the cop that had brought Charlton over. 'Take him somewhere quiet and get every detail you can. What height did the voice come from, what angle was the rifle barrel at, did he have an accent? Everything. Tony, come with me. We start on the fifth floor and work our way up. That fucker must have left something behind that we can use.'

It turned out that he hadn't. By the time they got to the tower, Narey had already ordered a floor by floor search and found that a door to an office on the seventh floor had had its lock picked. A window had been left open with a clear line of sight to the smouldering remains of the white van but forensics didn't fancy their chances of lifting anything worthwhile. There were a hundred and one fingerprints and various hair samples snagged on the back of chairs but they were sure they belonged to anyone but the shooter. The area around the open window was meticulously wiped clean and it looked like he had covered whatever tracks he'd brought into the room. They'd file and test anything and everything but whoever did this knew exactly what he was doing.

So Winter photographed a near-empty office knowing that the scene examiners were right. He also slipped on his biggest zoom and shot the car on the edge of George Square, just as the sniper had done. Easy peasy. One click.

He heard footsteps behind him and looked at the window to see Rachel's terse reflection looking back at him.

'What is this guy up to?' he asked her without looking round, seeing just a shrug of the shoulders in return.

'He's taken a van full of coke off those mules,' he continued. 'Beaten the shit out of them then shot them as they ran at Harthill. He's done all that to get hold of that cocaine. And it's worth how much?'

'A million is what the drug squad is guessing,' she answered. 'Twenty-four kilos, about £40 a gram.'

'A million quid's worth of cocaine. He's driven it into town, forced that poor sap to park the van in the square then blown the whole fucking lot up. He couldn't have made it more public if he had burned it in the centre circle at Celtic Park on a Champions League night. What's he up to?'

Narey shrugged again but this time offered up an answer.

'Whoever he is and whatever he's doing, he wants to make sure everyone in Glasgow knows about it. Us, the bad guys, the media, Joe Public, the lot.'

'No such thing as bad publicity?' Winter suggested lamely.

'Not buying that,' she said with a shake of her head. 'He's not trying to take over the Glasgow trade. If that was his game then he could have flooded the market with this, given it away free to every junkie in the city and put the opposition out of business. This headcase is not trying to become number one. And he is certainly not trying to make money because he's just smoked a million pounds of it in public.'

'Well, there's one thing you can be sure of,' said a voice from the doorway. It was Addison. 'The press are going to have a field day with this. Bad enough that he kills gangsters, now he burns seven figures worth of drugs. They are going to make this guy a poster boy for vigilantes.'

Winter couldn't help thinking that maybe wasn't such a bad thing but he knew it wasn't what his pal wanted to hear.

'So what do you think, Addy?'

'I think I'm going back over to Harthill to see the Temple and then grab some food before the game tonight. I take it you're still going?'

'Well, aye, but are you not going to be a bit busy with that lot out there?'

'Wee man, you know the score. There's murders, there's

shootings and there's the Celtic. Glasgow can manage fine on its own for a couple of hours. This shit isn't going to get any shittier tonight. Get you in the Oak sometime the back of seven?'

'No, I'll see you in the ground. C'mon though, what do you think is going on?'

Addison looked beyond them and through the window to the last flurry of the snow scene on George Square.

'An hour ago, I didn't have a clue but now, now I think I might at least know what this fucker is up to.'

'Care to share?' Narey asked him.

'DS Narey!' Addison replied with a wide grin, as if seeing her for the first time. 'Is my mind playing tricks on me or did we not speak about you working full-time on the Wellington Lane case?'

'We did, sir. You were very clear on the matter.'

'Ah, I thought so. So why . . .'

'I was in the area, sir. Just passing.'

'Really? Keep on passing then, Sergeant. We've got this under control.'

Aye, it fucking looks like it, she thought.

CHAPTER 17

At Harthill Services, word about the bizarre scenes in George Square had filtered back to those still meticulously poring over the scene in search of evidence. Shirley and Baxter had both demanded that their officers concentrate on the job in hand and not let their minds wander to the city centre.

Numbered yellow photo evidence markers dotted the scene showing where Winter had started the process and, following the news of the white van and the cocaine, the crime scene examiners had finished it. The examination was structured and sequential, by the book, and they would gather every available piece of physical and trace evidence.

Amidst the scrupulously organized fury of the examination, no one noticed Jan McConachie edge quietly to the perimeter of the crime scene to take the phone call that had been buzzing angrily in her pocket for several minutes. She had already seen the name on the phone's screen and there was no way she could take that call within earshot of anyone else. Not that she wanted to take the call at all. There were four missed calls by the time she was safely out of anyone's range. She could imagine his rage rising with every failed attempt to talk to her and knew that could never be a good thing.

'About fucking time,' he shouted at her when she picked up. 'Do you know how many times I've called you?'

'Yes, I know,' she answered quietly. 'There's been another two shootings. Well, three. Two of Quinn's guys, Stevie Strathie and Mark Sturrock plus an old boy who just happened to get in the way. I'm at the scene now.'

'Fucking hell.'

Jan could hear the shock in his voice and was relieved to hear that he hadn't known about the killings. That was at least one weight off her mind.

'What the hell is going on?' he continued. 'I've been watching Sky News and some fucker has just blown a shitload of cocaine up in the middle of George Square.'

'Yes, I know.'

'That's not much fucking good to me, Sergeant. I don't pay you to know things that I already know. I pay you to tell me things that I *don't* know. Who's doing this? And more to the point, who the fuck is he intending to knock off next?'

She hesitated. She had nothing to tell him.

'I don't know,' she finally admitted. 'We don't know.'

'That's no fucking use,' he raged. 'Things are crazy out there right now and I need to know who's behind this. I'm shedding no tears for Quinn or Caldwell, far from it, but this is all bad for business. Do I need to remind you of our arrangement?'

'No, you don't. All I can tell you right now is that it was the same gun that killed both of them. It was almost certainly the same person who shot the three in Harthill today. When I get more I'll tell you.'

'Immediately.'

'Immediately,' she agreed.

He hung up and she closed her eyes and made a silent prayer for all this to go away. Right at that moment, there was nothing that Jan wanted more than to be at home with the door locked and she and Amy safely behind it watching cartoons on television. Her mind raced to school finishing time and she prayed again, this time for Amy to be standing safely inside the school gate when she went to collect her.

CHAPTER 18

Winter was in his seat at Celtic Park by twenty past seven, kick-off still twenty-five minutes away. The old place was pretty full already and the atmosphere was building up nicely. That familiar sense of expectation and togetherness was buzzing through the ground and he liked to be in there in plenty of time to soak it up.

Not Addison though. His mate was doubtless still supping in the Oak, the nearest pub to the stadium and guaranteed to be wall-to-wall packed with sweating bodies trying to fuel themselves for what was to come. The Oak faithful would stream in at the last minute or beyond, pushing apologetically past people in the middle of 'You'll Never Walk Alone', ducking under scarves and stepping on feet. It was always the same and unless Winter dragged him into the Lisbon Lions Lower early then Addison would be one of those guys.

Winter loved European nights at Parkhead and always had. Ever since his Uncle Danny first led him by the hand through crowds of giant drunks to watch Celtic draw 2-2 with Ajax in 1982. McStay, McGrain, Burns, Nicholas, McGarvey, these were his first heroes. Them and Uncle Danny.

It was a couple of minutes before kick-off and everyone was on their feet as the teams trooped out onto the pitch. At the end of the row, fans began stepping back reluctantly as someone pushed by them towards his seat. With a huge grin and regular apologies, he edged along until Winter could feel Addison's beery breath on his face just as the team went into their pre-match huddle and a huge roar erupted around them.

'About time,' Winter remarked.

'Hey, this is early for me, wee man. Anyway, I've had a busy day in case you hadn't noticed.'

'You and me both. So what happened this afternoon?'

The referee blew his whistle for the start of the game and another huge, extended shout drowned out any reply that Addison could have made. Instead, he shook his head and leaned in towards Winter as they both sat down.

'Later. One thing though, I know what this fucker's game is.'

'Aye? So what's that then?' Winter shouted back, trying to be heard above the noise of the crowd.

The DI just looked down at him, winking and tapping the side of his nose, and then turned back to the game as Celtic immediately launched into an attack down the right wing. People were on their feet around them and the pair were forced to stand as well. Winter was bursting to ask more but knew he wasn't getting anything until Addison was ready.

There was wave after wave of attacks on the Bulgarian side's goal but Celtic didn't manage to score until five minutes before half-time. A cross from the left was met by a header down in front of them and when the ball hit the back of the net, Celtic Park erupted. Everyone was on their feet, Winter and Addison hugged each other and were clapped and bumped into by those around them. Songs soared round the old stadium and minor chaos ruled. The place was still jumping five minutes later when the half-time whistle blew, another mighty roar filling the night sky, and fans began streaming towards the toilets or the food outlets.

There was suddenly a bit of space round them and both men knew they could now talk without having to shout at each other.

'So what's happening?' Winter asked.

Addison hugged himself into his jacket before answering in as low a voice as he could get away with.

'Nothing good. Is it not your turn to go and get the pies?'

'Forget your stomach for a minute,' Winter countered. 'What's going on?'

'If I tell you, then you'll go for food?'

'Aye, okay. Spill.'

Addison looked around and moved closer.

'Looks like the killings at Harthill have made the natives restless and the pantomime on George Square obviously hasn't helped. Jo-Jo Johnstone's wee brother Jason was found with both his legs broken and Jo-Jo is spitting blood about it. Two of Tookie Cochrane's boys were hit by a car and are in the Royal. One of them is in a coma. There's also a guy supposedly gone missing named Harvey Houston who works at Ally Riddle's scrapyard. Riddle's saying he knows nothing but Shirley's pulling him in tomorrow for a chat.'

'Christ. Sounds like it's getting crazy.'

'Those are just the ones we know about. Fuck knows what else is happening. My guess is that there's much more that the bastards have swept under the carpet.'

'A lot going on this afternoon. Have to wonder why I didn't get a call to photograph any of it.'

'Oh fuck off. You will get to do your dirty little thing with whatever that twat does next but this is fall-out from it and you'll just have to get used to someone else pushing the buttons. Cool your jets.'

Addison's eyes were flashing the way they did when he was pissed off and Winter admitted to himself that he had a point. Much as he wanted to capture every bit of grisly shit that went on in the city, he knew he couldn't. There was just too much of it.

'So what happened when you got back to Harthill?' he asked the DI.

'The lovely Ms Fitzpatrick said that Strathie and Sturrock had had the shit kicked out of them professionally. Nothing obvious at first sight but abrasions and contusions to the neck, knees and chest. A few blows but well chosen. Lesions to the wrists, duct tape marks on their faces. They'd been bound up good and tight.

'The bullets are at the lab and we'll have a match in the morning. They will be from the same gun though. No doubt about it. Be the same with the rounds they found at George Square. The Temple had everyone jumping through hoops. He called for every bit of CCTV he could, on the motorway and in the services. The Harthill cameras picked up the pair running and falling so we were able to work out the direction of the shots and have crawled over every inch in a straight line but got nothing. They're going to try again tomorrow.'

'What about the motorway cameras?'

'Bits and pieces. They've got the white van at different times along the road and at a couple of places in town. No shot of it going into Livingstone Tower though.'

'So have they got any kind of pictures of the driver?'

'I can't really say.'

'What do you mean? You don't know?'

'No, I mean I can't say. Won't say, if you prefer it that way.'

'You are fucking kidding me. I'm on the team.'

'Nope,' Addison corrected him. 'You are *with* the team. Big difference. If you don't like it you can go back to photographing broken windaes.'

'Fucksake, Addy. I don't like it but I don't suppose I've got much choice.'

'You don't. I'll tell you some stuff, some stuff I won't. Time you went and got those pies.'

'Wanker.'

'That's Detective Inspector Wanker to you. Get me a burger as well, I'm starving.'

Winter told him what he could do with his burger but they both knew he'd buy it even though he was pissed off at him. Winter wanted every bit of info he could get and Addison was his best chance of it. Shit, he thought, if he was going to be this much hard work then Rachel was going to be a fucking nightmare. She was so wrapped up in the secrecy about them being together that she was paranoid about the need-to-know shit. As far as she was concerned, he didn't need to know. Addison was just enjoying pulling his chain.

Winter made it back before the second half started, his hands filled with two pies, a burger and a couple of Cokes. Addison enthusiastically helped lighten his load.

'So were you winding me up when you said you couldn't tell me about having pictures of the van driver?' Winter asked him.

'Maybe.'

'So are you going to tell me?'

'Nope.'

'Okay, so what's his game then?'

'Eh?'

'You said you knew what the fucker's game was.'

'Oh aye, that.'

'Aye, you know?'

'Aye.'

'Aye, you're going to tell me?'

'Naw. That also falls into the category of stuff I'm not going to tell you. Not yet anyhow. I'm sure I know what his game is but I still don't know what it means. But I will. I fucking will.'

Winter looked at him for an age but knew he was getting nothing more. As if to make sure of it, the teams ran back out and another deafening chorus of 'You'll Never Walk Alone' swept them up into the noisiest of silences.

Celtic scored twice more in the second half and the stadium emptied happy and bouncing. Addison and Winter made their way down the stairs and out onto the concourse.

'Pint?' Winter asked.

Addison looked at his watch with an exaggerated stare.

'Just a couple. It's getting late.'

'What?'

Winter looked at his own watch and saw that it was quarter to ten.

'What's up? You turn into a pumpkin at eleven?' he guessed.

'No, but I'll be pumping something by twenty past,' he grinned. 'She finishes shift at the hospital at eleven and will be naked by the time I get there.'

'Spare me the details.'

'You couldn't handle the truth, wee man.'

'I'm not sure you can handle her with the amount of drink you'll have put down your neck tonight. She might be disappointed.'

'Nae chance. The Addison Express runs well on firewater. The overnight train with no sleeper. I'm going to hit every station.'

'Mind when I said, spare me the details?'

'At least I haven't turned gay. Not that I'm prejudiced, Winter, each to their own. Whatever floats your boat and all that.'

He bristled but knew Rachel wouldn't thank him for blurting out a retort that used her as ammunition.

'Oh just fuck off, will you,' he settled for. 'Some of us don't feel the need to broadcast our conquests.'

Addison roared with laughter.

'Conquests? How is life in Elizabethan England? Are you ready to plight your troth or hoist your petard?'

'I'll hoist *your* fucking petard in a minute.'

'Temper, temper, wee man. Too easy.'

'Aye? Tell me, how many of these easy rides is it going to take before you find some measure of self-esteem?'

Addison's eyes flashed with anger and Winter knew that his jibe had stung. He glared at Winter for a second before the grin emerged again.

'How many? Let's see ... so far this month there has been Alison, Helen, Denise, Ali and ... what was the blonde's name ... oh aye, Moira. How could I forget? All Babes. Thank goodness for Bacardi. Another few should do it for September.'

Addison was beaming all over his face but it quickly disappeared when his mobile rang. He answered with a series of nods and shakes of his head and monosyllabic answers.

'Fucksake,' Addison growled as he finished the call. 'There's no fucking end to it.'

'Another shooting?'

Winter realized he'd said it almost as much in hope as anything else and that Addison had heard it in his voice.

'Don't get excited, wee man. No, that was from Monteith. Some muppet has firebombed Terry Gilmartin's place. His five-year-old son was right in the firing line and he's in intensive care. They don't think he's going to make it.'

'Jesus.'

'Probably not. More likely to be the Quinns. Colin's pulled overtime and is on the case so we can all sleep easy in our beds tonight. Well, you can sleep. I've got other things in mind.'

'You're a nightmare, Addison.'

'Thanks.'

Addison threw three pints down his neck in the forty minutes that they were in the Oak, the place buzzing around them with post-match post-mortems. Winter could see that he was on edge, full of jokes and bravado but he was under strain. His drinking levels had stepped up big time and something was weighing heavily on his mind.

They squeezed their way out of the pub and tumbled back onto the street where the two taxis they had ordered were waiting for them. Addison was heading for the nurse's bed and Winter said that he was going home. Except that he wasn't going home, of course, he was going to Rachel's flat on Highburgh Road.

As both cars were ready to move off, Winter wound down the window in the back of his cab and beckoned for Addison to do the same.

'You reckon you know what this guy is up to, right?'

'I've got a fair idea, yeah.'

Winter looked him straight in the eye.

'Is it good or bad?'

'That's the million-dollar question, wee man. A million dollars. It could be both.'

Addison wound his window up again and turned to direct the driver towards the waiting nurse without another word.

CHAPTER 19

Jan McConachie stared at her mobile phone and tried to summon up the courage to answer it. She dreaded doing so but knew that delaying it would only make him angrier and she could imagine how incensed he was already. He was a scumbag but he did love his son and she, more than most, knew just how desperate that could make a person.

She answered.

She'd expected that he might be ranting and raving, the way he often was, but instead his voice was low and measured and that scared the shit out of her. He was anxiously trying to keep his emotions in check but she could hear the fear and the rage bubbling under the surface.

'You better have some news for me,' he breathed.

'I heard about your son,' she replied. 'I'm so sorry.'

'Shut it. I don't want to hear you even mention him. I want information.'

'We don't know for certain but what we are hearing suggests that it is Quinn's people that were behind it.'

'I fucking knew it,' he seethed. 'That bastard Riddle organized this.'

'We don't know that for sure,' she insisted.

'Well, find out,' he roared. 'Do your fucking job and find out.

It's what you're paid for. Both by the polis and by me. My wee boy is fighting for his life and I'll have revenge for this.'

He lowered his voice again.

'My son means the world to me. You know what that's like, don't you?'

Jan's heart pounded and she could hear the blood rushing in her ears.

'I'll find out everything I can. You don't need to threaten her. You know she's done nothing wrong. She doesn't deserve this. She's only eight. Please.'

'Deserve? Don't give me that pish. My boy doesn't deserve what's happened to him and don't think for one second that I won't use whatever I can to sort this. I don't give a fuck about your daughter but you do. So find out what I need to know and I'll keep putting bread on your table. If you don't then someone else will be picking her up from school soon.'

CHAPTER 20

Highburgh Road was always a wee bit too west-end trendy for Winter's liking. Sure, the rooms had all the Victorian wood panels, stained-glass windows, cornicing and character that you'd want if you were into that kind of thing. But he never really saw the point in boasting that your flat had a butler's pantry when you couldn't get parked within a mile of the place. There were a ton of pubs and restaurants on its doorstep but it wasn't a whole lot of use for him seeing as they weren't allowed to go to them together. It was like being a liver-damaged eunuch serving champagne in a bordello.

Rachel liked it, though. She'd always wanted a pad in the west end and the truth was it was much more her style than his. When she spent all day, or sometimes all night, chasing the bad guys she wanted to get home and lock herself away behind three inches of security door, pour herself a glass of Sauvignon Blanc and chill under twelve-foot high ceilings while eating Kettle Chips. He was happy to lay his hat there, so to speak, four or five times a week.

He rang the intercom and waited. He virtually lived there but he didn't have a key. It was her flat. Her flat, her remote control, her bed, her rules. If he had a key then the next thing he'd be expecting a say in what they watched on the television and that just wouldn't do. It took her a while to pick up the phone upstairs and, as usual, she didn't say anything, just left him listening to the crackly line.

'It's me,' he said wearily.

The buzz meant she'd pressed the entry release so he leaned against the door, went up to the second floor and through the open door into the flat where he found Rachel sitting back on the bed with a selection of newspapers spread out before her. She didn't look up when he went into the room, just tossed a paper to the side of the bed and picked another one up. She was wearing a pair of pyjama bottoms, a vest top, a seriously pissed-off expression and was almost shaking with anger.

'Wankers.'

'Today's papers or tomorrow's?' Winter asked.

'Tomorrow's chip papers,' she scowled. 'I don't know what I was thinking but I went out to Queen Street station to get the morning editions.'

'What? You've always said–'

'Aye, okay. I know that, alright? Just gimme peace. I'm annoyed enough as it is. They are making this sniper out to be some kind of fucking superman. I can't believe it. And in the middle of all this ridiculous glorifying of a killer, "Melanie" or whatever her name really is, gets ignored. I'm sick of this.'

'I was wondering . . .' he started.

She looked at him doubtfully, sensing something she wouldn't like.

'Go on.'

'If you had the choice, would you rather catch the guy who's been shooting gangsters or the one who killed your prostitute?'

'Jesus. What kind of question is that?'

'One I'm interested in the answer to.'

She pondered, wondering whether to give him an honest reply, even if she wasn't sure of it herself. Against her better judgement, she did.

'For the sake of my career, I'd rather catch the sniper. If that didn't come into it, then for the sake of the greater good I'd rather catch Melanie's killer.'

'Is that not some sort of moral fuck-up? To want to catch the killer of one person rather than the killer of five?'

Narey threw a copy of the *Sun* across the room, kicked the other papers off the bed and glared at him.

'So are you here to screw me or what?' she demanded. 'Because if you're not then I'm not really in the mood for talking. And if you are then hurry up, I'm on early in the morning.'

'Who said romance was dead?'

'Is that a no?'

'Fucksake. You are a pain in the arse. It's a yes but think yourself lucky.'

'Oh aye, I'm so flattered.'

With that she pulled her vest top over her head and tilted her head to one side questioningly. It was discussion over. It was hard for a man to argue with perfect tits and she knew it.

He pulled his clothes off with an attempt at a grudging look on his face but another part of his anatomy gave the lie to it. Maybe he was cursed by the fact that she never looked better than when she was angry and those nut-brown eyes blazed. He grabbed the waistband of her pyjama bottoms and hauled them off her, throwing them to the side of the room. In turn, she grabbed at him and massaged him to the desired state, pulling him down and onto her. It was fast, furious and completely lacking in any social niceties. They wrestled, grabbed, slapped, swore, stabbed and thrusted. Speed, for once, seemed to be rated way higher than subtlety or technique. He pinned one of her arms with one hand and kept a tight hold of her hair with the other. It was enough for her to be pushed and pulled over the edge, coming a good bit before he did, barely bothering about waiting for him to join her.

She was asleep two minutes later, out like a light. Winter liked the idea that he had worn her out but he knew it was someone else that had done it. He had maybe sorted out her body but her mind had been fucked by the sniper and the prostitute killer. He also knew a lot of it was down to the Cutter murders and how badly she had come out of that. It was all happening again and she felt like she was chasing a runaway train.

He knew full well what was winding her up and, although it wasn't his doing for a change, he was always going to be the one in the firing line. Which was ironic.

He got out of bed and sat on the floor with his back to the wall, leafing through the newspapers that she'd kicked away. A quick look was enough to confirm the source of her anger.

The *Sun* had started it the day before when they began sneaking words into their reports of the killings. *Vigilante. Clean up. Crackdown.* They liked the last one a lot and the pun helped. Then the phrase that was the real killer – *anti-hero*.

The *Evening Times* had carried on the good work that afternoon. From the minute that he blew up the cocaine and gave Glasgow city centre a high it would never forget, he went from being a murderer to a maverick.

Now the morning's *Daily Mail* had done it in a heading. *Crackdown continues.* It implied something good, something that should have happened a long time ago. The *Daily Record*'s editorial followed suit. It was a carefully crafted piece but it could neatly be summed up as saying, 'We could never condone murder but . . .' It was open season on drug dealers and that was fine by them.

The prize went to the *Daily Express* though. It was them who came up with the name that was to stick, *Dark Angel.* He supposed that it suggested someone good doing something bad.

Winter had heard a couple of radio phone-ins before he went to the Celtic game and they were the same. Callers didn't hold back and at first the stations cut them off when they came out with lines like, 'Serves them right', 'Not before time', and 'Good riddance'. The presenters pretended to be outraged and were all apologetic about how they couldn't support such opinions. At first. That didn't last long though and when the calls became more regular and more insistent then they couldn't and wouldn't stem the tide. The Dark Angel was doing what the cops couldn't, doing what they were paid to do but were too scared or too incompetent to do. Presenters shooed them along when callers suggested the cops hadn't done anything because they were in the dealer's back pockets but they didn't stop them from saying it.

Sky held a discussion panel on *Hard News* debating the moral values of a bad man doing bad things to bad people but Winter could see that it was the *Daily Star* that had now jumped off the high board. *NEW AGE HERO*, they screamed. No anti, just plain old-fashioned *hero*.

No wonder Rachel was mad. Every new notch on this Dark Angel's credibility scale was a rat's bite at the collective police scrotum and they didn't like it one bit. The impression Winter got from her was that some of them agreed with the media line that dead drug lords was a good thing but they didn't want it said publicly. They'd felt hamstrung for years at not being able to get at the bastards they knew full well were responsible for feeding the city's habit. The cops didn't give a toss that Caldwell and Quinn had been shot but they'd be fucked if some trigger-happy psycho would get praise for doing it and at the same time caused them to get a slagging.

They could even live with all the knock-on effects of gangsters taking each other out as retribution although it would be a pain in the arse to clean up the mess. But now this Dark Angel had burned the cocaine and made a statement of intent. He was the one doing the cleaning up and the police didn't like that one little bit.

All the papers carried the hooker killing too but it was pushed way back. Some only had half a dozen paragraphs and it was obviously just getting in the way of the real story.

Winter must have rustled the paper too much because Rachel woke with a start and saw him sitting on the floor, his eyes fixed on the *Daily Star* and its shrieking banner headline. She glared at him.

'What are you reading that pish for?'

He'd had just about enough of this. He knew she was stressed but to keep taking it out on him was out of order.

'But it's okay for you to read them?' he replied testily.

'It's work for me. You seem to be enjoying it too much.'

'But it's not work for you,' he blurted out. 'You're not on the case.'

As soon as he said it, he regretted it but it was too late.

'Maybe you should just go home,' she spat.

'Yeah, whatever.'

He really could do without this and heading to his own place suited him just fine. Going home meant the opportunity of a couple of guilt-free drinks and the chance to have a guilt-free look over his photographs. Staying meant getting a hard time from a stressed-out maniac. No contest. However he wasn't about to go without leaving a cowpat of guilt behind.

'No problem, I'll get out of your way. I know how hard it is with everything that's going on at work and it's only fair you get some rest.'

'Fuck off, Tony.'

'No, no, I completely understand. You've had a tough day being removed from a high-profile case so it's perfectly reasonable that you get me round here, get shagged, fall asleep and chuck me out onto the street. Nice.'

'Don't even bother trying to make me feel bad.'

But he had, though, and they both knew it. He didn't slam the door behind him, realizing full well that she wanted him to. Instead he closed it with as much indifference as he could muster and phoned a taxi from his mobile. It was about two and a half miles to his own place in Charing Cross and he couldn't be bothered with the walk at that time of night.

His own place, that was a bit of a joke, he thought. It was his official home but it was empty more than half the time. He was usually only there to get a change of clothes or when she had friends or family visiting. Or when he wanted to do some work with his photo collection. Or when she was a total pain in the arse. The rest of the time he was chez Narey even though no one was supposed to know.

He was her guilty little secret and that annoyed him. Not just because he couldn't agree with her insistence that it was better for everyone - by which she meant her - that they kept their relationship quiet, but also because as secrets went it was poor. He knew he had her beat easy on the guilt front. Try having killed both your parents and see how that compares.

CHAPTER 21

The taxi dropped Winter off at his front door and he was inside a minute later, sighing at the mess the flat was in. Tidiness wasn't a natural instinct for him and the only time the place tended to be presentable was when he knew someone was likely to visit.

He put on the light in the living room but went straight on through to the second bedroom that doubled as his office. He tumbled back onto the bed, hands behind his head, and surveyed the far wall, taking it in impassively as he always did. He'd never been quite sure what anyone else would make of it but then that didn't matter; only Rachel and Addison had seen it and they were both, usually, on his side.

It wasn't that the sight of it didn't move him, it always did. It was just that he chose, forced himself, to try to look at it with as little emotion as possible. He believed there was a solution in there somewhere, an answer to be found even if he wasn't entirely sure what the question was.

Wall-to-wall death and misery. Twenty carefully positioned and evenly spaced photographs in five rows of four. It was the best of his collection, eighteen of his own and two by Metinides, each photo mounted on white card and framed in black ash, most in black and white but a few in colour. Usually the colour was varying shades of red.

Exhibit number one was his first, Avril Duncanson, wearing her shroud of glass near Muirhead. What made the photograph for him was the stunned look on the face of the middle-aged witness who couldn't take his eyes off the body. He'd obviously never seen anything like it and was praying to his God that he never would again. It was that and her face, all but unmarked, her eyes screwed shut hoping for the best but not getting anywhere close.

It was his own version of what was Metinides's most famous shot, the photograph of the death of Adela Legaretta Rivas. The poor photocopy he'd had blown up of that hung next to his own poor imitation of it. Life imitating art imitating life.

Edgar Allan Poe once wrote that 'there is nothing more beautiful than the death of a beautiful woman' and Metinides had the proof of it.

Adela was an actress, walking across the Avenida Chapultepec when she was struck by a white Datsun that had crashed into another car. Metinides caught her right on the cusp in a twisted pose between a metal pole and a concrete slab, eyes open, almost expressionless but for a trace of mild surprise and slight disappointment, as if she had forgotten her umbrella and there was a chance of rain. Her shiny red nails were manicured, her blonde hair perfectly coiffured, her clothes elegant and her jewellery understated. She looks alive, maybe caught in the car's headlights like a startled rabbit. All that gives it away is the unnatural angle of her right arm, the line of blood that runs from the bridge of her nose to her cheek, the trickle of crimson slipping from the corner of her lipsticked mouth and the faraway look in her eyes.

The photo shows a paramedic standing over her and about to gently, almost reverentially, place a blanket over her mangled body. Other people look on staring and you can't help but gawp alongside them. It's unsettling, intimate and terribly beautiful.

Winter felt there was beauty in his own work too and he looked at the photograph on the far right of the top row for evidence of it: an old man slumped at the foot of a tree near the People's Palace on Glasgow Green. He'd taken it first thing on a bitterly cold morning in the depths of January, just an hour after the man they called the Bridgeton Elvis had been found frozen to death. The cops said they all knew the old bloke pretty well and it was obvious they were choked up at seeing him like that. One had said that he'd always greet them with a chorus of 'Jailhouse Rock', dressed in a great coat that usually had the bulge of a bottle in one pocket or another.

Elvis must have had a fair share of the bottle inside him because he'd bedded down for the night with nothing more than a balaclava, his coat and some cardboard and newspapers for warmth. Temperatures dropped suddenly during the night and the old man didn't wake in the morning. Winter's photograph showed ice on Elvis's beard and his balaclava, the powder-blue of his cheeks and the frosting on his eyelashes that had brought the shutters down. Elvis had left the building for good but there was something noble about the way he sat there, sanguine about the indignities thrown at him by a spiteful world, quite literally frozen in the moment between life and death.

The beauty in some of Winter's other photos was perhaps more difficult to see. An Asian boy named Salim Abbas had been kicked and punched to death by a gang of white kids in Pollockshields. They'd chased him through the streets, throwing whatever they could at him before finally falling on him like a pack of hyenas, weighing in with boot and fist. The little bastards probably thought they'd given him no more than a right good doing but Salim never got up again.

The photograph documented every bruise and cut, the bloodied mouth, broken teeth and smashed ribs, as well as the small pool of falu that had formed below his jet-black hair where his skull had crashed against the pavement. The boy had been curled into the foetal position for protection but by the time Winter had arrived he'd been laid out flat on the ground to let a paramedic fight in vain to revive him. All that was left for him to do was record the injuries and shake his head in wonder.

It was the same with the battered wife whose photograph was on the bottom row, her face lacerated with the cuts delivered by her drunken husband and a broken glass. Neighbours had heard her screams and called the police or else the attack in her plush home in Newton Mearns would have gone unreported. Middle-class Marie whose face was a road map of sliced skin and whose eyes shouted shame and resentment.

She lived a long way from the ned in the neighbouring photo who had a screwdriver embedded in his skull. For him, it was all part of the job. Winter had photographed the little scrote in A&E at the old Southern General and the picture was mostly notable for the scowl on his pockmarked face and the raised fist of triumph. You should have seen the other guy, he'd said.

Above the ned was a photograph of a junkie mother whose partner's flat had been raided. Winter had been there to photograph the four bags of ecstasy found stashed under the sink. The woman - her name was Ashleigh, old way before her time and had already lost the looks she once had - screamed at them for taking away her boyfriend and asked how she was expected to cope and look after her wee girl. The daughter was about five or six, a pretty thing but in torn clothes and in need of a good wash.

Winter had asked if he could photograph the two of them but maybe she had sensed he was over-eager to take their picture because she immediately asked for a hundred pounds to do it. Addison had been there and laughed in the woman's face but Winter had agreed. Of sorts.

He left and returned twenty-five minutes later with four full bags from the nearest supermarket, putting them down in front of the mother. It was a hundred pounds worth of shopping. Milk, bread, food to get them through the week, plenty of fresh fruit and vegetables, a few T-shirts and other clothes for the girl. The mother had sworn and ranted but eventually agreed when he said it was that or nothing. She hadn't known he would have given her the stuff even if she'd said no.

Her anger at not getting what she'd hoped for had earned Winter the aggrieved glare that looked back at him from the photograph on his wall now. Ashleigh Morgan, junkie-chic skinny, eyes drained and wasted, her teeth soft and disappearing. Six-year-old Tiffany smiling happily. Hopefully both still alive and well but a couple of bags of decent food could only do so much.

Next to angry Ashleigh and her daughter was a black-and-white photograph of an empty street.

Arlington Street was in the west end, just off Woodlands Road. It ran long and narrow with sandblasted traditional tenements on one side of the road and red-and-cream modern versions on the other. You could see the Twenty's Plenty sign at the beginning of the street and around eight parked cars on each side, but that was it. No people, no blood, no guts.

He didn't think of it as his favourite photograph and it was far from the most eye-catching, but it was probably the most important. It was the progenitor, the catalyst, the reason for all of it.

The other Metinides copy he had was of his haunting photograph of a woman hanging from the tallest tree in Chapultec Park. It is otherworldly, quite surreal and you have to really look to see what is in front of you. The tree is obvious enough but it is only when you look again that the penny drops and you think, oh my fucking God. The realization eats away at you.

Metinides's secret was the knowledge that people are so used to seeing death in the cinema or on television that, often, the real thing just doesn't feel real. So he puts it right there in a photograph and messes with your mind, leaving you uncomfortable, unsettled, unsure. Winter had felt that way for a long time and knew that was why the Mexican's photographs resonated so much with him.

It turned out that the woman had gone to Chapultec, asked which tree was the biggest, pulled a rope out of her purse and hanged herself. When they took the body down, they found a photograph of a young girl in her purse along with a note explaining that her husband had taken her daughter away six years before. That day was the girl's birthday and she couldn't take the pain any longer. It was a sad little story in a big city full of sad little stories and that was something Winter knew all about.

He loved what Metinides did and what a photograph could do. A picture painting a thousands words and all that. Recording history, exposing lies, showing life in the raw, witnessing reality, framing the shit and the shitters. But a photograph can do more than that, it can also give up hidden truths.

He didn't claim that he could do what Metinides could but he was a witness to his bit of the world. There were rules though. Roughly speaking they ran along the lines of see no evil, hear no evil, speak no evil. He was there to observe and to document. Sometimes, though, whether you sought it or not, when you bent down to photograph the gutter, reality crept up and bit you on the arse. Something had nagged away at him from the moment he photographed Stevie Strathie but this was the first chance he'd had to do anything about it.

The A5-sized print that he'd run off showed Strathie lying in his own life spill. And he couldn't help but be pleased at the way he'd flash-filled it, making his bloodless face contrast with the sangria puddle that lent him an unholy halo. Those shit-scared eyes locked fast in the very moment that he crossed over – seeing his past, his future and nothing at all. He was bloodless and blood, empty and full, life and death. The bastard had made a career out of selling it and now he'd met it face to face.

The mark on the right of his chest was a little more than half an inch wide, maybe two centimetres in new money. It curved as if it would make a complete circle although it only punched a crescent into his chest. There were other distinct marks within it and they looked like they formed some sort of pattern. Winter realized that he'd probably known as soon as he'd seen it, maybe in the back of his mind, but he knew.

He sat the print next to the photograph he'd taken of Rory McCabe, the teenager who'd been battered around the knees with a baseball bat, the photo that hadn't been worthy of a place on his gallery wall but was now lying on the desk on the other side of the room.

There it was on McCabe's chest, shown up by the infrared on his IS Pro, a circular bruise the size of a five-pence piece. It also had marks within the circle that Winter hadn't noticed before. A darker, horizontal indentation that he guessed could have been vertical depending on the angle that it had hit the kid's chest at. The raised marks caused by the vertical/horizontal feature were maybe three millimetres wide. Same as the mark within Strathie's crescent.

As per procedure, he'd placed a photo scale at the side of both shots when he'd taken them so that sizes could be accurately measured. He was already sure of the answer he'd get but a quick calculation showed that the two circular marks were identical in size.

Winter breathed hard and thought harder. He wasn't much for believing in coincidences and Addison had always told him that they were to be trusted as much as a chimpanzee with a tin opener.

Rory McCabe. Stevie Strathie. A victim of neds with a baseball bat. A victim of the Dark Angel.

No doubt about it, he thought to himself. They had got absolutely nothing to do with each other. Move on here, nothing to see. Nothing to tell.

Look but don't touch. Record but don't interfere. Observe but don't violate. Chronicle but don't contaminate. He focused, he shot, he looked but he wouldn't tell. Not just yet anyway.

CHAPTER 22

Friday 16 September

The road to hell is also paved with bad intentions. Winter's mobile rang a few minutes before eight, bringing him crashing out of a deep sleep peppered with dreams of flashbulbs and bodies.

It was Addison. He sounded as rough as a badger's arse.

'Drop your cock, pick up your sock and meet me at Glasgow Harbour five minutes ago.'

'What the hell?'

'He's done it again. Two more dead. Glasgow Harbour. Now.'

'Christ. By the way, that old joke doesn't work in the singular. It would need to be . . .'

Addison had already hung up.

Glasgow Harbour is a relatively new residential development on the side of the Clyde, opposite the Govan shipyards. It's all upmarket, funky and modern, part of the urban waterfront regeneration and sitting in the shadow of the Finnieston Crane, the iconic symbol of the city's engineering heritage. It maybe wasn't quite the same as having an apartment on the edge of the Seine but it was nice enough.

You couldn't argue with the views, remnants of hundreds of

years of shipbuilding wherever you looked along with silvery glimpses of new Glasgow in the shape of the Science Tower, the Clyde Auditorium and the Squinty Bridge. And the river itself, wide enough to turn a 150-metre Type 45 destroyer but not as wide as most Glaswegians, stretching away as far as the eye could see.

When Winter arrived at half-past eight, there was a quite different view, the kind that money wouldn't want to buy. He was looking at two men lying dead either side of a gleaming black BMW, its paintwork daubed in splashes of vermilion. There was a lot more of the stuff on the ground and over the clothes of the two guys that wore it.

Addison, Colin Monteith, Campbell Baxter and his forensics plus a whole bunch of uniforms were already there when he arrived. Tenting was getting assembled and by the look of the skies it was going to be needed. It was going to chuck it down any second.

'I know this one,' Addison was muttering, nodding at the man on the left of the car, a heavy-set gorilla, well over six feet tall. 'Jimmy Adamson. They called him Gee Gee because he was a big punter on the horses. He's an enforcer for Terry Gilmartin, broke legs for a living.'

The DI was shaking his head and chewing on his lip, obviously not best pleased.

'He was shot first then the other one,' he murmured, looking from one body to the other. 'The second cunt is familiar too.'

'It's Andrew Haddow, Gilmartin's accountant.'

Winter turned to see who belonged to the female voice behind him and saw Jan McConachie glowering out from her white bunny suit and blue overshoes.

'He kept the books and put Gilmartin's money in piggy banks from here to the Cayman Islands,' she added. 'He also ramped up interest payments on loans owed to Gilmartin and put people in the poorhouse. He was a piece of shit and I hope he burns in hell.'

'And a good morning to you too, DS McConachie.'

'Piss off, Inspector.'

'Someone didn't get any last night then,' sneered Addison.

'With respect, sir, fuck off. For your information, I've been taking a statement about one of Caldwell's dealers, Jake Arnold, they call him Beavis. His people weren't for saying but I heard he'd disappeared off the face of the earth. Some think he's done a runner with some of Caldwell's money but others say he wouldn't have the bottle. Either way no one knows where he is. Sir.'

The tone was full-on mock sincere, guaranteed to get right up the DI's nose and it was a dangerous game. Winter recognized that Addison looked like he was suffering a raging hangover but McConachie had gone for it, delivering her information with an exaggerated smile before turning away from him.

'Right, if you two could just play nice,' he said, trying to break the tension before anyone else got hurt, 'I've got some photographs to take.'

'Just get on with it then, camera monkey,' snarled Addison. 'Leave the talking to the big boys. And girls,' he added with a condescending nod to McConachie. 'Jan, get a best guess out of Two Soups. Don't take any of his shit, just get an answer on where he thinks the shot came from, and flood the area. I've had enough of this cunt. Tony, hurry the fuck up.'

Winter ignored him and turned the lens of his Nikon onto Adamson, lying half on his side and half on his back where the impact of the bullet had sent him spiralling. The man they called Gee Gee had a purplish tinge to his cheeks, a drinker by the look of it as well as a gambler. His fingers also had the telltale orange glow of a smoker. A true Scotsman, not judged by what he wore under his kilt but by how he abused his vital organs. Winter imagined that if he looked in the car there would be half a dozen

Scotch pies, some square sausage and a litre of Irn Bru. Breakfast of champions.

The man had hands like shovels, huge meaty paws that had made a career of meting out justice according to the laws of Terry Gilmartin. How many legs had he broken, how many kneecaps had he smashed, heads busted, jaws punched or eyes gouged? Winter looked at every scar and bump on his hands and wondered if they related to a dealer, an addict, a granny with a bad bingo habit or a rival thug.

His full-length leather coat looked like it weighed a ton, a heavyweight article that gave him the look of a rock-star gunslinger. It was soaking up his rosso corso and Winter couldn't help but think it was a waste of a cool coat. But then again this guy had been a waste of a pulse.

His eyes didn't register much except astonishment, unlike the accountant's. His were terrified. Haddow had seen Gee Gee get shot in the head and would have known instantly who did it and what was coming next. He would have had the time it took an expert to reload the L115A3 and take fresh aim. Time enough for his arse to empty, his life to flash before his eyes and for him to take a couple of fruitless steps back towards the flats.

The difference between his hands and Adamson's were all too obvious. Smaller, softer and weaker. Still covered in blood though. These hands had never punched anyone or picked up a baseball bat but they were guilty all the same.

He was in his early forties, small and slight, dressed in a black pinstriped suit with an open-necked white shirt. It must have been the season's colour for getting shot in.

If Adamson was a waste of a pulse then the accountant was a waste of an education. The bits of brains that were littered over the pathway could have been put to much better use. Keeping Gilmartin's books was the job for a lab rat. In many ways that angered Winter more than Gee Gee making a living out of his muscles. McConachie was right, the man had been a piece of shit.

Winter walked back twenty paces and framed the whole scene before it was covered by the tent. The Beamer was nearly new, the two men lying on either side of it in a way that BMW probably never considered using in an advert. The Ultimate Dying Machine didn't have quite the same ring to it. With the expensive Glasgow Harbour pads as a backdrop it all yelled money. A caption for his photograph sprung to mind, hardly original but apt. Crime Doesn't Pay.

He took some more scene-setting pictures. Cop cars, residents hanging over their terraces at a view they hadn't expected, a local drunk who had wandered over for a nosey, forensics picking their way over the pathway. He managed a cracker of a man in a suit on one of the balconies, cigarette hanging from the corner of his mouth and a quizzical look on his face as if he'd been looking for *Cash in the Attic* and turned on the wrong channel. As he was taking them, Winter sensed a presence over him and looked up to see Campbell Baxter glowering at him. The forensic had not softened to him in the slightest.

'Mr Winter,' he sneered. 'It is my understanding that you have been assigned to this investigation in order to photograph the victims so as to help facilitate a successful prosecution case in the event of it proceeding to trial. Perhaps you could enlighten me as to how your photographs of local residents or passers-by, no matter how *expertly* taken, will be beneficial in that regard. Can you tell me that? Can you?'

Winter didn't need this.

'It is a procedure known as scene setting,' he began to bluff.

'Really?' The scorn in his voice suggested that Baxter was unconvinced. 'Please do enlighten me.'

'There are, er, various benefits. It provides scale, local character germane to the crime scene, all helping to create a, eh, panoramic image rather than simply a one-dimensional approach based solely on evidence photographs. Also the subjects within them may prove to be vital witnesses that might otherwise be missed by the investigating officers.'

Baxter gazed at him in mild confusion.

'Panorama? Local character? It is not in my nature to indulge in intemperate or coarse speech but this is bullshit, Mr Winter. Bullshit. I don't know what you think you are playing at here but this is not the sort of professional behaviour that I demand of my officers. I shall be speaking to Superintendent Shirley about this and expressing my continuing dissatisfaction with both your role and your methods. If I get no satisfaction from him then I shall not hesitate to take the matter higher. Do you understand me?'

Winter understood perfectly well.

'Yes, I do. You don't like me.'

Winter saw a vein in Baxter's temple throb and wondered whether the man was about to bust a blood vessel.

'Like you? *Like* you? Mr Winter, you have not the merest comprehension of what I like or dislike but I can assure you that my personal feelings have no bearing whatsoever on my judgement of a person's professional ability. None whatsoever. *Like* you? It would not occur to me to either like or dislike you. I dislike what you do and the way that you do it but do not dare to think that impinges on my professional assessment.'

'Okay.'

'What?'

'I said okay. I accept what you say.'

The vein in Baxter's head pulsed even stronger.

'I . . . I . . . This is not acceptable. Not acceptable at all. We are the dog and you are the tail and I shall not allow the tail to wag this dog. *We* are the dog. You . . .' he pointed a finger at Winter, 'you are the bloody tail. Get on with your work.'

As Baxter turned and left, muttering under his breath, Winter flicked a V at his retreating bulk and took one last picture of the scene, knowing while he did so that it was a bad idea but doing it anyway. McConachie was standing over Haddow, a snarl of disgust under her nose as she cast a shadow over the accountant's bloodied body. He couldn't resist it.

She threw up her head, staring at him, but the look of disgust didn't disappear; instead her eyes narrowed and Winter became the object of her scorn. He was no one's flavour of the month. Still, McConachie seemed much madder at Addison than at him and she was even madder at the corpses on the ground than she was at the DI. She glowered over them, seemingly resisting the urge to boot them as they lay there.

'What the fuck is up with that crazy bitch?' asked Addison, now standing at his shoulder. 'Does she not know they are already dead? She looks like she wants to kill them again.'

Winter didn't feel much like speaking up for the angry DS but the decision was taken away from him when Addison's mobile rang the Top Cat ringtone. He turned away from the photographer as he took the call. He was nodding and talking and nodding some more. What Winter could hear of his tone of voice meant it was no time for messing around. Alex Shirley was all business.

'Shirley,' Addison announced to the team as he hung up. 'He's just finished up with Ally Riddle, pulled him in first thing. It's why he's not here. Wasn't exactly best pleased at the news that there's two more of them. He's got steam coming out his ears. Says another of Riddle's team hasn't been seen for two days. Reckons one of the opposition has been balancing up the numbers and he's probably under a flyover somewhere.'

'What's Riddle saying?' Monteith asked.

'Seems he's playing it very cool. A smart cookie according to the Temple. He's being cooperative enough but giving nothing away. That's assuming he has something to give away.'

With that, Addison shooed both the detectives and the forensics in towards the bodies, walking to the side where Winter joined him.

'And you think he has something to give away?' Winter asked him.

'Who knows? Could be that he and the Temple have come to an understanding. It happens.'

'Like what? Shirley turns a blind eye to Riddle putting his feet under Quinn's desk in return for info?'

Addison gave him an odd look.

'Let's just say he's helping with our enquiries.'

'What? I'm getting the stock media answer now? I'm in the same boat as the twats from the tabloids?'

'For now anyway.'

'Thanks for nothing. There's no "I" in team Addy and there's no "Fuck U" in it either.'

'Oh calm down for fucksake. You know the score.'

'Doesn't mean I like it.'

'Christ, here we go again. Get over it.'

If Winter had been in any doubt then that made his mind up for him. Whatever it was he knew about the marks on Rory McCabe and Stevie Strathie was staying with him. He was Addison's mate and he reckoned that should have been reason enough for the DI to let him in. If he wasn't going to then neither was Winter. Of course, he knew that he was telling himself a steaming pile of shite but he didn't give a toss.

Addison must have bored of messing with him because he'd turned his fire on McConachie instead. She was still scowling at the two bodies and shaking her head.

'DS McConachie, any chance you could get your finger out your arse and join in this investigation. There's a hundred witnesses in those flats need interviewing.'

She nodded slowly, her eyes never off Adamson and Haddow.

'I'll talk to them, sir. I'm just wondering if it will be a terrible thing if they haven't seen anything.'

Addison spat on the ground.

'What, you buying into this "Dark Angel anti-hero" shite? I thought you had more sense.'

'No, course I'm not. But . . .'

'But what?'

'But maybe it's not the worst thing in the world that these two scumbags have been taken out. That's all I'm saying.'

'Is that right? Well what I'm saying is that I need a fucking breakthrough on this or the Temple is going to burst my baws. This fucker is taking the piss big time and he's not getting away with that on my watch so I want everything you've got whether you like it or not. We're the law round here, not some nutter with a rifle. Remember that, DS McConachie.'

The sergeant was stung and desperate to come back with something but she gnawed on her tongue and let her eyes blaze instead, settling for a stone-cold, 'Yes, sir' as an answer.

He was glaring at her and daring her to disrespect him. Addison would take plenty of banter at the right time and place but clearly this wasn't it. He wanted answers, not arguments.

Part of Winter was still bursting to tell him about the link, but he knew he wasn't going to. He was going home to look at photographs again instead.

CHAPTER 23

'Who is fucking doing this?' he raged. 'Who is fucking doing this to me?'

McConachie thought she could hear self-pity in the voice on the other end of the phone. It was beneath the fury and hidden behind the thunder but it was there. Self-pity wrapped up in fear. The Dark Angel, whoever he was, was getting closer and Terry Gilmartin was bricking himself.

That was bad news for Jan and she knew it. If Gilmartin was scared then he'd also be desperate and that put Amy at risk. There wasn't a single day that she didn't regret taking his money but few times that she'd regretted it more than right then. It had seemed so simple at first that she'd ignored just how wrong it was.

Amy had needed that tutor, she'd convinced herself of that and her class teacher had agreed. It wasn't that she wasn't bright, that was the thing – it was that she wasn't fulfilling her potential. It had been Jan's fault that her daughter had been badly affected by the break-up with Amy's dad. Her school work suffered as a result and she needed the tutor to catch up and be all that she could be.

She'd always told herself that if she hadn't needed that money right then she'd have told Gilmartin where to go. But he'd somehow sensed her desperation or her weakness. All he wanted was some information, an advance warning of impending trouble. Once the tutor was paid for then she'd get back on the straight path, he could look out for himself and no one would be any the wiser. How could she have been so stupid to think it could ever be that simple?

He had his claws into her and he'd never let go. When she'd sent one of his heavies back to him with the cash still in his pocket then Gilmartin turned the screw. Jan picked up Amy after school to find her beaming all over her face, happily showing off a new pair of trainers that her mum had never seen before. It turned out that a friend of Mummy's had got there before she did and given her the present, trainers that fitted perfectly. He'd told Amy that he could bring her presents any time because he knew where she lived. Amy was much happier at that prospect than her mummy was.

From that day, Terry Gilmartin still paid her for information but there was never any doubt that he no longer had to. She would do what he wanted and Amy wouldn't get any more visits from her new uncle George. Instead George Faichney initiated regular meetings with her, sometimes in person but usually by phone, to get whatever it was that Gilmartin wanted that week. Jan's co-operation kept Amy safe. Until now. Now Gilmartin wanted more than she was able to give and that made everything dangerous.

'Who is fucking doing this to me?' he repeated.

'It isn't just to you,' Jan told him. 'This guy is targeting every senior drugs figure in the city.'

'Don't tell me it isn't me,' he screamed down the phone. 'My son is in intensive care. Jimmy Adamson and Andrew Haddow are dead. This bastard is knocking on my front door. You tell me what the fuck is going on.'

So she did the only thing she could do. She told him everything that the police knew and everything that they didn't. It didn't please Gilmartin that there was much more of the second than the first.

CHAPTER 24

Thursday 15 September

Winter had Rory McCabe's address in his records from his visit to see the teenager in A&E at the Royal. The boy lived with his parents in a close in Whitehill Street, just a couple of hundred yards from where his mates found him lying in Craigpark Drive with a busted knee.

Dennistoun was tenement land, built by the Victorians to house the middle class but instead taking in respectable working-class families when they couldn't attract enough white collars. Whitehill Street was in the heart of it, a long line of four-storey terracotta-and-blonde stone buildings behind neatly hedged gardens. Mostly there were eight families to a close, hiding secrets behind lace curtains.

Winter hadn't exactly worked out what he was going to say or how he'd explain being there. But he figured that saying little was the way to go. In this case, less was more. He parked up outside, climbed the stairs of the tenement to the second floor, knocked sharply on the door and prepared to wing it.

A blonde woman in her late-forties answered almost immediately, well dressed and polite.

'Yes? Can I help you?'

Winter held his SPSA identification up in front of him, hoping she wouldn't look too closely at it.

'Mrs McCabe? I'm Tony Winter, I was part of the investigation into the attack on your son and spoke to him while he was in hospital. I was hoping to speak to him today as part of a follow-up enquiry.'

'Oh. Has there been a development?' the woman piped up excitedly. 'Do you know who did it?'

'Not yet, but we are still investigating. Today's visit is partly to reassure you that we haven't given up on finding who did this.'

This seemed to please the boy's mother because she smiled at him and pulled the door wide, standing back to let him in. The house was tidily kept and looked as if it had been recently decorated. Mrs McCabe ushered Winter into the living room from where he could hear the noise of a movie or maybe a computer game.

It turned out it was both. Rory was sitting on a couch with a PlayStation 3 in front of him while a crappy afternoon movie was thundering away on the television. A pair of crutches rested on the wall behind the settee. The boy didn't bother looking up till his mother told him for a second time that he had a visitor.

He knew Winter right away which explained why he got a glare. Either that or else he simply wasn't best pleased at having to interrupt his game.

'Rory, this is Mr Winter from the police. Oh, I'm sorry, Mr Winter, I forgot what rank you were.'

'It's fine, Mrs McCabe,' he said with as much authority as he could muster. 'Thank you. I'll just talk to Rory now if that's okay.'

The woman flustered a bit and backed away.

'Oh yes, yes. Of course. Can I get you a cup of tea?'

'No, thank you.'

'Coffee?'

'No, I'm fine. Thanks.'

She gave up her mission of hospitality and closed the door behind her, leaving Winter alone with her stroppy teenage son.

'Hi, Rory. How you doing? That knee of yours getting better?'

The kid sighed.

'It's okay.'

'You able to get around on those things?' he asked, nodding at the crutches behind him.

'I can manage okay. Listen, I'm no' as daft as my mum. I remember you. You're not a detective, you're a photographer. So what you doing here?'

Winter gave him a smile intended to tell him that he recognized that the kid was smart. And it wasn't completely a lie. He wasn't going to get anywhere by treating him like an idiot.

'I didn't say I was a cop, your mum just assumed that. But obviously I do work with them. I wanted to ask you some questions about the person that did this to you.'

'I told you already and I told the cops. I don't know who it was.'

'Yeah, I remember. But I still think you know more than you're telling.'

Rory frowned and looked out of the window.

'The guy that beat you up, he had a ring on his finger, right? Must have hurt like fuck when he punched you in the chest.'

His head spun towards Winter, his mouth dropping. He quickly clammed it shut again but it was enough to let Winter know he was rattled.

'I don't know what you are talking about,' McCabe mumbled. As he did so, his mobile beeped, signalling a text, and he picked it up, punching in a reply.

'My mate across the road,' he said, without looking up. 'Wanting to know if that was a cop going into my house. He's looking out for me.'

'So what did you tell him?'

'Said you weren't a cop. But that you were hassling me for information.'

'Ach, it's hardly hassle, Rory. More like trying to help you.'

'Aye, right.'

Time to push his luck, Winter thought.

'Your mum seems really nice.'

He was wary. 'Yes, she is.'

'Looks after you pretty well I'd say,' he continued. 'Thinks the world of you.'

'Aye.'

Winter lowered his voice.

'It would be terrible if she found out about the drugs.'

He was reaching, guessing. It could have been game over before it had barely begun but he knew the link was there.

'Fuck off,' Rory hissed at him. 'That's not cool. You can't do that. It would kill her. She thinks I'm the only teenager around here that's clean. And I *am* clean. It was only a bit of weed.'

'Just a bit?' he guessed again.

'Okay, more than a bit but it's no big deal. But I don't want her to know.'

'No problem,' Winter smiled. 'You help me and I help you. And everything you tell me stays between us.'

The teenager stared straight through him, gnawing his lip and thinking hard. Tears began to run down his cheeks.

'Fucking bastard,' he choked. 'This isn't fair. If he finds out I've talked ... he'll kill me. I'm scared.'

'I know you are but he won't find out from me. I promise.'

He wiped at his eyes with the back of his hand, his cheeks scarlet with embarrassment and worry.

'You promise?'

'Yes,' Winter nodded.

'You better. You saw what he did to me last time.'

Rory nodded as if he'd come to a decision, dried his eyes again and began.

'Okay. First off, I don't know who he was. Just one guy. Six foot-ish. With a ski mask on. I really don't know who he was. Okay?'

Winter believed him.

'Okay.'

Rory swallowed hard.

'He just wanted information from me. That's all.'

'Tell me what he wanted, Rory.'

The boy swore, blowing bubbles through his tears, his eyes red.

'There was a mate of mine that died a wee while back. Keiran McKendrick. Died of an overdose.'

The words stuck in the boy's throat as if he hoped that if he hadn't spoken them then they wouldn't be true.

'What happened?'

He glared again. Winter was wanting more information than he was prepared to give. He was intruding on the boy's grief.

'Don't really know. He didn't do much more than I did. A wee bit of miaow-miaow, that was all. Hardly ever though. Then he overdosed.'

'Sorry to hear it. So what did that have to do with you being attacked?'

Rory swallowed hard again.

'The guy wanted to know who supplied Kieran with the gear. He beat the shit out of me till I told him.'

'That's all he wanted?'

'Aye.'

'And who did give your pal the drugs?'

'Never mind. The other guy had to knock the fuck out of me to get it. All you need to know is that was what he wanted.'

'Come on, Rory. Finish the job. Give me the name.'

'No, I've told you enough. Why don't you just leave me alone?'

'Look, Rory . . .'

The living-room door opened and Mrs McCabe pushed through with a pot of tea and a plate of biscuits. She immediately saw that her boy had been crying and looked at Winter sternly, the tigress coming out in the quiet housewife.

'Trauma,' Winter assured her. 'People underestimate the effects of re-living an attack like that. It's a form of post-traumatic stress disorder. Just leave him with his PlayStation for a bit and he'll be okay. Maybe a cup of tea and a couple of biscuits.'

The woman looked unsure but Rory nodded at her.

'It's fine, Mum. I'll be fine. He's just going, we're finished.'

The words were to his mum but they were said with a look at Winter. He wasn't saying any more. Not that day, anyway.

'You'll have a cup of tea though before you go, Sergeant Winter?'

'No, sorry, Mrs McCabe, but I have to go. Thanks, anyway. Take care of yourself, Rory, and I'll pop back and see you.'

'No need, *Sergeant*,' Rory said, emphasizing the last word.

He let Mrs McCabe show him to the door and back into the close. He started down the stairs, wondering why the fuck somebody was so determined to find out the name of a dealer that they would take a bat to the kid's knee. It had to be linked to the shootings though, it just had to be.

He heard footsteps behind him just a second or two before he felt a kick to the back of his legs. A second boot swiftly followed and he found himself tumbling down the stairs. As he fell, he could hear more feet approaching, from down the stairs this time, and a hard blow came at his shoulder.

'Keep away from Rory, ya cunt. What's your problem?'

'He's no done nothing, right. Leave him alane.'

Winter covered his head and pushed himself back up onto his feet, taking a boot to his right knee for his efforts. Pain shot through it, causing it to buckle and he sank down, half kneeling. He fired out a punch at the nearest person and caught him solid, hearing a groan and footsteps staggering back. He threw back an elbow and caught someone else somewhere solid. It gave him enough breathing space to get to his feet and see three guys in hoodies, two with scarves over their faces and the third, much taller and broader than the other two, was wearing a balaclava that showed only his eyes. Winter lashed out at the nearest one with a boot and caught him in the balls.

His success didn't last long though and he felt a fist crash into the side of his head, nearly putting his lights out. Bodies were on him like pack rats and he went down under the weight as boots and punches rained in on him. He could taste blood in his mouth. Pain chased pain over his body like an electric circuit. He heard Rory's name again but couldn't take much in. Fuck. A kick to the side of his head delivered a dull sting and he knew he was close to blacking out.

Maybe he had because he was suddenly aware of them having stopped and could only feel the aches that were in every bone. He still had his hands wrapped round his head but no more blows came.

'Sorry.'

Had the cunts in the hoods suddenly developed a conscience? He seriously doubted it. He lifted his head gingerly and peeled his arms away, seeing two wooden pegs with rubber soles just a few inches from his eyes. Crutches.

Rory McCabe looked terrified, probably as much for himself as for Winter. He tottered nervously above him, his damaged knee bent and his leg raised from the ground.

'Shite, I'm really sorry. I didn't ask them to do this. I really didn't know they were going to do anything.'

Winter looked up at him, wiping blood from his mouth and massaging his ribs.

'One of those guys was waiting at the hospital when I came to photograph you, wasn't he? The big guy with the balaclava?'

Rory blanched.

'He fits the description of the guy you said beat you up,' Winters persisted.

'No, no way.' McCabe hissed at him. 'Lee is just trying to protect me.'

He stopped, realizing he'd said too much. 'Look you won't tell the cops, will you?'

Winter knew he probably couldn't have told them even if he wanted to but Rory didn't know that. He looked the kid in the eye.

'I'm not sure. I might have to.'

'Fucksake,' the boy whispered, leaning back against the wall so that it held him up. 'He's just looking out for me. He's in the army and will be in big trouble if this goes to the cops.'

'I'm not sure I have any choice.'

'Right, I'll tell you who Kieran's dealer was, okay? Then you don't come back here again and you don't mention Lee to the polis. Right?'

That sounded like a great deal to Winter.

'Fair enough.'

'Okay. It was a guy named Sammy Ross. He's from Royston and . . .'

CHAPTER 25

A couple of phone calls was all it took for Narey to learn that Melanie's boyfriend Tommy Breslin was, as they say, known to the police. He had previous for theft, aggravated assault and possession with intent to supply but he also had a reputation for a violent temper. Colin Daly, a mate of Narey's at Maryhill cop shop said that basically T-Bone Breslin was a bad bastard who was quick to use his fists, his boots or whatever he had to hand. He was a dealer with a sideline in pimping and if he could combine the two then all the better. Daly reckoned chances were that all the money that Melanie earned on the streets went straight to Breslin for drugs, leaving her broke and dependent on him as well as crack cocaine.

Daly's suggestion that Narey would be better taking a couple of burly cops with her instead of Julia Corrieri was, inevitably, met with an indignant retort. In the end, though, Narey saw the benefit of having the added manpower at least to get the door open and that was why there were four officers standing on the doorstep of Breslin's flat in Summerston at seven that morning.

Corrieri stood at the back with the two uniforms in between her and Narey who was about to knock on the heavy door. It wasn't exactly the loudest of knocks but after a few seconds, the DS stood back and nodded at the constables to do their business. They advanced holding the enforcer ram and slammed sixteen kilos of hardened steel into Breslin's door. With a bang, the door flew open, leaving the remnants of hinges, bolts and chains scattered on the floor. The uniforms stepped aside and Narey strode into the flat, just in time to see Breslin burst naked, shaken and bleary-eyed from a bedroom clutching a baseball bat.

The DS stood her ground and just looked at him, flipping open her warrant card holder and holding it up in front.

'Police, Mr Breslin. I suggest you put that weapon down.'

He glared at her, still trying to take in what was happening. He held the bat in both hands, legs wide, swishing it through the air as he weighed up his options. None of the cops moved, letting him come to his own conclusion that he had no choice but to put it down or take them all on. Finally, reluctantly, Breslin tossed the bat against a wall where one of the two constables quickly walked over and picked it up. The dealer stood, breathing hard, unperturbed by his nakedness. He was a muscular six-foot tall, in his early thirties, with close-cropped fair hair and a scar under his left eye.

'Thomas Breslin,' Narey addressed him. 'I have a warrant to search these premises and I suggest you put some clothes on. Officers, go with him.'

'You've no fucking right being here,' roared Breslin. 'What the fuck is going on?'

'Where do you want to start?' replied Narey. 'Possession with intent to supply? Or should we talk about Melanie? Or rather Una?'

Breslin's eyebrows knitted over in what could have passed for confusion or being found out but either way it soon manifested itself in aggression. His face contorted in fury and he advanced quickly on Narey until his face was right in hers, his spittle pebble-dashing her forehead as he ranted at her. She waved the male cops back with a quick motion of her arm and stared the man down.

'The fuck are you talking about?' he bellowed, his eyes bulging. 'Coming into my house at this time of the morning. Fuck's your game?'

'Something to hide, Mr Breslin?' Narey remained calm. 'Was it the mention of Una's name that bothered you?'

Breslin snarled and took half a step back and pulled his right arm back, ready to throw a punch at her. In a split second, another arm was quickly bent over his and he was forced to the ground with his arm twisted behind his back and a foot placed behind his right knee.

'I'm impressed,' Narey admitted. 'They teach you that at Tulliallan?'

Corrieri looked up at her with a sheepish grin, tightening her hold on Breslin's arm and being rewarded by a pained grunt from the naked dealer.

'Evening classes,' she admitted. 'Kuk Sool Won and Pilates. I get a discount for doing them both.'

'Nice work,' Narey nodded. 'Mr Breslin, I think we should take a wee trip to the station, don't you?'

In response, Breslin bitterly spat on his own carpet and let off a string of expletives, most of which were unflattering remarks about female police officers.

Half an hour later, a bristling T-Bone Breslin was parked in a chair inside Stewart Street, glowering at Narey and Corrieri and complaining at the length of time it was taking for his solicitor to get there. The bravado that he'd lost when Corrieri had brought him to his knees had returned along with his aggression.

'Talk to us anyway, Tommy,' Narey was telling him.

'Go fuck yourself, bitch. You should be out on the streets trying to catch the fucker shooting people who are only trying to make a living by providing a service to the community.'

Yes, you're right, thought Narey, I should. But I'll settle for cutting your balls off if you've done this.

'I really don't see why you wouldn't talk,' she continued. 'When did you last see Una?'

'What the fuck do you keep bringing her up for?' he shouted.

'It's a simple question. When did you last see her?'

'I don't fucking know and I'm saying nothing till my lawyer's here.'

'You don't *know*? She's your girlfriend, right?'

'None of your fucking business. I'm saying nothing.'

'And she's the mother of your daughter, right?'

Anger flashed across his features.

'Leave my daughter out of this. Out of this!'

'When did you last see Una?' Narey persisted.

'I don't know. A week ago. Just piss off.'

'When would that be then? Last Friday? Last Saturday?'

'Saturday maybe. I don't remember.'

'Long time to go without seeing your girlfriend, isn't it?'

'She's a crackhead. She doesn't know where she is half the time so how am I expected to know?'

'Long time for your daughter to go without seeing her mother.'

Breslin's anger flared again and Narey could see his weak spot.

'Seems to me you don't care much about that wee girl if you don't even care where her mother is.'

'Don't talk to me about my daughter. I love her, right? You know nothing.'

'So where is she then? We know she's not with her mother and we know she's not in your flat.'

'She's with my mother, okay? Fuck all to do with you but she's with my maw. Leave her out of this. Nothing to do with that skank and fuck all to do with you.'

A vein was pumping furiously on Breslin's forehead and his anger was ready to boil over. There were one or two more buttons to be pressed though and Narey had her finger poised.

'See, that's interesting. That poor girl. An addict for a mother and a violent dealer for a father. I am sure Social Services would be very interested to hear that. What would you say are the chances of them being allowed to keep that child, DC Corrieri?'

'Roughly zero,' Corrieri answered impassively.

'Fuck off,' Beslin roared.

'We have a duty to report it,' Narey continued. 'Then it's out of our hands.'

'You fucking bitch! What do you want?'

'I want to know when you last saw Una. And I want to know where you were on Saturday night.'

Breslin screwed his eyes tightly shut and let rip a silent scream of frustration.

'I told you. Saw her last Saturday. She was going out to work.'

'To work?' Narey mocked. 'Okay. So what did you do when she went to work? Did you follow her, make sure she wasn't pocketing some of the cash that you wanted for yourself?'

'No.'

'And you didn't wonder where she was all that time?'

Breslin shrugged.

'Did you wonder?' Narey repeated.

'She wandered off sometimes,' he replied. 'Got off her face in some shithole with some dirty crackhead or other but she always came crawling back for the T-Bone.'

Narey shook her head at him.

'But she didn't come crawling back this time, did she?'

With that, she lifted a photograph off the table and turned it over, shoving it in Breslin's face.

It showed Melanie lying half-naked on the ground with the life choked out of her.

Breslin flinched. Narey couldn't quite be sure if it was shock at the realization that the girl was dead or at seeing what he'd done. Maybe it was both, the possibility that he had left her there thinking she was alive and would come 'crawling back' in her own good time. Either way, shock was all over Breslin's face until he reined it back into its customary snarl.

'Where were you last Saturday night around midnight?' Narey asked him.

'That's nothing to do with me,' he answered, pointing to the photo.

'Where were you? Last Saturday at midnight?'

'I didn't do that. No way you can pin that on me. That slag worked the streets. Any fucker could have done that to her.'

'I'm sorry for your loss, Breslin. Your anguish is so touching. Once again, where were you on Saturday night?'

'I was with someone. She can prove that.'

'Who?'

'A friend,' he sneered with a grin that Narey itched to smash off his face.

'Name?'

'Suzanne Wright. I was with her all night.'

'All night?'

He grinned again.

'All night. They don't call me T-Bone for nothing. You should try some, bitch.'

'No thanks. I'd rather stay disease-free if it's all the same to you. Give us an address for this young "lady". And you are going nowhere till we check it out.'

'Oh it'll check out okay. Suzy's not going to forget a night with the T-Bone. I'll be out of here by lunchtime.'

The fear ran through Narey that he would be. If the girl that he had lined up as an alibi said she was with him then he'd be walking free unless they could prove she was lying.

'Take this piece of shit out of my sight and put him in a cell,' she muttered to the uniforms waiting at the door. 'We'll be seeing him again soon enough. Oh, and Tommy?'

'Yeah?' he grinned.

'I'm just off to make that call to Social Services. Your "maw" isn't going to be looking after your kid for much longer.'

'You fucking bitch,' he screamed, getting to his feet and viciously kicking over the table. 'I told you what you wanted to know! You can't do that!'

'Watch me. Get him the fuck out of here.'

CHAPTER 26

Suzanne Wright, the girl that Tommy Breslin was using as an alibi, also lived in Summerston, just a few streets away from the man that called himself T-Bone. Narey had made sure that Breslin's one phone call wasn't to her and was now standing impatiently on Wright's doorstep in a block of flats in Torrin Road near John Paul Academy. She'd left Julia Corrieri behind in Stewart Street to search the PNC for Una and so had Constable Sandy Murray in tow.

On the third knock, Wright finally wrestled herself away from daytime TV and pulled the door open just enough on the chain to see who her unwelcome visitor was. One look was all she needed to make Narey for a cop and the chain stayed in place.

'Whit?'

'Suzanne Wright?' Narey asked of the pale face below the tousled mop of dyed blonde hair.

'Naw.'

'Funny, it's your name on the door.'

'Aye, okay. What do you want?'

Narey held up her warrant card.

'Police. Can we come in?'

The girl exhaled heavily and slid back the chain, huffily edging the door open for the DS and the constable to enter the flat. A television blared in one corner of the poky living room showing one of the mid-morning confrontation programmes that Narey hated but occasionally watched in guilty secret. Narey picked up the remote control and lowered the volume before placing it back next to Wright.

She was in her mid-twenties and wore a short denim skirt over bare legs and a halterneck top that showed off her cleavage. Dumping herself in an armchair without bothering to offer a seat to the police, she seemed utterly unfazed by their presence and Narey guessed it wasn't the first time that cops had knocked at her door. The girl picked up the cigarette that had been smouldering in an ashtray on the chair's arm and began drawing on it.

'You live here alone, Suzanne?' Narey asked, looking around the room.

'Yeah. Just me,' she replied with as much defiance as suspicion.

'You ever have friends staying over?'

'What is this? You're a detective sergeant, right? You're not here about whether I'm entitled to my single person's discount on the council tax.'

'No, I'm not,' Narey conceded. 'Do you know Thomas Breslin?'

A frown flickered over Wright's face but she quickly covered it with a heavy drag on her cigarette. By the time she exhaled, there was nothing to read on her face.

'Yeah, I know him. Why?'

'Stay the night sometimes, does he?'

'What's that got to do with you?' Wright challenged her. 'Not getting enough of your own that you have to stick your nose into other people's sex lives?'

'Does he stay over sometimes?' Narey repeated.

'Yeah. Sometimes.'

'When did he last spend the night here?'

'I'm not sure. He's stayed over a couple of times recently.'

'Try to remember.'

'The weekend.'

'Which part of the weekend, Suzanne?'

'Friday and Saturday. He was here both nights.'

'You sure?'

'Yeah.'

'You weren't sure a moment ago.'

Wright grinned at her.

'Well, it all just came back to me. They don't call him T-Bone for nothing.'

It was Narey's turn to smile.

'Funny, Suzanne. That's exactly what he said.'

The grin slipped off Wright's face.

'I don't know what you mean but he was here all night Friday and all night Saturday. Shagging my brains out.'

'You do know that he has got a girlfriend, don't you?'

'What, that skank Melanie? She's not his girlfriend. She's a meal ticket, nothing more.'

'Hm. A meal ticket and a punch-bag from what I hear.'

Wright continued to puff furiously on her cigarette.

'He ever hit you, Suzanne?'

'Never.'

'Never? A man with a temper like T-Bone's? Not even a little slap when you were arguing?' The girl's silence spoke volumes.

'He is a very violent man, Suzanne. Do you know why I'm asking you about last Saturday night? His girlfriend Melanie, the "skank"? She was murdered.'

Wright's eyes widened but she still said nothing.

'Strangled,' Narey continued. 'Someone killed her with their bare hands.'

The girl simply shrugged but the DS could see the fear in her eyes.

'Are you still saying that Tommy Breslin was with you all night?'

'Aye, I am. All night.'

'Okay. Just be careful, Suzanne. Breslin is vicious and this is a murder investigation. I'm going to leave you my card and if you have anything else to tell me then you can give me a call. I'll just leave it here on the telly.'

'You're wasting your time. You know the way out.'

She picked up the remote control and pointed it at the television screen, the volume booming out even louder than before. Narey took her leave and the constable trotted along quietly in her wake.

The similarity of Wright's statement to Breslin's was just too pat for Narey's liking but there wasn't a whole lot she could do about that for now. She was convinced that Suzanne had been schooled to say that Breslin was working his magic on her all night but she couldn't prove it. On the other hand, if Breslin had killed Una then she was damn sure that she would prove *that*.

At least the small amount of drugs that had been found in Breslin's flat was enough to keep him in custody for a while and it would probably also be enough for Social Services to take the girl into care. That gave her leverage against Breslin which she wouldn't hesitate to use.

As Narey settled back into the driver's seat of the car, watching Sandy Murray climb into the passenger seat, her mobile rang. It was Corrieri.

'Yes, Julia? What's happening?'

'Well . . .' the excitement in Corrieri's voice was obvious and immediately quickened Narey's pulse. 'As you know, I've been searching the PNC, missing person's lists and the General Register Office for Scotland for any Una that might be our girl.'

Narey knew by now that Corrieri was likely to give her

chapter and verse on any and every step in the process and she was sorely tempted to tell her just to get to the fucking point. Still, the DC had been working since the day before and probably deserved her drawn-out explanation, so Narey let her continue.

'There was nothing at all on the PNC that seemed a likely candidate nor on the Missing People website. I got a list of every Una born in Scotland within the parameters of our assumption of her age, i.e. between 1986 and 1990, and I drew up a subsection of these within the greater Glasgow area. None, however, had a surname close to McCulloch which was the surname that "Melanie" used.' Narey groaned inwardly. This was the nonsense with the weird offender fetishes all over again.

'But . . .' Corrieri paused. 'I thought I might try variations on the spelling of Una and did some research on the derivation of the name. It is believed to be Irish in origin, meaning either 'one' or 'lamb'. The anglicized versions of the name therefore include Unity and Agnes . . .'

'Julia . . .'

'Yes, Sergeant. Sorry. The Irish variations include Oona and Oonagh. So I started the process again from the beginning with both spellings. And . . . well, I got something.'

'Tell me.'

'An Oonagh McCullough. Born in 1988, making her twenty-three. She went missing from her home in Giffnock seven years ago and her parents haven't seen her since.'

Narey fell silent.

'Do you think it might be her, Sarge?'

'Every chance of it, Julia. Very good work but we'll need to get hold of dental records to see if we can get a match and then contact this girl's parents. Can you order up the records for me, please?'

There was a slight pause.

'I've eh, already taken the liberty of requesting them and I've got a telephone number for Mr and Mrs McCullough. I hope that's okay.'

Narey laughed inside. Her awkward, unco-ordinated DC was blooming into a swan.

'That's definitely okay, Julia. Remind me to buy you a drink tonight.'

CHAPTER 27

Winter's head was all over the place as he left Rory McCabe's flat and he must have driven a mile without noticing a thing, his mind buzzing. Names, times and dates were crashing into each other and he couldn't make much sense of them. If that wasn't bad enough then he hurt like fuck. He could taste blood and knew he must have looked a sight.

He drove straight back to his flat, dashing inside before anyone could see him and heading for the shower. The water stung but it felt good. He spat onto the floor of the shower, seeing a whisper of coquelicot spiral down the drain.

As he dried off in front of the bathroom mirror, grimacing at the rub of the towel, he noticed a fierce red mark under his right eye and wondered if his cheekbone was broken but reckoned if it was then he'd have really known. His lip had pretty much healed already and apart from a lump on the side of his head the rest of the damage would be easily covered up.

He looked like a patchwork quilt of red, blacks and purples across his ribs though. Staying at Rachel's place that night or even the next few was out of the question; the bruises would beg questions that he didn't want to answer. A couple of nights in his own bed and he could probably pass them off as a rough game of five-a-side as long as she wasn't looking too closely.

Fuck it, it would be fine. Anyway, he was now armed with

information that he wasn't sure what to do with. Sammy Ross. He dug out his photographs from Blochairn, the ones that he'd barely been arsed to take. Sammy boy staring into the abyss, a smiley slash biting his chest.

There was a close-up of his face and his pleading eyes. *What the fuck was it all about, Sammy? What did you have to do with any of this? You were nothing more than the shit on the shoes of someone like Caldwell or Quinn, way down the ladder from the rest of them. Stabbed not shot, you just didn't fit, yet it was your name that fell from Rory McCabe's lips.* Okay, maybe the wee shite had made it up but Winter doubted it. How, apart maybe from having read it in the papers, could he even have come up with his name unless he was telling the truth?

Another thought kept jabbing at Winter's mind though. Not just what did any of it have to do with Sammy but what did it have to do with him? His job was to take photographs. Keep telling yourself that, he thought, keep telling yourself that.

He moved the prints of the dead dealer from one folder to another. He'd had to die to achieve it but Sammy had finally moved up a league. He'd been promoted from mundane murder to headline news even if the only person who knew it was Winter. He was in six-foot deep with Caldwell and Quinn, Strathie and Sturrock, Adamson and Haddow. His mammy would be proud at long last.

Winter's phone broke the insufferable silence with a text from Addison.

Pub @ 8. Think of somewhere or else it's the TSB.

It would be the Station Bar because Winter couldn't be arsed deciding on another pub. He texted back to say okay, then phoned Rachel, bracing himself for the likelihood that her detective radar was switched on and she'd see through his flimsy half-lie. As it turned out, he didn't have much need to worry. Either she bought his story about not feeling great or more likely she was up to her ears in her own case and it suited her just fine to be alone that night. That was already three nights in a row, and he missed her. The speed with which she agreed and hung up suggested she didn't miss him quite as much.

It was okay. He knew there was another man in her life right now and that it wasn't one he should be jealous of. It came with the job and anyway, Winter now had another nine men in his. All dead.

He had a couple of hours before heading to Cowcaddens to meet Addison in the TSB so he decided to go online and see what he could learn about Kieran McKendrick. If there wasn't enough there then he'd head to the Mitchell Library and go through the back copies of the papers. There were plenty of people on the force he could ask but that was a no-no for now. He wanted to keep this to himself and there wasn't a reason for that he could come up with that didn't scare him. No reason that wasn't wrong, one way or another.

He booted up his laptop and googled the name, coming up with a selection of photographers, chip shops, pub landlords, football players and genealogy searches. He added 'drugs death' and hit enter. There were just three results. He picked the one from the *Daily Record*, all seven paragraphs of it. More than your average stabbing got.

'**Teen drugs death blamed on miaow-miaow**', ran the headline

The victim of a suspected drugs death in Glasgow has been named as Kieran McKendrick.

The 17-year-old was found dead in the entrance to a tenement block in the Dennistoun area yesterday. It is believed he was abandoned there by friends after having a reaction to the drug mephedrone.

Police say the teenager had taken mephedrone in the hours preceding his death. A full toxicology report has been called for and Strathclyde Police say they are trying to work out what

role, if any, mephedrone – street name miaow-miaow – played in his death.

Kieran's mother Rosaleen said her son was, 'a lovely boy who never did anyone any harm.'

Detective Chief Inspector Anthony Morrison, who is leading the inquiry, said family and friends have told him that Kieran had been taking the drug on the day of his death, possibly with other substances.

DCI Morrison is asking for anyone with knowledge of Kieran's movements on the day of his death to come forward. He is particularly keen to speak to the friends he may have been with that day.

The teen's family, his mother, brother and younger sister, are said to be devastated by his death.

Devastated? No shit, Winter thought. What a stupid fucking line. It would have been much more of a surprise if they'd been anything other than devastated.

All very routine. Someone was taking a powerful interest in this kid's death, though. Enough to beat the shit out of someone to get it, leaving the same mark as he did on Stevie Strathie. If Winter was right, the shooter, the man they weren't supposed to call the Dark Angel, was very interested in how Kieran McKendrick died.

Winter went back to Google. 'Kieran McKendrick funeral'.

The one result that showed was for the *Evening Times*. The local paper was the only one that gave a toss enough to cover the boy's service. Four paragraphs.

Drug death funeral

The funeral took place today of 17-year-old Kieran McKendrick from Whitevale Street in Dennistoun who died three weeks ago of a suspected reaction to the drug mephedrone.

The teenager's life was celebrated in a service at Lambhill Crematorium attended by a large number of family and friends.

Kieran's mother Rosaleen, his elder brother Ryan and sister Suzanne led a cortege of over one hundred well-wishers, including a number of his present and former schoolmates from St Mungo's Academy.

A police investigation into Kieran's death, which was linked to the drug miaow-miaow, proved inconclusive.

That was it. Seventeen years and all the entire World Wide Web can be arsed to run to was a grand total of four paragraphs. No one batted an eyelid and the Clyde still flowed towards Dumbarton. No one gave a fuck, the rest of the place ploughed on, blissfully unaware or uncaring about the latest stain on the pavement. Walking on by, stepping over it like a Tory MP dodging tramps on the way to the opera. This time somebody cared though. Cared enough to kill.

Winter put 'Ryan McKendrick' into the search engine and got businessmen, social workers, librarians and jockeys. 'Ryan McKendrick Glasgow' scored better though. It got him a couple of Bebo and MySpace hits then it got him 'Naval rating Ryan McKendrick'.

'Navy Ryan Kieran McKendrick' hit paydirt on another Bebo site. A friend of the family mentioned both of the boys in a tribute.

He found the McKendrick's number in Whitevale Street in the phonebook and was shaking slightly as he put 141 before the number to disguise where he was calling from then dialled, not sure what he was going to say. Or why.

A woman's voice answered, polite but tired, barely summoning up the energy to rouse herself enough to say hello.

'Yes?'

'Eh, hi. Could I speak to Ryan, please?'

'Ryan? Ryan's at sea. He has been for three weeks. Who's calling?'

Winter panicked.

'It's um, it's Tony. Okay, sorry to have bothered you. Bye.'

He ended the call before there could be any more awkward questions, appalled at himself for lying to a mother whose son had just died. Arsehole, he raged at himself, throwing his phone on to the chair in the far corner and shutting down the laptop. He needed a drink and luckily enough he knew a man who wanted one with him.

The Station Bar was on Port Dundas Road in Cowcaddens, near where the old STV studios used to stand. Just five minutes' walk from the city centre but far enough away that it was a local bar for local people. It got its share of cops from Stewart Street and journalists as well as firemen, civil servants, brickies, workies and assorted loonies.

As Winter pushed his way through the door, he saw Addison sitting at the table next to the open fire, stewing over a Guinness. He had obviously been counting bodies.

'Fucking eight of the bastards,' he muttered almost as soon as Winter sat down.

Nine, Winter thought to himself.

'So what is being looked at now?' he asked him.

'Anything and everything. No stone unturned. It's the way the Temple works.'

'Something that I shouldn't know?'

'Everything that you don't need to know.'

Fuck you, he thought.

'Fuck you,' he said aloud.

'You're welcome.'

Winter decided that if Addison was only going to give him partial information then that was going to be a two-way street. The names of Sammy Ross and Kieran McKendrick were staying with him for now but he did have something he wanted to share, as much for his own purposes as the DI's.

'Addy, when Cat Fitzpatrick went through Strathie's pockets at Harthill, she found his wallet and driving licence, right?

'Right. What's your point?'

'Well, I was thinking more about what she *didn't* find.'

'Let's hear it. We know the shooter had taken the car keys.'

'He didn't have a mobile phone on him, did he?'

'Nope, and someone like Strathie, doing what he did would have had at least one mobile, more likely two or three.'

'Addy, why do I get the impression you don't sound surprised?'

'Because I'm not. The same thing occurred to me. But I'm impressed though. We could make a traffic warden out of you yet.'

'Fuck you. I'm trying to help.'

Okay, so maybe he wasn't trying to help as much as he could. For a start he could have mentioned how Sammy Ross didn't have a mobile on him either when he was found.

'Thanks for that, wee man,' Addison laughed drily. 'Very public spirited of you. But the question isn't why Strathie, or Sturrock for that matter, didn't have mobiles. It's what the cunt that took them wanted with them.'

'And what's the answer?'

'Obvious enough. Most probably information. If this guy is doing what it looks like he is doing and cleaning out anyone and everyone at the top end of the city's drug operations then most of the names in those phones should be double-locking their doors at night. And they won't all be criminals either.'

Winter raised his eyebrows questioningly but Addison just shook his head wearily.

'Work it out for yourself when you are at the bar. Another Nigerian lager for me.'

Winter shook his head at him, kicked back his chair and headed to the bar. Derek the bar manager had seen him coming and had already stuck the first of two Guinnesses under the tap.

'Your pal alright, Tony?' he asked.

Winter immediately went on the defensive. Derek was the kind of barman who knew when and when not to ask questions. He knew his punters and wouldn't have stuck his nose in without good reason.

'Aye, he's fine. Why do you ask?'

The manager frowned.

'It's just he's been hitting it pretty hard. He's had a large malt with every second pint. That's heavy going even by his standards.'

'He's just got a lot on at work. You'll have read about the shootings.'

'The Dark Angel? Aye, of course. It's all anyone that comes in here is talking about. It's time someone sorted those bastards out if you ask me. They've had it coming for years. The guy deserves a medal,' he sighed softly.

'Well, don't let Addy hear you saying that. I'll keep an eye on him, Derek. He'll be no bother.'

The bar manager nodded and Winter took the pints back over in time to see Addison knock back the last of the glass in front of him.

'What's he saying?' he asked as Winter returned.

'Derek? Nothing. He was just talking about the Celtic game.'

'Don't kid a kidder, wee man. Especially not when he plays at being a detective for a living. He on about how much I'm drinking?'

'No.'

Addison eyeballed him.

'Aye,' Winter conceded.

'He should keep his nose out and just count the money,' Addison snarled. 'Stressful job, don't you know?' He paused and slugged some more. 'Getting more stressful by the day.'

Winter let the comment hang there, drawing deep on his own pint, letting the silence settle both of them for a bit.

'Who else then?' he asked at last. 'Who else should be worried about their numbers being on those mobile phones?'

'Know what I miss?' the DI replied. 'Being able to smoke in here. Just being able to light up and have a fag without dragging your arse out into the cold.'

'You don't smoke.'

'I used to. Haven't had one for eight years but I'm still a smoker at heart. Still miss it. See, wee man, you don't know everything. And that's my point.'

'It is?'

Winter was pleading ignorance even though he was pretty sure where Addison was going with the conversation.

'It is. You don't know who else was listed in those phones. And neither do I. But the nature of the business that Strathie and Sturrock were in it stands to reason there are people in those mobiles who wouldn't want anyone to know they knew drug dealers. Especially a big bad wolf with a gun.'

'Uh huh, people like who?' he persisted.

'You no listen? I told you, I don't know.'

'Cops?'

Addison's hand and pint were halfway to his mouth but he stopped and placed the tumbler back on the table, looking into its murky depths for an answer.

'Maybe. Probably. I don't know.'

They both looked at their drinks rather than each other and it stayed that way for an age till Addison eventually broke the silence.

'My round.'

'Just pints, Addy, eh?'

He gave Winter his best undertaker's smile.

'Just pints, wee man. Not a problem.'

He barely missed a beat on the way to the bar, just a slight brush against the chair hinting that all wasn't as it should be. He signalled Derek towards him and Winter saw him grimace before setting up the two pint tumblers. But as they were pouring, he shoved a glass under the optic, twice, and set it down in front of Addison. He had his back to Winter but Winter still saw his arm come up to shoulder height then fall back down in one swift movement.

Seconds later he was back at the table, a Guinness in each hand.

'Two pints, wee man. Just what the doctor ordered.'

'Addy . . .'

Winter let his question disappear into the air. How can you ask just one question when there's a hundred of them battering at your skull?

'What is it, wee man?'

'Nothing. Cheers.'

Addison grinned widely and scooped half a pint of Guinness down his throat. Winter knew it was his round again.

CHAPTER 28

Saturday 17 September

Brendan and Margaret McCullough lived in a smart semi-detached bungalow in Merryburn Road in Giffnock on the city's south side. Driveway, garage and four bedrooms, it would set you back a quarter of a million or so. Not flash, just smart and cheaper than most houses in the area.

Oonagh McCullough's parents had lived there for twenty-five years, the two of them before their only daughter was born.

Narey and Corrieri pulled up outside the low wall and neat hedge, both unbuckling their seat belts before taking a deep breath.

'You ready?' Narey asked her.

'No.'

'Me neither. Let's go.'

The two women got out of Narey's Megane, walked up the driveway and climbed half a dozen steps to the front door. Narey raised her hand to press the bell but the door swung open before she could hit it and a stern-looking man in his late fifties looked at them doubtfully.

'Sergeant Narey?'

'Yes, Mr McCullough. This is my colleague, DC Corrieri. May we come in?'

The man didn't answer but pursed his lips and nodded them past him inside. Everything about him was neat. Closely trimmed reddish hair and a manicured greying moustache, immaculately ironed trousers and shirt and polished shoes. The front room that he directed them to was equally tidy, albeit in an explosion of floral chintz.

As they entered the room, an anxious-looking woman pushed herself up out of a chair and greeted them with a nervous smile, extending her hand to meet theirs. Behind them, her husband introduced the visitors although there was no doubt Mrs McCullough had spent the afternoon waiting for them to arrive.

'Margaret, these are the police officers,' he was saying unnecessarily. 'Ladies, Officers, this is my wife.'

Mrs McCullough smiled again.

'You said on the telephone that you might have some information about Oonagh?'

'We think we have, Mrs McCullough. Is that your daughter in the photographs on the mantelpiece?'

Six separate portraits showed the same auburn-haired girl at various ages. On one side of the shelf a baby picture, wide eyes and an unlikely mass of hair; a shyly smiley toddler in a short summer dress; then in school uniform aged about five. In the middle was a wedding portrait of her parents, the husband in army uniform and the wife in a white dress and veil. On the other, was Oonagh with a pony and rosettes; a birthday shot complete with thirteen candles on the cake; and finally a sulkier teenager looking bored in a family wedding photograph aged about fifteen. There was little doubt that it was the face of Melanie the hooker that was looking back at them.

'Yes,' her mother was confirming with another smile, this one managing to be at once proud and sad. Mrs McCullough was fearing the worst but hoping for the best. Narey knew it wasn't fair to prolong their agony any longer.

'Mr and Mrs McCullough, I think it would be better if you sat down.'

Her words slapped across the mother's face and Narey saw her recoil from them. The husband shook slightly but refused to budge.

'I'd rather stand, Sergeant,' he said soberly. 'Please, continue.'

'I really think it best that you take a seat too, sir.'

'I'll stand.'

'Very well. I'm afraid that we have some very bad news for you both. The body of a young woman, whom we believe to be Oonagh, has been found. She was murdered.'

Mary McCullough grabbed at her skirt and a hand flew to her mouth.

'Believe. Believe. You said you "believe" it to be Oonagh. You aren't sure, then. It could be some other poor girl. Right?'

'I'm sorry to say that we are quite sure, Mrs McCullough. We will need to ask you or your husband to identify the body but . . .'

The phrase produced a scream from deep within Mrs McCullough. As soon as it escaped she clamped a hand over her mouth and looked to her husband, eyes pleading.

'Where was she found, this girl that you think is Oonagh?' Brendan McCullough asked grimly.

'In the city centre, sir. In the area near Waterloo Street.'

'In Glasgow?' the parents chorused.

'She was living here all this time?' the father added. 'Living here but wouldn't come to see us?'

'We believe she has been here for the last few years,' Narey nodded. 'She disappeared when she was sixteen, is that correct?'

'Sixteen years and one day, Sergeant,' he replied. 'She left on the twenty-third of March 2004, the day after her birthday. We never saw her again. I can't believe she was so close all the time. We have never moved, she knew where we were.'

'I realize this is very difficult news to take in,' Narey continued.

'But we believe that Oonagh became a drug addict and this led her into a life of prostitution.'

'No. No, no, no.'

Mr McCullough's denial wasn't spoken in anger but more in an unwillingness to accept what had been said. He was dismissing the possibility out of hand. His wife had silent tears streaming down her face.

'I'm sorry, Mr McCullough, but there seems little doubt. We have already checked Oonagh's last known dental records with your local practice and despite considerable decay in the intervening period, there is a convincing match.'

'We always made sure she had a check-up every six months,' the mother burst in. 'Regular as clockwork, never missed an appointment.'

Her husband opened his mouth as if to scold her but his gaze softened and he just nodded in her direction instead.

'Have you had any contact at all with Oonagh in the past seven years?'

Brendan McCullough turned to his wife again.

'The postcard.'

At that Mrs McCullough jumped up, glad of something to do, and almost ran to a teak sideboard against the far wall. She opened a drawer and instantly brought out a card adorned with a photograph of the Eiffel Tower.

'It arrived four years ago,' the husband explained. 'May 2007.'

Narey took the postcard from the woman's trembling hand and turned it over.

Don't worry. I'm safe. O.

The card had a Paris postmark and was dated as the man had said.

'It is definitely Oonagh's handwriting?'

'Of course.'

'And this was the only time she got in touch?'

'Yes.'

'Is there anyone she was particularly close to before she left, someone that she might have stayed in touch with?' asked Corrieri.

The father shook his head impatiently.

'We spoke to all her friends, all the ones we knew of. The police did the same at the time. They knew nothing.'

'Brendan went out all the time looking for her,' his wife said, her red eyes staring at the floor. 'Day after day, night after night, scouring the streets. But nothing. After the postcard came we stopped looking, knowing ... thinking ... that she wasn't in the country any more.'

Mrs McCullough sprang out of her seat and plucked one of the photographs from the mantelpiece, the one of Oonagh in her first school uniform. She sat carefully back onto the sofa, cradling the framed picture to her breast. Her husband sat down beside her and put an arm around her.

'Mr and Mrs McCullough, might it be possible for us to take a photograph of Oonagh away with us, as recent as you have?' Narey asked. 'I'll ensure it gets back to you safely.'

The husband nodded without looking up.

'I'll get you one.'

'And could we arrange for one of you to identify Oonagh's body at the city police mortuary at the Saltmarket?'

'Yes, of course. I'll do it,' he replied.

'Thank you. I am so sorry to have had to bring you news like this. I will arrange for a family liaison officer to be in touch with you this afternoon.'

'There's no need,' he snapped at her. 'We'll be fine.'

'I still think it's best. I'll ask one to call by and you can take it from there.'

'Yes, yes, whatever. Let me show you to the door.'

Brendan McCullough squeezed his wife's shoulder before

rising from the seat and leading the two officers out of the living room, closing the door behind him.

'You're absolutely certain that it's Oonagh?' he asked them quietly.

'Yes,' Narey replied.

'And you are sure that she was an addict and . . . a prostitute?'

'Yes, Mr McCullough, we are.'

The man's face darkened.

'Whatever she had become, I need to know that you will still do your job. No one cares about those working girls, do they? The police always have more important things to do.'

'I can assure you that we do care,' Narey answered testily, her mind chiming with the force's resources being eaten up by the sniper killings.

'And you will catch the man who did this to my wee girl?'

'Oh we will, Mr McCullough,' Narey assured him with a lot more certainty than she knew she could promise. 'We will.'

CHAPTER 29

Sunday 18 September

Winter woke up feeling sore. Sore head, sore body, sore Sunday morning. Both head and body had taken different kinds of pounding the day before and the price was now being paid. The shower helped one but only succeeded in stinging the other. A cup of coffee at least helped both a bit.

He struggled into some clothes but resisted the temptation to head for the newsagents. His bruises had won the fight against the hangover and woken him early enough that he had time to read over the previous day's newspapers before going into Pitt Street. There was a morning meeting of the Nightjar team but he wasn't needed for that and was to wait for a call to arms if their man struck again.

The killings of Adamson and Haddow were splashed over the front pages of the papers and most of them had large photographs of the pair. The *Daily Star* was the exception but even it squeezed the photo of some reality TV bimbo to the side in order to get in a head and shoulders of the dead accountant. For Winter, though, the real eye catcher was the *Sun*'s headline.

HE'S DONE IT AGAIN

Fuck. That left plenty of scope for interpretation. It was as if a striker had scored his twentieth goal of the season, not that there had been another double murder. The paper had a new logo for it too. A large D in a red circle made to look like a rifle sight. Winter could imagine Alex Shirley spitting blood, Addison too for that matter. He'd been in a black mood by the time they went their separate ways the night before, the whisky having him in a near rage about the sniper. The hero status that the papers were serving up would have had his hangover at bursting point.

The crackpots had come out of the cupboard, too. An inside page of the *Record* had the leader of the English Defence League jumping on the bandwagon. He was calling for an amnesty for the Dark Angel and even issued a 'rallying call' for someone in England to do the same job there. He wanted 'an English knight to rid the streets of drug-dealing scum in the same way that the Scottish hero is doing'.

Right-wing American Republicans had picked up on the killings too. A Senator from Texas hailed it as a 'prime example of people power in reclaiming their freedom from hoodlums'. He went on to make references to his ancestors and *Braveheart* that made Winter want to puke. The pompous prick had no idea who was doing this, far less that it should be lauded as a good thing. In the end, Winter picked up a copy of the *Sun*, the *Record* and the *Herald* and took all of them to work with him. The *Herald* had easily the best photographs from Glasgow Harbour. A staff snapper had made it to the scene while the bodies were still warm and although he'd been chased, he'd gone to the other side of the river and his long lens had done the trick. The main shot they'd used had McConachie standing over Haddow. Of course the pictures weren't a patch on Winter's own, given that he had the luxury of standing right over the victims. He printed off a glossy image of Gee Gee Adamson laid out in his heavy, black leather coat with his meaty chops and gobsmacked expression. The coat soaking up his spilled blood like a leathery sponge, making it heavier and heavier with every life drop that it tasted. Gee Gee the gambler and his final losing bet.

He pinned it to the wall alongside a bloody close-up of Haddow in his pinstripe and white. The terrified smart man who died without the brains he was born with. Already on the office wall were his favourite shots of Caldwell, Quinn, Strathie and Sturrock. His Dark Angel gallery.

He so wanted to put a photograph of Sammy Ross there too but couldn't let himself do it. Some screwed-up version of see no evil, hear no evil, speak no evil was playing in his head and he had no idea what the rules were. All he knew was that Sammy's picture couldn't go up there, not yet. For now it stayed in a drawer along with his blown-up images of the marks on McCabe and Strathie.

Sammy was a dot, a bloodied dot along with McCabe and the McKendrick kid and they were joined to the other six killings somehow. Just how, he had no idea and maybe he didn't really want to know. Record but don't interfere, observe but don't violate. It was getting harder every day to remember the mantra.

Saturday morning stretched into afternoon and no call came for him to join up with the team. Apart from a couple of calls from Addison, he had heard nothing from them all day. His mate was clearly on edge, a cat on a hot tin roof, bouncing from word to word and from subject to subject. One second it would be a mention of Malky Quinn, the next it would be how Celtic were going to do in the next match. He was telling Winter how a guy named Harvey Houston who worked for Ally Riddle had supposedly gone missing and then he just switched to what he'd like to do to the barmaid in the TSB. Not that night though because he was seeing someone else and was worried he'd not be able to get away from work on time, worried because she was a sure thing, or so he reckoned. Talking about women or Celtic, he was fine; it was the case that had him dangerously grouchy. He flew into a rage at any mention of the new hero that was cleaning up the streets and Winter knew he'd been slicing people in two with cutting remarks. Nobody except Winter talked to him or went near him unless they had to. On the Friday, he'd almost decked Colin Monteith when he suggested they just let the Dark Angel get on with it. Even the use of the nickname had Addison's hackles rising.

Rachel was crabbit as fuck too, snapping at him left, right and centre. Too busy to talk, only time to bite his head off. He finally managed to persuade her to go for some Italian food at Gambrino on Great Western Road on Saturday night but it was a waste of time for both of them. He'd hardly got a word out of her and knew her mind was on both cases every minute they were there. He wouldn't have minded so much if she had shared it with him but her guard was up, saying nothing. It was obvious she'd rather have been back in the operations room.

Her phone was out on the table and her eyes continually flicked to it as if willing it to ring, saying only that she was waiting for results to come through from some DNA test. Finally, she turned down the offer of dessert and got Winter to drop her off at home, sending him on his way to his own place. He made the mistake of making some comment about no sex and she nearly strangled him.

Saturday night became Sunday morning and Glasgow woke to no more news. It must have been a pisser for the Fox News team that had parachuted in from the US as well as the Japanese and German TV crews that were in town now. Six dead criminals might not have been a lot but sniper killings made headlines everywhere, especially when the person carrying them out was being held up as some kind of people's champion. Fox had tried calling him the Dark Knight but DC Comics threatened to sue so they had to settle for the Dark Angel as well.

Winter didn't hear much from either Rachel or Addison

throughout Sunday, just the odd text and brief phone call. The little he was being told, it seemed Alex Shirley was running the Nightjar team ragged, having them pore over every bit of CCTV footage they could lay their hands on. They studied every camera anywhere near Central Station, Harthill, George Square and Glasgow Harbour. Every access road and possible escape route, every bit of motorway they could see. All the usual suspects and some unusual ones were run through face-recognition technology but it came back empty.

Forensics were working round the clock, analysing the little that they had. The room at Livingstone Tower had been brushed within an inch of its life but Winter hadn't heard of anything turning up that was of any use. The bullets had all come from the same gun and manufacturers were being pressured to turn over lists of stockists and owners.

The mood among the few cops Winter spoke to, uniform and CID, was odd. They were all nervy, that much was obvious, but he couldn't figure out just what they wanted to happen. In the end, he realized they just wanted something, anything, to happen. And if that meant another dealer, mule or boss had to get shot then that wouldn't be the worst thing in the world.

He'd heard they'd hauled in everyone they knew connected to the drugs trade and squeezed them for all they were worth. Half of them were scared shitless even before they were brought in and knew the shooter could do a lot worse to them than any cop could. In fact they knew they were safer in the cop shop than out of it. Even without what the Dark Angel was doing, they were getting tanked into each other. Their own attempts to find out who was doing the killings continued by way of drive-bys and beatings, everyone suspicious of everyone else. Another of the Gilmartin clan, cousin Billy, had ended up in hospital; an enforcer for Tookie Cochrane named Colin Sinclair was reckoned to be wearing a concrete overcoat somewhere; and the mother of a well-known dealer named Benjo

Honeyman walked into Baird Street greeting that he had missed her birthday. The natives were both restless and revolting. One of Terry Gilmartin's lieutenants, George Faichney, had done a bunk and Gilmartin was supposed to be desperate to find him.

After seven killings in four days, there hadn't been anything for two days in a row and it seemed like a lifetime. It should have eased the tension but instead it racked it up a few notches till the city was a pressure cooker with the lid twitching like a rabbit's nostrils. That's why when the dealers and the doers-in were dragged into stations across Glasgow, they weren't too fussed about being questioned. In fact, by the time they got hauled in, not only did they have nothing to tell, it was them demanding to know what the police were going to do about it all. The problem was that nobody had an answer for them.

Winter spent most of Sunday afternoon filing everything he had to file so he popped into the Nightjar operation room late on and was basically chased along. If you're needed, we'll call you, otherwise fuck off, camera boy. He got the message.

Winter could feel the sudden chill, the wind picking up and the grumble of approaching thunder. His *sgriob* was itching and he couldn't ignore the voice that was whispering in the back of his head. It's quiet, too quiet. The calm before the storm. Be calm before the storm.

He got a drunken phone call from Addison late on Sunday night after the DI had emerged empty-handed from Viper, more or less demanding to know why no one had been shot while he'd been inside trying to get his end away.

'What is it with this fucker?' he slurred at Winter. 'Where's he hiding himself? Eh? Where's he hiding, wee man?'

'I've no idea, Addy. You looked under the bed?'

'Ah, a comedian, just what I need. And for your information, the night is still young and I'll be looking in a bed before it's finished. The mountie always gets his woman. Anyway, that's not why I phoned. I know you're up to something you little scrote. I know your game. You're hiding something.'

What the fuck? Winter hesitated a fraction too long.

'I don't know what you're talking about, Addy. You're pished. Away and get yourself home.'

'You know what I'm talking about alright, wee man. That bang on the cheek you had on Friday night? Slipped in the bathroom, my arse. How do you explain the big bruise at the back of your head?'

'Fuck off, Addy. I don't need this.'

'Can't answer, huh? You're up to something and first thing in the morning I'm gonnae find out what it is. I know you and it's something to do with your photographs. You know something you're not telling.'

'You're mental. Get yourself some chips or something.'

'Good idea, wee man. I'm starving. Might nip over to the Philadelphia. Hey, you know Graeme Forrest, the inspector that works out of Anderston? Never showed up for his shift today and no sign of him anywhere. I reckon he's done a bunk with that wee blonde WPC, whatsername, Sandra something? You know her?'

'Nope. No idea who she is.'

'Tidy wee bit of stuff, can't say I blame him. Anyway, don't change the subject, wee guy. I'm gonnae find out what you're up to, whatever it is. And what about the shooter? What's his game now? He's been far too quiet for my liking.'

'Maybe he takes the weekend off?' Winter suggested.

'Yeah, very fucking funny. Now fuck off. I'm starving.'

And with that Addison hung up and disappeared somewhere into the night leaving Winter wide awake and wondering what was to come.

CHAPTER 30

Monday 19 September

The Nightjar operation room lay dark and empty, the last person having called it a day just before midnight, six hours earlier. All that could be heard was the impatient hum of technology: fax machines, telephones and computers on stand-by, all left to guard the shop and await any news of the man who rendered the same office full of noisy, nervous energy during the day. If an empty room could ever be described as a coiled spring then this was it.

At 6.04 a.m. the quiet was disturbed by the angry ringing of a telephone in the middle of the office. It was the hotline set up for members of the public to call if they had any information on the sniper killings. On the eighth ring it stopped and the answering machine kicked in, a flashing red light the only indication that a message had been left. For a further hour, the red signal throbbed in the gloom of the locked-down office like a lighthouse sending out a danger signal that no one could see.

Nancy Anderson was first through the door at seven, the civilian admin assistant in before any of the CID. She had worked on farms all her days, first in Glasgow then in the Borders at Lauder, before her MS had forced her to finally take an office job. She could never get out of the habit of rising early though and was almost always first into work. Her husband Colin was forever telling her to take it easy but she knew he was already up too, doubtless ready to fuss over their grandchildren.

She threw on the lights and pulled her hand through her greying hair as she tutted at the mess the cops had left the place in the night before. There were coffee cups everywhere and newspapers lying on the floor. She guessed she would have to be the one to tidy the room up as per usual. So much for swapping the farm for an easier job, this one brought its own problems.

She picked up a tray and began piling paper cups inside each other, going from desk to desk and making a mental note of the worst offenders, fully intending to pull them up about it when they came in. It was only when she got to the desk in the middle of the room did the flashing light register. There were unlikely to be any officers in for another hour so she would have to deal with that as well. Oh, it could wait another few minutes, she had to open the blinds and let a bit of light into the room. That done, Nancy grabbed a notepad and turned almost reluctantly to the phone, trying to guess whether it would be a message from a nutter, a timewaster or both. She punched the message button and listened.

The first few seconds was nothing more than crackling on the line. Then a man's voice spoke, slow, deliberate and heavily muffled.

'More bodies.

'End of Lawmoor Road.

'Dixon Blazes Industrial Estate.

'Courtesy of the Dark Angel.'

Nancy stood stock-still for seconds that seemed like minutes. She looked down at her notepad and tried to make sense of what she had just heard and written down. She began to edge away from the phone but took a deep breath and returned to press the play button again with a shaky hand. The same muffled voice delivered the same measured words. With a final glance at her pad, she spun on her heels, nearly slipping to the floor as she ran across the room as fast as she could to her own desk where she knew her phone was programmed with the speed-dial numbers she needed. Seconds later, the tired and testy voice of Superintendent Alex Shirley came on the line.

'Nancy? What the . . . this better be good!'

'It isn't, sir.'

Within minutes, unshaven cops dived into cars across the city. Addison had given Winter two minutes to be ready and said that if he wasn't on the pavement when he turned up then he was going without him. Winter was ready and waiting before he arrived.

He jumped into the passenger seat, the Audi lurching away long before he'd closed the door. They'd burst through the red light at the slip road to the motorway by the time Winter managed to fasten his seat belt. By the look on Addison's face and the drift of beer and whisky that was coming Winter's way, the DI probably shouldn't have been driving. Just as well there was no cop likely to be asking him to blow into a breathalyser.

He looked rough, eyes strained and red as if he'd knocked back his last half just five minutes before. There was a fierce anger around his eyes. Winter knew the look. Addison was trying and failing to hold it back, he wanted to burst, ready to boot someone's head in. Instead he kicked his foot to the floor, battering the car towards Rutherglen.

He only spoke once all the way there. He didn't take his eyes off the road, just spat the words at the windscreen.

'I'm fed up with this cunt. I'm going to bring him to his fucking knees. He's finished. Last job.'

He didn't utter another word until they hammered into Dixon Blazes and roared down to the far end of Lawmoor Road, passing warehouses, offices and industrial units, heading for the last plot before the railway line.

Two blue and yellows and a couple of unmarked cars were the X's that marked where the spot was. Addison didn't bother locking the Audi and was out and onto the tarmac before Winter had even opened the door. He was still fishing his camera gear out of the back when he heard him utter:

'What the fu . . .'

It was only then that Winter took in the look on the faces of the handful of cops that had beaten them there. All looking at them with something approaching pity on their faces. Addison couldn't have noticed them either because he had blundered round the corner and straight into the face of whatever it was. Now he was standing stock-still with his mouth open.

Winter sprinted to the corner, aware that his head was slowing it down like it was some nightmare version of *Baywatch*. He caught his feet in time to follow the gaze of Alex Shirley, Jan McConachie, – fuck, Rachel was there too – Julia Corrieri, two other CIDs and four uniform, including Jim Boyle and Sandy Murray.

Thirty yards away was the door to what looked like a half-finished warehouse. There was no sign on it and an unpainted roof sat on top of unpainted walls. Standing hard against the door was a man, arms wide as if he was being held at gunpoint. His head was slumped against his chest like he had fallen asleep but his arms said that couldn't be the case. It filtered through to Winter's brain slowly, the only way it could because what he was really seeing was just so terrible.

The guy wasn't standing or leaning against the door, he was being held up by it. He was somehow pinned against it and his arms were out straight as if . . . as if he were crucified against it. That's exactly what it is, Winter thought. The itch on his lip was competing with a thud in his heart and the potential collapse of his bowels.

He was aware of Shirley beckoning him forward, waving him

towards the door, everyone else standing back to let him by, almost reverentially. He was aware of grim faces and quizzical looks, someone was saying something but he didn't hear it. He was zeroing in on the door, focusing on it as if he'd fall unless he concentrated on it. His camera came out of his bag on auto-pilot and he looked down, surprised that it was in his hand.

As he approached, he saw dress shoes and suit trousers, a pale-blue shirt open at the collar, no tie. He saw tousled dark hair that had been wet or sweaty and had dried that way. Blood. He saw falu red at the man's open palms and daubs of it at his feet. He got closer and saw nails driven through his hands, and his gut tightened and his breathing became harder. There were nails through his feet, too, driven through the black leather of his shoes and causing the unholy puddle beneath him. There wasn't just blood in that spill though, it ran with the fear that had soiled the front of his navy-blue trousers. He'd been alive when some of this had happened.

Closer. Winter's nose picked up sweat, blood, urine and fear. And death. His nose wrinkled at the smell of it just as his lip itched. He stopped, focused and shot, stepped a few yards to the side and repeated the process. He circled right, snapping as he went. Every detail from every angle. This was a new one even for him, no amount of Glasgow could prepare you for this. His mind flew back to Father Mulroney at St Simon's in Partick Bridge Street. Mark Chapter 15. 'And they crucified two bandits with him, one on his right and one on his left.'

He was no more than six feet away and the man filled his viewfinder. Switch, zoom, focus. His hands punctured and still bleeding, slowly, ever so slowly, dripping away what was left of him. The nails that pinned him were bog-standard B&Q specials, intended to be driven through planks of wood, not flesh and bone. Right hand, left hand, neither knowing what the other had done. Closer.

Winter knew before he finally saw it for sure. Every angle, every detail. He'd seen it in his camera's eye but had shut it out, willing it not to be so but there was no getting away from it. He kneeled before the man, careful to avoid the pool of blood and piss at their feet. His lens turned to the man's face in a final act of supplication and saw Inspector Graeme Forrest look despairingly back down at him, his last hope long since dripped onto the concrete.

Forrest's mouth was stuffed with twenty-pound notes, his cheeks bulging with them, and a hundred, maybe two hundred quid's worth hanging from his lips. Used notes stuffed between his teeth, either ensuring his silence or choking him to death.

Graeme was staring at the pavement as if it offered some kind of answer, fear in his empty blue eyes. Winter closed in on one of them, a photo that would never appear in any evidence submission. He saw alarm and guilt and pain.

Forrest had always been a bit of a devil yet here he was crucified like Our Lord. Father Mulroney wouldn't have approved of this. Who the fuck did he think he was?

Forrest's mouth looked sad, loose and wide with the bank notes and turned down at the corners. All that, whatever it was, for this. Police college, being nice to his mum, catching criminals, always brushing his teeth. All that just for some bastard to nail him to a door. He looked fat, his head slumped down like that and his cheeks bulging – whatever blood he had left had been rushing there too and left him looking like a chipmunk. Poor bastard.

Winter could hear Forrest telling him not to photograph him like that. Always was a vain bastard. Forrest would have wanted a better angle but there weren't any more of them. There was only one shot. Anyway, God help him, but he'd never looked better. Frozen for time immoral in the biggest case in town.

Winter stepped down and back, easing himself out from under

the dead cop, vaguely aware of more voices behind him. He could pick out Rachel - what the hell was she doing there? - and Addison among them but hadn't a clue what they were saying. More pish, no doubt. It was all pish. Pictures painted a thousand words so why talk? He turned away from Forrest to let the vultures in to pick over his bones. He'd recorded him for posterity and for the high court, now they were going to rip him to bits. If he was thinking it then so were they - the crucifixion and the cash, shades of Jesus and Judas, saint and sinner. They'd crowded in on Winter, watching him work. Rubberneckers. Gawpers. They weren't rushing forward to get to Forrest though and for a moment Winter thought their reluctance was down to it being one of their own until he realized there wasn't a forensic among them. Baxter, Cat or whoever was on duty hadn't got to the site and the cops would have to wait. Graeme's dignity was spared for a few minutes longer.

He was in a world of his own again and it was the first ring of the mobile phone, no, phones, that made him jump. Two ringtones cut through whatever talk was going on among the cops, the sounds jumbled together, but Winter recognized one of them, his brain trying to unscramble it from the other. CID and uniform were looking at each other and hands started to reach into pockets to pull out the phones, some stopping when they realized it wasn't theirs.

It was Jan McConachie, standing maybe ten feet to Winter's right, who emerged with a phone first, looking at the screen display with puzzlement and discomfort. She was still looking at it when a shot rang out and a bullet took her clean off her feet. She fell straight back, a circle of pure candy-apple red bursting her forehead.

Winter spun instinctively to the left where the other ringtone, the familiar one, was coming from. He turned just in time to see Addison holding his mobile and trying to move, to dive, to duck.

He was too late and another gunshot exploded from somewhere over Winter's shoulder and sent Addison spinning. Winter saw the gush of blood like an oil well being struck, a burst of scarlet showering him before he hit the deck.

CHAPTER 31

Winter heard the thud of Addison hitting the tarmac then nothing. His ears were full of gunshot, ringing with horror. The cops who were still standing, some having thrown themselves to the ground, were frozen to the spot. He looked over Addison's stricken body and saw Rachel looking back at him, her eyes locked on his. He held his breath for another shot and in the hour that seemed to flash by in a split second, or the split second that lasted an hour, he had time to hope the next bullet would hit him and not her.

Shirley found his voice, piercing the hush and roaring at everyone to get down. Lying flat, Winter saw the spurt of blood pooling round Addison, gathering quickly round him like a shroud. He thought his heart was going to burst. Death didn't seem so beautiful after all.

What was he doing lying there, he thought? He got back to his feet, shakily, turning to face away from the warehouse door where Forrest was hanging. Turning to face where the shots were coming from.

'Get fucking down, Winter,' Shirley bellowed. Winter ignored him, staring out to wherever the bastard with the gun was, his heart hammering at his ribs and his throat dry. He stared the shooter down even though he couldn't see him. He gave him ten long seconds and then made his move, turning towards Addison with his camera in his hand. The sniper with the rifle wasn't going to shoot him, he'd have done it by then.

A few feet in front of Addison, Winter stopped and took a photograph, realizing for the first time that he had tears in his eyes. Addison was lying on his back, one leg caught under him, one arm at his side, the other across his chest, his mobile a foot away.

His skull was torn and bathed in red, his eyes wide in shock and his mouth contorted in a final grimace. Fuck, he was tall, stretched out long and getting cold. Winter ripped off his jacket and knelt beside his friend, suffocating a scream that he could feel building up inside him, trying to stem the wound with the coat but only succeeding in getting it saturated with blood in seconds. Addison's eyes were lost somewhere and though Winter turned his cradled head towards him, he couldn't see. How could this be? Then he felt it, a kicking somewhere below him. Addison's legs were convulsing like a man suffering a mild electric shock. Did it mean he was alive, did he mean he was dying? Winter was panicking.

From behind him, he felt an arm on his shoulder. He tensed, ready to tell whoever it was to fuck off. The voice surprised him though.

'Ease his head back down slowly. You could paralyse him, you fool. Then get out of the way. Please.'

Winter looked back and saw that it was Campbell Baxter. He hadn't heard him arrive. The tone of his voice was gentle and understanding but firm. Winter looked from him to Addison and back, unsure.

'Look, Winter. I know I'm more used to dealing with dead bodies but I have more knowledge on how to help him than anyone else here right now. The ambulance is two minutes away. He's still alive. Let me help him.'

Winter nodded wordlessly, helplessly, pushing the sleeves of his jacket on the ground below Addison's head and letting Baxter reach his hands underneath his and place the DI gently on it. Sound rushed into his ears again, hearing Shirley roaring to get every cop within miles to the spot they thought the shots had come from and to shut off every road leading to and from it.

Baxter took Addison's wrist in one large paw and searched for a pulse, finding it and declaring it very weak. Winter felt more hands on his shoulders, pulling him up and away. He gave in to them, letting the hands turn him. He stood and looked and fell into Rachel's arms. His face was smothered in her hair and the smell of it filled his senses, making him realize how much he'd missed it. She hugged him tight, facing him away from Addison, seemingly not caring that they were in public. He wanted to kiss her, lifting his head to do so, but she grabbed him back towards her, locking his head to her shoulder.

It was only the blare of the arriving ambulance that made Winter rip himself away, pulling free to see paramedics jump from the vehicle and run to Addison. Baxter had already wrapped something round the wound and had seemingly stopped the flow of blood. He spoke quickly to the paramedics then stepped aside as they secured his neck, eased a stretcher under him and lifted him into the ambulance. Rachel held Winter again as the doors closed, a last glimpse of tubes and wires being fitted as the engine fired up and it left, siren blaring.

The ambulance turned the bend and disappeared out of sight. Winter looked around and saw Alex Shirley standing over the body of Jan McConachie, realizing that the ambulance hadn't taken her because she was dead.

'Let me go,' Winter told Rachel.

Her eyes pleaded with him not to but he leaned in and whispered to her.

'It's okay. I'm okay. Let me go.'

She nodded, reluctantly releasing him and looking to see who had been watching them. He didn't know and he didn't care. He had other things to do. Jim Boyle, the PC, saw him coming and cut across his path. Boyle was a burly big guy, shaven-headed under his hat, and Winter couldn't have pushed him aside very easily but he would if he had to.

'You don't have to do this, Tony,' he was telling him.

'It's my job, Jim.'

'Fucksake, Tony. There will be others on their way. Get someone to take you and follow the ambulance. Addy's your best mate.'

Winter shook his head.

'Work to do. It's the only thing I can do for him now. Let me past.'

The constable held Winter's eyes for a second or two then stepped back, letting him push on by. Superintendent Shirley heard his footsteps and turned, looking Winter up and down. His face was set, grim and angry, chewing on his bottom lip, and Winter couldn't tell what he was thinking. The look on his face could have been disgust or understanding; Winter didn't know or care. They were pretty much the same feelings he had about himself.

Jan McConachie was flat on her back, arms and eyes wide. Winter's hands were shaking as he framed the full-length shot but steadied with the first click. She was almost expressionless beyond the confusion she had registered at the phone call.

His mind was full of thoughts of Addison but he shook them out of his head. No time for that. McConachie was stone-cold dead, the circle in the middle of her head already turning fire-engine red before his eyes and her lost life juices spreading under her. Black trousers, flat shoes, a green blouse under a black waterproof jacket. Waterproof but not bloodproof: it was already soaking. Her phone was a couple of feet behind her right hand.

Winter didn't know her beyond a few shared words. A hard ticket, a woman in a man's world, just as good as any of the guys, swore like a fucking trooper but a good mum to her kid. Hair dyed blonde, a conceit offset by the careless cut. Dress-down clothes, nothing overtly sexual. Male cops probably thought her a hard bitch. Female cops probably thought her a cold bitch. Winter circled McConachie, using the spherical camera for the R2S as he swept round behind to photograph her in situ with the whole warehouse in sight. Not just it but the cops as well. Rachel, Shirley, Corrieri, the uniforms. They knew he had them in the shot but said nothing. They were frozen like they were when Addison was shot, frozen with fear and helplessness. Shirley was stern and glaring, Rachel was looking right into his lens, worried and on the edge, Boyle and Murray were both looking round like sentries, scared and strong.

Where was the beauty in this? He shifted a foot to the right and focused again but saw the other movement through his viewfinder. All bar Rachel had turned their backs away from him and from McConachie and were walking quickly towards the now-open warehouse door where Forrest still hung. Baxter stood beside it, a look of utter confusion on his face as the cops filed past him and inside. Seconds later, Sandy Murray appeared again, waving at Winter. The look on his face didn't encourage Winter at all. He looked like he'd seen a ghost.

Without a final look at McConachie, he followed the wave of Murray's arm. His bag over his shoulder and his Nikon now in his hand, he hustled through the door. No more than a few steps inside, he ran straight into the broad back of Shirley, bouncing off him and almost falling to his knees. He looked where Shirley was looking and saw four men tied to four chairs arranged in a sort of semi-circle facing the door. All dead.

CHAPTER 32

The first was a bloody mess, his face battered beyond recognition. Lips burst, nose flattened and cheekbones smashed, his shirt soaked so deep in blood that you couldn't have guessed what colour it had been originally. The whites of his lifeless eyes were like beacons among the blood, staring emptily into nowhere. Behind the gore he might have been nineteen, he might have been thirty. His jeans were damp with God knows what and his shoes seeped. Most of what had been inside him was now leaking out.

To his right sat a wiry ginger-headed guy in his mid-thirties, tied with wire at his hands and feet, unmarked compared to his neighbour but alabaster-white on account of the deep slashes at his wrist through which every drop of blood had poured. His lips were the palest blue, as if he'd been left out in the snow too long, his eyes rolled back in his head. The swimming pool at his feet was purest crimson, a gorgeously horrendous bath of unadulterated *jus de vie*. His blood streamed to the feet of the third victim. Not that the next guy needed it, he had plenty of his own. He had been gutted, a deep vertical incision into his chest from which gushed a mess of lust. His head was back staring at the ceiling or beyond, his last act maybe, screaming or straining against what was being done to him. The tips of his fingers were bleeding too from where he'd been gripping onto the chair for dear life. He was in his early twenties, a skinny ned with flinty features and a shock of dirty, blond hair. Winter looked at the cut in his chest and wanted to get Baxter to check something that he couldn't ask. Was it the same knife that had been used to kill Sammy Ross? He couldn't ask because he should already have told them of the link between Ross and Strathie before now. Before McConachie and Addison were shot and before Forrest and these four were murdered. Before it was all too late . . .

The fourth man had a hood over his head, his neck slumped at an unnatural angle. There was something wrong about his legs too, dangling askew from the knees down, bones seemingly jutting out where they shouldn't. He wore jeans and a sweat-shirt, both dirty as if he'd been rolled on the ground, maybe taking a kicking as well as what was most probably a baseball bat beating.

'Photograph him, Winter,' ordered Alex Shirley. 'And get a fucking move on. I want that hood off him.'

Winter found his feet the moment the superintendent spoke, glad to be able to move and not simply standing and staring. He circled the broken man, snapping as he went, aware of the open-mouthed, fearful cops in the rear of his shot. 'Right, enough,' barked Shirley. 'Out of the way.'

Winter was done, anyway. He wanted to see the guy's face as much as anyone else. Shirley strode forward, pulling the hood off the guy's head and dropping it into an evidence bag that Baxter held out for him.

The right side of number four's face was caved in, his eye out its socket, the skull and jaw both smashed. It brought images of Addison's head screaming into Winter's consciousness and he had to banish them fast. Had to concentrate or he'd be in deep shit. He knew he was close to losing it completely.

He stared at the guy's left eye, saw that it in turn was staring away from the damage to the skull, either looking out for trouble from the other side or just desperate not to see what had happened. For a second he wished he was wherever number four was looking, somewhere safe, somewhere out of sight and out of mind. He snapped back into reality.

The guy only had half a face left but it was enough for him to be identified.

'Harvey Houston?' asked Shirley, looking for confirmation.

'Yes, sir.' Sandy Murray was the first to answer. 'I've run into him a few times over the years.'

Shirley made a small nod of his head, looking angrier than Winter had ever seen him.

'And the rest of them? Get them all fucking photographed, Winter. Names, people. Now.'

Winter focused on Houston's shattered skull and photographed as he heard names being confirmed by Murray, Boyle, Williamson and Monteith, the last two having joined the party along with another two forensics that he recognized: Paddy Swanson and Lucy Stark. They would have their hands full.

The bloody mess was Jake Arnold, known as Beavis, bleed-to-death guy was Ginger George Faichney, and the gutted-stomach victim was Benjo Honeyman. All as expected and nothing that anyone could have seen coming. Four missing men and one missing cop, all snug as bugs in the same rug. Winter's stomach was rumbling in a way that meant he was either very hungry or about to puke.

He moved from one man to the next as if he were in a dream, sidestepping the forensics as everyone tried to do their job at the same time. No sooner had he finished photographing every angle of Arnold's battered-in nose or Faichney's sliced veins than Swanson was daubing them with Luminol and waiting to see what developed. Winter snapped at Honeyman's stabbed chest, zooming in on the signature rip of the knife, standing back to be replaced immediately by Baxter dusting the chair for prints that they both knew wouldn't be there. None of it was futile but none of it was going to help.

Winter heard the shout from somewhere over his left shoulder.

'Sir!'

It was Murray, his face ashen. Everyone followed his arm to the far corner of the warehouse and saw the homemade poster on the wall. Letters and cuttings from newspapers. From a distance all that could be made out was a headline, *THE DARK ANGEL.*

As they all moved closer en masse they could make out the two words that were pasted below.

Dirty

Cops

They were drinking in those words, swallowing hard on their implications, when another voice burst through the door. Narey. She stopped in her tracks for an age when she saw the four bodies, her jaw dropping before she recovered her composure and went up to Shirley.

She spoke to him quietly, out of earshot. Winter watched Shirley's face wrinkle and his brow furrow. His eyes were blazing but he gave her a curt nod, before placing a reassuring arm on hers. He stood for a moment, weighing up his options before coming to a decision.

'Constables,' he barked, looking at Boyle and Murray. 'Will you excuse us, please? Mr Baxter, your people, too.'

None of them looked too pleased but they had no choice. They left the warehouse and closed the door behind them.

Shirley looked at Winter, narrowing his eyes.

'I think you should hear this too,' he said, hesitating before going on. 'The calls that DI Addison and DS McConachie received a few minutes ago have been identified from their phones.

McConachie's was from George Faichney. Addison's was from Mark Sturrock, the mule from Harthill Services.'

Winter wanted to throw up the emptiness in his stomach or to deck Shirley. The two words on the poster screamed at him, mocking him.

Dirty. Cops.

CHAPTER 33

They were sitting on the bedroom floor in Highburgh Road, holding each other tight, head on the other's shoulder. Him looking north and her south, neither seeing anything. They'd been like that for an age without saying a word. His guess was that they were silent because there was just too much to say.

It was only nine at night but it felt like past midnight. From the early morning dash to the industrial estate to the final visit to intensive care at the Royal, it had been a long, long day. Addison was alive but only just. They said the next twenty-four hours would be critical.

They'd both wanted to wait but Shirley was having none of it. He understood why they wanted to be there but his job was to catch the shooter and to do that he needed his team rested. There was also the small matter of whether Addison was shot because he was involved with the dealers. Shirley was insistent: they were to go home and get some sleep whether they liked it or not.

Sleep. That was a joke.

They'd climbed the stairs to the flat and Rachel had the fridge door open before the front door had shut. She cracked open a bottle of wine, picked up two glasses and poured. Winter didn't even have the energy to make his usual moan about white wine.

She'd kicked off her shoes then fell out of her trousers and her blouse, causing him a pang of guilt at watching her body when he should have been thinking about Addison. Then he remembered that Addison would have been exactly the same, if not worse, and he'd laughed out loud before he knew it, strangling it once he caught the thought. Rachel threw him a look of surprise but didn't bother asking. Instead she pulled on pyjama trousers and a T-shirt and padded into the bedroom.

Winter followed her through, losing his own shoes and got down on the floor where Rachel knocked her glass of wine back in one gulp. She immediately poured a second but left it untouched. She put her arms out without looking at him and he fell into them. That's the way they were nearly an hour later. It was Rachel who finally broke the spell.

'Can I ask you something?'

'Of course you can,' he replied.

'You probably won't like it.'

He tensed.

'Go on.'

How much worse can things get, he thought?

'When Addy was shot, why did you get up and take his photograph? Why did you do that when the Temple told everyone to stay down? You knew that maniac was probably still out there.'

'It was my job.'

'Bollocks, Tony. I need you to do better than that. Why did you get up?'

'It *was* my job. It was the only small thing I could do to help catch whoever did that. Make sure the evidence was there when it goes to court.'

He could feel her head shaking against his.

'Okay, I buy part of that. But that doesn't explain it all. You could have been killed. What was so important that you risked that?'

He hesitated, partly because he wasn't sure what the answer was. Or maybe because he did.

'Is that all I'm getting? Silence? An answer would be nice.'

'I don't know.'

Her voice softened.

'I think you *do* know, Tony. Trust me.'

'I . . . I just got up and did it. I didn't feel like I had much choice. My legs were there before I knew it.'

'Okay. But that's still only half an answer. Why did you want to do it?'

He shrugged. She swore.

'Fuck, Tony, for as long as I've known you, you've never been more alive than when you're photographing death. We both know that's the truth. I used to accept that it was your thing but now, today, it's freaking me out. When you risk your life to photograph someone else's death then I can't accept that. I'm just not sure I can deal with that at all. I'm not sure I can be part of that.'

He was glad he couldn't see her face. He didn't want to see the look on it. He knew ducking it again wasn't going to work but he tried.

'Look, Rach, I don't know. Okay?'

'Not okay. Let me keep it simple. You tell me why the fuck you did that or we're done. I can't handle it if I can't understand it.'

'You know I'm not good with ultimatums.'

'Tony, I'm beginning to wonder what you *are* good with.'

'Cheers.'

'Sorry. I didn't mean that. But I need to know. And I need to know now.'

He closed his eyes and screamed silently into her shoulder.

'Tell me.'

He breathed hard.

'Okay, I'll tell you best as I understand it myself.'

'Okay.'

'When I see something like that, when I get to photograph something like . . . you're right, it does make me feel alive. It's like I'm seeing the other side . . . like I'm getting a glimpse into . . . into death. It's as if there's a chance to make sense of the whole thing, you know?'

'Maybe,' she said. 'Go on.'

'Life doesn't make much sense on its own so maybe . . . I don't know. Maybe if you can understand death then you can get a handle on the rest of it. Maybe if you can get your head round it then it won't seem so bad and there'd be nothing to be scared of. Maybe death's what it's all about.'

'Christ, Tony. Why would you think that?'

'Because death . . .'

He hesitated.

'Death what?' she demanded.

'You want to hear this or not?' he shouted at her. 'It's because of my mum and dad, alright? It's because my parents were murdered. You fucking happy now?'

She gasped, trying to snap her head away and round so she could see him but he held her tight. He wasn't ready to be seen. She fought it but he was too strong and she finally let her head rest on his shoulder again.

'You told me that your parents died in a car crash.'

'I lied.'

More silence. More thinking.

'So what happened? Who killed them?'

He screwed his eyes shut, wishing the moment away.

'They were killed. That's all that matters. It might be hard for a cop to understand but sometimes the dead are more important than the killer.'

She thought about that for a moment and he felt her nodding.

'I do understand that. But tell me what happened, Tony. Please? Who killed your mum and dad?'

He took a deep breath. 'I did.'

He could feel her tense, frightened. Not of him but of what he might say. It wasn't going to stop her asking though.

'Tell me.'

Winter bit on his bottom lip, pinching the skin hard with his teeth, trying to make it bleed, trying to bring pain. He deserved pain, he craved it.

'I killed my mother. They say it wasn't my fault but I know differently.' He released a small, bitter laugh. 'Cars don't kill people, people kill people.'

'She died in a road accident?' Rachel asked.

'No, you've not been listening? She was *killed* in a road accident. By me.'

Rachel was desperately trying to keep the shock from her face.

'Okay, Tony. It's okay. Go on.'

His eyes were closed.

'She was just twenty-three. Really pretty. My dad was a school teacher, history. She was going to train to be a teacher too. Till I got in the way.'

Rachel tried to interrupt but he didn't let her.

'We lived in Arlington Street. You know, just off Woodlands Road?'

She nodded.

'I was five and was always dashing off to play in the street as soon as she turned her back. She was always on at me not to do it. Always. If she'd warned me once about running across that road when cars were coming then she'd done it a thousand times. I never listened though.

'This particular day, she was washing dishes and I sneaked out of the house with a football and was booting it from one pavement to the other. Cars were always coming round the corner fast at the Arlington Bar but I always thought I had time to get out the way. This time though . . .' He choked back the memory. 'This time I was too busy watching the ball and by the time I heard the engine, this car was nearly on top of me. The driver hadn't seen me till he was just a few feet away. All I could see was the front of the car, it filled the world.

'The next thing I was flying through the air away from it. I didn't know what had happened but I heard the crunch, this terrible, terrible noise . . . Then she landed on top of me.'

'Your mother?'

'Yes. She'd seen me playing outside and had come out to call me back in. When she saw the car about to hit me, she threw herself into its path and pushed me out of the way. She was hit full on the head. I was lying there, her blood dripping onto my face. She died on top of me. I could see the guy get out of the car with his mouth hanging open and neighbours running out, screaming their heads off but I couldn't hear a thing. All I could feel was her blood hot on my face.'

'You were in shock,' Rachel soothed. 'Tony . . .'

'The neighbours eased her off me to see if I was alright. Of course I was. Barely a scratch. I had nothing more than a grazed knee. She . . . she . . .'

'Tony, that wasn't your–'

'Oh it was. It was my fault. She'd told me a thousand times but I still did it. If I'd just done what she'd said then she'd have been alive. She didn't deserve that. I didn't deserve her.'

A single tear was running down his cheek.

Rachel hugged him fiercely.

'What about your dad?' she asked eventually, almost fearful of the answer.

'He managed to drink himself to death in under four years. Good going, even by Glasgow standards. Can't blame him. Bad enough that he had lost his wife but he also had to put up with the miserable wee bastard that had killed her. I was greetin' my eyes out every moment I was awake, which was most of the day and the night. He just couldn't bear to look at me. Must have driven him crazy. Certainly drove him to drink.

'He got sacked two years after she went. My uncle Danny says the school was sympathetic but just couldn't put up with it. He started turning up drunk in class and took a swing at some kid who was winding him up. That was it finished. All it meant was that he had more time to drink.'

'And who was looking after you?'

'Him, until it got too bad. Till the whisky and the sight of me had him in the boozer full-time. My auntie and uncle, Janette and Danny, took me off him. Think he was glad. All I ever did was remind him of what he'd lost. His liver packed in. Alcohol hepatitis leading to chronic liver failure. Dead at twenty-nine.'

'Jesus Christ, Tony. I'm so sorry. Why on earth didn't you tell me?'

'Not the easiest thing to tell. Not when it's your fault.'

'It wasn't!' she insisted, tears soaking his shoulder.

'Don't think I haven't tried telling myself that. Don't think psychiatrists and psychologists haven't told me. But it doesn't change a thing. It was my fault. Killed my mum. Drove my old man to death. Only memories I have of him, he's unshaven and rough as fuck, shouting at me to shut up. Just made me cry all the more.'

'So you stayed with your aunt and uncle?'

Winter nodded.

'Until I was seventeen and got out of there as soon as I could. Went straight to university from fifth year. Janette and Danny were great but I probably drove them daft too. I wasn't the easiest kid to bring up.'

'That's not really surprising, Tony.'

'Maybe not. But I must have been a pain in the arse. I remember I was in primary three or four and a big black crow was found lying dead in the playground. I think some wee bastard had hit it with a stone. Everyone had gone to look at it, poking it with a stick and turning it over. Everyone else got bored soon enough but I couldn't stop staring at it. Looking at those empty black eyes and wondering what they could see. Wondering about its soul and its ghost. Wondering where the life inside it had gone to.

'Guess it made me a weird wee boy. It was just that though, nothing else. Every other way I was the same as the rest of them but I had this wonder about death and it sorted of infected other stuff, made me miserable and lonely.'

'But that's not the guy I met,' she said.

'University cured me.' He laughed a bit. 'I discovered beer and girls and snooker and that life could still be fun. I drank and shagged my way through uni and things looked brighter. I didn't learn as much about algorithms as I should have done but I learned how to put a face on things. How to stop being the morbid kid.'

'But it's still there?' she asked. It was as much a statement as a question. 'It's why you got into this job and why you want to photograph death?'

'Yep. Still poking the crow with a stick in the playground. Still looking for answers. Trying to make sense of it. Like with Addy. Makes no sense at all.'

She couldn't help herself.

'Okay, I'm going to tell you something I probably shouldn't. And I'm telling you because this isn't down to you. Not what happened to your mum and dad and not what's happened to Addison. When we were at Harthill Services, Addy said he didn't know or recognize Mark Sturrock.'

Winter didn't want to hear this.

'And he got phoned by him. So what?'

'Tony, we know he got phoned by him because the name showed up on his phone. Sturrock's name and number are in Addison's phone.'

It hit him like a hammer.

'Okay, so what does that prove and what are you going to do?'

The blue-and-white police tape went up between them again.

'Just leave it to us. Let us do our job.'

Winter nodded and let her hold him but he didn't mean it. He didn't mean it at all. For a start, she'd been wrong. What happened to Addison was down to him. Unlike with his mother though, it wasn't what he did but what he didn't do. Now it was down to him to put it right.

Rachel was thinking hard, trying to decide if one more thing was better out in the open. She resolved that it was.

'Tony, there's something else.'

He heard the waver in her voice.

'What is it?'

'I wasn't going to ... but I can't ... I have to tell you. Those phones that the shooter took off Strathie and Sturrock ...'

'Go on.'

She was struggling.

'As I said, Addy and Jan McConachie, it seems certain their names were listed as phone contacts.'

'Means nothing.'

'Tony, it means everything. Listen to me. It was why they got shot. It's obvious. And ...'

She left a chasm of silence as she tried to force out the words that were stuck in her throat. She finally managed it.

'Tony, I'm scared.'

'You're scaring me too,' he told her. 'What is it? Tell me.'

Rachel put the palms of her hands to her forehead and clamped her eyes shut.

'A couple of years back I caught Mark Sturrock with gear in his car. It was small beer stuff compared with what we knew he usually ran. It wouldn't have been enough to put him away for serious time but it would have blotted his copybook big time with Malky Quinn. It gave me leverage with him.'

Winter said nothing but could feel the fear growing inside him as he watched her speak behind hands that trembled ever so slightly.

'So I suggested to him that I could make the possession go away if he was prepared to co-operate. He was. He gave me enough information that I was able to bust a bigger deal. Terry Gilmartin had a lorry-load of skunk coming up from Manchester and thanks to Sturrock we intercepted it. So much for honour among thieves.'

Winter's heart was thumping in his chest and his mouth was dry. He didn't want to hear any more of this.

'Jesus Christ, Rach. Why didn't you tell me this after Harthill?' he asked. 'Have you told Shirley about it?'

She shook her head and continued.

'So after that, Sturrock and I had a quiet little arrangement. He knew that if I could nail him for something major then I would. No question. But if it was small stuff then I'd let it slide as long as he would help the police with their enquiries.'

Winter asked the question that he didn't want to hear the answer to.

'So you and Sturrock . . . kept in touch?'

'Yes.'

'How?'

Rachel peeled her hands away from her face and returned his stare.

'It wasn't often. A couple of times a year, if that.'

'How did you contact him?' Winter persisted.

She looked back at him.

'By phone?' he asked her.

Rachel's gaze fell to the floor before she answered.

'Yes.'

Winter pulled her head up so he could look her in the eyes again.

'So your mobile number could be in his phone?' She shook her head slowly.

'No, not *could be.* Is. My number is definitely in his phone. I'm scared, Tony, I'm very scared.'

CHAPTER 34

Sleep overtook them eventually but not before Winter demanded that Rachel go to Shirley with everything she knew and that she stayed off the street and out of harm's way. Rachel was having none of it though.

She told him that if she went to Shirley then she wouldn't get within a mile of the Dark Angel case and might be out of a job entirely. She'd never registered Sturrock as an informer and worse than that, had never told Alex Shirley about it after Sturrock was shot. She kept it to herself, thinking it didn't matter because she was clean and there was no point in dragging it up. Now it was too late.

Anyway, she wasn't one for hiding away. Even if the maniac that was running around shooting people found that her number was in that phone and knew who she was, she'd take her chances.

They woke early, both bad-tempered and fearing the worst about the day ahead, following one another into the shower without a word being said. The television and the radio were replaying the previous day's horrors and that was more than enough without either of them adding to it.

The morning was dreich; grey, wet and miserable to match their moods, as they went their separate ways towards Pitt Street and Stewart Street, both fuelled by a growing sense of urgency and apprehension and with thoughts of Addison and Sturrock's phone writ large in their minds.

Winter was in the office before eight, meaning he had the place to himself for the best part of an hour and he could get on with what he'd decided to do undisturbed. He'd stopped to pick up a paper and threw it on his desk, seeing BLOODBATH in large red letters across the front of the *Sun*. They didn't have any photographs from the scene at Dixon Blazes but they'd used their gun-site logo half the size of the page. There were only a few paragraphs of the bare facts and a whole lot of conjecture.

Thank God they didn't have a photograph of Addison, he thought. A quick scan of the story showed there was no mention of any accusation against him, instead the keywords were 'near fatal', 'severe head wounds' and 'critical but stable'. He couldn't get the image of Addison out of his head and it didn't help that he was going to have to file the photographs. That was part of his reason for getting in so early, to get the admin done and get out of the office before some fucker began noising him up with questions he didn't want to answer.

But he also wanted in and out as quickly as he could because he had other things to do. As soon as he got in, he had left a message on Cat Fitzpatrick's answerphone, asking if he could stop by and see her as soon as possible. He wasn't sure what she'd think of the message but it didn't really matter, not compared to the rest of it. If it became complicated then it was too bad.

The full-length shot he'd taken of Addison was on screen in front of him, uploaded from his camera. It was surreal. His best friend stretched out, cut down, dark suit and crimson collar. He struggled to match the person lying there with the one that he went to the pub with, went to the match with, the one that called him 'wee man' and chased anything in a skirt. He could only see someone on the cusp of eternity, one foot in the grave and the other limping badly. It wasn't Addison, it was too lacking in life for it to be him.

He cropped a section of his face, trying to make it look more like him, to make the connection with the Addison he recognized but still all he got was skull and blood and bone and concrete and shards of being. None of that added up to him. It was a subject, a still life.

Jan McConachie was different. She'd already crossed the threshold and the bullet that had taken off the top of her head left no room for argument. Flat on her back with arms and legs spread wide, she pleaded for a redemption that would never come. Her lights had gone out so fast that it didn't register on her face. It seemed her life had been stolen from under her nose and she simply hadn't noticed. The only evidence of it was a vaguely stupid, open-mouthed look as if she didn't know the answer to the final question. She was looking to the skies for the answer but Winter doubted she would find it there.

The phone made him jump, a testament to his state of mind.

'Yes?'

'Hi Tony. How are you?'

'I've had better days, Cat. I need a favour. Can I come to your office?'

'Sure. I'll be in all morning. Whenever suits you.'

'I'll be there in ten minutes.'

Cat Fitzpatrick looked up from a microscope as he pushed the door open, the hint of a sympathetic smile on her face, then turned her eyes back to whatever was under the glass. It gave Winter a few seconds to look at her without her noticing. The weak sunlight that struggled through the window still managed to pick out highlights in her flame-red hair which was tied back severely. Even in a lumpen, white lab coat she looked stunning. The second-best looking woman in Strathclyde polis, he told himself.

'Sit down,' she said, without looking up. 'Two minutes.'

Winter cast his eye around the lab, never failing to be amazed at how there always seemed to be a new piece of kit every time you visited. These guys had to go back to school every five minutes or technology would outstrip them. Dinosaurs like Baxter were continually in danger of being left behind as they clung on to what they knew.

Cat pushed the scope aside and looked up, studying him.

'How is Addison?'

He sighed and closed his eyes.

'Not good. He lost a lot of blood and the bullet passed through his skull. They think it missed his brain, though, and there's some hope. They are giving him a thirty per cent chance of survival.'

Cat looked at him, another question waiting to be asked, but when he didn't offer an inroad she let it go.

'What can I do for you?'

'It's awkward. But it's important.'

'Go on.'

'There was a drug dealer killed last week at Blochairn. A guy named Sammy Ross.'

She shrugged.

'The name doesn't ring any bells.'

'No reason it should. He was found stabbed Saturday night, Sunday morning. Nothing out of the ordinary.'

'So?'

'So I think that there might have been more to it than there first appeared. I might be completely wrong but I'm guessing that something might have been missed in the post-mortem.'

Her mouth opened then closed again.

'That's . . . I'm not sure if I'm more astonished by the possibility of something being missed or that you have some reason for thinking it. What's this all about?'

'I can't say, Cat.'

'Then I don't see how I can help you.'

'Look, it's important. If I'm wrong and there was nothing missed then there will have been no harm in checking, right?'

She weighed it up.

'Maybe. Has this got something to do with Addison being shot?'

'It might have. I can't be sure. But I need to find out. I need your help, Cat.'

'If you need help then what the hell are you standing here for? You should be going to Alex Shirley with this, not me. You know that.'

'I can't, not yet anyway. Addy is lying there half dead and I need to do this for him. There are things I need to sort out for him.'

The look on her face told him she'd heard some of the shit that had leaked from the warehouse in Rutherglen. She sighed.

'I must be off my head . . .'

He smiled at her.

'Don't get carried away,' she scolded him. 'I'm only going to check his file and see if this is possible. You are going to have to tell me at some point what's going on here. When was this Ross killed?'

'The body was found last Sunday morning, the eleventh.'

She kick-started her chair and wheeled across a few feet until she was in front of her computer screen, shaking her head as if she couldn't believe what she was doing. Her fingers flashed across the keyboard and within seconds she had what she was looking for.

'Samuel Kenneth Ross. Cause of death blah blah, puncture of major organs caused by a knife or similar sharp-bladed instrument. Pronounced dead at the scene by Campbell Baxter. Time of death estimated at 3.15 a.m. The body's still in the morgue. Okay, what else am I looking for and how do you suggest I find it?'

He grinned at her apologetically.

'I don't know. I think there might be something else there

beyond the stabbing, something that no one knew to look for. Or bothered to. And I was kind of hoping that you could have a second autopsy done.'

'You have got to be kidding me. On the basis of what? Some half-arsed guess that you won't explain to me?'

'Yes. And I was also kind of hoping that no one would need to know about it.'

She gave a derisory laugh.

'You are crazy. Give me one good reason. And it better be good.'

It was his last gambit. The card he was hoping not to play.

'The only reason I've got is what we had together.'

She rolled her eyes.

'Christ, I was wondering if you would try that one. What we had? What we had was one drunken night of admittedly fabulous sex. And you think that entitles you to a voucher for a free post-mortem at a time of your choosing? Not to mention a career-threatening cover-up?'

'You did say it was fabulous ...'

She smiled ruefully.

'Arsehole. Anyway, I exaggerated for the sake of your ego. It was merely very good. Tony, what we had was sex—'

'Fabulous sex,' he interrupted.

'Sex followed by awkwardness and tension and sly looks and no explanation of why you never came back for more. Or why you never thought to ask me out. That's what we had. And you think that's good enough to get help like this?'

'I'm hoping it is. It's all I've got.'

'Arsehole,' she repeated. 'Okay, okay. There is someone who could be persuaded to have a look. There's a junior pathologist in the morgue who ... well, let's just say he likes me. A lot.'

'Okay.'

She smiled wickedly at his discomfort.

'I'm sure he will help me out if I ask very nicely.'

She was enjoying watching him squirm.

'I'll call him.'

'Thanks, Cat. And I'm sorry about . . .'

'Out. I'm not speaking to him when you're here. I'll call you back in when I'm done.'

A few minutes later, Winter was back in the lab, like a naughty schoolboy called before the headmistress. 'Okay, he's going to do it. I didn't quite promise him anything but he seems to have got the idea that he is in with a chance. If you know what I mean.'

Winter knew exactly what she meant and a steel toe-capped boot of inappropriate jealousy kicked him in the nuts.

'You'll call me if he finds anything, Cat?'

'If he does, I'll call. It will probably be tomorrow before I can get back to you. Okay, go. Run along now. I've got things to do.'

She turned her head back to the microscope and, duly dismissed, he turned for the door.

'Tony,' she called at his back.

'Yes?'

'I really hope Addison is okay. I don't know what's going on but I've heard the rumours. Whatever the truth is, I hope he makes it.'

He nodded at her silently and left.

CHAPTER 35

Tuesday 20 September

Narey had half expected, half hoped, for the phone call that she received that morning when she got into the office but it brought as many problems as it did promises. With Addison shot and Jan McConachie dead, the Nightjar team were two officers down and Alex Shirley needed her back on the team.

She couldn't help but think it was where she should have been in the first place. It was a thought that scared her; she'd seen with her own eyes what had happened to the officers that were on it. More than that, whoever did it, whoever it was that had the phones that once belonged to Sturrock and the others, had her number too. Had her name. She shouldn't have told Winter about it the night before, it was information he didn't need and now he was going to plague her to keep out of sight. Fat chance of that.

For a start, the pressure was on to get the McCullough killing wrapped up as quickly as possible. The message was clear: it was way down the priority list compared to Dark Angel and if necessary it would be put aside until there was time to deal with it. Narey wasn't for having that. As desperate as she was to be part of the sniper investigation, with her own neck on the line, she hated to let this one go completely and leave the McCulloughs without an answer.

She had to get back to the basics. It was all she knew to do when she ran into a brick wall and that was what was staring her in the face this time. Oonagh's parents hadn't been much help and Pamela had told her all that she knew or was willing to tell. All that was left was to go back to the slog of going through the CCTV tapes from the night that Oonagh was killed. Addison had already been through them but that was no excuse not to try again. It was the only bit of available footage they had and there just might be something he'd missed.

She felt a surge of guilt for doubting Addison when he was at death's door but the truth was he was probably thinking about nothing other than Quinn and Caldwell when he watched the tapes so missing something was a real possibility. Christ, she hoped he pulled through. The tapes made for slow, depressing viewing. There was just her and the CCTV operator, a WPC named Imelda Couper, and neither had much stomach for frame-by-frame examination of the life forms that crawled through the red-light area. What made it bearable was the thought that they might just be able to put one of these pervs away.

The two of them watched every frame for half an hour before the estimated time of Oonagh's killing and every frame for half an hour after it. Nothing but half-hidden sleaze bags and passing cars. Nothing that held out any real hope of finding a murderer among the punters. Still it was all Narey had, so she'd keep going, jotting down meagre notes and hoping for the best.

When they had exhausted the two half-hour windows, Narey had the WPC go back till an hour before Oonagh was killed, with the intention of doing the same for an hour after it. It meant they would have been sitting there three hours in all by the time she was done. Narey's bottom was already starting to go numb and she could see that Couper's eyes had glazed with boredom.

They were half an hour into the second sitting, back to the point where they'd started and the temptation was to skip that rather than going over it yet again but no, she'd make herself sit through it. She owed it to Oonagh's mother and to prove to the father that some of them *did* actually care.

Twenty minutes before the estimated time of death and something, someone she hadn't quite noticed before.

'Hang on, Imelda. Back up a bit,' she said quietly, trying not to get ahead of herself.

'What is it, Sarge?' said the WPC. 'You see something?'

'Maybe . . . back a bit further.'

She saw the shadowy figure that had caught her eye.

'There. Freeze it.'

'The guy in the dark jacket?'

'Yes, that's him.'

Narey didn't speak for a bit, but studied the man on the screen. About five foot five, lanky fair hair and upturned collar. The glint from a pair of steel spectacles causing an orange tinge under the streetlight. Was it him? She couldn't be sure but it looked promising.

'Do you know him, Sarge?'

'Yeah. I think I might, Imelda. Can you close in on him?'

The operator picked out an area around the man and a larger image appeared in front of them.

Narey laughed out loud.

'Rubber Johnny,' she sniggered. 'And here was me thinking he had retired and got out of the pervert business.'

Couper turned and looked at her in confusion.

'His name is John Petrie,' explained Narey. 'A long-time customer of Her Majesty's Constabulary. God knows how many times he's been collared over the years. He's a freak-out creep of the first order. Hadn't heard of him in ages. Thought he had lost the taste for it.'

'The taste for what?' the WPC asked warily.

'He likes to frequent the work space of the ladies of the night,' Narey told her. 'Rarely approaches them, never lays a finger on them, but likes to spy on them when they get down to business. Sometimes he gets charged, sometimes he just gets chased and that's the end of it.'

'What a weirdo,' remarked Couper.

'It gets worse,' Narey said. 'Rubber Johnny got his nickname for one very good reason. He watches the girls getting it on with the punters, waits for them to leave then ducks back down the alley, picks up the discarded condoms and makes off with them.'

'That is fu– That is gross, Sarge.'

'You were right the first time, Imelda,' Narey agreed. 'He's the grossest of the gross. Takes the used rubbers home with him and keeps them as some kind of freaky souvenir. You have to wonder what he does with them.'

'I'd rather not know,' the WPC replied.

'Ah well, that's where we differ. Because I really do want to know what he does with them.'

Narey swung over to the computer that sat behind her and punched Petrie's name into the PNC database where she found his current address. She pulled her mobile from her pocket and found Corrieri's number in her address book.

'Hi, Julia. Where are you? Okay, good. Meet me in Summerston, say twenty minutes. Islay Street. I don't want to count any chickens because this could be nothing but on the other hand it might be just what we need.'

Corrieri asked what the lead was but Narey wasn't for telling. Partly because she wanted to get straight in her own head how to play this. And partly because she was quietly pleased with herself and wanted to savour it.

Rubber Johnny lived in a block of flats deep in Summerston. It was a first-floor hellhole with broken bikes and bags of rubbish on the landing and junkies for neighbours.

There were people hanging out of windows shouting to those sitting smoking on the front steps, kids running around half naked and everyone yelling when speaking would have done.

Narey briefed Corrieri quickly on the street outside Petrie's flat, enjoying the look of confusion on Corrieri's face when she mentioned Petrie's name.

'The condom guy?' she'd asked doubtfully.

'The one and only,' Narey replied.

'You think he's our man?'

'I doubt it. He's a watcher, not a lover or a fighter. He's never so much as touched one of them so it doesn't seem likely he'd start bumping them off now. No, I'm interested in Rubber Johnny for his collection rather than for the murders.'

'Fucking gross.'

'Funny, that's exactly what Imelda Couper said. Come on, let's go in.'

They climbed the steps to the first floor where Narey knocked sharply three times on Johnny's door. They soon heard soft footsteps coming towards the door and the shadow under it gave away that someone was standing there. The footsteps didn't retreat but the door didn't open.

'Open the door, Johnny,' Narey said gently.

There was a pause before the sound of a chain being pulled back and the snib turning on the door. It swung back and revealed a sandy-haired man in his early fifties with steel specs and a few days' growth on his face. On someone other than Rubber Johnny it might have qualified as designer stubble. He was wearing a dark, baggy T-shirt and there were slippers sticking out from beneath his faded jeans. It was obvious that he recognized Narey but was weighing up Corrieri with suspicion.

He didn't say anything, just turned and walked back into the flat with the two cops following behind him. Johnny knew the routine and couldn't be bothered arguing the toss on his doorstep.

With a wave of his arm he directed them to a settee before falling back into a well-worn armchair.

'Well? What do you want?'

'Nice to see you too, Johnny,' said Narey.

'I remember you,' he muttered, looking at her. 'Detective Sergeant.'

'DS Narey,' she reminded him. 'This is DC Corrieri.'

Petrie managed a barely perceptible nod in Corrieri's direction.

'What do you want?' Johnny repeated. 'I've not done anything wrong,' he continued. 'Done nothing. We've been through this a hundred times and the judge said that as long as I didn't go near the girls then there was "no state of fear and alarm". Anyway the samples were in a public place.'

Narey knew she and Corrieri were thinking the same thing, smiling inwardly at his legalese and self-delusion and their skin crawling at the thought of his little hobby. Whatever some twat of a judge said, Rubber Johnny was a gold-plated weirdo.

'Nobody's arguing about that, John,' soothed Narey. 'We're not here to do you for that. Truth is we could do with some help. We'd just like to take a look at one or two of your samples.'

'No, no. No way. No. Judge says there's nothing wrong with it. Nothing you can do. No.'

He was getting hysterical.

'Calm down, John. It's okay. We don't want to take them all away,' said Narey. 'There's one we think can help us with a case and I can take it if it is evidence.'

'For fuck's sake. Fuck's sake. Show me a warrant. I want to see a warrant. No, no, no way.'

'Johnny, you know the routine by now,' said Narey, her voice firmer. 'I can go away and come back with the paperwork and a really bad temper or you can just help us out seeing as we're already here.'

Petrie looked doubtful. He looked between the two of them trying to suss out if there was another agenda than the one they were laying before him.

'You're not in any bother, John. We're just looking for your help,' Corrieri chipped in. 'Someone has been messing with the girls,' she continued. 'Some not very nice stuff. We want your help to catch the guy.'

'And I'm not in trouble?'

'Absolutely none,' Narey confirmed.

Rubber Johnny stood up, scratched his head and sat back down. He got to his feet again and nodded towards the door off the living room and for them to follow him.

Petrie held the door open behind him and the three of them traipsed into what turned out to be the kitchen of the tiny flat.

He paced across the worn lino to where an upright fridge freezer sat in the corner, stopping with a hand on the fridge door before he turned and stared at Narey again.

'And if I help you, you'll only look at the sample you need and leave me the rest?'

'Just the one that we need, John. No interest in anything else.'

The man nodded, satisfied.

He swung back the upper door to the fridge and proudly stepped back to let them see what was inside. It was unbelievable.

There were four white, evenly spaced, moulded plastic shelves. On the top one sat two supermarket ready meals, a jar of jam and a tub of margarine. The other three were neatly packed with sealed, transparent sandwich bags, each labelled and ordered, maybe a dozen bags to a shelf. Each containing what was very obviously a used condom.

There seemed an obsessive precision about the way they were

laid out, all overlapping each other by the same amount. The numbered sticky labels were placed in exactly the same position in the top left-hand corner of each bag and the painstakingly neat, handwritten numbers were colour-coded.

In the fridge door were two cans of lager and the remains of a pint of milk.

Narey suppressed a laugh at the look on Corrieri's face. She looked like she would have taken a pair of rusty shears to Johnny's bollocks there and then before locking him up and throwing away the key without handing him a sticking plaster.

She was now at the fridge door and was beginning to reach out towards the sandwich bags.

'No, no, no. No! Don't touch them,' shrieked Johnny, pushing himself between Corrieri and the fridge. 'They're in order. Don't mess them.'

Corrieri couldn't help but snigger and that got her a black look from both of them. Narey tried to make up for it.

'Johnny is very particular about order. Aren't you, John?'

'It's important,' Petrie said. 'Need to be in the right place.'

'Well how are we supposed to . . .'

Narey cut off Corrieri's objection by holding a photograph up in front of Rubber Johnny's face. It was the photograph of Oonagh McCullough that they'd got from her parents.

'You know her, Johnny?'

He looked confused for a few moments but then he nodded.

'It's an old picture. But that's Melanie.'

'Okay. And would you have any . . . samples in there of her?' asked Narey.

Petrie nodded again. Didn't have to give the matter any thought. 'Three,' he said.

'When was the most recent, John?'

Johnny looked briefly to the ceiling as if seeking confirmation of the day that flashed up in his mind.

'Sunday.'

'You sure?' asked Corrieri.

Petrie glared at her.

'Of course I'm sure. Got a very good memory. Anyway, it's in my log.'

'Can you get the log for us, John? It's important.'

Rubber Johnny nodded at them and opened a chipped, wooden kitchen drawer and carefully produced a ring-bound black folder which he placed open on the kitchen table.

They saw columns of meticulously tidy script, all in the same hand as the numbers on the condom-filled sandwich bags, each column under the headings of sample number, date, time, place, girl and customer.

Petrie ran his index finger down a column and stopped with a point. 'Melanie.'

They ran their eyes across the line he indicated.

Number 476. Sunday 11 September. 11.42 p.m. Wellington Lane. Melanie. Black anorak man.

'You didn't know the punter then, Johnny?'

'I'd seen him a couple of times but he wasn't really what you would call a regular.'

'Do you remember what he looked like?' Narey knew that he would but wanted to fluff Johnny's ego a bit.

'Course. He was tallish. Maybe about five foot ten with short hair. Wore a dark anorak and trousers. Medium build. It was very dark, though, and he kept out of the lights.'

'So tell us what you actually saw, John,' prompted Narey. 'Don't be shy about it.'

'Well, I didn't actually see them … at it. The guy was glancing over his shoulder all the time as they walked down the lane, like he was nervous. I just stayed round the corner and …' Petrie's voice trailed away.

'You listened to them, John?'

The man had the cheek to look a bit sheepish, dropping his eyes away from them.

'Aye.'

'So tell us what you heard,' Narey demanded.

'Well, they were talking a bit. Couldn't really hear what they were saying. Prices, I suppose. Then there was a bit of heavier breathing . . .'

Neither of the cops really wanted to hear this.

'And I guess he was getting going. Melanie was moaning a bit but I'm sure she was just putting it on for his sake.'

Petrie was excited now and Corrieri felt the urge to punch his head.

'I heard him gasp and then it sounded like Melanie was getting it good and hard because she got loud. Muffled like, but much louder.'

Narey and Corrieri swapped glances but said nothing.

'Loud like what, Johnny?'

'Like . . .' he cleared his throat and mimicked the prostitute. 'Ahhh, AHHHH, then higher pitched and louder, AHHHHH then hnnnuuuh, muffled. Then I thought he had finished off, cum real quick, like, 'cos it got quiet and that was sort of it.'

'Nothing more? Narey asked.

'Well, there was the noise of clothes again. Them sorting themselves. And a metal bang like one of them had hit the metal door that's there. Oh aye, and there was a noise like someone falling against one of those big bins they got out there. Thought maybe he was just drunk and had walked into it.'

'Johnny, did you hear Melanie say anything after you heard her get loud?' the DS asked.

'Naw. She never said a word. Why, what's happened?'

'And you didn't hear him speak either after they were finished?'

'No. What happened? Tell me. Did that guy do something to Melanie?'

'Thing is, John, Melanie's dead. We think the punter killed her.'

Petrie opened his mouth and closed it again. He was struggling to take it all in.

'So when ...' the penny had dropped. 'When I picked up the condom, Melanie was already dead? But where was she?'

'She was behind one of the bins.'

Petrie's face turned to fury.

'That fucking bastard. Bastard.'

'Did you see him leave, John? Did he go past you again?'

'No, he must have gone down Wellington Street towards Bothwell Street.'

'Did you see the guy's face, Johnny?'

'No.'

'But you'll testify in court about what you did see and what you heard?'

'Too fucking right I will. Too fucking right. I can't believe I ... and she was dead when I went in there. Fuck's sake. I'll testify, don't worry about that.'

'Okay, Johnny, here's what I want to do,' Narey said. 'I'm going to call forensics and get them over here to take the sample from your fridge. They won't move anything else while they're at it, I promise, and then take the bag down the lab to run some tests. Okay?'

'And can I get it back after that?' Petrie asked hopefully.

'No, John. Sorry. We need to keep it.'

'Aye, okay.'

Half an hour later Cat Fitzpatrick was standing in Rubber Johnny's kitchen, the look of utter professionalism on the forensic's face hiding the disgust that burned behind her eyes.

Fifteen minutes after she arrived, they were all making their way down the stairs and back to their cars.

'Sometimes,' Cat was saying, 'Sometimes ...'

'Is this going to be a sentence that involves the word men?' guessed Corrieri.

'I can see why you're a detective, Julia,' the forensic answered with a rueful smile. 'This has been a day of strange job requests. Just when you think it can't get any weirder, you get dragged away from *EastEnders* to pick up bags of days-old spunk from an autistic pervert's fridge.'

'Autistic?' Corrieri asked.

Cat shrugged.

'Petrie. Autistic. The precise labelling. The obsessively ordered bags. The extraordinary memory for detail. The near-hysteria when his perceived reality is challenged. Almost certainly autistic. I'm dropping this off at the lab then I'm going home to have a long shower.'

Narey wasn't sure why but she was annoyed by their chummy chat. She wanted to get this done and not piss about. She knew the condom was easily the best lead she was going to get.

'What are the chances of getting a positive DNA result out of that?' she asked Cat.

'Very good, I'd say. Disgusting as it is, the fridge is the best place he could have kept it from our point of view. I'd say the seed in this condom will be nearly as fresh as the day it was sown. If this is your killer then I'll have his DNA on a plate within a day or two.'

CHAPTER 36

Wednesday 22 September

Winter and Narey's mobiles went off within seconds of each other, although neither realized it. He was in Charing Cross and she in Highburgh Road. His was the call that they were both hoping it would be. Cat Fitzpatrick. Hers was the last call that she needed.

'Morning, Cat. You got news for me?' Winter asked as soon as he picked up the phone.

'What happened to, "How are you?". I'm fine, thanks for asking.'

"Sorry, I'm just a bit anxious to hear what you've got.'

'It's okay, I'm kidding. Although maybe you're right to be anxious.'

'What is it? Have you got the results?'

'What I have got is only one pair of hands. You and DS Narey need to learn some patience.' The reference to Rachel threw him completely.

'Ra– DS Narey?'

'Yes. She wants everything yesterday as well. I can't say what it's about but it's Weirdsville. Even stranger than what you wanted.'

Winter's mind was in a whirl, thoughts of mobile phones and

snipers scaring the shit out of him. Whatever it was, it probably made it all the more urgent that he got what he needed to know.

'So do you have the results?' he tried again.

'I don't have anything that I'm going to discuss over the phone. Meet me in an hour.'

'Your office?'

'No. Too many busybodies wandering in and out. Meet me in the car park. My car.'

An hour. Winter was going to drive himself crazy before an hour was up. He needed to know what Cat's pet pathologist had found. Too much was depending on it.

Within moments of ending his call to Cat, his mobile went again and, with a pang of guilt, he saw that it was Rachel.

'Hi. I phoned just now but you were engaged.'

'I was on to the hospital,' he lied.

'Any change?'

'No.'

'Okay. Listen, there's been another one.'

Rachel sounded more nervous than he'd ever heard her. It wasn't like her at all.

'Where? Who?'

'Jo-Jo Johnstone. He was shot at the front door to his detached villa in Bishopbriggs. We're sure it's our man but he's missed this time. Jo-Jo's got it in the neck and he's bleeding like a geyser but they think he'll live. There's more though. Terry Gilmartin's kid died in hospital this morning. The poor wee bugger never regained consciousness after the firebomb.'

'Christ.'

'It's out of control out there, Tony. Those animals are ripping each other apart. It's kicking off everywhere.'

'Okay, what's Johnstone's address? I'll be there as soon as I can.'

'No you won't.'

'What?'

'The Temple says you're off the case. I shouldn't even be phoning you.'

'You're kidding. What the hell has he done that for?'

'Tony, he knew how close to Addy you were. From his point of view it makes sense. I've got to say I understand why he's done it.'

'Thanks a fucking bunch.'

'I'm on your side, you know that. But he can't take any chances. If Addy was on the wrong side of this . . .'

'He wasn't.'

'You don't know that for a fact and neither do I. If he was wrong then you're going to be at arm's length till we know otherwise. Look, I've got to go. This is fucking terrible. Speak later.'

And she was gone, his reply cut off before it started. He gripped his mobile tight and resisted the temptation to hurl it to the ground. Mobiles, fucking mobiles. Addison had been shot because he'd answered his phone, McConachie too. He couldn't stand the thought of Rachel being out there and at risk.

Shit, he so wanted to be at the scene. And he knew that he wanted to be there for all the wrong reasons. It wasn't just about joining the dots that were Ross, McCabe, Strathie, Sturrock and McKendrick. It was also about his *sgriob* and the itch to see the Dark Angel's handiwork. He needed to see it but knew Shirley was going to let him nowhere near it.

He hustled into his clothes and made for Pitt Street as fast as he could. He couldn't afford to wait an hour on Cat. As it turned out, his office was empty, no doubt because of the Bishopbriggs shooting.

Winter hurriedly fished out the blown-up sectionals of the bruise marks on Sammy Ross and Stevie Strathie, showing the identical circular marks and scanned them into his PC. He cursed himself for not doing it before then, realizing he'd put it off but now couldn't do it quickly enough. The computer let him crop and scale until the two images were the same size and there was clearly no doubt that both had been caused by the same thing. It was like the men had been branded, although he was sure it was far from deliberate.

He popped the first image, Sammy's, into Photoshop and used the software to map out the rest of it. He filled in where the lines disappeared and made guesses where they were needed. He adjusted the tone, removed the purplish colours of the contusion and eventually had a complete image which he was able to separate from the original photograph.

It was almost certainly a ring, a signet ring of some sort. The symbols on it seemed to be a sword or a dagger, with two wavy lines on either side. An insignia? He desperately needed to find out.

A look at his watch told him it was nearly time to meet Cat and he closed the image down and hurried towards the car park. He quickly found her sporty green MX-5 and saw that she was already sitting behind the wheel, the look on her face suggesting she had news.

'You were right,' she started as soon as he'd climbed in beside her.

'I don't know how you knew and I'm not sure I want to know but you were right. There was something else with Ross. Something that was missed.'

His heart dropped through his stomach and he struggled to find an answer but thankfully she didn't wait for one.

'It might not be much but it *is* odd. We found pollen fibres in his nose and in his throat which we think come from something like a face cloth, the kind of thing that you might find in any bathroom. There was also some unexplained damage to his lungs which would have been easily overlooked if you hadn't been actively searching for it. It had routine stabbing written all over it though. My friendly man in the morgue was a bit embarrassed because he was the second hand on the original PM.'

'What sort of damage to his lungs?'

'It's difficult to say. I think *he*'d define it as "distress". Nothing major in itself but it would probably have caused him severe breathing difficulties in years to come if he'd lived that long.'

'And the cloth fibres?'

'Well, I have a theory but without more information from you, that's all it is. What's this all about, Tony?'

'I don't know yet. What's your take on it?'

'You know more than you're telling me, Winter, that's my take on it. The cause of death was definitely the stabbing. The blood coagulation was consistent with that and it would have stood out like a sore thumb otherwise. But tell me one thing, do you think someone was trying to get information out of our Mr Ross?'

Winter's heart missed a beat with excitement.

'Yes. That's exactly what I think.'

Cat tilted her head to one side and upwards as if thinking the answer she sought might be up there somewhere.

'Okay,' she said finally. 'Unlikely as it may be, it fits with something like waterboarding. You know what that is?'

'A torture technique? Something to do with Guantanamo Bay?'

'Not just a pretty face,' she smiled grimly at him. 'Yes, but not limited to Gitmo. It's a Special Forces favourite, used in operations from Baghdad to Beirut to God knows where. It's classed as a professional interrogation technique. You put a wet cloth or cellophane over the subject's face and pour water over it till they start telling you whatever you want to hear. It triggers the mammalian reflex and makes the subject believe they are actually drowning. The average that anyone lasts before they give in is fourteen seconds. The beauty of it is that it doesn't leave a mark. Not so much as a bruise.'

In Winter's mind, one dot just joined to another.

'So who would have the knowledge or the skill to do something like that?' I asked her.

'The CIA, MI5, MI6, SAS, Barlanark Boy Scouts. Take your pick.'

'The Navy?'

'Yes, maybe, but it would more likely be the Special Ops boys. SBS or US Navy Seals. What the hell is going on, Tony? What has this got to do with what happened to Addison, McConachie and the others?'

He knew that she deserved an answer but he didn't want to get her into trouble. He was likely to be in enough for both of them.

'How about I do us both a favour and don't tell you?' he answered. 'And you don't tell anyone else? Ross was just a two-bit drug dealer who got stabbed. No one cares.'

'Okay, that's obviously a lie. And you know I could lose my job over this. You're asking a lot.'

'I know. But I *am* asking. I need you to do this for me, Cat.'

She held his gaze for an age, trying to read his mind and make her own up before shaking her head slowly at him.

'Are you involved with someone, Tony?'

'What?'

It wasn't the response that he was expecting.

'It's a straightforward question. Yes or no would suffice.'

'Well . . .'

'That was neither yes nor no. Are you involved with someone? I'm not asking who it is.'

Thank God for that, he thought.

'Why do you ask?'

'Just answer the question, Winter. I'm serious.'

'Yes. Yes I am.'

'There, that wasn't too difficult, was it?'

She looked him over again, finishing her deliberations.

'Okay, I won't tell anyone about Sammy Ross and neither will young Alastair. I think he'd just as rather no one knew. But don't make me regret it. You do and I'll have no hesitation in making you pay.'

He believed her.

'Thanks, Cat. I really appreciate it.'

'You should.'

'I do. Honest. But . . . why did you ask . . . what you asked?'

'God it's like talking to a teenager. Because if you are involved with someone else then it gives you a valid reason for not shagging me again. Okay? If it was because you didn't like it then I'd have been very offended.'

'I did. I mean I . . .'

Winter stumbled over his embarrassment, realizing it was probably not best to mention that he fell for Rachel so shortly after his dalliance with Cat. It wasn't what she wanted to hear.

'Oh shut up,' she stopped him. 'Okay, here's the deal. If you are involved then you stop looking at me the way you do. It's not on. I like you, Tony, and can now forgive you for being so stupid as to not know a good thing when you saw one, but you keep your eyes off my ass in future.'

'It will be difficult.'

'At least you didn't say it would be hard. I might have had to change my mind about the deal if you had. And I mean it, don't give me cause to regret this. Whatever it is, sort it soon. This deal might expire.'

'I intend to.'

'You be very careful. You're a photographer, not a cop. Promise me that if you are in over your head then you will go to someone who actually knows what they are doing and get this dealt with properly.'

'I will,' he said, knowing almost certainly that it was a lie.

CHAPTER 37

Smeaton Drive in Bishopbriggs was a family residential area and the neighbours were never likely to take too kindly to having anyone shot on their doorsteps, let alone someone who turned out to be a major gangster. By the time Narey arrived, Jo-Jo Johnstone had been rushed to hospital and what was left behind was a pool of blood and a shocked and unhappy group of locals.

The crime scene examiners were busy at work and the police were going door to door to get every bit of information they could. No one doubted who had done it but they still didn't know who that someone was. The word Dark Angel went unsaid.

Narey sensed the strange mood that pervaded the scene and couldn't help but share it. She'd known of Jo-Jo Johnstone for as long as she'd been on the force and knew just what a bad bastard he was. Every officer there was aware of the money laundering, extortion, violence, brothels and drugs.

It had been the same with Caldwell and Quinn, and to a lesser extent with Strathie, Sturrock, Haddow and Adamson plus the four at Dixon Blazes: Houston, Faichney, Honeyman and Arnold. Every cop knew of them and knew they were no loss to society.

The shock wasn't the same in Smeaton Drive as it had been with some of the others. It was just the latest and there wasn't enough sympathy on that street to fill a teaspoon. Narey could smell it. They didn't give a fuck that Johnstone had been shot and what was in the air was the whiff of disappointment.

She saw the TV crews and press pack that were being held back at the end of the street, vultures in a feeding frenzy, delighting in the latest kill but probably sharing the dissatisfaction that there was a survivor this time. The Dark Angel was going to claim yet more headlines. Deadlines, she thought darkly.

There was a difference too in the work of the forensics. They were meticulous as ever but she sensed they were cutting with the dull blade of someone who knew what they would find. Baxter would ensure that their standards didn't slip but they somehow lacked urgency as they laid out yellow markers – for photographs that Winter hadn't the chance to take, she reflected – measured blood spatter and calculated angles. She wondered if they too had come to the conclusion that a gangster being shot wasn't perhaps the worst thing in the world.

Then she saw a child being hugged in a mother's arms a few doors away from Johnstone's house, a neighbour whose daughter had got out of the front door and seen the blood that soaked the steps where Jo-Jo had stood. Johnstone had kids, she remembered, and wondered where they might be now. With one of the neighbours, maybe, or waiting anxiously at the hospital. Whatever their dad did for a living, they were still children and she couldn't wish this on them.

The thought triggered memories of Jan McConachie and her daughter. What was her name? Amy. Narey wasn't sure if she believed that Jan was dirty, whatever the evidence of the phone call from George Faichney suggested, but either way, her heart bled for that wee girl.

She realized someone was standing next to her and turned to see Corrieri and Colin Monteith at her shoulder.

'All the neighbours have been interviewed,' Corrieri was saying. 'Only one of them actually saw Johnstone being hit, the others only heard the shot. It gives us a firm time of the shooting but nothing much more.'

'Okay, thanks, Julia. What do you think, Colin?'

Monteith shook his head at the scene before him.

'I think it's a hell of a waste of manpower for a scumbag like Johnstone.'

'You don't mean that,' Narey chided him.

'Don't I? How many people here do you think actually feel sorry for him? Not the neighbours, I mean. Us, the police. If any of them are sorry it's that the Dark Angel didn't finish him off.'

'Yeah well, keep that to yourself,' she hissed at him. She nodded at the woman cradling her crying daughter. 'There are people here who are upset even if you're not. That kid probably played with Johnstone's children.'

'You want me to feel sympathy for a gangster's kids?' he mocked. 'Where did the money come from for the big house that they lived in? What paid for their toys and their holidays? Other people's fucking misery that's what. Don't lecture me about what to think, Narey.'

Maybe it was the guilt she felt at having let similar thoughts pass through her own head earlier but Narey bit back at him.

'And what about Terry Gilmartin's kid? You heard that his boy died in hospital this morning?'

'Same answer,' Monteith snarled. 'He was a gangster's son. Don't lay that emotional blackmail pish on me.'

'That kid was five years old!' she blasted.

'Dry your eyes, Rachel. I'm not losing any sleep over what some scumbag did to a scumbag like Gilmartin. He has fucked this place over for years without any of it bothering his conscience. Well, what goes around comes around. Fuck him.'

She stared at him, bothered as much by the fact that so many people seemed to be in agreement as by what he had said. She hadn't read one ounce of sympathy for the victims of the Dark

Angel and she doubted she'd read much the next morning about Gilmartin's son. It certainly didn't make what Monteith said any more appropriate though. She didn't know how many wrongs it took to make a right and she wasn't sure she wanted to find out.

She didn't have an answer for him that he'd understand or want to hear so she settled for the only answer she could muster.

'Fuck you.'

CHAPTER 38

The moment Cat Fitzpatrick left, Winter hurried back to his office and jumped back onto his PC, bringing up the Photoshopped image of the ring that had punched its mark into McCabe and Strathie. He hadn't known what it was but now he had a fair idea where to start looking. Special Ops, Navy, waterboarding, torture techniques.

His first guess turned out to be the right one. He typed 'Special Boat Service' into Google Images and hit enter. Twenty pictures leapt up onto the page, men on dinghies, men wearing balaclavas and night goggles, men dark and unknown, armed to the teeth, men getting on and off boats and paddling canoes.

There was a group shot of six guys, all menacing in their anonymity and their machine guns, strapped up with pocket after pocket of kit, looking like they were ready to retake the Falklands. Another showed eight men in a dinghy on high seas, every one of them except the one at the helm had machine guns or pistols pointed at some poor fucker who had no chance. Another had four men launching themselves into the sea from the back of what looked like a transport carrier. It was accompanied by some info. 'The Special Boat Service is one of the Royal Marines' two Special Forces units, the other being the Mountain and rctic Warfare Cadre. SBS Marines are proficient at demolitions, parachuting, and various weaponry and specialize in intelligence, observation, reconnaissance and sabotage. The SBS motto is "Not By Strength, By Guile".'

But three of the images, three of them were different, and they had leapt out at him right away.

Set on a black background, it was a silver-gray dagger with a scroll either side of the handle and two thick blue waves behind the blade. The insignia of the SBS. He downloaded the picture, bringing it up full size then switching between that and the image he'd created from the bruise marks. Insignia, bruise mark, insignia, bruise mark, insignia, bruise mark. Identical.

Back to the search engine. He typed in 'weapons used by the SBS' and up it came. A long list of deadly weapons.

'The Diemaco C8 carbine, the HK MP5 Sub Machine Gun, the HK53 Assault Carbine, the G3 Sniper/Assault Rifle, the Sig Sauer P226 Pistol, the FN Minimi Para Light Machine Gun, the GPMG Machine Gun, the L115A3 Sniper Rifle . . .'

His heart stopped then thudded against his chest. He read on for reasons that were beyond him, as if doubting the evidence of his own eyes. 'The HKP11 Underwater Pistol, the Flashbang Stun Grenade.'

He clicked the link to the L115A3.

'Shown to be accurate up to 2.4km, the British made L115A31 AW sniper rifle is a fearsome weapon, especially when placed in the hands of an SBS sniper. Like most sniper rifles, it is a single-shot bolt-operated weapon. The L115A3 is typically fitted with a Schmidt & Bender 5-25 x 56 telescopic sight. It is a large calibre weapon which provides state-of-the-art telescopic day and night all-weather sights, increasing a sniper's range considerably.'

Winter pulled out his mobile and flipped through his contacts until he found his uncle Danny's number. Three rings and it was answered.

'Hullo?'

'Hi, Uncle Danny. It's Tony.'

'Jeezus, how many times are we having Christmas this year? You've phoned me twice in a week. Am I about to die and leave you money that I don't know about?'

'I hope not, Dan. There's been enough deaths lately without adding you to the list.'

'Is it this Dark Angel case? You done any work on that?'

You could never get much past Danny Neilson.

'Yes, I've done some photographs. Nasty stuff.'

'You know any of these cops that were shot, Tony? It doesn't exactly look good for them.'

Winter hesitated. This wasn't where he wanted to go.

'Not really, Dan. Cops and photographers, you know how it is.'

It was Danny's turn to hesitate.

'Aye, sure. So, seeing as it's not Christmas, what can I do you for this time?'

'If I'm remembering right, you had a mate that was in the Royal Navy a while back. Jim something.'

'Jim McKenzie, aye. Died about five years ago. He was a good guy. Why you asking?'

'Just wondering about something and needed some info. Thought you might know.'

'Okay, shoot.'

Bad choice of words.

'You told me once that he had mates that had been in the Special Boat Service. If guys like that were in the Navy but were members of the SBS, what would they tell people? Outsiders, I mean.'

'That they were in the Navy. Nothing more. Yeah, Big Jim knew a couple of guys that had been in the SBS, never any names mind, and he said they were the hardest bastards he'd ever known. And Jim was from Possil. Why do you ask?'

Winter ignored the question and pressed on.

'And if someone was on operations, maybe something in another country or something undercover, where would the Navy say he was?'

'At sea. Standard reply, I'd reckon. If he was in Russia or a lap-dancing club in Edinburgh, they'd give the same answer. They wouldn't be giving anything away.'

'That's what I thought.'

'Tony, you getting yourself into any bother?'

'No, I'm fine, Uncle Danny. I'm fine.'

'Aye? Well, make sure you stay that way. Whichever of those cops that were shot that you were close to, I hope they rest in peace but it's not worth you getting yourself into trouble over. You hear me?'

Danny was the smartest man he knew.

'I'll be careful, don't worry. How did you know that?'

'Tony, you can't teach an old dog how to suck eggs. I did my job a long time.'

Winter laughed.

'Aye, fair enough.'

'You be careful, son. And you know where I am if you need me.'

Winter thanked him and hung up.

Five minutes later he was in the car before he could change his mind. It was less than an hour since he spoke to Cat but it seemed so much longer. He was driving back out to Dennistoun, his hands gripping the steering wheel tighter than he knew he should have with no idea what was in front of him.

What he was about to do was wrong but he couldn't get away from it, it was the only thing he could do. What had happened to Addison and, God help him, what might happen to Rachel meant he had no choice.

He turned right off Alexandra Parade just after Alberto's Café but instead of going directly down Whitevale Street, he turned off onto Ingleby Drive to get onto Whitehill Street. The road that the McCabes lived on ran parallel to Whitevale and something inside him wanted to drive past their house first to get a feeling for what he was doing.

He glanced up at the window of their red-brick tenement as he slipped by, wondering if Rory was sitting in front of his PS3, his crutches at his side. Maybe his mum was busy making tea. Maybe Rory's mate Lee, the one that liked to wear balaclavas and was handy with his boots, was nearby too.

In front of Winter was the tower of the church with Duke Street beyond it, cars queuing at the junction and most of the way down the street no doubt. He headed that way, taking the long route and putting it off as long as he could. Past the self-service laundry and the Neptune chippy on the left, Coia's Cafe on the right at the corner and then left onto Duke Street.

The street was mobbed and it made him anxious to get there quickly even though at the same time he was glad to be held up. The lights changed and he crawled past the discount stores, tanning salons, off-licences and bookies, the barbers and Greggs until at last he turned left onto Whitevale, past the other side of the church and up the street.

It was a four-storey bleached stone building that looked like it had been recently sandblasted into submission. He parked up, telling himself to keep calm. He took a deep breath and pressed the second-floor buzzer with McKendrick on it. It took an eternity until a tired-sounding voice crackled through the intercom.

'Yes?'

'Hello, Mrs McKendrick? Hi, I'm sorry to bother you.'

'Who is it?'

'I'm Tony. A friend of Ryan's. We've met before but it was years ago.'

'Oh right. I'm sorry but Ryan's not here.'

'I, uh, I heard about Kieran ...' he stammered.

'Oh.'

'I just thought I'd ... that I should ... I'm really sorry.'

'Thank you.'

'I just wanted to pay my respects,' he continued, the self-loathing growing inside him.

'You better come up.'

The security buzzer blared and he pushed the door open. It was dark inside the close but he could see ancient yellow ceramic tiles in some art deco style lining the walls. They were probably fashionable once but they looked pretty awful to him. The close wound its way to the second floor and by the time he got there, Rosaleen McKendrick was holding the door open for him.

She was a small, weary-looking woman with reddened eyes that looked him over to see if she recognized him. He got the distinct feeling the path to her door had become well-worn and she was tired of it.

'I think I remember you now, Tony,' she lied generously. 'The boys have so many friends. It's hard to keep up with them all, especially the old ones.'

Her voice was frail, as if she was exhausted by the fight. She'd almost certainly been crying and the knowledge of that didn't exactly make Winter feel good.

'We used to play football together,' he told her. Surely Ryan played football.

'Oh right. He hasn't played in years, not properly since he joined the Navy. He used to love it though.'

Winter was guessing that Mrs McKendrick was only in her mid to late forties, fifty at the most, but she looked nearer sixty. Her brown hair had hints of gray and was largely unkempt while nicotine stains were licking at her fingertips and snaking towards bitten nails. Losing a child would do that to you, he supposed. That and not sleeping for a month. He wasn't happy with the thought that he could cause her a lot more sleepless nights but it wasn't his choice any more.

Mrs McKendrick didn't really want him in her house, much as she tried to hide it out of politeness. She probably thought her days of dutifully receiving well-wishers were behind her but here was a straggler, another well-meaning pain in the arse. She led him through to the front room and tried not to look too relieved when he turned down her offer of a cup of tea.

The living room was neat and tidy. Fading flowers packed four or five vases round the room and the mantelpiece overflowed with condolence cards. In the middle of it was a silver-framed photograph of Mrs McKendrick with two young men either side, both towering over her, and a younger girl in front. The younger boy was obviously Kieran, longish fair hair and wide cheeky grin, happy and only faintly embarrassed to be hugging his mum. Ryan was taller and broader, his dark blond hair close cropped with an air of confidence about him. Undoubtedly the man of the house. There was a determination about him too, a steely look in his eyes and a protectiveness. You wouldn't mess with him, that was for sure. In front was Suzanne, gazing up at Ryan with undisguised admiration.

'That was taken on my birthday,' she said from behind him. 'Ryan was home on leave and with Kieran about to go to university, well it just seemed a good time to get a photograph of the four of us. It turned out to be the last one.'

'I'm sorry I couldn't be here for the funeral,' Winter told her after he sat down. 'I was away.'

She nodded distractedly as if she couldn't care less and began to light a cigarette, her hands shaking.

'I haven't been able to get hold of Ryan,' he added. 'Is he back at sea?'

'Yes, yes, he's back at sea.'

Something about the speed with which she answered made

him doubt her. It was just too quick, too keen to confirm. She either knew that was untrue or else she doubted it herself. He wasn't going to call her on it though.

'I'm really sorry I missed him. Did he have to go back straight after the funeral?'

'No, he was allowed back for three days after it. To look after me and Suzanne, I suppose. Then he had to go again.'

'How was he, Mrs McKendrick?'

She looked up from a thread in the carpet that she'd been studying and considered the question as she dragged on her cigarette.

'Not himself. Not himself at all. He blames himself for not being here when Kieran ... but he couldn't be. He's got his career. But ... he's, he's ... he was ...'

'Kieran's big brother?' Winter guessed.

'Yes. I kept telling him that it wasn't his fault but he wouldn't listen. He took it really badly. He wanted to know how it had happened and why Kieran's pals hadn't looked after him. He just couldn't let it go.'

'I guess he went to talk to them?'

'He said he did but he was angry when he came back because they wouldn't tell him much. Too scared of the police, I suppose. He was like a tiger in a cage when he was here. All he would do was talk about Kieran and things they'd done. Spent so much time in Kieran's room. And he was always talking about Grahamston.'

'Grahamston?'

'Yes, he kept going on about it. It was like he was obsessed. He kept saying how terrible it was that he and Kieran would never be able to go to Grahamston again. How he'd promised Kieran that he'd go with him one more time and how you should always keep a promise.'

Winter realized that the woman wasn't really talking to him any more, she was looking at the floor reminiscing. Her mind was probably full of images of two wee boys playing together, best pals, all their lives before them.

'Grahamston, Grahamston. It was all he talked about. As if it could bring Kieran back. As if . . .'

She stopped mid-sentence, remembering for the first time in a few minutes that her youngest son was dead and suffering the shock all over again. Tears welled up in her eyes and Winter felt a complete bastard. He had to ask one more question though, despite the fact that he had a good idea what the answer was.

'Did he tell you what that was all about, Mrs McKendrick. Did he say where he meant by Grahamston?'

'No. He never told me. Neither of them ever did. It was always this silly secret they had since they were wee. I'd hear them mentioning it but they'd always shush up. I think they were worried their dad would give them trouble over it whatever it was. Do you know what it was all about? Did Ryan ever mention it to you?'

'No, never,' he answered truthfully. 'He never mentioned it to me.'

It was a half-truth though. A lie in other words. He was pretty sure he knew what Grahamston meant and if he was right then he was about to do maybe the stupidest thing he'd ever done in his life.

Mrs McKendrick nodded at him sadly, flicking the smouldering end of her fag into the ashtray below.

'You can always ask him when he gets home, I guess,' he murmured.

'Eh? Yes, yes I can. When he gets back from sea. I'll ask him. Is there anything else, Tony, because I've got to make Suzanne's tea. She'll be in soon and she'll be hungry.'

'No, nothing. I'll get out your way.'

Winter got to his feet and she led him to the front door, her eyes welling up with some new memory. It was an awkward moment as they both hesitated, unsure what to do. He offered an uneasy handshake which she began to reach towards before changing tack and taking another half-step closer and giving him a brief hug.

'It's always good to see the boys' old friends again,' she mumbled. 'You take care of yourself now.'

The door shut behind him and he made his way down and out of the close as quickly as he could.

CHAPTER 39

There were two Grahamstons. One in Falkirk, about twenty-five miles away, with a railway station, a crumbling football stadium and a retail park. The other was right underneath Glasgow and over 100 years away. It was possible that the McKendrick boys were always talking about running off to Falkirk together but that didn't seem very likely. Vegas it wasn't.

Winter remembered when he was wee, Uncle Danny telling him about the secret village that existed underneath Glasgow. Grahamston used to be a thriving community, a couple of thousand people living in a commercial and industrial hub right at the heart of the city. All roads led to Rome but in Glasgow they all went through Grahamston. It stood on the main east-west route and then later it was on the main north-south link as well. The roads to all the main towns of central Scotland, and from the Forth and Clyde canal to the ships at the Broomielaw, they all went through Grahamston.

It was at the crossroads of Union Street and Jamaica Street with Argyle Street and it was one of the busiest in Europe. Some Glaswegians will tell you it was the busiest intersection in the world at one time. There was only one street in Grahamston itself, Alston Street, and it ran the length of the village. The first permanent theatre in Glasgow, the Alston Street Playhouse, was built there in 1764, although technically it stood just outside the then city boundary.

Alston Street had a sugar refinery, warehouses, carters' yards, pubs, houses and three hundred shops all crammed between Mitchell Street and Waterloo Street. It was famous for its breweries and that endeared it to many a man in the empire's second city. It was some place, alright.

Winter remembered Danny showing him this old map one afternoon in the Mitchell Library. It was Glasgow in the late 1700s and to his young eyes it was amazing. This tiny city mapped out where there ought to have been the giant metropolis that he lived in. Some of the streets that he knew so well were still there and that just made it all the stranger. Buchanan Street and the High Street cutting great swathes south while one big street ploughed east to west. It started in the east as Gallowgate Street then became Trongate Street and, finally, Argyle Street.

He could remember the map like it was yesterday. He'd said it looked like had been soaked in tea and Uncle Danny had laughed. There were hardly any houses and so many fields. The big street that ran to the west, ended at a place that was spelt out in capitals as GRAHAMSTON. It had even fewer houses than the middle of the city and he'd asked Uncle Danny if it was still there.

'Well, wee man,' he said to him. 'There's a very interesting question. Some say it is and some say it isn't.'

Winter's eyes had grown large with wonder and Danny promised he'd tell him all about it on the way home. He had him hooked on every word as he told him how the village had grown from a row of thatched cottages to this important place, of all the people that lived there and how, with a wink, he told him of the vital role of its breweries in the life of the city.

But then came growing industrialization and Grahamston simply got in the way. Glasgow was getting bigger and bigger and people wanted to travel to and from it to the rest of Scotland and beyond. The Caledonian Railway wanted to build a huge new station to service the trains and the people. In the late 1800s they began building Central Station, moved the people out of Grahamston and the demolition crews in. They constructed the giant station right on top of the old place. Some say they knocked down Alston Street, some say they didn't.

Danny told him how some people believe that Grahamston was still there, right under the platforms and the arches of Central Station. They say that Alston Street is intact, just the way it was the day they moved the people out. He spun this marvellous tale, making Grahamston out to be Glasgow's version of Pompeii, a place frozen in time by the intervention of progress rather than molten lava. What got him was that there were still two buildings from old Grahamston actually standing in modern Glasgow, the Grant Arms beside the Heilan'man's Umbrella and the Rennie Mackintosh Hotel in Union Street, the one that used to be Duncan's Temperance Hotel. Makes you think, if they are still there . . .

Mind you, Danny also told him how people said that there was still silver in the shops because the shopkeepers were moved out so quickly that they didn't have time to take it all away with them. When he was eighteen Winter realized that was bollocks but when he was eight, he truly believed.

He never forgot the story of Grahamston. It was easy to see why boys like Rory and Kieran would be drawn by it, the sense of mystery and adventure, the lost silver and the thought of Alston Street still standing, waiting to be explored. The temptation to run away to Grahamston must have been huge.

From the instant the name fell from Mrs McKendrick's lips, it reminded him that Central Station was where the first of the shootings took place. Cairns Caldwell shot down within a couple of hundred yards from the Rennie Mackintosh Hotel and right above the tracks of the station, right above the old village. And the man that fired the shot had simply vanished as if he'd dropped into the bowels of the earth.

There was little doubt in his mind. Grahamston was where he'd find McKendrick. The only real question was whether he *wanted* to find him.

Winter was scared, there was no getting away from it. He was a photographer, a recorder, a witness. What the fuck was he doing? The fear was in his chest, like a battalion of butterflies eating away at him. It was only images of Addison and Rachel that were making him go on. If he was right then McKendrick had shot his best mate who was lying wired up to a machine that was keeping him barely alive. He had tortured Sammy Ross to get the names, places addresses, whatever it was he needed to let him take out the people at the top, the middle and the scummy bottom of the drugs trade. Now he had mobile phones that had provided him with a death list and maybe Rachel's name was on it. No way could Winter stop now.

He had next to no idea what he was going to do when he got to Grahamston, or at least to wherever McKendrick was hiding in the maze under the station, but he knew he was going to look. Maybe he could find enough proof to take Alex Shirley there, catch Ryan and clear Addison, save Rachel. Fuck it, he didn't know.

Over the years he'd heard various stories of how to get into the areas below ground at Central that the public aren't meant to. Uncle Danny had got him interested enough that he had always listened out for the tales that spilled from office workers, engineers, electricians and plumbers that had been down there for one reason or another and said too much once they'd had a drink. All the shops in the Argyle Street area had large areas below them and many, maybe most, had access that led to others, although most were blocked off these days.

Some guys told of knowing someone who had been down there and seen the street with shopfronts intact. Some had seen a butcher's shop, others mentioned a spirit merchant. Another who said his uncle was a telecom engineer and did work down there said the access was via the stairs from platform 3 and that under the platform was a lift that took you into the bowels of the place. It opened up into a pitch-black area with tunnels going off in all directions. Down one of those was Alston Street. According to him it ran from the edge of the foundations of the station to the edge of where Debenhams stands. But it was always a friend of a friend; he'd never met anyone who claimed to have been down there themselves and seen it. Probably with good reason.

There was truth in the spaces down there though, he was sure of that much. He knew there was a massive maze-like area under the Arches because he'd been down there once while a friend that worked in the Argyle Arcade said there was a tunnel that ran the length of it too, below all the jewellers' shops. There used to be a basement below the old What Every's that allowed you to go down one side of Argyle Street, inside the shop, and back up on the other. More tunnels than the Great Escape and Colditz combined. Whatever lay below the station, old street or not, there was no end of places that a man could hide if he had a mind to. Or if he was out of his mind.

The most likely story he'd heard of how to get in came from someone who didn't believe a word about Alston Street and that was maybe why Winter believed him. A pal of his, Jamie Rowan, said that there was a passage which ran behind McDonald's at the corner of Argyle Street and Jamaica Street, across the road from the Grant Arms and right above the heart of old Grahamston. Jamie said that when he was young, he and a couple of mates used to lift this metal sheet in the middle of the passage and spend their day below ground getting full of Buckie and White Lightning and wandering around feeling the reverberation of the trains.

That was years ago though, Rowan would only have been about

fifteen and he was over thirty now. Chances were that health and safety had put an end to it. But you never knew.

The passage itself was easy enough to find coming in off Jamaica Street and the bits of bush that sprang across the entrance wasn't a problem. Winter waited till there was no one passing by and pushed his way through. The place was a tip and there was the usual collection of broken bottles and used condoms at his feet. It was narrow, just enough space to walk through, and there wasn't much light but he was happy enough with that as it hid what he was up to. He edged along warily until he got about halfway back and, sure enough, he heard metal ring beneath his shoes.

It was partly overgrown but he ripped the weeds back and found the edges of the half-inch thick, rusted cover. It must have slipped through the safety net because it wasn't bolted to the ground, just lying there. Maybe because it wasn't covering anything, he thought.

He managed to get his fingers under a corner of the sheet but could barely budge it. Then he got both hands under, wondering if he'd ever get them out again, and heaved. Christ it was heavy. He could only lift it a few inches but pulled it to the side, rested then lifted and pulled again. He lifted and yanked it best he could till he'd moved it maybe a foot from where it was. He looked and couldn't believe it: there was a hole beneath it. Jamie had been telling the truth. It took him ten minutes but he wrestled with the sheet enough till he could see the top of a flight of wooden stairs and had made a space big enough for him to get through. Shit.

It was starting to get dark which didn't do much for his confidence. Not that there was exactly going to be much in the way of sunlight anyway down in the old foundations of Alston Street or the disused platforms of Central but it made him even more unsettled. He'd seen enough old horror movies to know that going into the monster's lair as the sun went down was a really stupid idea.

One last look to make sure no one was watching and he dropped onto a step a few feet down, glad of the torch that he could feel nestled in his back pocket, and began to descend. He climbed down maybe a dozen steps then felt his feet hit level ground. He turned and saw he was in a room like a hallway with a corridor leading off to the right, north he was guessing it was, towards Central Station. It was why he was there and no matter how shit-scared he was, he was going on.

The torch picked out walls that were tiled to maybe four feet high in yellow ceramic and painted in dirty yellow above that. Other parts were whitewashed and it rang of a Romanian hospital or a lunatic asylum. All of a sudden, there was unexpected daylight and he realized he was under one of the reinforced glass walkways on the street above. Footsteps rang over his head and his guess was that he was somewhere under Union Street. He could see double doors at the end of the current corridor and made his way tentatively towards them. Thankfully, they were unlocked and he went through. The walls in the next passage were white tiled to above shoulder height but clearly hadn't been touched for donkey's years. They led to another set of double doors then another. He edged along in the gloom, having no idea what was in front of him or behind.

At the next set of doors were stairs and he followed them down two flights, all too aware of the growing chill and the smell of damp. He could hear dripping water too and had the impression that it was running behind the wall nearest to him. Abruptly the wall on his left shrunk back and he could make out a large recess that held the remains of what looked like a generator, some polystyrene blocks and planks of wood. A storeroom of some sort. After flashing his torch into the corners, he moved on, becoming aware of every footstep rattling round him. He determined to walk as softly as he could. If there was anyone down there then he was in no hurry to warn them that he was coming.

A sheen of dust covered the walls and the floor, giving off a stale odour that mixed unpleasantly with the damp. His nose tickled and the hairs stood up on the back of his neck but his *sgriob* didn't budge. All he sensed was his own fear and uncertainty. Another pair of doors and another set of stairs. It was colder, damper and darker. He had a choice of two ways to go and followed his nose, passing low brick walls, no more than a couple of feet high which he took to be old boiler supports. Other walls held the ghosts of doors long since vanished and behind them were what seemed to be the arches of the foundations. He surely couldn't go much lower.

Wary of his footing as the ground below him got rougher, he flashed the light on the floor and saw the nestle of dust had been disturbed. He crouched and was fairly sure it had been footsteps but the big question was how recent they were. Days or months? He nibbled his lip and looked ahead into the darkness, realizing he had no real idea of how long he'd been down there - fifteen minutes maybe - and only a vague idea of how to return to the surface. At the end of that corridor, he again had a choice of directions but was able to see that on only one of them did the dust seem to have been displaced. That was the way to go.

It was much wider down there now, the narrow hospital corridors having been replaced by large spaces that seemed to have no edge and he hugged close to the wall for fear of staggering in the wrong direction. Then something else caught his eye, picked out by the torchlight amid the murk. He reached down and picked it up, an empty two-litre bottle of Diet Coke. It looked pretty new. Everything else down there was covered in the dust of a hundred years, or at least since the last time anyone had ventured down to clean up the rubbish. He picked up the plastic bottle and checked the sell-by date. January 2012. It had been dropped very recently. Shit, wasn't he the proper little detective?

So he knew he was probably on the right track. He threw the bottle back onto the ground a few feet away, knowing immediately it had been a mistake as it rattled off the floor and the sound reverberated up to the arches. But as the sound settled, it was joined then taken over by something else. The noise made by the bottle moved seamlessly into a growing crescendo of squeals that came from his left, squeaks that became a screech rising from behind a closed door. Then in an instant he saw them. Rats.

They stormed out from the space beneath the door and towards him, fleeing, angry, scared. Christ, there was an army of them and they were huge, the size of large puppies or small dogs, but much fiercer and scurrying at top speed.

Winter froze, his heart racing and yet stopped at the same time, every hair on his body on edge. He was scared shitless of rats. There must have been twenty of the little fuckers and they scuttled across his path at a hundred miles an hour. Two, maybe three of them actually ran across his feet, scampering across his shoes without giving a damn.

He couldn't breathe, couldn't move, just had to stand and watch them run. They'd vanished from sight in an instant, the only evidence that they'd been there at all being the distant sound of their shrieking but he was still rooted to the spot, silent, wary of breathing too loudly, shaking. The only wonder was that he hadn't crapped himself. He had to try and slow his heart down.

Stop shaking, he told himself. Get a grip.

What was behind the door? Much as he didn't want to, he had to know what had made the rats interested enough to go in there in the first place. He was guessing food. Maybe whatever had been washed down with the Diet Coke. Only one way to find out, he thought, and cursed himself for thinking it.

There was an image from the movie *Ben* that was growing

stupidly large in his head. The one where the kid goes into a small room and stands up to see the entire place filled with rats. Every shelf filled with the dirty little bastards, surrounding him. That scene scared the crap out of him for years. And now, he was actually going to go in there and perhaps be confronted with exactly that.

He steeled himself, grabbed the door's handle and pulled, stepping quickly back as far as he could as he did so in case they came running out. Nothing moved and there wasn't a sound. He skirted slowly past the edge of the door, bringing what turned out to be a large storage cupboard into full view. There wasn't a rat to be seen, thank God, but there was plenty else there.

In the gloom he could make out a blanket bundled in the corner, a cardboard box that looked like it had packets of food in it. On a shelf sat not rats but a notebook and a pile of photographs. There were boxes too, four of them about a foot square, marked *Naval Issue*.

He was in the tight grip of his shallow breathing, a pounding heart and a head crowded by creeping fear but despite all that, his brain still functioned enough to know that he was undoubtedly in the right place. And the wrong place. His senses were overloaded by what he could see but slowly the others were kicking in too and he realized that the cupboard smelled. It was an odour that he knew fairly well but worse, much worse, than he normally experienced.

He wanted to run but he couldn't, his feet didn't know how and anyway, he'd as likely run into McKendrick coming back to his lair. He had to stay and he had to deal with something. The voice in his head was telling him to do it, to stop ignoring what was in front of him and just do it. He reached down and took a hold of the corner of the blanket with the ends of his fingers, wary of it. He pulled it slowly towards him but realized he was just making things worse by delaying.

He swallowed hard, gripped the blanket properly and whipped it away in one movement, unveiling what lay below. But no matter that he tried to do it quickly, he still saw it inch by revealing inch. A foot, a leg, fingers, blood, chest, head, eyes, blood, mouth, blood, hair. A whole body, yet not whole. He staggered back, crashing into the shelf behind him and cracking his head off the wall. The shock spiralled through him, stealing his breath away. Now he knew what the rats had been doing in there.

His hands went to his temples, holding his head tight. He wanted to scream but couldn't. His breathing was rapid, trembling, wheezing like an old man or an idiot. He'd seen death, seen lots of it but nothing like this. Usually, he was ready for it, called to it, but this, this was different.

Maybe it was because of the mess that the rats had made. The man's right eye had been eaten away completely, a hole left where the soft tissue had been munched from. His pale lips and cheeks had been partially eaten, half a feast that had been interrupted. His fingertips had been chewed too and the soft of his belly gnawed, all tasty morsels for hungry mouths.

No, it was all of that but it was more to do with the fact that as Winter recovered his breath and his heart restarted, he looked at the body and knew beyond a shadow who it was.

CHAPTER 40

The face in front of him, what was left of it, wasn't the good-looking, confident young guy from the photograph on his mother's mantlepiece. The pride that Winter had seen in his eyes was gone from the one that he had left shrunken in his skull, the close-cropped hair was grimy and stained with blood, the strong determined jaw was slack and bore the sharp incisor marks of the rats. But it was definitely him.

Ryan McKendrick. His brother's avenger. The man-boy who ran away to Grahamston. Dirty and dead and half-eaten by rats. Winter's head spun. Whatever he had expected, it wasn't this.

His head had been full of some straight-line thinking that was all too simple. McKendrick wanted to even the score for his wee brother's death and became some kind of human wrecking ball against the scum that fed drugs to Keiran. He was Special Boat Service, he had the training, the motive, the access to the hardware. He'd tortured Sammy Ross and pumped him for information before he'd killed him. He'd then shot drug dealers, gangsters and crime bosses and he was hiding out somewhere in a hellish version of Brigadoon.

It was McKendrick. He'd been sure of it. The Dark Angel. The new-age hero. The killer. It was all so fucking simple and he was the smart-arse who had worked it out.

The only problem was the evidence in front of him. Winter was no expert on forensics but he'd regularly ridden shotgun with Baxter or Cat so he was more informed than people who watched *CSI*. He knew enough about rigor and lividity to be able to confidently predict a time of death that wouldn't look foolish in court.

There was a greenish-blue tinge to McKendrick's head and neck, large blisters were starting to form on his skin from the gases below, he was beginning to bloat, rigor had been and gone, fluids were beginning to seep from all visible orifices and he smelled. Really bad.

McKendrick wasn't killed in the last few hours, he hadn't been killed in the last twenty-four. Winter's guess, his very educated guess, was that he'd been dead for two days, more likely three. Days. Before Addison was shot, before Forrest, McConachie and Johnstone were killed, before those four guys were tied to chairs and tortured to death.

Whatever Winter thought he knew, he clearly didn't. This guy hadn't shot Addison. But someone had and someone had also killed McKendrick. And what was he doing down here if he wasn't the Dark Angel?

Winter took a deep breath then quickly lifted McKendrick's shirt to see that there were dark red-purple pools across his back, meaning he'd been moved after he was dead. The dark pools were lividity. When the heart no longer pumped blood around the body then gravity caused the heavy red cells to sink through the serum. If McKendrick had been killed where he lay then the hypostasis would have settled more on his side.

Winter didn't think he could have been moved too far. Ryan was too heavy to carry any kind of distance – unless it was more than one person – and manhandling him up and down the narrow staircases seemed a big job. His guess was that he was killed down there but maybe out in the main passageway then dumped in the storage cupboard a few hours later.

The Dark Angel or killed by the Dark Angel? Hero or villain? Or both?

Winter reached, almost self-consciously, into his back pocket and drew out the compact camera that was tucked in there. It was beyond him why he felt at all bad about it but he knew this was a different kind of death, more real. More frightening.

The compact had twelve megapixels and a decent flash yet it fitted into the palm of his hand. Which suddenly struck him as ironic because what he was about to do was some form of photographic masturbation. Maybe Rachel had been right, maybe it was necrophotographilia after all.

He stood with his back to the wall, letting as much light in as possible and also because he was scared of what might creep up behind him. He flicked the zoom up then down again, focusing and framing as best he could, aware of the tremble in his fingers and took a full-frame shot of McKendrick's hunched body.

What a mess the nasty little fuckers had left him in. The thought hit Winter that he was glad Ryan's mother couldn't see him now. Poor tortured Rosaleen had suffered enough already and no mother should ever, ever see what was in front of Winter at that moment. Chewed, eaten, bitten, gnawed. None of that was what had killed him though. Not unless rats had learned how to break a man's neck. The tortured angle of his head to his body left no doubt. Winter's guess was that the blood that matted his hair could have been from another blow before he was snapped or as he fell to the ground.

Mouth open, lips ashen, his one good eye rolled back and distant. Limbs tucked beneath him in an unnatural fashion where rigor had set in then reversed itself. The splashes of blood were far from being red, they were carmine, almost maroon, dirtier than rust and just as uninviting. His skin was purple and tight, his nails white, his clothes dirty. That poor wee woman could never see this.

Winter had photographed more than his fair share of death but this was horrific. He was normally there when they'd just gone, when they had one foot in the grave and one in the gravy. McKendrick was long gone and although that was hardly a first for Winter, the mess he was in made it so much worse. Cold compassion wasn't the option it might otherwise have been.

He zoomed in as much as the compact would allow him and photographed McKendrick's blotchy, algae-green neck. Snapped it. The ugly bulge of the broken vertebrae under the discoloured skin. He moved to his other wounds, the ones caused by the rats, and photographed them too. The position of the body, its place in the room, the blanket, the shelves, the printed photographs and the boxes. Everything from every angle. He had no idea how or if this could ever get to court without landing him in deep shit but he knew his job.

Having done it, he looked through what else there was in there. All the time with an ear to the door and the corridor, waiting for footsteps, either on two legs or four. A corrupted line from *Animal Farm* flooded his mind. Four legs bad, two legs worse. Whatever happened to McKendrick, someone had taken the trouble to move him and cover him up yet hadn't taken away the stuff in the cupboard. That someone could be coming back.

The cardboard box held the remains of packets of energy bars, chocolate, brown biscuits, cheese and meat spreads, instant coffee and water purifying tablets, instant soups and oatmeal block. Some were intact; some had been ripped open and eaten, probably by the rats. They were survival rations but hadn't allowed for the eventuality of a broken neck.

Winter fingered open the boxes marked *Naval Issue*, lifted up the cardboard flaps and peered inside. Ammunition. Lots of it. He took out a single bullet and felt the weight of it in his hand, coming to the conclusion that it was heavier than whatever it measured in grammes. Mindful of not leaving any more traces of himself than was strictly necessary, he wiped the bullet on his shirt and popped it back into the box still clutched in the cotton. Mindful too that it was probably a complete waste of time.

They were obviously the bullets for the L115A3. Three of the boxes were full, the other one less than half so. There was no knowing if there had been other boxes or if the someone who had killed and covered up McKendrick had taken away a box or two of ammo. One thing was certain, there was no sign of the rifle itself. He'd looked everywhere, including under the body, but could see nothing. If it had been here, and his betting was that it had, it was gone now. Which had to make him wonder if it was being used. There would be no point in taking it out of this perfect hiding place for no good reason.

He knew he'd been avoiding the stack of photographs on the shelf, leaving the best or worst to last. He picked up the top one, annoyed at the obvious tremble in his hands, and began to study it. It was printed on plain paper in black and white, straight from a computer by the look of it. Right away, he knew where it had been taken. Smeaton Drive in Bishopbriggs, recognizing it immediately from the television pictures when they covered the Johnstone shooting. He could make out Alex Shirley and Baxter, then there was a bunch of indistinct figures in bunny suits.

He placed the print down next to the pile and lifted another one, his eyes growing wide. It was taken at Dixon Blazes and Rachel and McConachie could just be made out looking at each other in disbelief. He worked his way through the photos, fingers and eyes moving faster. Harthill Services. Glasgow Harbour. Central Station. Smeaton Drive. Kinnear Road. Location photos taken with a zoom. Some had been taken before the killings, either reconnaissance or trial runs with the camera rather than the gun. Others were taken after. He'd gone back, somewhere, somehow, and photographed his hunters. Or were they the hunted?

There were groups shots of the Nightjar team. There were some individual pictures too, some close enough and over-extended enough that you couldn't see where or when they were taken. Alex Shirley looking furious. Addison pissed off. Jan McConachie worried. Colin Monteith transfixed. Winter himself, busy. Baxter serious. Cat Fitzgerald detached. Rachel.

Rachel.

She was in a white coverall at Central Station, standing over the body of what he knew to be Cairns Caldwell. Winter's throat choked with the bile of trapped anger. He swallowed it back down just as he fought the urge to kick McKendrick's corpse or throw something. He suppose he should have expected a close-up of her too but the sight of it still hit him hard. Rachel. Christ.

Shakily, he put her picture on the pile, aware of the tension rising in him, and the hairs on the back of his neck electrified.

The next photo was of him. It was a side-on view, barely making out his face, and at his feet was a dark object that he knew to be the leather coat that Jimmy Adamson was wearing when he was shot. The photo was taken at Glasgow Harbour as Winter lined Jimmy up in his heavy leather cowl. Was it irony that someone had photographed him as he photographed the body? Or just threatening?

He saw the next photo, again taken at Dixon Blazes industrial estate. It was slightly out of focus as if it was rushed but it showed the whole group of cops looking at the warehouse door where the unseen crucified body was hanging. He and Addison weren't there and it must have been before they entered the fray. Winter put it down, wondering just how the fuck the Dark Angel had the nerve or stupidity to stay to take that, and lifted the next one. Rachel again. Close up.

This time emerging from the front door at Highburgh Road. Home. Business suit on, going to work. A realization exploded in Winter's mind. He knew where she lived.

CHAPTER 41

The room spun and Winter's senses rang as if he'd been smacked over the head with something heavy and hard. The wall behind him was holding him up and he slid down it till he was on his arse, the photograph in his hands. He wasn't scared for himself but he was terrified for her. Terrified and ready to fight. If it was McKendrick that had threatened her and he'd still been alive then Winter would have killed him himself. If it was whoever had killed McKendrick then he'd kill him instead.

There was no doubt where the photograph had been taken. He'd seen that door a thousand times, the red brick, the four steps to the intercom, the hedge to the left with the lamppost in front, the lace curtains to the right. The low, black railing, the 'Please Close The Door' sign stuck inside the glass pane and the beginning of the cycle lane on the road. The photograph had been taken from Caledon Street which ran at right angles to Highburgh and faced right onto the close at number 21 where Rachel's flat was on the top floor.

She was in a dark trouser suit with a dark-green blouse under it, pushing her hair away from her face. When had she been wearing that blouse? He racked his brains, knowing it was the sort of thing she'd rebuke him for not paying attention to. Was it just yesterday? Either that or the day before. The more recent it was the better, he reasoned. Less time for whoever it was to do whatever . . . He couldn't finish the thought. It wouldn't happen anyway, he'd see to that.

Suddenly something hissed to the side of him and he spun his head to see a single rat standing on its hind legs in the doorway. It didn't flinch when Winter looked at it, maybe sensing his fear or just angry at him for keeping the hordes from their meal. What it couldn't know, whatever it smelled, was that Winter wasn't afraid of it. The rat might have scared the shit out of him earlier but now it was way down the list of things that frightened him.

He got halfway to his feet and began to move towards it, like a dog chasing a car, having no idea what it would do if it caught one. It was enough and the rat whipped round, disappearing in a whisk of its pink tail as if it had never been there.

Winter fell back, letting himself thud into the wall, comforted by the chill of it, and considered the paucity of his options. He decided that if the rat was a hint for him to get the hell out of there then he was going to take it.

He fished the compact out of his back pocket again and, calmly as he could, photographed each of the print-outs in turn. Any pretence at calm disappeared at seeing the pictures of Rachel. He needed to get out of there and back up above ground. He needed to do that really quickly. Grahamston, Alston Street, Central Station, wherever he was, it was closing in on him fast and he was developing a claustrophobia that he'd never known before. He had to get out.

He tossed the blanket back over McKendrick's body, not particularly worried about replicating the placement of it as the rats had doubtless already moved it and would do so again. The printed photographs were back in their pile and the boxes were back where he'd found them. Exhaling hard, he backed out of the storage cupboard and set his sights on the way he'd got there. He was pretty sure of the way back out, knowing there were only two points at which he'd need to choose between alternative ways to go. The thought made him realize that there must have been a number of ways in because the metal sheet that he'd moved behind McDonald's looked like it hadn't budged in a long time. Not only that but he only noticed the footprints that had disturbed the dust on the floors once he was a fair way down and in, obviously having picked up another path.

He knew he could try and follow the footsteps and see where they'd entered but didn't want to hang around down there and anyway, it wouldn't matter. He'd got in, McKendrick had got in and so had his killer. It didn't make any difference if there was one entry point or three. All that mattered was Rachel.

He scuttled through the passageways as quickly as his legs and the light would allow him. Round, along and up. Double doors and damp hospital corridors, by the recess with the generator, the white tiles then the yellow ones, passing under the walkway on Union Street which was now lit by neon. It was only then that the fear gripped him with the realization that someone could have replaced the metal sheet over the hole. Either a deliberate ploy to keep him in there or just some civic-minded twat with nothing better to do with their time. Getting out again had never occurred to him but if the sheet was back over the hole then he'd never shift it.

It was only when he passed through to the faintly moonlit hallway that he breathed again, knowing that the sliver of pale light meant the sheet was as he'd left it. He climbed the stairs gratefully and popped out onto the overgrown corridor behind the burger joint.

As soon as he was out he reached for his phone and was glad to see that the buildings weren't cutting off his signal. He didn't have time to go through his contacts and trusted his fingers to punch in the numbers quicker. Come on. Thank Christ, after four rings she answered.

'I can't talk just now. I'll need to phone you back.'

She hadn't used his name, meaning there was probably someone else there. Someone who couldn't be allowed to know she was talking to him.

'No. I need to talk to you now. Right now.'

'I can't do that, sorry. Things are really busy.'

She lowered her voice.

'There's been another shooting.'

'Fuck. Who? In fact it doesn't matter, just listen to me.'

'I have to go.'

'No! This is really important, Rachel... Rachel. Rach! You have to get away. Listen to me–'

'I'm going into a press conference. I'll call you once I'm home. Bye.'

'Fucksake, Rach!' He was talking to himself. She'd already hung up. He switched the phone to text and began frantically typing in a message.

He scrubbed it. Would just scare the hell out of her. And pose too many questions. He started again.

Don't go home. Go to my place and text when on way.

Again he deleted it. The press conference would last a while and it would be at least half an hour, probably longer still, before she left Pitt Street. At least she'd be safe there. Instead he hurried back to his car where he'd left it off St Enoch's Square, immediately turning the radio on when he got there and pushing the button for Radio Clyde.

Good timing. The presenter was announcing that they were interrupting the programme to go to a live news conference at Strathclyde Police Headquarters where there was news about the killing which they'd exclusively told their listeners about earlier. Another voice took over but only got out a few whispered words of unnecessary explanation before loud familiar tones began to talk above it. Alex Shirley.

'Ladies and gentlemen, thank you for attending at such short notice. I am going to read a prepared statement then take questions but I must warn you in advance that there are operating issues that I cannot and will not discuss. I'm sure you understand that and I thank you in advance for your co-operation in this matter.'

Shirley paused and Winter could imagine him glaring at the press and daring them to disagree.

'At 20.30 hours this evening, officers received a 999 call from Causewayside Street in the Tollcross area, just off London Road. On arrival outside the premises of Eastern Salvage, they found the body of a man they identified as Alastair Riddle, the owner of the scrapyard. He had been shot in the head at point-blank range and was already dead when officers reached the scene.'

Winter could hear a flurry of background noise breaking out and Shirley paused until there was silence again.

'Mr Riddle was twenty-five years old and a known associate of members of Glasgow's criminal fraternity and had close connections with Malcolm Quinn. Owing to the specific characteristics of Mr Riddle's injuries and the nature of his business, we are – subject to full and proper forensic examinations – linking his death with the others under the remit of Operation Nightjar.

'The investigation into the other killings are ongoing and a matter of the utmost priority for Strathclyde Police. We are working round the clock to apprehend the person or persons responsible for these killings and will not rest until they are in custody. We are determined this will be done as quickly as is possible.

'Now I'll take questions.'

'Who found the body, Chief Superintendent?'

'Two local men heard the shot and they were first on the scene. I am not prepared to release their names at this stage.'

'Will they be available for interview later?'

'I doubt it. We'll let you know if that situation changes.'

'Can you reassure the public that you have firm leads in this case?'

'I can reassure them that everything that can be done is being done. We have several leads and every one of these is being fully explored. I cannot say that an arrest is imminent but I can say that we are closer to an arrest than at any other time during this investigation.'

'Can you tell us what information leads you to say that?'

'No.'

'Can you tell us the nature of this information?'

'No.'

'Chief Superintendent, the Dark Angel case has attracted worldwide publicity. Is this something that Strathclyde Police are comfortable with?'

'The Nightjar investigation has now involved the deaths of fourteen individuals and that is something we are not comfortable with. The extent of the publicity these killings has received is perhaps inevitable but it is not something that affects this force one way or the other.'

'Chief Superintendent, are you happy that drug dealers and crime bosses are being shot? Many members of the public say they are not unhappy with what the Dark Angel is doing.'

There was nothing but dead air coming from his car radio. Eventually Shirley responded icily.

'Thank you for attending, ladies and gentlemen. This press conference is now at an end.'

The station cut back to the studio where the presenter segued slickly into 'Psycho Killer' by Talking Heads. Winter switched it off.

He sat looking out of the car window and drumming his fingers. He gave it five long minutes until he couldn't stand it any more and called Rachel back. Straight to voicemail. Winter swore at the phone then paused, waiting till he could leave a message.

'It's me. Call me back as soon as you can.'

Ten minutes passed that seemed to last an hour. He called again and again but only got the answering service.

He fingered through the contacts book looking for another number even though he knew it off by heart. As usual, it picked up on the third ring.

'Hullo?'

'Uncle Danny? It's Tony.'

'I know who it is,' he growled back at him. 'Are you going to tell me what it is this time?'

'Danny, it's complicated . . .'

'Fuck off, Tony. Let me rephrase, you *are* going to tell me what it is this time. What kind of trouble are you in?'

'It's not me.'

'So is it the guy in the Special Boat Service or is it your mate the cop who's been shot? Or is it to do with the latest guy that's been shot and just been on the news?'

It stunned him into silence.

'I did this for a living, son.'

'I need your help, Danny.'

'I'd kinda gathered that. Okay, what do you need?'

'There's a friend that I . . . my girlfriend. I need you to look after her.'

Danny paused, taking the information in.

'Okay, so who is she?'

She wasn't going to like this but it was too late for that.

'She's a cop. A detective sergeant.'

'I need her name, Tony.'

'Rachel Narey. DS Rachel Narey.'

Danny laughed lightly.

'I know her. You've done well there.'

Despite everything, Winter laughed too.

'Cheers, Danny. You can tell her that yourself. I want you to pick her up from Pitt Street. You still know enough people in there that you can get past the front desk, don't you?'

'Course I do. And where do you want me to take this girlfriend of yours?'

'Somewhere safe. She won't want to go with you and she'll not be happy when you tell her who you are. Danny, I want you to not take no for an answer.'

'Okay. You going to tell me why?'

'We need to get her safe because she might be next. I know that this Dark Angel guy knows where she lives and I think he might be looking to shoot her.'

A long pause.

'Why would he want to do that, Tony?'

'She's not on the take, Uncle Danny. I'm as sure about that as I can be. But one of her informants had her name in his mobile and the cunt that's doing all the killings has that phone.'

'Tony, you should be going to the cops with this. I know Alex Shirley, he's sound. You can talk to him.'

'No. I can't. I can't go to anyone in Strathclyde with this.'

'Why not?'

'Because . . . because I've fucked up and I need to sort it.'

'That's not good enough, Tony. People are dying here. It can't be about your pride being hurt.'

'It's more than that. I owe it to people. Give me two days and keep Rachel safe. If I've not sorted it by then, I'll go to Alex Shirley. I promise.'

'No need to promise,' Danny growled at him. 'If you haven't done it by then, I'll drag you there myself.'

CHAPTER 42

It was well after dark o'clock and Winter knew it was no time to be going visiting but then again it was no time to be standing on ceremony.

Just minutes after phoning Danny, he was driving up the High Street past the cathedral, his head full of Rachel and Addison, safe houses and hospital beds. He could still hear Danny's warning, knowing he was right and only managing to shut him out when the lights at the Royal turned green and the road before him swung right and down the hill onto Alexander Parade. It felt like he'd been in Dennistoun more often than he'd been in his own flat the last few days and he was beginning to get sick of the place.

Maybe Mrs McKendrick would be out or in bed but his guess was that she was in her flat, peering into the bottom of a glass of brandy or gin and wondering how the hell it all happened. She'd be up half the night, doped up on Prozac and booze and too tired to sleep. Whether she wanted a visitor to share her misery was another matter but he had to find out.

Winter parked on the other side of the road and looked up. Sure enough, there was a light on in the McKendricks' flat, a dim light like that given off by a table lamp. He crossed the road and pressed the buzzer, hoping that it wouldn't simply scare her. Stepping back, he saw the curtains twitch as a shadow looked down onto the street. It didn't pay to let someone know you were in at that time of night without checking them out first. Rosaleen couldn't have been happy with what she'd seen because there was no voice through the intercom and he had to buzz again. Another minute passed and finally a crackle and she spoke, her voice weary and slightly slurred.

'Who is it?'

'It's Tony. Ryan's mate. I was round yesterday.'

'Oh.'

She fell silent and for a moment he thought she'd walked away.

'Are you still there, Mrs McKendrick?'

'Yes.'

'I want to speak to you.'

'It's very late.'

'I know but it's important.'

'About Ryan?'

'Yes.'

There was a pause as she deliberated then he got his answer as the intercom buzzed loudly. He pushed against the open door and made his way quickly but quietly up the stairs. She was standing just inside the door, holding it to her as if it was some kind of ill-considered protection. He read the look on her face and immediately felt like shit. She thought he was there to bring her bad news about her son.

In some ways, it was the exact opposite. He was there to not tell her the bad news that he knew. He wasn't protecting her for her sake but for his. And Rachel's.

'Do you . . . is Ryan . . .' she faltered.

'No, no,' he reassured her, lying through his teeth. 'I haven't heard anything.'

She fell against the door frame in her relief, immediately making him feel even worse, and burping out a small, fake laugh. Her eyes were frazzled and either prescription medicine or alcohol had been hard at work. She looked at him again, trying to remember who he was.

'Tony?'

'Yes, could I come in Mrs McKendrick?'

She shrugged and turned, leaving him to follow her once more into the flat. Winter closed the door behind him.

Rosaleen fell back into her armchair, a half-full/half-empty glass within easy reach. It had only been a day since he'd seen her but she was already two years older, a greyer and smaller version of her yesterday self. He knew he could make her age another ten years with a few careless words but he wouldn't.

'Can I get you a cup of tea?' she asked as if startled by remembering her manners.

'No thanks.'

'Coffee?'

'No, thank you.'

'Something stronger?'

It was tempting but he said no.

'I just needed to ask you a few questions.'

'Oh.'

'About what we talked about yesterday.'

'About Ryan.'

'Yes. You said he was always on about going to Grahamston.'

'Did I? Yes, that's right, he was always talking about it. How he and Kieran wouldn't be able to go there again. How he'd promised Kieran. Grahamston. That's right.'

The woman was all over the place.

'Mrs McKendrick, has anyone else come to visit you?'

'Oh yes, lots of people. The boys have so many friends. It's been non-stop. People have been very kind. Although, to be honest with you,' she lowered her voice conspiratorially, 'it's all a bit much and I'd rather they didn't any more. Oh I didn't mean you though. Sorry.'

'No it's fine. I understand. But has someone else come to visit you and talked about Grahamston?'

'Oh no. Why would they? Nobody else knew. Just the boys.'

'Yes, but has anyone come to speak to you and maybe Grahamston came up in conversation. Like the way it did with me?'

'Oh, I see. No. Wait, yes. Yes. Oh, it wasn't you, was it? Yes, you as well as the other man.'

Winter's heart skipped a beat.

'When was he here, Mrs McKendrick?'

'Who?'

'The other man.'

'I don't really remember, son. A few days ago.'

'And . . . was it someone you know?'

She reflected for a bit, seemingly not sure how to answer.

'No. I hadn't met him before. He came to ask about Ryan. Like you.'

'What was his name, Mrs McKendrick.'

'You know, I can't remember. There's been so many people round.'

Part of him wanted to strangle her.

'Please try and remember. It's really important.'

'Is it? I don't see how it can be. But I don't remember. I'm sorry. I've not been too well.'

'Can you remember what he looked like? How tall he was? Anything at all?'

She shook her head sadly.

'No. He was maybe . . .' She looked Winter up and down. 'Maybe as tall as you. Maybe not. I'm not sure. Do policemen not have to be a certain height to join?'

His heart stopped briefly.

'What?'

'I thought they had to be tall. Well they used to be anyway. Mind you, you see some . . .'

'He was a policeman?' he interrupted her.

'Oh yes, didn't I say that? He was here to talk to me about how I was after Keiran, well you know. Family liaison, that's what they call it. He was very nice.'

FLOs wouldn't be likely to be still visiting relatives of an overdose victim, not after this length of time. It smelled fishy.

'Was he on his own, Mrs McKendrick?'

'Call me Rosaleen. Was he what? On his own? Yes, yes he was. Just wanted to make sure that I was okay and that Ryan was coping with things.'

'Did he ask you a lot of questions about Ryan?'

'Did he? Yes, I suppose he did. Wanted to know how he was. If I'd heard from him.'

'And had you?'

She looked up at him nervously.

'He's at sea. Can't contact him when he's at sea.'

'No, of course not. And this policeman wanted to know about Grahamston?'

She looked very tired, as if the trouble of remembering things just wore her out.

'I can't really mind, son. I think he asked me about places that Ryan liked to go when he was at home on leave. I must have mentioned Grahamston. Ryan was always going on about it, you know.'

He knew.

'This fellow did seem very interested when I told him about it. He said he'd been there when he was a boy too. He wanted to know all about Ryan and Kieran going there. He was such a nice chap. Very interested.'

I bet he was, Winter thought.

'Try and think, Rosaleen. What did he look like? Anything.'

She frowned and sipped at her glass with an exaggerated thinking pout of her lip before shaking her head firmly.

'Sorry, son. No. I told you. I've not been too well. I can't remember his name or anything. Sorry.'

It was pointless pushing her any further.

'Thanks, Mrs ... Rosaleen. It's late. I'd better be going.'

'Oh. Okay, Tony. I'll see you out.'

She began to push herself out of her seat and stopped halfway, looking puzzled.

'But what was it that you wanted to talk to me about Ryan? You haven't really said. Have you?'

'Yes, yes. About Grahamston and just making sure he was doing okay.'

She looked doubtful.

'But you said it was important.'

'It was.'

'And Ryan's okay?'

'Like I said, I haven't heard anything.'

'You'll let me know if you do?'

'Aye. Of course I will. Of course.'

She smiled, ten years dropping off her in an instant. He wasn't sure if that should have made him feel bad or good. Bad, he decided.

She led Winter to the front door and opened it to let him past.

'Thanks for coming,' she said. 'I didn't mean what I said about not wanting people to come round any more. Not you anyway.'

With that she lifted her head and looked Winter straight in the eye and he took an instinctive half-step away from her, hoping she wasn't hinting at what he thought.

'It gets lonely on my own and my daughter is with friends,' she added.

'I'm sure you won't be on your own for long,' he blurted out. 'Ryan ... I'm sure you'll see Ryan soon.'

Mrs McKendrick managed to look pleased and disappointed all at once. He backed away with a nod of his head and an embarrassed wave, turning to the stairs and hearing the door click shut as he was four steps down. He didn't breathe until he was outside and had opened the car door, not daring to look up at the McKendricks' window.

He started the engine and drove a couple of hundred yards before pulling into the first space he saw and stopping again. His hands gripped the steering wheel hard and he resisted the temptation to batter his head against it. Addison had said to him something once about being careful about asking questions that you didn't know the answer to. Addy.

Whoever it was that had asked Mrs McKendrick about Grahamston it wasn't Addison and it wasn't Rachel. One too tall and one too feminine. It left a whole lot of other cops though.

Winter pulled out his phone and called the number of the intensive care unit. It was late but they were used to being bombarded with calls from worried relatives round the clock. When the young female voice asked, he said he was family. It probably sounded true because he meant it.

'Mr Addison is still stable,' she told him when she came back to the phone.

He said nothing.

'That really is good news,' she continued, sensing his anxiety. 'They were very worried yesterday but he's come through that and they think he might even be able to breathe for himself very soon.'

'Really? I . . . that's . . . Thank you. Really, thank you.'

'He's still very ill,' she warned. 'Stable but serious. I don't want you to . . .'

It was too late, she couldn't take back the only bit of good news he'd heard in a long time. He was going to need it to see him through whatever was coming next.

He glanced at his watch, seeing it was almost half past eleven. There was a good chance that there wouldn't be anyone in the office at that time of night. It wasn't going to stop him going in anyway but he'd just as rather there was no one there to ask him what was going on and where he'd been all day.

The alarm bells that had sounded in his head when he'd seen the photo print-outs had been ringing their heads off from the moment that Rosaleen McKendrick had said the word policeman. They couldn't be ignored any longer, no matter how much he'd tried to rule it out of his thinking, scared of everything it implied.

His mobile phone rang, jumping out of the night's silence and making him nearly soil himself. The name that he hoped for flashed up on the screen. He grabbed it and answered quietly.

'Danny. Have you got her?'

'I've got her. She'll be safe, son.'

'What did you tell her?'

'Enough. She's a feisty one, all right. But like you said, I didn't take no for an answer.'

'Where have you got her?'

'Probably best you don't know, Tony. If you don't know then you can't tell.'

Winter could see the logic of it, even if he didn't like it.

'Fair enough, Uncle Danny. I'm going to get this sorted as soon as possible.'

'Don't sort it quick on account of me. I'm happy looking after a beautiful young woman for as long as it takes.'

'Have I got to keep my eye on you?'

'You better believe it, son. Seriously, get it sorted quickly but get it done right. You watch yourself. I mean it.'

'I will.'

He didn't mean it though. He only had a vague idea of what he intended to do and he had absolutely no idea if it was going to work.

'Tony, I've said this already but you should be taking this in to Shirley. Rachel thinks the same. She was all for taking you to him herself. I must be off my head but I told her we had to trust you. Don't make me regret it.'

'Thanks. But I can't go to Shirley or anyone else in Strathclyde come to that.'

'Why not?'

'I've got to go. Things to do. Look after her for me.'

Danny started to speak but Winter had already gone.

CHAPTER 43

It was just off midnight when Winter got to Pitt Street. There were still a few people hanging around but he kept his head down, avoiding eye contact and the questions that would follow. He didn't have either the time or the energy for that; instead he made straight for the office, switching the light on and closing the door behind him. He needed a bit of privacy.

He booted up the computer, urging it to go faster, and linked up his phone with a USB cable. In a couple of minutes, he had the photographs he'd taken of the photo print-outs from the storage cupboard and printed them off. Sweeping everything off the desk top, he laid them out and added a selection of photographs of his own. Central Station. Harthill Services. Glasgow Harbour. Dixon Blazes. The Dark Angel's portfolio.

For many reasons, the pile of photographs had been burrowing away at him since he saw them. The pic of Rachel coming out of Highburgh Road was the biggest one but Danny had put that right, for now at least. Then there was the fact that two of them were his, or copies of his. He'd recognized them right away.

One that he'd taken of the Nightjar team as they stood near to Addison and McConachie after they were shot. And one of the three cops laughing in the background over the body of Mark Sturrock at Harthill. He hadn't filed them for evidence, on the basis that there was no immediate prospect of a prosecution, so it meant they hadn't left the office. Some fucker must have taken them from his desk and copied them.

Apart from other members of the SPSA, the only people who could get in there were police. Even they weren't supposed to but it wouldn't be difficult to do considering the amount of time they were around the place.

One thing was for sure: Ryan McKendrick couldn't have got in. If this was the Dark Angel's portfolio then it wasn't his alone.

The real kicker was that some of the photographs had been taken from behind the police tape lines. Not from a distance, not from where the killer had been but right there, inside the lines. Four of them in total, taken at Dixon Blazes and at Smeaton Drive. The ones at the industrial estate definitely weren't Winter's and he hadn't been at the Johnstone shooting. They weren't much good and looked like they could have been taken on a mobile phone without much in the way of framing.

If his amateur forensics were right then McKendrick was already dead when they were taken and in any case, it was impossible to see how he could have got past the cop tape. Maybe, just maybe, whoever had copied his photos had done the same with these ones but Winter didn't think so. He who smelt it dealt it, they used to say in the playground. He who took the shots fired the shots, that was his guess.

Rosaleen McKendrick's mystery visitor. The person who was able to get in and copy his pictures. Whoever it was that could take snaps at the crime scene.

It all seemed to add up to the C-word. The question was, which cop was the cunt in question? The answer was in the photographs, he was sure of it.

He looked at Central Station first. The poor pictures he'd taken on his mobile when he made such an arse of himself. There was Campbell Baxter, Daz McKean, Harkins and Simpson,

Paul Burke and Rachel. It was before the Nightjar team had been put together so it was just whoever had been on duty and got the call.

His eyes lingered on the wound in Cairns Caldwell's skull, the dark puncture that oozed dark life. The Nokia hadn't done too bad a job, picking out the hole in his head that he had disappeared into. He had to stop looking though. There was no time for wallowing in that any more.

Nightjar at Harthill. Alex Shirley. Jan McConachie. Addison. Monteith. Cat Fitzpatrick. The uniforms that he didn't recognize. The bodies of Strathie and Sturrock. Pools of rioja and rufous.

Glasgow Harbour. Addison. McConachie. Monteith. Two Soups. Uniforms. Gee Gee Adamson in rosso corso and his leather shroud. Andrew Haddow in a black pinstripe with soft hands and terrified eyes. The black Beamer.

Dixon Blazes. Carnage. Forrest crucified to the front door with blood money stuffed in his mouth. The Temple. Jim Boyle and Sandy Murray. Paddy Swanson. Lucy Stark. It was a real party all right. The four stiffs were there too. Jake Arnold, Ginger George Faichney, Benjo Honeyman and Harvey Houston. McConachie and Addison lying shot, one dead, one dying.

Smeaton Drive. The images behind those he'd seen on TV. Caroline Sanchez. Paul Burke. Rachel. The Temple. Iain Williamson. Baxter. A whole host of bunny suits and uniformed cops making up a one-ring circus.

Blood and people. Death and crowds. Watchers and the watched. The guilty and the innocent and the guilty. Blood and snot and tears. Everything and nothing. Twelve souls separated from their mortal coils in one easy shuffle and two men who almost managed to dodge a bullet. He scanned every face, every expression, looking in the shadows of the eyes of the dead and the grimaces of the living. Looking for something, anything, aware he might only know what it was once he saw it.

Then it struck him. It wasn't about what he could see. It was about who he couldn't.

Winter had never read any Sherlock Holmes but he'd seen the films and he knew the lines. Well, two of them. 'Elementary, my dear Watson', of course was one. The other was, 'Once you eliminate the impossible, then whatever remains, no matter how improbable, must be the truth.'

Eliminate. Take away. Deduct. He wasn't a cop, he was certainly no detective but that didn't mean he knew nothing.

He looked through every photo again, moving them quickly from one hand to another, faster and faster. Harthill, Dixon, Central, Dixon again, Smeaton Drive. From the first to the last then back again. His brain was ahead of his eyes and his hands, jumping from photograph to photograph and to a conclusion.

The most blindingly obvious thing of all was the one that had escaped him till then. The one person that wasn't in the photos at Dixon Blazes and Smeaton Drive was the person behind the camera. He looked at them again and again and again, ticking off names on a list in his head. He wiped the whole lot from his brain and began going through them again from the beginning, coming up with the same name as before.

He pushed past the desk, sending some of the photographs spinning, and back to his computer. He brought up his pictures file and clicked on the entire set that he'd downloaded from the industrial estate. Sixty-two photos in all. He calmed himself as much as he could and began working his way through them, frame by frame.

A scene-setter as soon as he got out of the car. A group shot of Shirley, Rachel, McConachie, Boyle, Murray, three other CID and two other uniform. Open mouths and anxious glances. Distance shots of Graeme Forrest standing against the warehouse door. Close-ups of nails through his hands and feet. McConachie and Addison lying sprawled. Shock and fear on so many faces. Quickly past his frames of Addison to the butchery inside. Jake Arnold's battered corpse with Sandy Murray standing behind him as if he'd never seen anything like it in his life. On past the bloodless ginger ghost, the bloody gutted stomach and finally the broken bones of the man in the hood. Alex Shirley and Colin Monteith stood by the last of the four, angry and spellbound.

Finally he logged into the Return to Scene images from all the crime scenes and viewed the virtual copies of who was where and when. He was pretty sure but he needed to be certain and it suddenly struck him how he could be.

CHAPTER 44

When Danny had finished telling Winter that he would look after Narey and that he had convinced her to get off the streets and stay somewhere safe, he turned and looked her in the eye.

'Happy?' he asked her.

'No, I'd hardly say that. I don't like lying to him any more than you do. But I don't see that we've got any choice.'

'There's always a choice, Rachel.'

'Yes, and I'm choosing to do it this way.'

'Tony thinks you are in serious danger and he thinks I've got you somewhere safe. At least one of these things isn't true.'

'Hopefully both of them.' She tried a laugh but he didn't buy it.

'He says this Dark Angel guy knows where you live and that you're on his hit list. You sure you want to be out there and give him the chance to shoot you?'

'Danny, with all due respect I'm a cop, not a kid. I don't need a babysitter and I don't need the advice of the halfwit that happens to be my . . . boyfriend. Christ, I don't think I've ever called him that before.'

'So this Dark Angel, he thinks your name is in some drug dealer's mobile phone?'

'He knows it is.'

'Uh huh.'

'I'm not corrupt, Danny. Never have been.'

He nodded.

'I know you're not. But I can see why it looks bad. That why Tony can't take this shit to Alex Shirley or someone else in Strathclyde?'

She shook her head.

'No, I don't know how he knows what he does but I'm sure that somehow Tony's got a handle on what's going on. For all that he's a halfwit, I think he's managed to work out the same thing as me.'

'Which is what?'

Narey held her head in her hands for a moment or two, suddenly feeling very tired.

'The call to the Nightjar operation room from the Dark Angel came in at 6.04 but wasn't picked up by the admin assistant until she started at 7.00. Every available CID officer was roused out of their beds and got there as fast as they could. By the time they got there all five men were dead but the bodies were still warm. You with me?'

Danny nodded slowly.

'If the call had been picked up right away,' he said, 'and the cops were there an hour sooner, then the Dark Angel might not have finished his work and wouldn't have been in place to make the shots. Whoever placed the call knew the shift system and knew he had that hour to spare.'

Narey smiled.

'Tony always says you are the smartest person he ever knew.'

'Yeah but he's a halfwit so what the fuck does he know?' he laughed. 'You sure you shouldn't stay somewhere safe?'

'No chance,' she replied. 'Would you?'

'No. Okay, so what are we going to do?'

'We're going out and we're going now. This could be a long night.'

CHAPTER 45

Winter took all the photographs that had been spread across his desk, put them back into the drawer and stuck the prints that he'd made of the storage cupboard copies in beside them. On top of them he stuck a piece of paper with a single name written on it. Insurance. Just in case.

The thought of locking the drawer crossed his mind but so did thoughts of stable doors and bolted horses. He should have done it before. Anyway, there was a good chance that he'd need someone to be able to find what was in there.

He logged off and shut down his PC, knowing that the tech guys could get in there no problem without his password if it came to it. Once inside, it would take them all of two minutes to find the explanatory file he'd left for them.

He walked out of his own office and down the corridor to the stores where the various items of hardware that he needed were kept. During the day it was guarded over by the stores manager and nothing went in or out without his say so. Nights were different though and he had a swipe card that got him in if he was short of equipment and needed replacements in a hurry. Lenny Lewis, the stores Nazi, hated it when anyone did that but he was the least of Winter's worries right now.

The place was like a warehouse and held everything that the different departments within the SPSA needed. Lewis kept it like a maze so that only he knew where everything was in an effort to hold on to his silly little power base. It didn't matter though; even if it took him a bit of time Winter would find what he needed.

He went past evidence bags, batteries, bunny suits, nitrile gloves, casting kits, lifting tape, tweezers, swabs. He saw dictaphones, tents, ink-remover towels, UV inks, release sprays and feather dusters. It was an Aladdin's Cave for forensics. At last, at the far end of the second aisle, he found what he was looking for. Motion sensor cameras.

It maybe wasn't the best plan in the world but it was all he had. He'd go back down into the bowels of the city and place one of these little beauties somewhere it couldn't be seen. The sensor nodes would do the rest, triggering the camera and hopefully proving his theory. It needed to work because there was no plan B.

He hadn't used these things much because there was generally no need but he knew a thing or two about them. In the early days they had video camera tubes as sensors but now they were more likely to have a CCD, a charge-coupled device, or a CMOS, a complementary metal-oxide semiconductor, basically active pixel sensors. Those evening classes had come in useful after all.

The office issue had a five gig CMOS sensor chip, a wireless USB receiver and it was small. Perfect, in fact. He could set it up so that it ran to the laptop and because it was wireless he could hide the lappy somewhere else away from the camera. It would even have sent to his mobile phone but for the fact that he'd be so far below street level.

The beauty of it for Grahamston was that it had built-in infra red LED. It took colour pictures during the day – or outdoors – but at night or down in the gloom below Central Station it would photograph in black and white. But colour or mono made no difference to what he wanted. He only needed to see the fucker and to capture him. On film at least.

He liberated the camera from the store. For something as expensive as that, he should have filled out forms and sent in a request but somehow he didn't see either Lewis or Baxter okaying a midnight requisition demand. But the important thing was that he needed it to catch a bad man and that was what the job was all about. If Baxter understood that then he'd have said yes so it was all good. Lenny Lewis would explode but he could go screw himself.

The temptation was to wait till morning before going down into Grahamston and the little common sense that Winter had left told him that attempting to find his way back to the cupboard where McKendrick's body was stowed was going to be difficult enough with the little daylight that filtered through but nigh on impossible in the dark. The key was to get the first few turns right and he knew he probably needed the initial help from the glass walkways above.

He was knackered too. It was a toss-up whether his legs or his eyes were heavier and his energy levels were as drained as his emotions. Adrenalin could only take you so far.

But for all that, he wasn't for waiting. Too much at stake, too much that could go so badly wrong if he did wait. Addison, Rachel, too many people that he owed to put things right. It was now or never.

Anyway, night was the one time that Winter figured he could be fairly sure not to bump into the shooter if he went down there. Sure it was possible that he'd be there overnight but he doubted it. McKendrick needed to hide there but he didn't. Quite the opposite, he needed to be seen, needed to be visible in his everyday world, above ground and above suspicion.

He still had a job to do after all. He had shifts to fill and villains to catch. He was the cop chasing the killer and the killer chasing the cops. Winter was going to catch this bastard or . . .

The thought stopped him in his tracks. Catch him or die

trying. That was what he doing here, that was the gamble he was taking. But he wasn't afraid of it. It was all about death to him so what could there be to fear?

No, whatever the sense of it, he wasn't for waiting. How would he sleep anyway with his head full of Rachel and worry? He wondered about calling her, hearing her voice but she would just demand that he abandoned his half-arsed plan and let the professionals do it. He'd tell her how they hadn't exactly done a good job of it so far and that would start an argument. No, tempting as that was, he wouldn't do it. That really could wait till morning.

He put the stores back into darkness and slipped out again, back along the corridor and straight past his own office towards the exit. The guy on the desk looked up half-heartedly and gave him a disinterested nod.

'See you later,' he mumbled.

Hopefully, Winter thought.

It took him all of three minutes to drive from Pitt Street to where he parked outside Fat Boab's on Dixon Street and the same again on foot to McDonald's. Late as it was, there were still plenty of people around, having tumbled out of pubs or clubs, but they weren't paying him much attention. CCTV cameras crossed his mind but if anything he'd be happy enough if they'd picked up on him.

He didn't even bother looking around when he got to the end of the lane, just walked straight through the bush-strewn entrance like a late-night drunk who was looking for a piss stop. It was virtually pitch-black down there with little in the way of either neon or moonlight finding their way down into the alley. As well as the camera, Winter had also liberated a torch from the stores but he was keeping that until he was below decks; there was no point in drawing unwanted attention.

It meant he couldn't see where he was going but it was narrow enough that there was nowhere to go but forward with a hand on either wall for balance. His feet crunched over glass and squelched on God knows what as thorns pulled at his trouser legs. He was going slower than he'd done the previous time when there had been some light in the passage, edging ahead a shuffled step at a time. The different pace and the darkness made it harder to judge how far he'd gone . . .

Shit. His left foot suddenly dropped from beneath him, causing him to pitch forward and down, bumping off a succession of stairs, his right knee crashing down onto the edge of the metal sheet that now only half covered the opening and sending an almighty bang reverberating round the narrow passage and down into the depths below. He was left dangling, one leg a few feet below him, pain shooting through his kneecap. He eased himself back up onto his arse and nursed the torn scraps at his knee, feeling blood oozing through the skin. He couldn't see it in the dark but he was guessing it seeped candy-apple red. His left ankle also throbbed and he might have sprained it. He cursed himself for being such an idiot; it wasn't as if he hadn't known the hole was there. The pain was bad enough but the noise that he'd made was even worse. He could definitely have done without that.

Fuck it. If anyone was coming to investigate from Jamaica Street then it was better he wasn't there when they had a nosey. He dropped down through the opening, ignoring the pain in both legs, and made his way down the wooden stairs into the tiny hallway below. He stood there for a bit, waiting for noises from above that meant someone was in the passage but there was nothing. Glasgow either didn't hear or didn't care.

He could see next to nothing down there but with a bit of memory and groping around, he located the corridor that headed off to the right towards what he had thought was north. As soon as he was in the corridor, he switched on the torch, glad of the comfort it brought him, glad even to see the grubby asylum yellow walls and ceramic tiles. When the wash of neon appeared in front of him, oozing down from the walkways above, he hastily put the torch off again although who the fuck he thought was going to notice it staggering along Union Street was beyond him.

He went through the first set of double doors, then the second and the third, becoming more confident that he knew where he was going. The two flights of stairs down rang more bells and so did the cold and the damp that attacked his nostrils. The thought occurred to him that there might be areas of this underground maze that mirrored each other and that one wrong turn could have taken him to somewhere that looked just the same but was hundreds of yards away. For all he knew, he was getting further away from McKendrick and the storage cupboard with every step he took.

But his self-doubt washed away when the recess with the generator suddenly appeared at his left. There might have been more than one such space down there but the assembly of polystyrene and wood were exactly the same. He was on the right track after all. That realization made him emboldened and wary all in one go. His *sgriob* wasn't tingling but the hairs on the back of his neck were disco dancing.

This time the increase in cold and damp came as no surprise: he was getting deeper and darker into Grahamston or the Central foundations or whatever it was. The low brick walls, the boiler supports, the rough ground, the arches, the running water and the years of dust. He was getting close.

He found himself looking out for the discarded Diet Coke bottle. That would be his landmark, the X that marked the spot. The narrow corridors had gone and it was all open and dark with unseen horizons. Close, very close. The bit he was in now looked familiar but then lots of it did in the dark. He switched the light from left to right, picking out what was around him as much as what was in front. There it was! Two empty litres of sugar-free soft drink with aspartame. He moved the torchlight to his left and sure enough it found the contours of the storage cupboard that he was looking for.

For a few seconds, he steeled himself and waited for a scurry of rats to appear under the door frame and charge towards him but thankfully none appeared. Just him and the dust and the Coke bottle and the body of Ryan McKendrick.

The obvious temptation was to look inside the cupboard but he doubted he was any more dead than he was the day before. Anyway, the rats had probably furthered their feast and he wasn't too sure he wanted to see the effects. It could wait. He was down there to rig up the camera and get the fuck out. It was more than enough to be getting on with.

Where was the best place to position the camera? Facing the cupboard or from it? Or inside it? Suddenly he found himself wishing he'd brought more than one, if only for the certain heart attack it would give Lenny Lewis when he found they were gone. But one was all he had so the location was going to be crucial.

He scanned the room with the torch and spied a likely looking beam where he could get a decent angle towards the cupboard door and probably even inside if he got the angle right. There was a support column too that would hide the laptop and let it record the images without anyone seeing it. Yes, that would do the job.

The angle was going to be the vital bit and he lined up a spot at a height that he was sure would let it see straight through the door, assuming it was open. The further the camera was away from the object then the less light it would throw on the subject but that could always be improved later. The tech guys couldn't turn water into wine but just about anything else was within their capabilities. His guess was that this was easily close enough that the camera would grab whoever came near that cupboard.

He took one last look towards the door, making sure that he'd positioned it just right when he was aware of something in his peripheral vision to his right. Nothing more than a flicker of shadow or movement and no time at all to react.

It meant the crash against the side of his head came as a surprise. In the split second that he was aware of his brains rattling against the inside of his skull and his senses spinning out of control, he had just about enough time to taste blood in his mouth before plunging into a pool of darkness that swallowed him up.

He was vaguely aware of a second thump as his head hit the floor but that was all happening to someone else as he drifted far away.

Someone was standing over him.

CHAPTER 46

Consciousness came slowly, along with confusion and a crashing headache. Behind closed eyes, Winter sensed the mother of all hangovers pounding at him and it took a moment to remember that he hadn't drunk ten pints of Guinness and half a bottle of Ardbeg. Instead there was the vague recollection of the dull blow to the back of his head and the sudden realization that he was still alive. And in trouble.

As he peeled back his eyelids, the world came back into focus an inch at a time, from blurred views of his own chest to fuzzy horizons. Shaking his head warily and screwing his eyes shut again in an effort to focus them, he became aware of someone beside him and another in front. He could also feel his hands behind him, tight together, tied together. The person next to him was lying motionless. Still and bloody and smelling bad. Ryan McKendrick. Winter was inside the storage cupboard.

He lifted his head slowly, seeing his own feet bound together with cabling, then someone else's legs standing there, then hands, hands holding a rifle pointed at him, a chest, shoulders, face. Expressionless, cold, looking for shock on his face and disappointed when he didn't see any.

'You don't look surprised to see me,' he said quietly.

Winter just shrugged.

'Was it me you came looking for, Tony?'

He sounded anxious, more nervous than a man with a gun needed to be.

'I came to find the killer.'

'Well, you found him.'

He motioned with his head towards McKendrick's body.

'Aye?' Winter asked him.

'Aye,' he answered. 'I know that you found out about his brother. Can't blame him for wanting revenge really. Can you?'

'Probably not. I never had a brother, wouldn't really know but I guess you'd want some pay back.'

'Pay back?' The man's eyebrows shot up scornfully. 'Revenge, that's what you'd want. Fucking justice. I've got a brother, ten years younger than me. Anyone did that to him I'd be after them. Can't blame him at all.'

'Did something happen to your brother?'

He lashed out a boot, catching Winter hard on the ankle, making him recoil with the pain.

'Don't try to psychoanalyze me, you prick. Nothing happened to my brother. What the fuck are you doing here anyway? You take a couple of photographs and you think you are a cop? Is that it? Always wanted to be one of us?'

'No. I told you. I just came to find the killer.'

'But why? What the fuck has it got to do with a wanker like you?'

Colin Monteith was getting less anxious and more angry. Winter realized that probably wasn't good.

'Too many people have been killed. And shot. I thought I knew where to find the guy that was doing it.'

'Shot? Your bum chum Addison. Is that it? That long streak of pish had it coming for years. It's only a wonder that no one tried to kill him before now. And how the fuck can you say that too many have been killed. Eh? Too many drug dealers and scumbags are dead? Halle-fucking-lujah. It's barely a fucking start.'

Monteith's eyes were wide now, almost bulging.

'Too many?' he continued ranting. 'Well, seeing as you've never been a cop. Too many my arse. Too many of these bastards have got away with it for too long. Killing people with that shit that they peddle, getting minted and we've been able to do fuck all. Don't greet for those cunts, Winter. They don't deserve it.'

'So you think it's okay what McKendrick did?'

'He should get a fucking medal. I've spent years cleaning up the mess left by bastards like Quinn and Caldwell. Couldn't lay a fucking glove on them even though we all know what they do. They bring drugs into Glasgow, we can't touch them. They sell the shit, we can't touch them. They have people killed, we can't touch them. They launder money, run protection rackets, break legs, bribe cops, we can't touch them. It makes me fucking sick to my stomach.'

Winter was suddenly reminded again of Addison's lecture about only asking questions that you know the answer to.

'So why didn't you stop them? Why didn't the police do something before McKendrick started killing?'

Monteith laughed derisorily.

'You think it's that easy? You stupid sod. We can do nothing. The law's there to protect these bastards and stop us doing our job. They've got better lawyers than we have. More expensive lawyers. Vermin. And even without them, too many cops are just too scared to do anything about it. They've got families and are scared shitless that the bampots will come after them. It's a small city and it's awfy easy to find out where they live.'

A picture of Rachel flooded Winter's mind and he tensed his wrists, causing the ties to bite into them.

'Not everyone can be too scared,' he said. 'You're not scared are you, Monteith?'

A tight grin stretched across the cop's face, followed by another vicious kick to Winter's ankle.

'Don't taunt me. You're in no position. No, I'm not scared. But for every cop that's got the bollocks to do something about it, there's another one in his way that's deep in the pockets of scumbags like Quinn and Caldwell and Riddle. It makes me fucking mad. I've never taken so much as a penny but there's cunts who have.'

He levelled Winter with his stare. 'Like your pal Addison.'

'Addy isn't dirty.'

Monteith laughed again.

'How do you know that? What the fuck do you know? Addison's name and phone number was in Sturrock's mobile. In his contacts folder. How do you explain that? That cow McConachie, she was on the take too.'

'I know Addy enough to know he wouldn't.'

'Bollocks. You know nothing. Snap your clever little photographs and fuck off home and think you're part of it all. You're not. You're just an annoying wanker that gets in the way of cops trying to do their job. Sturrock had your pal's number right there in his phone and now I've got his number. I've seen it with my own fucking eyes.'

He stopped, realizing he'd said too much.

'With your own eyes?' Winter asked. 'Sturrock's phone? The cops don't have that. They only have Addison's. How did you see it?'

Monteith bit his lip and spun away from him, as if hiding from some unwelcome truth. He came back full circle, staring him down angrily and directing his rifle at Winter's head, lifting the barrel up and down a couple of times as if making his mind up. He held his breath. He clenched his teeth.

Monteith must have made a decision because he pointed the rifle straight between Winter's eyes then spun on his heels again and left the cupboard, the door swinging closed behind him. The silence that he left behind washed over Winter, leaving him in a cold sweat, breathing hard.

He sat still, waiting for Monteith to come back, his ears straining for any sound or suggestion of what he was doing. There was nothing beyond dripping and running water, the distant rumble of a train and the pounding in his chest. That was the loudest of them all, compounded by the blood thumping in his ears.

What the fuck did he think he was doing? Danny had tried to warn him off doing anything stupid, Rachel too by the sound of it, but he was just too pig-headed to listen. He was supposed to be behind the camera. The observer. See the city through a lens. That had been the idea.

Winter tested the ties on the cabling that held his wrists. There was a bit of movement but nothing too encouraging. He was stuck there, waiting. Monteith could do whatever he wanted.

The door burst open and the cop stormed through, the rifle still in his hands but – Winter breathed again – it was pointed at the floor.

'Well done, fuckwit,' Monteith scowled at him. 'I wasn't sure how I was going to let you get out of here but now I can't do it. What the fuck are you doing down here, you stupid bastard?'

Nothing to lose now, Winter thought.

'Looking for you.'

The cop stared at him.

'I came looking for you, Monteith.'

He just continued to stare.

'What happened to him?' Winter asked with a nod to McKendrick.

Monteith looked from him to the body and back again, wavering, deliberating.

'An accident,' he said finally. 'An accident.'

'Tell me.'

'Why the fuck should I?' Monteith barked at him, suddenly furious. 'Why the fuck should I tell you anything?'

'Because I think you want to tell someone and there's no one else here. You just said you can't let me go so there's nothing to stop you telling me.'

'You always were a smart arse, Winter. You and that twat you palled about with. In fact you can thank him for this. If he hadn't opened his big gob then I'd never have found McKendrick. At least not so quickly.'

Winter felt even more uneasy than he had up till then.

'Not as smart as you think you are though, eh?' Monteith taunted. 'Didn't know that, did you?'

Winter said nothing. 'It was your pal that mentioned the bruise on your cheek. The one that you made up some half-arsed excuse about. He said that there was no way you'd slipped like you said you had. He said you'd been punched or more likely kicked in the face. I didn't think too much about that on its own except that you probably had it coming.

'But then I heard of a woman phoning to complain about a Sergeant Winton giving her son a hard time. They got hold of Eddie Winton over in London Road but he had no idea what they were talking about and anyway he was on a course the day this McCabe woman said. Everyone else thought nothing of it but I thought of you. Winton . . . Winter. Close enough and I didn't like the smell. I thought maybe you were up to your eyes in it all.'

'You went through my photographs.'

'I sure did. Quite a collection of shite you've got there.'

Winter bristled and wanted to punch his lights out but that wasn't going to happen.

'All those pictures of car crashes and glassings and stabbings. What the fuck is that all about, eh? You get your kicks from all that blood?'

'Fuck off.'

'Hit a nerve, have I? You are a sick bastard, Winter. And what the hell is it with those photos of people in the background, especially cops? You've no fucking right to be taking those. None whatsoever. You're not fit to kiss their feet never mind photograph them when they are doing their job.'

He lifted the barrel of the rifle level with his head but this time Winter had no sense that he was going to use it. He was simmering but he wanted to shoot his mouth off, not the gun.

'Yeah? Well I was doing my job, too. You wouldn't understand.'

'Oh, I understand better than you think, sicko. I had a good look through everything you had stowed away there. You like it too much. All those close-ups of wounds, all that blood. You don't need that much detail for court. That's just for you, isn't it?'

Winter's stomach turned because he knew the answer was yes but he wasn't admitting that to this psycho.

'It's my job, I told you. And you had no right going through it.'

'No right?' Monteith laughed wildly. 'I am a police officer. I am investigating a series of crimes. I have the right to do whatever the fuck I want, look wherever the fuck I want. And I found even more than I could have hoped for. Didn't I?'

'You tell me.'

'Oh I will. Even though you know already. I found two photographs filed together. A kid called Rory McCabe and our old friend Steven Strathie. As soon as I saw the name McCabe I knew I was right. The picture of Strathie meant I'd hit the jackpot.'

He was grinning smugly. So smart. Winter wanted to smash his face in.

'There was a link right there. Those marks on their chest. Identical. The blow-ups of them that you had left no doubt about that. Now I didn't know what they meant but I knew they put McCabe in the middle of the case. Yet you didn't think to mention that to Alex Shirley or Nightjar, did you?'

'Fuck you.'

Monteith ignored him and went on.

'No, you didn't. Now that is either because you were too fucking thick to make the connection or because you were in thick with your crooked mate Addison.'

There was a third reason, a worse one in many ways, but Winter wasn't for sharing it with Monteith. He wasn't going to give the cop anything never mind the shameful fact that a bit of him was happy to let the Dark Angel carry on at that point. He just looked back at him blankly. Monteith could think what he wanted.

'Nothing to say, eh?' he smirked. 'Idiot or up to your neck in it. Has to be one or the other.'

'So what does that say about you, Monteith? 'Cos I'm betting you didn't take that bit of info to the Temple either.'

Winter knew it was a mistake the second the words were out of his mouth and winced as he took another kick, to his right knee, the one he injured earlier. Monteith put his weight right through it and it stung like hell.

'You don't tell me what I should have done, you cunt. You don't get to tell me anything. I am a cop. I get to do what I want, you don't.'

'Anything you want?' Winter asked him. Monteith shook his head.

It was Winter's turn to stare back at his captor, but Monteith wasn't for biting just yet.

'I checked the case file and the kid McCabe was beaten up in the street. Stupid wee fucker done over by other stupid wee fuckers. I read through it but it seemed no big deal. But then I ran McCabe's name through the computer and found out that he'd been interviewed after his best mate died of an overdose. A kid called Keiran McKendrick. Sound familiar?'

Winter shrugged but Monteith just laughed.

'Doesn't matter either way. It was more drugs and I knew right away it fitted. Not sure you would have the brains to do that.'

Winter took the bait.

'So that's why you went to see Mrs McKendrick in Whitevale Street, is it, Monteith?'

The cop looked surprised but it was quickly replaced by a sleek grin.

'You know that? Yes, of course you do. That's how you found out about this place. The old bat must have told you about it the same as she did to me. Silly cow barely knew what day it was but she remembered the place her precious son kept banging on about. If only she could see him now, eh?'

'What happened to him?'

'Accident. I told you.'

'Tell me what happened.'

Monteith closed his eyes briefly then opened them to look right through him.

'Winter, you know that Mafia line about how if I told you then I'd have to kill you?'

He nodded.

'Well if I tell you then I'll have to kill you.'

Winter let the suggestion settle on him. He'd already come to the conclusion that he'd had it anyway.

'Like you killed McKendrick?'

He shook his head at Winter with what looked like a rueful smile.

'Have it your way, dead man. But like I said, it was an accident. Not going to be worth your life.'

Winter wasn't sure what would be worth that but he knew he wanted to hear it.

'Like I said, as soon as I knew the McKendrick kid was involved with drugs then I knew I was on the right track. A wee bit of digging and I discovered he had a brother in the Navy. That was pure gold. Nightjar had already identified the L115A3 as military issue, probably Special Ops. The boxes just kept on getting ticked. I put in a call to Northwood and learned that Ryan McKendrick was officially off active duties after suffering from post-traumatic stress disorder. Unofficially, they didn't have a fucking clue where he was.

'But I did. Thanks to you and his mother. I wasn't sure what she meant by Grahamston, not at first, but a couple of phone calls and a visit to Google and I was certain. The only problem was finding exactly where he was hiding down here. It's a big place.'

'How did you find your way in?' Winter asked, somehow still hoping that the answer wouldn't include the lane behind McDonald's.

'Through the front fucking door, what do you think? Never you mind, you won't need to find your way out. You'll be spending the rest of your days down here. The good news is it won't be for long.'

'Oh you're a funny man, Monteith. You should be on the telly.'

He laughed in Winter's face, a cackling laugh that disappeared in a flash and was replaced by a snarl and a rifle barrel shoved against Winter's forehead. He felt it rough and hard and cold, scraping against his skin, pushing his head back.

'Maybe I will be on the television, Winter. Maybe I am already, maybe all over the world. And I'll tell you what, I'll be having the last laugh. Is that all right with you? Is it?'

The bastard was losing it and Winter didn't want to give him any excuse for squeezing that trigger. He knew he was halfway to dying but as much as he wanted to meet his mother again, he didn't want it to happen any sooner than it had to. He nodded his head the best he could.

When Winter gave in to him, Monteith seemed to calm down a bit. He pulled the rifle off Winter's head with one last scrape of the barrel for good measure leaving a tear of skin and a squeeze of blood.

'As I was saying. I had to find McKendrick down here. Big place but not that hard, even a fuckwit like you managed to do it,' he sniggered. 'I wandered around till I found this place; it was obvious he had been here and then all I had to do was wait.'

Monteith hesitated to allow Winter time to be impressed but he wasn't giving him that satisfaction.

'The way the sound reverberates down here you can hear someone coming from a long way off, especially if they don't expect you to be waiting for them. And if they are as stupid as you are. McKendrick was no better.'

He smirked at Winter, daring him to answer but he didn't.

'He walked in here and virtually begged me to club him over the back of his head with this four by four. He had a rifle so I had to put him down in one go. He went out like a light. The man was twice your size but went down just the same. There he was, the man they called the Dark Angel, the man they were all talking about, at my feet.'

This guy was seriously fucked in the head. Winter could hear his sense of himself growing with every word that spewed from his mouth. He was boasting that he had managed to knock McKendrick out when the man hadn't been looking. In his own head, he'd done what no one else could. But what had he done next?

'Did you talk to him when he came round?'

'Of course I did. That's my fucking job. Think I don't know my job? Of course I talked to him. I wanted to know everything he had to say. He wasn't exactly shy about it anyway. He was . . . he was pleased with what he did. And so he should have been. He should have been fucking proud of it.'

Monteith was wandering on the spot now as he talked. It was spilling out of him like blood from a wound. Just to be sure, Winter was going to stir his pot even further.

'What did he have to be proud of?'

He paid for it with the butt of the rifle being spun and crashed against the outside of his left knee. It wasn't as bad as the kick had been to the other one but the hurt still shot through him, sharp and deep.

'Are you kidding me? He took out the bastards that were responsible for the shit that was going through the veins of all those kids out there. Quinn and Caldwell got rich, fucking minted, by selling death. They had been fucking up this city and so had the cunts that went before them and those that would have come after them. They'll think twice now though. Maybe not be so quick to push out drugs if they know there's someone out there who's going to take them out.

'What did he have to be proud of? You're only a fucking photographer but you've still been out there, you've seen what that stuff does. Stick insects chasing powder up their nose or firing shite into their veins. Their kids starving and half naked, their chances completely fucked of doing anything other than following in the footsteps of the bampots that spawned them. Entire communities screwed because of that stuff. Stealing off each other, walking round like zombies, no fucking interest or energy in getting a job even if they could stay clean long enough to find someone stupid enough to give them one.

'Drugs have killed this place. You walk five minutes in any direction from Buchanan Street and all those million-pound shops and you'll find some poor bastard who barely has the strength to pick up their giro because their body is shot to pieces. You drive five minutes from George Square and you drive past shitholes full of people who never had a fucking chance. You drive fifteen minutes and you hit schemes where those who aren't on drugs aren't trusted by anyone else.

'Do you really think these poor bastards want to spend their lives stealing a fiver from some prick that's got a fiver more than they have? You really think that girls want to go on the game and blow some fat drunk for a tenner? Think they wanted to grow up and be skanky whores? It's the fucking drugs and it's the fucking bastards that push it at them. Of course he should have been proud. He did something when everyone else did fuck all.'

Monteith fell back against the wall, the exertion of his rant leaving him momentarily breathless. Maybe Winter should have known better but he recognized a soft spot when he saw one.

'Is that why you took over where he left off?'

The cop lifted his head off his chest slowly, his eyes suddenly full of fire. His lip curled back and Winter wished he hadn't said what he had but that thought was quickly overtaken by pain as Monteith rushed towards him, rifle butt high. He turned his head to the side to avoid the blow but Monteith had fooled him. The kick came to his balls and the pain seared through him like lightning. Winter doubled over as much as the bindings would let him, his balls throbbing and screaming. His eyes watered and he spat out the ache that soured his mouth.

Monteith stood over him, the rifle still clenched between his fists, raising it up and down threateningly but Winter doubted he could hurt him more with the gun than his boot had.

'I'm telling the fucking story,' he raged. 'You just shut up and listen. Just keep your questions to yourself.'

'Fuck you.'

Monteith giggled at that. An off-the-wall, manic giggle that worried Winter far more than the threat.

'Listen to the big man. McKendrick did more for this city in a few days than you could do in a lifetime. He took action. He avenged his wee brother and he did so much for this place while he was at it. He had reason to be proud.'

Winter settled for just lifting his eyebrows by way of a question. Monteith was doing fine without prompting. Winter didn't need any more hurt before the cop did whatever he was going to do.

'He was more ... angry, though. Just very angry,' Monteith continued. 'Like he had unfinished business. That bothered him more than the fact that I'd knocked him out and taken his rifle off him. He didn't seem to give a fuck what happened to him except that it stopped him from doing what he'd planned. He just sat there fuming, ready to rip Monteith's head off the first chance he got. Like a caged bear. I told him that I didn't blame him for doing what he'd done but it didn't wash with him. He just wanted to have a go.

'He kept going on about his brother. How it was his job to look after Kieran and that he'd let him down. How he'd failed him and how he had to make up for that. The poor bastard had lost it. I think the post-traumatic stress disorder thing from the Navy was only half a lie. If you ask me, he was probably wired to the moon before his brother died and it just pushed him over the edge.

'I asked him how he knew where to get at Caldwell and Quinn and he was happy to tell me. He roughed up some two-bit dealer, the cunt who sold the gear that killed his brother. Shook him down for every bit of info he had, which was plenty. The guy squealed like a stuck pig, told McKendrick everything he needed to know. Places, likely times, habits. Told him about couriers and their schedules. Told him the entire hierarchy of firms across the city. The lot.

'Then when he had Strathie and Sturrock, he learned more. Beat the shit out of them until they coughed as well. He felt bad about the old boy Turnbull at the services. Shooting him had been a mistake. Still, it all helped lead him to Haddow and Adamson. Bang bang, another two scumbags down. He had a list, a long list. He had all the stuff that we should have had. But even then we couldn't have taken these bastards down within the law. He didn't need to bother about that though.'

Monteith stopped and looked at his watch.

'So what happened to him?' Winter asked.

'It's time for me to go.'

It wasn't an answer, it was an aside. Winter decided he was going to push his luck.

'So what happened to McKendrick's list?'

Nothing.

'Did someone decide to finish it for him?'

Monteith looked at Winter blankly before coming over behind him and taking his watch off his wrist. Monteith fished into Winter's left pocket then his right where he found his mobile phone. Standing up again, he dropped both onto the ground in front of him. He looked Winter in the eye again briefly before stamping on first the watch and then the phone. Both lay in bits.

'I've got work to do,' he said softly. 'Don't miss me too much.'

He turned and closed the door behind him, leaving Winter trussed on the floor next to the rotting corpse of a killer, somewhere deep in the bowels of the city. A key turned in the lock from the outside. A bad day had just got a lot worse.

CHAPTER 47

Winter listened to Monteith's departing footsteps, trying to work out which way he'd headed so that he'd know if he used the same entrance or a different one. It was hopeless though. He'd no idea if the cop had gone straight out or had done something else first. He'd obviously taken the rifle out of the cupboard with him but if he was going on duty then surely he wouldn't take it above ground with him. That might mean he had planked it somewhere and then headed in another direction. Although the 'job' he had to do might have been something else entirely from police work

Winter hung intently on to the ever-diminishing noise of Monteith's shoes clacking against the foundations, catching the point where it merged with the sound of the dripping water then was subsumed by it, leaving him alone in the bowels of hell.

He put his head back and screamed silently, roaring nothing at no one. Monteith leaving should have made him feel safer but it did anything but. Bound hand and foot in the half-light from the hurricane lamps, he felt like Jonah in the belly of the whale with another misbegotten soul, the remnants of an earlier meal, lying by his side.

McKendrick was reeking. Winter had been trying to block it out but there was no getting away from it, the body seemed to be getting riper by the minute. It was like a piece of rotting steak meat had been left in the sun for days on end and had been sprinkled with a couple of drops of cheap perfume to make it sweet. Monteith's speech had taken his mind off it while he was there but now there was nothing else to occupy his mind. It invaded every inch of the cupboard and attacked his nostrils like a snake.

His gag reflex was working overtime and he wasn't sure how long he could go without chucking up. Once the horror of the smell lodged itself in his brain he could think of nothing else. His cheeks puffed out and he swallowed back down the bile that wanted to escape. He turned his head away from the body in a futile gesture because it was everywhere. The longer he sat there, the more it crept into his clothes, his hair, his skin. He edged away the little he could, shuffling on his arse so he was at least not touching him.

His stomach eventually let him down. He pulled his head to the side as it tightened its grip and he threw up. Fucking great. As if the stench of McKendrick wasn't bad enough, now he had the smell of vomit to contend with as well. The only consolation was that at least it was his own sick. This didn't seem much of a comfort as a second belch rose from his stomach and joined the rest. Emptied, he spat the last of it from his mouth.

The effort exhausted him, causing him to inhale and immediately bark out the smell again. His stomach had no more to give and disgusting as the stink was, he could handle it. Maybe vomiting had broken the hold that it had on him.

He looked around the cupboard and saw that apart from him being a prisoner, nothing seemed to have changed from his last visit. The cardboard box with the remains of the Special Ops' survival rations. The four boxes of ammunition. The notebook and the photographs that had led him back here to Monteith. What a smart idea that had turned out to be.

He sat and listened. The dripping water was through the door and to his left, maybe twenty yards away. Way above him, Glasgow was still there and doubtless still awake but he couldn't hear it. He didn't know what time it was but the last train had gone for the night and the sounds of the cars and the food vans wasn't making it down this far.

No, apart from the water and his heart, all he could hear was the darkness beyond.

His phone was just a couple of feet away but useless to him. Danny and Rachel were on the other end of that mess of broken technology, maybe wondering where he was, maybe not. Why hadn't he listened to them?

Suddenly there was noise and his ears twitched at it. A scrape. A number of scrapes. Then silence. The wind? There was water down here so why not wind too? Then there it was again, closer, louder, more of them. The light of the hurricane lamps picked out the space below and beyond the bottom of the door and in the shadows he saw the shapes approach. Maybe it was the smell of vomit that attracted them. Maybe it was McKendrick, their unfinished meal. Maybe it was him.

There was either one big fucking rat or lots of them because the shadow moved and whispered as one. The scrapes that they had made across the floor were slowly, feverishly replaced by their chatter to each other. The squeaks soared to the roof as they had obviously decided that the time for deception was past. He could only imagine that they were considering the merits of charging into the room.

His breath was fast and shallow and he realized he was truly terrified. He'd seen what they'd done to McKendrick and didn't fancy some of the same. Ryan hadn't exactly been able to fight back but with his hands and legs tied, Winter wasn't going to be much better off.

They were getting louder and nearer. Instead of just shadows, he could now see tails and feet and the odd inquisitive head darting below the door frame. Fuck this.

He roared at them. He put his head back and bellowed with every bit of energy that he had left inside him.

His face must have been the colour of beetroot as he threw a random collection of angry swear words at them but he was determined that they'd get the message. It wasn't enough to be loud, he needed them to hear rage and danger.

It must have worked because they shrieked and turned, disappearing from the doorway as soon as the explosion of noise hit them.

He continued to shout like a madman until he ran out of breath. His head collapsed onto his chest and he panted like a rabid dog. He didn't know how long he sat like that, weary and fretful, wondering how the fuck he'd got there and how he'd get out.

His head occasionally lifted enough to sneak a glance at the door but the little furry bastards were elsewhere, doubtless hatching a plan. He stayed quiet and tried to think.

He watched the hurricane lamps. One was burning much brighter than the other and maybe it was his paranoia but the weaker one seemed to be on its last legs. From where he sat, he couldn't see the length of the wick on it but he worried it would burn itself out before too long. He studied them. Watching how quickly they burned, trying to gauge how long they had left.

Not that he had any real concept of time any more. With his watch and phone smashed and no passing of daylight, it could have been crawling or racing for all he knew. He guessed it had been maybe two hours since Monteith left but it could have been half that or twice it. He was fucked. He heard another squeal.

His head flew from the lamp to the door in time to see pink feet and ink-black eyes steal fearlessly into the room. Just one rat rather than the pack. An advance party, perhaps.

The little bastard scanned the room, nose twitching, giving him no more than a contemptuous glance in the passing. Winter roared again but it didn't flinch, just looked at him curiously wondering what he thought he was achieving. Maybe it was because it could see that the noise wasn't connected to movement or had worked out that he couldn't move. Either that or they'd just sent in the bravest or the stupidest one they had.

It was well inside the room now and on the move. He pulled his legs instinctively towards him but it scurried past and made for the cardboard box with McKendrick's rations. The black tail disappeared from view as it slipped inside and in seconds the sound of munching came from the box. Energy bars or biscuits, he guessed. The crunching stopped and he saw the rat's head pop up into view, checking to see if Winter had found the ability to move. When it saw that he hadn't it must have encouraged it to be braver still rather than go back into the box because, just as the first of the lamps gave up the ghost and flickered no more, it hopped out and onto McKendrick.

Standing on its hind legs, it sniffed at the air then in a flash buried itself under the blanket that covered the body. The squelching sound that floated over to him made his stomach turn. It was like fingers being stuck into blancmange then pulled back out. Judging by where the bump of the rat was on the body, he could only imagine, hard as he tried not to, that the munching slurping sounds were coming from McKendrick's face. The image of Ryan's half-eaten lips already scarred his mind and it seemed the rat was now finishing the job.

He screamed at it, as much to block out the hellish sounds as in any hope that it might scare it off. He bawled at it till his lungs were fit to burst. Whatever McKendrick had done, he didn't deserve to be dessert for a rodent. And he didn't deserve to listen to it. The last tired bark left him but the damnable noise was still escaping from the blanket and molesting his mind. Then it stopped, the bump moving from McKendrick's head and slithering towards the edge of the blanket. The rat reappeared and looked at Winter with renewed interest, sitting up and testing the air with its nose.

Its snout still quivering like jelly, it hopped off McKendrick and onto him. Winter shouted and squirmed, trying to throw it off by rocking side to side as much as he could but it easily maintained its balance and all he was doing was slowing it down a bit. He screamed at it as he realized it was heading for his knee and that it was the dried scrapes of carmine blood that was grabbing its attention. He rocked almost all the way over and, yes, managed to shake it off but it simply leapt back on again.

Winter rolled the other way but it was ready for him this time, digging its claws into his legs and holding on, getting nearer and nearer to his bloody knee. He tried going up and down and side to side, almost absently noticing that the wriggling was loosening the ties at his feet, but couldn't shake the rodent off again. Then, its target in sight, the rat almost lazily sunk its teeth into his exposed knee and bit. The pain shot from his kneecap to his teeth and back. It was like being stabbed with a rusty knife. He was being eaten alive by a dirty rat, sharing whatever diseases it had.

He screamed again and rolled right over onto his side, sending the rat spinning onto the floor. He kicked and scrambled and rolled, desperately trying for perpetual motion in a bid to stop it sinking its teeth into him again. Being on his side made him vulnerable but the movement was saving him. The cabling was becoming looser round his legs and the more he kicked, the more he was sure he could get them off. The rat circled and jumped but he was trying to get on a bucking bronco now. As long as Winter had the energy to keep going then he could keep it off but when he stopped the rat would have him. He had to kick the cabling loose and quick.

He thrashed more, feeling it give bit by bit, his feet easing further apart until with a final shake it was off him and his legs were free. As soon as he'd rid himself of them, he rolled onto his side and heaved up unsteadily onto his feet. The rat didn't fancy it so much once Winter was standing and tore off under the door, easily avoiding the kick Winter swung at it.

He looked down at his bleeding knee, thinking that it wasn't crimson, it was dirty, diseased red. If he ever got out of there then he'd need to see a doctor right away. But as he looked at the still-locked door and tested the cabling on his hands to no avail, he knew it might be the least of his worries.

He paced around, again trying to shake the ties on his hands the way he'd done with his feet, but he got nowhere.

He ended up slumped back against the wall, as far away from McKendrick as he could, waiting and watching and wondering. He hadn't been like that for long when he heard it. Faint but getting louder and closer. Footsteps. Despite all the bad news that they were probably bringing, he was glad to hear them. After so long of nothing but water and squeaks, they were somehow deafening as they neared until finally they crashed down outside the door and in the dim glow of the single remaining lamp, he could see the long shadow of human legs.

CHAPTER 48

The key turned slowly in a lock weighed down by a hundred years of rust but with a final clunk it drew back the bar and the door swung open. Rifle in hand, Monteith came in looking stern, anxious even. He seemed surprised to see Winter sitting in a different position to when he'd left and immediately looked to Winter's feet where he saw them untied. Monteith immediately lowered the rifle till it was trained on him.

'Turn and show me your hands. Now.'

'Nice day at the office, dear?' Winter asked him, paying for it with a sharp kick to his right ankle. He was really getting fed up with that.

'I said fucking turn round.'

Winter obediently swivelled at the hips, ducking forward and to the side so Monteith could see that his hands were still firmly bound together behind him.

Monteith nodded, satisfied. It was only then that the smell from McKendrick hit him and he turned away sharply, his hand covering his nose and mouth.

'You get used to it after a while,' Winter told him.

Monteith looked down at the covered body, shaking his head slowly.

'How did he die?' Winter asked again.

'I told you. An accident.'

'You accidentally broke his neck?'

'He went for me. The crazy bastard leapt at me when I had the gun on him. I didn't want to kill him, wouldn't have shot him. Not dead anyway. I might even have . . .'

'Let him carry on?'

'No. Yeah, maybe. I don't know. It didn't come to that. He got both hands on the gun and it became him or me. He ended up in front of me with the rifle across his neck, both of us holding it, grappling for it. I tried to pull it into his throat just to choke him a bit but then I twisted it and . . . there was a crack and he slumped. I didn't mean to kill him.'

'So you took over where he left off?'

Monteith ignored him.

'How many did you kill, Monteith? Eight? Oh and you shot an innocent cop too. That make you proud?'

'Shut the fuck up, Winter.'

'You said that McKendrick should have been proud of what he did so it should be the same with you. Are you proud? Are you?'

'I told you to shut it.'

He was getting louder, angrier.

'Come on, Monteith. It's just you and me. You said McKendrick should have got a medal for what he did. He did something when everyone else did fuck all, that's what you said. So you did it too, didn't you?'

'You're talking yourself into the grave, you stupid bastard. And there was no innocent cop. Your arsehole mate Addison was guilty as sin. I've never taken a dirty fiver in all the years I've worked and the idea of cops working for these bastards makes me want to puke. They are no better than the scumbags that pay them.'

Winter tensed his wrists against the cabling ties, wishing they'd been loosened so he could punch him in the face.

'Addy wasn't dirty. You've got nothing to prove that because there isn't anything. What about Forrest and McConachie?'

'No doubt about it. They were up to their eyes in it. Those four scumbags in the warehouse at Dixon Blazes? They couldn't wait to talk about the dirty cops. Full of it they were. Wanted to save their necks and gave chapter and verse about how Forrest had been taking backhanders for years and turned a blind eye any time he was told to. He was well known in the saunas that Caldwell owned, got freebies from the girls in there. I'd heard that about him so it all fitted. They said that bitch McConachie had been tipping off Gilmartin whenever we tried to move against them and she had a pile of cash in her bank account.'

'And Addy?'

'Your mate's number was in Sturrock's phone. Why the fuck do you think that was there?'

'That's it? That's all you had?'

'It's all I needed.'

'Bollocks it is.'

Winter swallowed hard before what he was going to say next.

'And what about Rachel? Rachel Narey.'

Monteith looked at him hard.

'What about her? How did you know about her?'

'I saw the photograph you'd taken. The one outside her flat.'

'I'd have to wonder how you knew that was her flat but yeah, I took that. She was on the short list.'

Winter tried to keep a lid on his temper but it was becoming impossible.

'McKendrick's list?'

'No, mine. I found her name listed in Sturrock's phone as well. I've been keeping my eye on her. Not a hard thing to do, she's tasty. If she wasn't shagging drug dealers, I wouldn't mind giving her one myself.'

That did it.

Winter got to his feet. Ignoring Monteith's warning shout, he pulled one leg under the other and let his weight fall to the side till he was able to push himself up. Unsteady but upright, he was facing Monteith eye to eye for the first time and the cop didn't like it.

He took half a step back. It wasn't much but it was the first sign of a defensive move on his part, the first time that he'd displayed anything other than full confidence in what he was doing. Maybe he realized that too because he immediately came forward again to where he'd been.

'Get back on the floor. Get back on the fucking floor.'

Winter stood his ground.

'Fuck you, Monteith.'

'What makes you so sure I won't just put a bullet between your eyes, Winter? It is a hell of a lot closer than this thing is designed for but you shouldn't be in any doubt that it can do the job. From here it would blow your head off.'

'And you can do the job, right? Maybe you will. But the ones you killed deserved it, didn't they?'

Winter took a couple of steps towards Monteith and was pleased to see him backing away towards the open door.

'Stop right there, Winter. Stop now. You stop or I will fucking kill you here and now.'

'I don't think you've got the balls for it, Monteith.'

'You know nothing, Winter. Nothing. Not about what I'm capable of or what the fuck happens in the real world. Talking about whether I'm proud when you don't have the first clue about what needed to be done.'

'So tell me.'

'I'm going to kill you right now.'

'I told you. I'll take my chances.'

'You're an arsehole. Yeah I'm proud. I've got every fucking right to be proud. I've done more in the last week than in fifteen years in this job. Glasgow's a better place for it and that's what I'm paid to do.'

'You're not paid to kill.'

He aimed straight at Winter's head, his eyes blazing with anger.

'Don't you dare fucking tell me what I'm paid for. Faichney, Houston, Riddle, Honeyman. Those cunts had bled this town dry for years.'

'So how did you get them into the warehouse?'

'Easy. I'm a cop, remember. I rounded them up and had some fun with them. Suddenly I had what every cop in the city wanted. A licence to take out these bastards with no comeback. However many of them I removed, they'd all be chalked up to McKendrick's slate. Turned out these guys weren't so untouchable after all.'

'So you killed them.'

'Yes, I killed them. I took his list and I followed it through. I did what I could do, what I had to do. Those scumbags had to go. Every one of them has to go to give people a chance to get out from under. It's like cutting the heads off the hydra but that's the way it's got to be. You cut off as many fucking heads as you can then one day the new heads will stop popping up.'

'So who does that make you? Hercules or was it Jason and his fucking Argonauts? Who appointed you the head cutter?'

'Opportunity, that's who. McKendrick set it all up, put it on a plate for me. You've seen what they do, the misery they cause. It was my job. You understand, right?'

'No, I don't understand. I don't understand how someone whose job is to uphold the law can take it into his own hands and kill people. Murder people. It makes you as bad as Caldwell, Quinn, Riddle, the lot of them.'

'I didn't kill Riddle. I'm sure that was Terry Gilmartin. He shot him for firebombing his place and killing his son. He just did it before I could. But you're wrong, it's not the same at all. They deserved everything they got.'

'You're a murderer, Monteith.'

Winter took another step towards him and Monteith edged further back.

'Yeah? Well if I am then one more won't make any difference.'

Winter kept walking.

'You're a dead man, Winter.'

'But I'm innocent, Monteith. Done nothing. Just like Addy didn't. Just like Rachel.'

Monteith hesitated, the rifle barrel quivering.

'You really want to kill an innocent man?'

'No, you … no. But it's too late. I told you to stop. Told you what it would mean.'

'It doesn't have to mean that. Hand yourself in to the cops.'

'No! I can't stop now. There's more to be done.'

'You better kill me then.'

'Don't think I won't.'

His voice was cracking but his jaw clenched and his eyes narrowed. Winter saw him standing stiller, stiffer, his finger caressing the trigger. Primed.

Winter took another step forward.

Monteith's face contorted as he squeezed his finger, his eyes closing briefly as he pulled the trigger. When he opened them again, he just looked surprised. He quickly tried to fire again, then again. He looked down at the rifle dumbfounded as if he just couldn't understand why it hadn't fired and why Winter wasn't dead.

'No bullets,' said the woman's voice behind him.

Monteith whirled to see Narey and Danny Neilson standing there, staring at him intently. He turned the gun on them and instinctively fired off a shot at each. Nothing.

'We took them out of the rifle while you were off pretending to be the good cop,' she continued. 'You could have found a better place to hide it. It took us about two minutes to find it.'

'What the fuck are you doing here?' Monteith shouted at them.

'I would have thought that was fairly obvious even for a retard like you,' Danny grinned at him. 'Tony's getting out of here and you're going to jail.'

'No. No way. That's not going to happen.'

'Oh it will happen all right,' said Narey evenly. 'Your hands all over that gun, we are both witnesses and so is that camera up there.'

She pointed to the wall where the remote was busily recording everything through the frame of the storage-room door.

'And don't even think of destroying it,' Winter told him. 'The whole lot's already being relayed via my laptop. You're officially fucked.'

Suddenly, Monteith rushed forward and switched the rifle quickly so that he was holding the barrel and swung the butt viciously, catching Danny on the shoulder and sending him crashing back towards Narey, sending them both to the ground. Monteith raised the rifle again, this time looking to smash it down towards Narey.

Winter ran forward, hands still tied and hurled himself at Monteith, barging hard into his back and knocking the rifle from his hands. It flew a few feet away and he scrambled across from where he'd fallen and threw himself over it as if it was a grenade about to explode.

Monteith screamed abuse at him then, seeing Danny and Narey starting to get up, he turned and ran off to the left where he disappeared into the darkness of a corridor. They were both quickly on their feet, Narey shooing Danny away when he tried to check she was okay. Instead she made Winter turn and released the cabling, freeing his hands.

'You could have done that when you first came into the room,' he told her, the three of them immediately heading in the direction Monteith went, Narey leading the way as she was the one with a torch.

'Oh stop moaning,' she retorted. 'I told you he'd check as soon as he saw your feet were untied. Did you manage to look as shit-scared when he came in as you did when it was us?'

'Very funny. Obviously when I saw the shadow outside the door before I thought it was him. Can't tell you how pleased I am to see it was you two.'

'Me too,' she said softly, looking at him with real worry in her eyes.

'Get a fucking move on you two,' snarled Danny. 'There will be time enough for that later. Let's catch this guy.'

'He won't be getting far, Danny,' answered Narey.

'Yeah well let's make sure of it,' he puffed.

The corridor was narrow and they jogged along as quickly as they could in single file, picking out footsteps carefully, treading over loose concrete and trying to avoid the potholes and steps, all the while listening for the noise of Monteith up ahead.

'Uncle Danny . . .'

'What?'

'Thanks.'

'Don't worry about it,' he breathed heavily. 'That's what I'm there for.'

'And thanks for taking care of Rachel,' Winter added.

Danny burst out laughing despite the exertion of running.

'Take care of her? Christ, son, that woman of yours doesn't need looking after. It's you that needs the babysitter. Just as well she took the ammo out of that rifle for you. Now shut the fuck up, I'm too old to run and talk at the same time.'

They suddenly came to the end of the corridor and found it led off in two directions. They stood for a moment, Narey shining the torch as far as she could in each direction, and listened for the sound of him. Monteith must have known they'd have the choice to make though and had stopped or slowed so as not to make any noise. There was just running water and there in the distance the abrupt rumble of a train. They shrugged at each other and Winter was about to guess one way or the other but there, off to the left, a clang that was so close it had to be Monteith.

Narey took off in front again, the others struggling to keep up because she was far fitter than they were.

'We took a few wrong turns when we came down here after you,' panted Danny, obviously struggling now. 'We followed you to the corner of Jamaica Street but then lost you. By the time we went into the lane you had disappeared into thin air. It took us a bit to find the opening and we had no idea where it would take us.

'We must have taken a few wrong turns when we got down here too. It's a big old place. How the hell did you find it anyway?'

'You remember my pal Jamie Rowan?'

'Cheeky wee toerag with long hair?'

'That's him,' Winter replied. 'He told me about it years ago but I never had a reason to check it out. Then I found out that Ryan McKendrick was always going on to his mother about Grahamston.'

Danny smiled at him through his efforts.

'You did well. Always told you that you should have gone into the polis.'

Narey shot an angry look over her shoulder.

'He did well? My arse he did well. He nearly got himself killed. He should have gone *to* the polis not *into* the polis. He's an idiot and he knows it.'

Danny smirked at him behind Narey's back. He obviously approved. They were getting higher now, slowing as they climbed and ran out of breath. They could still hear Monteith ahead of them but they didn't seem to be closing on him. A couple of times they ran into things in the corridor, a box then a breeze block that Monteith had obviously dragged into their path. Narey crashed her shin into the block but only let out a yelp and a swear then carried on.

They charged through a set of double doors and found themselves confronted by a tall set of stairs that the torch suggested went up a couple of flights. There was some daylight swarming around the top of them too and for the first time since Monteith ran, they could see him above them. The higher they climbed the clearer it got above them and they saw him turn and look back. A plank of wood and some stones came hurtling towards them causing all three to flatten against the wall and see them thud harmlessly by. A minute or two later though, half a brick came down and caught Danny unawares on the same shoulder that Monteith had clouted with the rifle butt, making him groan loudly.

'I am going to kill that fucker when I get my hands on him,' he gasped. 'But you will need to catch him for me. Go on without me, I'm holding you back. Don't worry, I'll follow on.'

Narey and Winter swapped glances but knew Danny was right. She turned and started up the stairs again, him following on closely and thinking it wasn't really the time to admire her bum but he couldn't help himself. With Danny left behind, they were at last gaining on Monteith.

They could have been no more than twenty feet below him when he reached the top of the stairs, bathed in light now from the street walkway, and burst through a door on his right. They were at it in moments and pushed at it, only to find it blocked and barely budging. Winter took a few steps back and charged it with his shoulder, knocking it open far enough that they could get through, sprawling on the ground and seeing the breeze block Monteith had placed there.

'My hero,' she laughed.

'Fuck off,' he grinned.

She pulled him up and they took off after Monteith, maybe fifty yards behind him now. He went through another door and they headed for it too, finding this one opened easily. The tiles on the wall were a similar murky yellow to the hallway that Winter had entered just below street level near McDonald's and he was sure they were near the surface. They charged on, hearing Monteith's footsteps and knowing they were close behind.

A bang rang out, like a door hitting against a wall and sure enough when they rounded the next corner, there it was, a fire door flapping open, and they burst through it and found themselves in what had obviously been a gents toilet but looked like it hadn't been used for years.

They hurried through, the smell of stale urine nothing compared to the stench Winter had been putting up with in the storage room, and found themselves facing a small set of narrow stairs and they hurried up them. There was noise everywhere now, Monteith's feet loud on the tiles, a buzz of people, then suddenly the clang of metal. At the top of the stairs was an open set of rusty green gates and behind them was the concourse of Central Station itself. Monteith was standing there, anxiously fiddling with a padlock, obviously trying to lock them in. They were only a few feet away though and he had to settle for swinging the gate towards them. He hurtled into the crowded station, pushing people aside and heading for the main entrance.

They were after him, Winter's eyes blinking at the light that flooded in through the glass ceiling, past the white beams and the famous four-faced clock that hung from one of the supports. Monteith was making his way towards the stone arches that led onto Gordon Street, sliding as he ran along the floor and clattering into more and more people. Behind him, Winter and Narey pushed apologetically past the same passengers, desperate to get to him. Monteith skidded to a halt and changed direction, hurtling right. They looked beyond where he had been going and saw a dozen uniformed cops at the main entrance and knew that he had seen them too.

'He's going for the Union Street entrance,' shouted Narey,

frantically waving towards the police and urging them to cut him off. They were nearer and faster though, gaining on Monteith with every step. He knocked a little old lady flying and she fell into their path. Narey hurdled the woman without breaking her stride but Winter caught the whack of her walking stick as he ran round her. Monteith plunged into the narrow doorway of the entrance and hurtled down the stairs towards Union Street. They were just a couple of feet behind and could see a uniform positioned at the bottom the stairs with his back to them and Monteith. Narey shouted out but too late and as the cop half turned, Monteith barged past him, the momentum of coming down the stairs taking the officer clean off his feet.

Monteith ran again and they were after him, emerging to see a number of cops further down the street towards Gordon Street and knowing he was not going to get away. He stopped and looked round anxiously and saw his options severely limited at either end of the street. He dashed between two cars into the four lanes of one-way traffic, causing a series of others to slam on their brakes in a cacophony of squeals. Monteith edged to the right and saw an opening, looking back to see where his pursuers were before running straight in front of a silver Golf. The car slammed into Monteith, whipping his legs away and throwing him back onto the bonnet with a sickening thud and a shattering of glass.

The Golf came to a screeching halt a few yards further on with Monteith splayed across the bonnet and puncturing the windscreen.

Winter and Narey were on him immediately but there was no need to hurry, the rogue cop was going nowhere. Blood trickled from his mouth and a violent gash on his temple. His legs were surely broken and probably his pelvis as well, but he was alive if only just.

In seconds, the car and Monteith were surrounded by uniformed cops. A heavily panting Danny Neilson pushed his way through to join the party. Behind the wheel, a young woman sat open-mouthed and completely frozen.

Winter reached into his pocket for his mobile phone, patting it down until he remembered that Monteith had smashed it hundreds of yards below them. He reached an arm across Narey, neither of them taking their eyes off the man on the car, patting at her pocket to get her attention.

'What?'

'Phone. Please.'

Without looking at him, Narey found her mobile and handed it over.

Winter quickly found the camera function, briefly shaking his head at the miserable four megapixels that it offered, and framed Monteith's broken body through the viewfinder.

'Got him?' Narey asked as the sound of an approaching ambulance closed in on them.

'Yes, got him.' Winter replied. 'I got him.'

Narey nodded at him before continuing.

'Colin Monteith, I am arresting you for the murder of Jan McConachie, Graeme Forrest, Harvey Houston . . .'

CHAPTER 49

Going along the corridor to Ward 52, it struck Winter that he hadn't been in the Royal since he'd gone to photograph the baseball bat damage to Rory McCabe's knees twelve days earlier. A nothing photo of a nothing injury, so routine that it had bored him but he ought to have known better. Every bit of everyday crime feeds into the whole rusty machine.

He pushed through the doors into 52 and saw him straight away, sitting propped up in bed with a huge grin on his face and a nurse by his side. The jumble of gauze, bandage and scaffolding on his head didn't seem quite as shocking now that he was awake and talking and didn't seem to be bothering him in the slightest.

'Awrite, wee man? Thought you were never going to make an appearance.'

His voice was slightly slurred but Winter was used to that with him. He shook his head ruefully, thinking that some things never change.

'Good to see you, Addy.'

'And you too, wee man. I'm forgetting my manners. This is the lovely Tricia,' he said with a wave of his hand towards the petite red-haired nurse. 'Tricia, wee man, wee man, Tricia.'

She giggled and left them alone, doubtless aware that Addison's eyes followed her as she wound her way down the ward.

'As soon as I'm out of here I'm in there,' he grinned.

'Are you not supposed to be ill?' Winter asked him.

'Oh aye, I am. But I'm only ill, not dead. A man would need to be dead not to look at that.'

'Aye well, there are enough people dead to be getting on with.'

'Amen, brother.'

'What's the prognosis on that then?' Winter asked, nodding towards Addison's broken skull.

'I've got to keep the turban on for a while but I'll be fine. They'll put a plate in to replace the bit of skull that the bullet took out and they say there's no brain damage.'

'How can they tell? You got shot in the head and it manages to miss your brain, what does that say? I knew all the space in there would come in handy one day.'

'Size doesn't matter,' he chipped back. 'It's what you do with it.'

'Addy, you keep telling yourself that if it makes you happy.'

Addison looked away for a moment and when he turned back his face was much more serious.

'You know what would make me happy?'

'That nurse?'

Addison ignored him.

'If that cunt Monteith was dead instead of taking my bed in intensive care before it even had the chance to get cold. It makes me sick that he thought he could just pish all over the force by doing what he did. It leaves the rest of us smelling as bad as he did. That bastard had always been bitter about what we could do and what we couldn't with the likes of Caldwell and Quinn. He was even more frustrated than I was that we couldn't get at the bawbags and just put them away once and for all. But I'd never have thought he'd . . .'

'Addy, what if it was you that had found McKendrick rather than Monteith?'

'What? Would have I taken on the job and done what Monteith did? Is that what you are asking me, wee man?'

'I'm just asking.'

'Well don't be such a dick. Ask something else.'

'When did they tell you what Monteith had done?'

'Right after they asked me about Sturrock. That was the first thing they asked me when I came round. There was no, "How are you, how's the head, can we get you something to eat?" No, it was "What's your connection to Mark Sturrock?" straight off the bat. I had no idea what the fuck they were talking about so I just told them. The wee dickhead is an informant, my snout, my grass and why the fuck did they want to know. So they told me how the phone call that I answered was from him. Must admit I hadn't seen that one coming.

'You're supposed to declare grasses on the official informants list but toeing the party line's never really been my thing. Sturrock gave me a few tasty tidbits over the years and there's a good few locked up in Barlinnie thanks to him. I didn't think it was in his interest for people to know that. I'm not completely stupid though and I had documentation locked away at my lawyer's, signed and dated, in case the shit ever hit the fan. Not that I expected it to be like this. Anyways, they checked it out and it turns out I'm not a dirty cop after all.'

'I never thought you were.'

'And I'd fucking hope not too. They tell me you've been a right little boy scout while I was asleep. I knew you were up to something but I didn't figure it would be that. I leave you alone for two minutes and you go off chasing murderers. The sooner I get back to keep an eye on you the better. Seems like our Rachel Narey isn't up to the job of looking after you.'

'She did okay,' Winter hit back, more defensively than he should have done and seeing the hint of a smirk on Addison's face. 'She's close to clearing up that prostitute killing and managed that while you were in here sleeping. She's already made an arrest in the case.'

'But not the killer?'

'Maybe that too but she's nicked the girl's boyfriend. You know Tommy Breslin?'

'Mental twat that calls himself T-Bone? I know him.'

'He was Oonagh McCullough's boyfriend and Rachel has busted him.'

'How did she manage that?' The DI looked confused.

'Arithmetic,' Winter answered. 'Breslin was the father of Oonagh's daughter. The daughter is seven, the mother was twenty-three, Breslin is thirty-two. He was twenty-five and she was still fifteen when he got her pregnant before she ran away from home. She has done him for statutory rape.'

Addison burst out laughing.

'Nice one,' he admitted. 'Sounds like you are becoming quite a fan of our Rachel.'

Addison looked at Winter knowingly, waiting for a response but he could go to hell as far as Winter was concerned. As far as anyone else knew, Narey had got a call from Danny who was worried about him and they followed him below the station. Nothing more they needed to know, she said. Addison was just fishing, probably thought that being the hero of the hour might have got Winter a sneaky lay.

'Aye well, you better get yourself back on your feet then,' Winter said, changing the subject. 'I need someone to drink with in the Station Bar.'

'Oh don't, you're killing me. I'd give another bit of my head to be in there right now. Talking of the TSB, that night you walked into there with that boot mark on your cheek and that load of old bollocks about slipping in the bathroom, I knew you'd taken a kicking. I made the mistake of mentioning it to Monteith though. I'm thinking that helped you get into this mess.'

'Maybe a bit, yeah. But it helped me get out of it too. Let's just leave it at that.'

Addison laughed.

'Listen to Joe 90. Am I going to have to be looking out for my job?'

'Nah, you're safe on that count. I'm sticking to taking photographs. I know which side of the lens I want to be on from now on.'

'Wise words, wee man. Best not to get carried away thinking you've cracked the crime of the century. Anyway, something Alex Shirley said to me made me think he was on to McKendrick as well so you weren't the only one.'

'What? You think Shirley knew about McKendrick? How can that be? You must have picked him up wrong.'

'Aye, probably. I can't even remember what he said, it was more the way he said it. I don't know. I'm probably talking rubbish. I was still a bit woozy when they spoke to me.'

'Aye, probably. And you're a bit woozy at the best of times.'

'Funny, funny. Why don't you do something useful for a change, wee man?'

Addison lowered his voice.

'Go and see if you can smuggle me in a can or two of Guinness? Purely medicinal, you understand. And how about getting me some proper food, maybe a cheeseburger and fries? I'm starving.'

'Addy, you're *always* fucking starving.'

CHAPTER 50

The sound of the October rain lashing against the window just made it all the better to be inside. Rachel was standing by the window with one of Tony's shirts on, watching the cars go by on Highburgh Road down below. Winter was lying naked on the bed looking at her, in no doubt that he was the one with the better view.

He stole quietly from the bed and padded over, hoping to sneak up behind her but, ever the detective, she saw him coming in the reflection of the window.

'Hey, you,' she smiled at the glass.

'Hey.'

He snuggled in behind her, pressing himself against her and letting his lips fall onto her neck. She purred appreciatively and thrust back against him. He reached round with both hands and fondled her through the shirt.

'Hey,' she said again. 'Who said you could do that?'

'It's my shirt, remember.'

'That's a very good point. Carry on.'

Winter didn't need to be asked twice, squeezing at her, running her nipples between his fingers and gently biting at her neck. He was rising to meet her and she was beginning to moan. Then suddenly the name came from the television and they both froze.

Winter tried to pretend he hadn't heard it but she eased herself out and away from his grasp.

'Leave it,' he urged her.

'No. I want to hear this.'

She pulled his shirt over her head once she was away from the window and threw it aside, sprawling out on the bed to watch the news. He sat down behind her, no less interested in what was happening.

'... a spokesman for the Crown Office said that Detective Sergeant Monteith has been charged with thirteen counts of murder and three counts of attempted murder. He has also been charged with attempting to pervert the course of justice and unlawful possession of a firearm.

'The Crown Office spokesman listed each charge individually. They were namely the murders of Cairns Caldwell, Malcolm Quinn, Steven Strathie, Mark Sturrock, Alasdair Turnbull, James Adamson, Andrew Haddow, Inspector Graeme Forrest, Detective Sergeant Jan McConachie, George Faichney, Benjamin Honeyman, Harvey Houston and Jacob Arnold. The attempted murders were of John Johnstone, Detective Inspector Derek Addison and civilian worker Anthony Winter.

'The Crown intimated that it intends to offer both witness testimony and video evidence to prove that Detective Sergeant Monteith carried out the killings. The case attracted global publicity and it is thought that media from many countries will attend the trial which is expected to last several months.'

'That's what they think,' murmured Rachel.

'He's definitely going to plead guilty then?' Winter asked.

'So he says. And there's no reason not to believe him. He's adamant that's what he'll do and he'd gain nothing by changing his mind at the last minute to throw the prosecution. He's bang to rights and he knows it.'

'And he'll cough to the lot of them?'

'Yep. He's a mad bastard but he's sane enough to know that he's as well being hung for a sheep as a lamb. And he still thinks that he should be getting some kind of reward for getting the scum off the street. He wants every bit of credit that's going.'

'That's just so wrong.'

'Is it? Maybe it suits everybody.'

'What do you mean?'

'It doesn't matter.'

'Of course it does. After all this shit, everything matters.'

The news presenter broke into the conversation again when he mentioned the name Chief Superintendent Alex Shirley.

'. . . of Strathclyde Police said that his force was fully satisfied with its performance during a "difficult and extremely complex" case.'

The camera cut to Shirley looking suitably grave.

'This has been a very trying time for Strathclyde Police and for the city of Glasgow,' he said to camera. 'Given legal constraints, I am clearly limited as to what I can say on this matter at the current time, however I will say that it is with deep regret and personal sadness that I learn of the confirmation that a serving member of this police force has been charged in connection with this series of killings.

'Strathclyde Police pursued this case diligently and vigorously. If we had known that it was one of our own that was involved then we would have been no less conscientious in doing so. It was not until after the shooting of John Johnstone that, through good old-fashioned police work, we began to suspect DS Monteith's involvement. Until that point, we were keeping all our options open.'

Winter turned Rachel round so he could see her face.

'What the fuck? He's talking bollocks.'

'Maybe. He's smart enough not to say anything that could

come back to bite him on the arse later. He's worded that very carefully and the truth's probably in what he's not saying.'

'Such as?'

She pulled her bottom lip over her top one and shrugged.

'McKendrick? He knew?' Winter asked her.

Rachel shrugged again.

'I don't know for sure. He's hardly going to let me in on it, is he?'

I'm surprised you're letting me in on it, Winter thought to himself.

'But you think he did? Or might have?'

'Might have,' she nodded. 'The look on his face when I told him it was Monteith wasn't just someone who was surprised. It was way more than that. And it wasn't just someone who thought he'd get his bollocks fried because one of his officers had done what Monteith did. He thought I was wrong and wanted to tell me why but he couldn't. He'd thought it was someone else. I'm guessing he'd thought it was McKendrick.'

'But how could he have known?'

'Christ, any number of ways. No offence, Tony, but you found out so it should hardly be beyond the bounds of possibility that a detective super could do the same. Even if he hadn't found out on his own.'

'Fucksake.'

'Couldn't have put it better myself.'

'So the obvious question is that if he'd thought it was McKendrick . . .'

'Then the obvious answer . . .'

'Is that he was singing from the same hymn sheet as Monteith.'

'Except that he just hummed the tune and didn't go on to actually kill anyone.'

'He might as well have done.'

'But he didn't,' she said flatly. 'And the media and the streets are full of people who think that Monteith didn't do the worst thing in the world. They think that the people he killed did far worse. My guess is that he will be out in ten years. Probably less.'

Before Winter could answer, the news programme butted in again.

'And in other news, the funeral took place today of a Scots naval officer who displayed what has been described as "outstanding bravery in defence of his country".'

'Leading Hand Ryan McKendrick from Dennistoun in Glasgow was cremated in a ceremony accompanied with full military honours.

'A lone piper played the lament "Flowers of the Forest" and naval colleagues formed a guard of honour as his coffin was carried into Our Lady of Good Council, and then on to Lambhill Crematorium.

'Lieutenant Commander David Wallace told the congregation that they had lost a brave and determined young man who had suffered personal family loss but found the strength to act in the interests of others. He said that he could not give precise details of LH McKendrick's actions for reasons of ongoing national security but said that his family and friends could be assured that he had shown conspicuous courage and decisiveness and was a shining example to other young men and women.

'Lieutenant Commander Wallace also took the opportunity to announce that LH McKendrick is to be posthumously awarded the Military Cross and that this will be presented to his mother Rosaleen at a ceremony in Buckingham Place later this year.

'Despite being in obvious distress, Mrs McKendrick also addressed the congregation and told them of her pride in her son. She said that she was finding it very difficult to come to terms with the loss of Ryan so soon after the death of her younger son Kieran but that she found comfort in knowing he had died bravely helping others and was grateful for Ryan's senior officers in privately sharing the circumstances of his passing.'

Rachel grabbed the remote control and switched the television off, falling back onto the bed, her eyes on the ceiling. Above her, Winter saw the three framed original Metinides prints that she'd bought him. The woman hanging from the tallest tree in Chapultec Park, the man electrocuted on the wires and the beautiful Adela Legaretta Rivas after she was knocked down and killed by the car on the Avenida. The most romantic presents anyone had ever bought him.

'That was the right thing, wasn't it?' she asked him.

'The right thing? I'm not sure what the right thing is any more but I know it's right that poor woman doesn't get any more shit in her life that she doesn't deserve. If Monteith taking the hit for everything means that she gets a moment of comfort in thinking her boy's a hero then I can live with that.'

Narey thought for a moment, still examining the contours of the ceiling.

'I can live with that, too,' she said at last. 'But can you live with me?'

'What do you mean?'

'What do you think I mean?'

She reached under the pillow and produced a key.

'It doesn't mean you're moving in and it doesn't mean I want to broadcast it but it does mean you could let yourself in now and again. If you can live with that.'

Winter smiled.

'Yeah. I think I can live with that.'

He leaned in towards her but his attempt to kiss her was interrupted by her phone ringing.

'Ignore it,' he pleaded.

'No can do,' she replied, picking it up and looking at the display screen. 'Cat Fitzgerald,' she said with a finger to her lips to indicate he should shut up.

A pang of guilt surged through Winter and he was grabbed by

an irrational fear at the forensic scientist phoning Rachel at home. What did she want?

'Hi, Cat.'

'Hi, Rachel, sorry to call you so late. I hope I didn't disturb you.'

'No, you're fine. What's up?'

'I've finally got those DNA results for you from the condom we recovered in the Oonagh McCullough case.'

There was something in Fitzpatrick's voice that bothered Rachel but she couldn't place it.

'Okay … I'm guessing that there's something wrong if you're not leaving this till the morning. Bad news?'

'Not bad news, Rachel, no. More like very strange news.'

CHAPTER 51

Narey and Corrieri were already in the city mortuary in the Saltmarket, the Arctic chill licking at their skin, waiting for Brendan McCullough to join them to formally identify his daughter. Corrieri's hands were stuck firmly in the pockets of her overcoat and she shuffled from foot to foot as much to fend off her nerves as to keep warm.

'The first time is always the worst,' consoled Narey, sensing the DC's edginess.

Corrieri was grateful for her words but she wasn't altogether convinced that she'd ever get used to this bit of the job. The pervasive clinical smell that she took to be disinfectant and perhaps formaldehyde was turning her stomach and she was worried that she'd be unable to hold onto it.

The pair fell quiet again, the only sound being the faint buzz of the fluorescent striplights on the high Victorian ceiling.

The door creaked open behind them and the desk sergeant ushered a tense-looking Brendan McCullough into the room. The man's eyes immediately flew to the covered body in the centre of the room and the two officers saw his mouth drop open in shock before he firmly closed it again. Oonagh's father stood, almost to attention, dressed smartly in collar and tie beneath his anorak and stared at the shape that he had been summoned to see.

'Thanks for coming, Mr McCullough,' opened Narey. 'We realize how difficult this must be for you.'

The man didn't look at her but pursed his lips and sternly nodded.

'Would you like to take a moment to prepare yourself?' Narey continued, her eyes on McCullough's.

'No. No need,' he replied briskly. 'I'm ready.'

As if to prove it, he took two steps forward towards the table and stood still again awaiting for Narey to act.

Narey swapped glances with her DC and got a brief nod from Corrieri suggesting that she was ready too.

The DS went to the end of the table, placing herself to one side and indicating to McCullough to take his place on the other. The man moved forward and with a deep breath positioned himself opposite Narey, with Corrieri at his shoulder.

With her eyes on him, Narey reached down and took hold of the cover and slowly pulled it back to reveal the head and shoulders of Oonagh McCullough.

Her father's eyes opened wide and a gasp escaped from his lips. After a momentary waver, he stood stock-still but shut his eyes tight.

'Mr McCullough,' said Narey firmly, 'I have to ask you to look.'

After a few seconds, his eyes opened again and for the first time since he entered the room, he turned towards Narey, reproachful at her tone.

'I am sorry, Mr McCullough,' she continued, 'but I *do* have to ask you to look. Is this your daughter?'

The man held her gaze for a few moments longer before switching back to the table. Oonagh's eyes were closed over and her face stripped of the make-up she'd worn when she was killed in Wellington Lane. Her skin was bloodless pale and the livid purple strangulation marks on her throat stood out angrily.

The father looked at the mortal remains of his daughter, his jaw clenched and seemingly determined to avoid any more sounds of weakness leaking out. He stared at the lifeless form in front of him, almost glaring, resentful that she was dead.

'Yes,' he barked loudly, his voice ringing round the mortuary. 'Yes,' he repeated, quieter this time. 'It's Oonagh.'

Narey nodded, her eyes never leaving his.

'It's been a long time since you've seen her, Mr McCullough. She will have aged considerably in seven years. Are you sure it's Oonagh?'

'Yes.'

'Her hair was auburn but this girl's is dyed. And there has been dental damage that has altered her expression . . .'

Narey let the question go unrepeated but it hung in the air between them.

McCullough snapped his head round to her angrily.

'It's my daughter!' he replied sharply. 'It's Oonagh. I should know my own daughter.'

'Indeed,' Narey agreed softly.

'Has she changed much, Mr McCullough?' asked Corrieri at his shoulder. 'Excessive drug use can have such an effect on a person's appearance.'

He turned to look at her, his eyebrows knotted in momentary confusion.

'I don't really . . . yes, of course she has but it's Oonagh. It's Oonagh.'

'It must have been hard to discover what she'd been doing,' chipped in Narey. 'That she'd been working on the street.'

The father's eyes blazed at her furiously.

'My wee girl wouldn't do something like that. She wouldn't be some kind of cheap whore.'

'Things happen, Mr McCullough. People change,' replied Narey.

He stared at her, saying nothing.

'Oonagh had changed so much,' she continued. 'It would be perfectly understandable if someone didn't recognize her right away.'

'Especially if it was dark,' added Corrieri.

Brendan McCullough continued to stare at Narey.

'Look at her, Mr McCullough,' Narey told him.

The man glared at the DS, battling her gaze. She saw him gulp hard.

'Look at her!' she ordered.

McCullough turned hesitantly to look at his daughter.

'I remember her in those photographs at your house,' Narey said behind him. 'Such a pretty thing. She didn't need all that make-up she wore, did she? Not really.'

The father shook his head, agreeing.

'She looks better without it, don't you think? More like your wee girl.'

'Yes,' a faint voice came back at her.

'That's why you tried to scrub the make-up off her cheek, wasn't it?'

'She was such a sweet girl when she was younger,' he replied. 'The best daughter you could imagine. Never got herself into any kind of trouble and was always quick to do something for someone else. She was . . . happy.'

'It must have been hell for you when she left.'

He smiled sadly.

'Broke my heart. Her mother's too. Tore me up inside. My wee girl.'

'She was always that wee girl in your head all those years, wasn't she? In the picture in your head she was still sixteen.'

'Yes.'

'Hardly surprising that you didn't recognize the woman that she'd become.'

McCullough's face crumbled and the shake of the head was of a man lost.

'When you scoured the streets for Oonagh after she left, you went down to the red-light district to look for her, didn't you? Knowing that a lot of lost souls end up down there.'

He nodded, his eyes still on his daughter but now welling up with tears.

'I suppose you needed some kind of comfort,' Narey continued, her voice soft. 'Maybe an escape. They tell me that you can get a taste for it. Is that how it was with you?'

The man gave a shrug and she nodded thoughtfully at him in return.

'I was wondering, there's so many girls working out there. Do you think maybe that you picked "Melanie" because, possibly subconsciously, she reminded you a bit of Oonagh?'

McCullough's eyes fired red at the suggestion but the flames quickly died and she could see in his face that he was considering that it might be true.

'Oh God. Oh God.'

'At what point did you realize that it was actually Oonagh? Not at first obviously. Not in the dark, not with all that make-up on and with that platinum-blonde hair.'

'I was drunk. I wouldn't have gone down there otherwise. I always felt disgusted with myself when I sobered up. I was drunk.'

There were tears streaming down the man's face.

'So when did you realize it was Oonagh?' Narey repeated.

McCullough was shaking his head from side to side and beginning to tremble.

'When I woke on the Monday morning, I'd convinced myself it wasn't her. That I'd got it wrong. Even coming in here I wanted it not to be her. Not my Oonagh.'

'But you knew, Mr McCullough. Didn't you? Was it when you climaxed?'

The man suddenly bent double, his stomach retching and his hand going to his mouth. He didn't vomit but it must have been close.

'Yes,' he whimpered as he stood upright again.

'I really was drunk and it was so dark, especially down the lane. And she didn't know who I was, she was so out of her head on whatever she'd taken. We ... well, *I* did what I did. The business. But when I ... finished ... it was like something cleared in my head and I saw her. Oonagh. I'd looked for her for so long but ... not like that, not like that. I tried to rub off that hideous make-up. Tried to see if she was still underneath it. I'd never have ... you know, if I'd known. You've got to believe that.'

Narey ignored his plea.

'What happened?' she demanded of him.

His eyes fell to the floor.

'I just lost it. I was ... disgusted. At me. And at her. I was furious. It was like I was angry at her for having made me do what I did. At her for what she was doing. I strangled her. My hands were on her neck before I knew what I was doing and ... and she fell to the ground.'

Narey let the silence echo round the sterile environs of the mortuary.

'You killed her.'

'Yes.'

'You strangled her and smacked her head off a metal door.'

'Yes.'

'And then you stuck your wee girl behind a bin.'

He looked at her, his eyes desperately pleading for understanding that he was never going to receive.

'I panicked. I couldn't believe what I'd done. I lost control and I just wanted out of there. I hid her and I got out of there.'

'Yes,' she snarled at him. 'You got out of there so quickly that you just took off the condom and threw it away without a thought to what you were leaving behind.'

McCullough's face fell, realization dawning on him.

'You couldn't even cover her up?' she challenged him. 'You left her with her fucking knickers round her ankles!'

The man gulped awkwardly twice and turned away from them, bending over and throwing up onto the polished marble floor of the morgue. Narey didn't offer a flicker of sympathy although Corrieri looked like she might follow suit.

'How could you do that to any human being?' Narey demanded. 'Never mind your own flesh and blood.'

McCullough wiped the back of his hand across his mouth, wild-eyed and fraught. His self-control and military bearing had disappeared.

'I didn't know what I was doing. I think maybe I thought that if I just got away then no one would know. Maybe no one would even find out who she was and then her mother wouldn't need to know . . .'

McCullough broke off, a desperate thought interrupting his confession.

'She doesn't need to know, does she? Not about what happened, I mean. But about what I . . . I . . .'

Narey shook her head at him, a mixture of disgust and wonder.

'Of course she will need to know. There's no way round that. You can explain it to her yourself.'

A pitiful wail came from the man then suddenly his hands flew to his face and he began to claw at himself, digging his fingers feverishly at his skin and eyes. His nails drew blood on his distorted features and he howled like an animal.

Narey directed Corrieri towards the door with an abrupt nod of her head and the DC went to bring in the two uniformed constables who were waiting outside. Narey could have restrained the man while she awaited their arrival but she didn't.

The PCs burst in at a trot and quickly pinned McCullough's arms to his sides. Blood leaked from the corner of one eye and vivid scratches marked his cheeks as his head lolled from side to side.

'Your own flesh and blood,' Narey rebuked him. 'And that's what you left behind. In every sense of the words. The science team were confused by the DNA that was retrieved from that condom you threw away. It was so similar a match to Oonagh's that they thought they'd perhaps made a mistake and mixed up samples. But they hadn't, had they, Mr McCullough?'

'I will kill myself in prison. You do know that?'

Narey just looked at him.

'That's someone else's problem, Mr McCullough. Not mine. Take him away.'

Corrieri led the officers to the door as they half pulled, half carried McCullough to it and on to the waiting police van.

Narey watched them leave then turned back to the body of Oonagh McCullough, standing over her for just long enough to wonder how the young woman had made the journey from Giffnock to the streets and to the morgue. She gently eased the cover back over Oonagh's head and wished her a silent goodbye before switching off the light and returning the room to darkness.

He was standing outside the mortuary room, with his back leaning against the wall. When Narey came out, he raised his eyebrows by way of a question.

She looked around before shaking her head ruefully in reluctant agreement.

'You've got two minutes, Tony, but if you get caught then as far as I'm concerned, you broke in here and you're getting nicked.'

Winter's eyes fell to his camera where they dallied in thought before he lifted his head again and studied the pain etched on Rachel's face. It was his turn to shake his head.

'No, you're right. There will be other times and other photographs. Glasgow isn't going to turn into Disneyland overnight. That girl deserves some peace. Come on, I want you to come with me.'

'Where to? I've got to deal with McCullough.'

'After, then. I can wait. I want you to come with me to my mum and dad's graves. It's about time you were introduced.'

'Okay. I'd like that.' She smiled for the first time that day.

As they emerged blinking into the glare of a watery September sun, Winter was reminded of the basic law of photography which dictates that the process is only possible because of darkness as well as light. For every thing of beauty there has to be an ugly truth.

ACKNOWLEDGEMENTS

Writing is a solitary occupation that is best done with the help of others. I am grateful for the skills, patience and kindness of my editor Maxine Hitchcock and all at Simon & Schuster, particularly Emma Lowth.

I must also thank my agent Mark 'Stan' Stanton at Jenny Brown Associates, not least because he moaned at not being acknowledged in my previous book. Stan's wise words dispensed over pints of a certain Irish stout were the foundation of much of the character that became Tony Winter.

Inevitably, authors steal from all around them; collecting ideas, information, phrases and stories then hoarding them like literary magpies. It is impossible to name all those that were stolen from but I'd like to thank Gordon Blackstock for introducing me to the word *sgriob*; Adam Docherty for alerting me to the remarkable work of Enrique Metinides; Brian Moran for the tale that became John Petrie's repulsive fridge; Dr Andy McCallion for his insight into torture methods; and Arlene Kelly for being the font of all Glasgow knowledge. All were fundamental to this story in their own way.

I must also thank photographers Chris Austin, Andrew Cawley, Barrie Marshall and Ritchie Miller for allowing me to steal from them over the years too. Tony Winter is all of them and none of them.

Finally but most importantly, I would like to thank my friends and family for their support and advice – and their recommendations of ways to kill people. Keep them coming.